BOYS OF WINTER

SHERIDAN ANNE

Sheridan Anne

Damaged: Boys of Winter #2

First Published in 2021

Anne, Sheridan

Damaged: Boys of Winter #2

Cover Design: Sheridan Anne

Photographer: Korabkova

Editing: Heather Fox

Editing & Formatting: Sheridan Anne

DAMAGED

To all those sorry suckers who've had to move houses while working on deadlines with children running around your feet, I feel for you. I really do.

How many bottles of wine does it take to finally feel human again?

Also, if this book seems extra harsh, blame a certain person who somehow convinced me to start boxing. My hands hurt, my feet hurt … my whole freaking body hurts.

Again … How many bottles of wine do I need?

1

His big hand curls around my throat as his eyes spit venom, the power in his hold like nothing I've ever experienced. I try to scream, but Carver's lethal stare holds me captive, and I find myself holding back, unable to look away from the horror and betrayal within his eyes.

They burn, pulsing with fury, daring me to try and get away as my nails claw at his strong hand. I'm lifted off the ground, and my feet dangle below, the black silk of my gown barely grazing the marbled tiles. "An eye for an eye," I tell him as I'm quickly running out of oxygen. "Let me go. I had to do it."

It's as though he doesn't hear me as he continues to stare, his gaze saying everything he needs to say—he fucking hates me. I betrayed him, just as they've done to me time and time again.

I killed his father, just as his father had killed mine.

I had no choice. I had to do it, and I'd do it again a million times over.

My heart races, my oxygen quickly dwindling as my throat begins to burn and bruise under his wicked hold. I need to breathe. He'll never let me go. Carver is all about the win, all about what's right, and he's too fucking stubborn to give in now. To him all that exists is black and white, there is no grey area, no in-between.

"Carver," I gasp, feeling light-headed as the gasps and horror continue around us. "I … I … can't breathe."

His lethal stare doesn't waver. He's going to kill me.

The music dies, and the screams instantly echo around the room. Every eye is on us and the dead body lying at Carver's feet, the pool of blood slowly seeping across the dance floor.

A body rushes into Carver's side, and like lightning, a loaded, brutal punch flies straight at his face. There's a loud grunt before Carver goes flying back, releasing his hold on my neck.

My body crashes to the ground as I suck in a deep breath, my throat throbbing from his bruising grip. My hip drops to the hard dance floor as my torso falls forward into the spilled blood. My hand lands just by the intricate dagger I used to end his pathetic existence.

I wince in pain, knowing that come morning, my body will be covered with deep bruising, but the boys move in front of me, not giving me even the smallest second to assess the damage.

King's strong grip curls around my upper arm and he yanks me to my feet. The blood runs from my body and I hold back a gag as King keeps his hands on me, holding me still for a few long seconds as my head spins from the lack of oxygen. He refuses to meet my stare as he throws his large body in front of mine, holding me close to his back, making me invisible behind him.

I grip onto his strong arm and peer around him, watching as Grayson throws another punch at Carver, sending him sprawling back onto the marble tiles. I suck in a breath, my eyes wide as Grayson comes down over him, delivering punch after punch as Carver desperately fights back, demanding to get to me.

What the hell is going on? Why is Grayson the one defending my honor? This is the kind of shit I expect from Cruz or King, but Grayson? Why does he even care?

People rush in from all sides, shouts, and gasps coming from every corner of the room as Cruz comes storming in. His eyes quickly scan over me before he flies at Grayson. Cruz grabs him by the back of his suit jacket, and in an incredible show of strength, tears him away from Carver.

Without Grayson's weight pinning him down, Carver flies back to his feet, storming for me again. He shoves his hand hard against Cruz's chest and forces him back a few steps, his stare fixed solely on mine.

He reaches King, but he won't dare move, keeping me protected from the raging heir in front of us. Carver grabs King by the front of his shirt and pulls him in, ready to toss him aside. "MOVE," he roars.

King pushes against his hold, forcing him back just as Carver had done to Cruz. "You'll have to fucking kill me to get to her."

Fury burns in Carver's eyes. There's no way in hell that he'd follow through on a challenge like that, but he'll sure as hell knock him the fuck out if he has to.

I see the exact second Carver decides that nothing will stop him from getting to me, and judging by the way King's body tenses against mine, he sees it too.

Just as Carver goes to make his move, Cruz and Grayson storm into his sides, grabbing each of his arms and holding him back. Cruz leans into Carver, keeping his furious stare on me, making it more than clear that the guys aren't exactly thrilled with my actions tonight. "Touch her again and I will fucking end you."

Carver pulls against their hold, desperate to get free and end me just as I did his father. "She fucking killed him," Carver roars.

I push out from around King, not one to shy away before rushing into Carver's chest. "He killed my parents," I yell as King's arm snaps around my waist, hauling me back away from the furious new head of Dynasty.

Carver roars, "YOU DON'T KNOW THAT."

"I SURE AS FUCK DO," I throw back at him, my throat instantly burning from my tone as I push at King's arm to get closer. "He just admitted it. He was boasting about it, telling me how my mother screamed when he slit my father's throat, telling me how much blood pooled in their bed. WHAT THE FUCK WAS I SUPPOSED TO DO?"

"NOT FUCKING KILL HIM," he roars, his face turning a deep shade of red in anger, his tone making me flinch. "DO YOU HAVE ANY IDEA WHAT YOU'VE DONE?"

"Fuck what I've done," I spit, not regretting it one bit as people rush into us, violently jostling me around. "I can live with what I've done. I avenged my parents and gave your father what he finally deserved. An eye for a fucking eye."

Carver shakes his head, the fury and rage pulsing out of his eyes and telling me that from this moment on, nothing will ever be the same between us. "Take out enough eyes, and soon enough, we'll all be fucking blind."

Tobias King pushes in between us, slamming a hand against his son's chest and Carver's before giving a harsh push and sending us all a step back. He turns a ferocious glare on me. "What is the meaning of this?" he demands as the other heads of Dynasty form a circle around us. "Why the hell is Royston Carver lying dead at my feet?"

High pitched wailing cuts through the circle as an older woman in a deep red gown crashes through and drops to her knees beside the body, her dress instantly soaking in the pooled blood. "NOOOOOO," she sobs. "No, no, my poor husband. What has she done to you?"

She throws herself over the body as though her own warmth will somehow pump life back into her disgraced husband. She sobs and I find the sight far too hard to watch. It's one thing to take a man's undeserving life, but taking someone's father, someone's husband … that hits differently. But is it enough to make me regret what I did? Hell fucking no.

My gaze instantly slices back to Carver's as his mother wails between us, but his stare is still there, still boring into mine and demanding retribution. "You will die for this," he tells me, making Cruz, Grayson, and King flinch. "I'll make sure of it."

"You don't mean that," I tell him, shaking my head. I see the pain in his eyes, but on closer inspection, it's clear that the pain isn't from the loss of his father, it's from my betrayal. And I think that cuts deeper than anything ever could.

Carver's mother throws herself to her feet and slams into her son, throwing her arms around him and sobbing into his neck. "She took him from me. She murdered my sweet Roy. You have to do something about this. You have to demand justice."

I hold back a scoff as Cruz and Grayson release their hold on Carver and his arms instantly wrap around his mother. King does the same for me but keeps his hand at my elbow.

Tobias surveys the area, trying to gain control of the situation before nodding at Earnest Brooks. "Close this thing down."

Earnest flashes his gaze at me before nodding back at Tobias. "Consider it done."

Just like that, Earnest turns to the crowd gathered around us, and with a simple nod of his head, every last person turns on their expensive heels and scurries for the door, leaving behind the boys, the body, the dagger, and the remaining fifteen heads of Dynasty. Sixteen considering that Carver just inherited his father's seat at the table.

Once the people are gone and the doors are closed behind them, Mrs. Carver's sobs come to an abrupt, appalling stop and she turns her glare on me. "You will pay for this, mark my words, girl," she spits, making it clear that her sobs were just for show. "You took from me and I will not stop until I find revenge."

Tobias raises his chin. "Remember your place, Ida. That's Elodie Ravenwood you're talking to, our leader."

"She is not my leader," Ida growls. "She's a murderer. She should be locked up and fed to the wolves for all I care. She's white trash and not worthy of being leader of such an organization."

"Watch your mouth," Earnest says, stepping into her side as my fingers curl into a fist and I long for my brass knuckles, desperately wishing that I could end this shit the one way I know how.

I raise my chin and take a step toward Ida as King's hand tightens on my elbow, silently telling me to back off. "Your husband just stood before me and told me all about the sick way he murdered my parents as they slept in their bed, relished in the way my mother screamed. He told me how he tried to suffocate me and then boasted about how he set fire to my home. That same man stood before me not twelve hours ago and declared his loyalty and stated that I will have his support in my search for my parents' killers. That is the man you're defending."

"That man was my husband of twenty-five years."

"Which makes me wonder just how much you had to do with this."

"Excuse me?" Ida demands, sucking in an appalled breath as Carver creeps in closer, his fingers tightening on his mother's arm.

I scoff at her little show, ignoring the way Carver seems to loom over me. "You were by his side every day for twenty-five years. So, you either knew exactly what was going on and are an accessory to his crimes, or you're just plain stupid. Which is it? Because judging by the little show that you've been putting on for the guests tonight, I'm going to go ahead and assume that you're a smart woman."

"I have no idea what you're talking about," she snaps, her eyes briefly flashing toward Tobias King.

"Oh, but you do," I tell her, drawing her attention back to me. "You knew exactly what his plans were for Dynasty, just as I assume your son did too."

Carver's stare hardens as Cruz, King, and Grayson look at him in confusion. "What is she talking about?" Grayson demands, his tone lowering in suspicion. "What was your father planning?"

"This has nothing to do with me," Carver growls, his anger at being questioned by his best friend as thick as the blood staining the dance floor. "I've seen my father once in the last six months."

"It's nothing," Ida cries. "My husband was dedicated to our cause. He was an upstanding member of our organization and as loyal as every other head of Dynasty. He did not deserve this. This … this … trash should be locked up. This was just some ridiculous stunt after her humiliation during this morning's meeting. You all saw how she targeted my poor husband. I demand an investigation."

"I agree," Carver says, raising his chin. "Lock her up. She's dangerous. Who knows who else she might go after."

"Take her to the cells," comes a voice to my left. I glance across to find Preston Scardoni with a scowl stretched across his face, his eyes narrowed on me in distaste. "After insinuating that I had something to do with the attack on the King property, it's clear that she's not fit for leadership. She's on a rampage, intent on destroying what our fathers built, and I refuse to be her next victim."

Cruz steps into my side and grips my other arm as King pulls me back into his chest. "You're not taking her anywhere," Cruz says, leveling Carver with a ferocious stare. "Hasn't she already suffered enough? You saw the fucking cell Sam Delacourt had her in, and now you're just going to throw her in another? Fuck you, man. Doesn't she mean anything to you?"

"Cruz," an older man reprimands from behind us, making me wonder if that's his father, but I refuse to take my stare off Carver's for even a second to check.

Guilt flashes in Carver's eyes and I know he's picturing that cell just as clearly as I am, but he won't budge. "I stand by my decision," he says, his comments sending a smug as fuck grin stretching across his mother's face. "Take her away. She needs to be somewhere secure where she can't hurt anyone else while we investigate her claims. All in favor?"

Hands raise from all around the room and as I look around, my eyes widen with fear, seeing that I'm outnumbered, even the eight men who are supposed to have my back have their hands raised high above their heads. "No," I panic, backing into King's chest as Cruz and Grayson move in around me, protecting me from the men who want to take me away. "I'm not going to some shitty dark cell. You can't make me."

"I'm sorry," Tobias says, leveling his son with a stare to release me. "You have no choice. This is how we deal with things. You've committed a crime and now we must hold you accountable. The cell is just a precaution so that you cannot run."

"I swear, I won't run," I say, shaking my head as Grayson and Cruz are pulled aside and held down by the men of Dynasty, desperately trying to get free. The panic rises heavily within my chest, and while Carver will never forgive me for what I've done here tonight, if I'm put into another dark, cold cell, I'll never forgive him. "Lock me in my house. Please, no. I can't go in another cell. Carver, please."

Ida waves her hand dismissively toward the door. "Get rid of her. She's a traitor to her own people. Royston will not die in vain. She will be punished."

Two men move into my sides as I frantically search for a way out. King's arm tightens around my waist, more than ready to fight his way out of this. "Hunter," Tobias snaps. "Release her now."

"No," he demands, fixing his father with a hard stare and proving that my well-being comes before these bullshit old policies and traditions of a corrupted organization. "I'll keep her at my place. She's not going down to the cells."

"She has no choice," Tobias hisses, pissed off with his son's lack of respect in front of the other heads. "Release. Her. Now."

Having the patience of a doorknob, two others move in and tackle King away from me, leaving me open for the taking. I try to fight them off, but every single one of them are professionally trained, and their skills up against the bullshit, weak as fuck punches I taught myself are absolutely nothing.

Two men grab my arms and I desperately try to pull free, but their grip is too tight. They pull me toward the door, my feet dragging along the marble tiles. I look back at the crowded bodies, taking in the boys who desperately try to get free, each of their concerned stares on mine, filled with regret, devastation, and defeat.

A lump forms in my throat as I turn my desperate stare on Carver to see nothing but pure rage in his eyes. "You said I could trust you," I cry, his betrayal hitting me harder than anything I've ever felt in my life. "You were supposed to have my back."

Something flashes in his eyes, but it's gone before I get the chance to figure it out, and before I know it, the massive doors of the ballroom open and I'm dragged back through them, feeling my freedom slipping away.

Then just like that, the big doors slam closed with a loud BANG, blocking me off from the rest of the world.

2

The big iron key slips into the lock of the cell, and as the door slides open, the metallic sound of bars scraping sends me straight back to that tiny, damp cell of Sam's.

How the hell did I get back here?

The hands at my arm grip me tighter as I fear what will come of this. How could Carver do this to me? Out of all the guys, he's the one who understands me the most. He's the one I would run to when the nightmares would come back to haunt me, yet he's the one who condemned me to this bullshit.

Fuck him. I'll never forgive him for this.

I'm dragged forward, and I do everything in my power to avoid being thrown into the open cell, but my attempts against these strange men are useless. It's like throwing around a ragdoll. My strength is laughable against theirs.

A hand slams into my back and I'm pushed roughly through the cell door. I fall forward, my body crashing down to the hard concrete ground with a loud thud, a pained grunt tearing from between my lips. My elbows scrape against the concrete and instantly sting as my mom's silk gown is torn.

Wicked laughter echoes through the cells, and as I go to push up onto my hands and knees, the door slams shut with a deafening BANG. The men walk out and all that's left is a dead silence that seems to go on forever.

I stare around the dimly lit cell, my breath coming in short, sharp pants as my eyes flick around the shadows. This world has destroyed me. I used to be so strong, but the second I came to Ravenwood Heights, everything changed. Some good and some were so fucking bad that no one should ever have to live through it.

I pull myself to my feet and look over my elbows to find them scratched up and bloodied, but it's nothing compared to the raspy soreness pulsing through my throat from the way Carver strangled it. Sure, I didn't think before pulling that knife on Carver's father, but I sure as hell didn't get the impression that he gave a shit. I thought he hated the guy. I thought he was on my side.

My gaze drops over my ruined dress and I quickly realize that it's not just my blood covering it, but Carver's father's from when his furious son dropped me on the ground. Disgust sinks heavily into my stomach and I reach around myself, desperately feeling for the flimsy zipper.

I drag it down my body and allow the ruined material to fall off my shoulders, leaving me in nothing but a black strapless bra and a pair of panties, that read 'It's not going to lick itself' across the front. I hate that the last time I was in a cell, I was also in nothing but underwear, but right now, it beats sitting in someone else's blood.

I kick my heels off and watch as they slam against the concrete wall, the sound echoing through my cell and down the long hallway, where no one will hear me screaming.

I'm in the underground world, and if I had to take an educated guess, I'd say that my cell is directly beneath Carver's property. Fucking perfect. Just my goddamn luck. I bet he's sitting up there with his moronic mother laughing about how they put me away so easily.

God, I want to hate him. Why is it so hard?

They'll fucking pay for this, especially Carver. I'll never be able to understand how he did this to me. Were the last two months all an act? Does he not care even a little bit? Because if that were true, then why the hell would he go out of his way to save my ass so many times? Why would he let me sleep in his arms, and live inside his home? It doesn't make sense. There's got to be something more going on here, something I'm missing.

I drop onto the small, hard bed and use the rough sheets to wipe away the blood that had seeped through the thin silk gown to my skin, desperately wishing that I could get out of here and take a shower. Hell, even the hose attached to the side of my house would be enough.

I'd do anything to get rid of the stain of that man on my body. I'd guess for guys like Carver and Grayson, wearing the blood of their enemies is like wearing a trophy, but for me, it only goes to remind me just how low I've sunk.

I curl into the hard bed, my eyes wide-open as I fear the faceless men that will come to haunt me the second I allow myself to fall asleep. It's got to be only six or seven in the evening, but it's been such a long, exhausting day that I feel as though I could sleep for days on end. But I won't dare; not here, and certainly not now.

An hour ticks by and quickly turns into two when I hear the distinct rhythmic sound of someone creeping down the hall. I suck in a breath, my heart thundering heavily in my chest.

There's only a small number of people who know I'm down here, and even a smaller number of people who would have a reason to come for me.

Fuck. Fuck. FUCK.

I glance around the small cell and dive for my stiletto heel. I'm not usually one to back down from a fight or even be fearful of one, but right now, I'm at a loss. I'm nearly naked in a cell that I can be easily cornered in, deep in an underground world that I don't know my way around, with eight different families seeking my painful and timely death.

I'm a sitting duck. I might as well have a fucking target painted across my forehead and a big arrow in flashing lights telling all the creeps where to find me. If someone wanted me dead, today is their lucky day.

The person gets closer and I find myself holding my breath as I cower in the darkest corner of my cell. Facing the door, I do everything that I can to give myself an advantage, but if it's Carver coming to get me, I'm fucked. I'll never be able to take him down, nor do I want to.

Carver means something to me, he's my safety blanket, the warm embrace at the end of the day. He might hate me, and I will do everything I can to make him pay for putting me in here, but I will never be able to hurt him. Carver is something special that I need to get out of my system.

A long shadow stretches over the room, distorted and changing with each step the stranger takes. My rising fear has me gripping onto the heel tighter. If this turns into a life-or-death situation, I can guarantee that I'll be the one living to tell the story, no matter how brutal I have to be with this stiletto.

Thump. Thump. Thump.

The person grows closer.

My breath slows, my hand tightening on the heel in the dim light.

Thump. Thump.

My eyes widen as the shadow pulls across my face, the fear crippling me.

Thump. Thump. Thump.

The shadow shifts just one step closer and without sparing me another second to figure out my game plan, the stranger steps into view.

Cruz's handsome face stares back at me, and the relief rocks through me so hard that I fall to my knees, the stiletto heel clambering across the cold concrete as I catch myself on my palms.

"Fuck, Winter, baby. Are you okay?" Cruz demands, panic lacing his tone as he races to the iron bars of the cell and grips them tightly, almost as though he's about to attempt to pull them apart with his bare hands. He stares at me, his eyes piercing into my body. "Winter? Please, what's wrong?"

I take slow, deep breaths, trying to calm my thundering heart before nodding and raising my head. I drop my ass to the cold concrete and fall back against the wall of my cell. "I thought you might have been Carver coming to finish the job."

"Fuck," he curses, rushing down to my end of the cell and reaching through the bars to take my hand. I latch onto it with everything I have, hating how desperate I must look. The guys have always seen me as a strong woman who doesn't take shit from anyone, but right now, I feel like a fraud. "You're safe down here, babe. I know you don't feel it, but you are. There's a fucking code on the door and the keys are locked away. No one can get to you down here."

I raise my head and look him in the eyes, knowing his words are only there to appease me. "You got in," I point out. "Carver's not fucking stupid, nor are the other dickheads who've been after me. If you could get the code for the door, so can they. I appreciate you trying to make me feel better, but you and I both know that I'm fucked."

Cruz lets out a sigh and drops his forehead to the bars before tugging on my hand and pulling me close enough that he can pull me into a tight hug. "I'm not going to leave you, Winter. You'll be safe with me. I won't let anything happen to you."

I breathe him in, loving his words but hating that I can't trust them. There's not a single doubt in my mind that Cruz believes every word he's telling me. He truly thinks he can keep me safe in this world, and that's a huge part of why I love having him in my life. He's always so optimistic. He's my ray of sunshine against a black, stormy sky. The rest of the guys, even me, all see the negatives, we see the world as a horrible, dark place, and without Cruz keeping our chins raised to the sky, we'd all be buying a one-way ticket to hell.

Not wanting to crush his spirit, I simply nod and drop my head into my hand, focusing on the softness of Cruz's thumb as it travels back and forth over my other hand. "What's going to happen?" I ask him. "You know, assuming they're not going to vote that I be sentenced to death for killing an asshole."

Cruz shakes his head. "That's not going to happen," he tells me, his tone soft and soothing. "They can't ignore that you're Elodie Ravenwood. You're our natural-born leader, and there are eight families who are going to take your side."

"But there are also eight families who won't."

"Not necessarily," he says.

My brows furrow as I raise my head from my hand and look him in the eye. "What do you mean?" I ask, studying every little line of his face.

Cruz's lips pull into a tight line as he shakes his head, deep in thought. "I don't want you getting your hopes up or anything like that, but Carver … I don't know. He wouldn't just side with his family like that. I think it was all for show."

"No," I tell him. "I know you want to see the best in everyone, but I felt his hand on my throat. *I couldn't fucking breathe, Cruz.* That's not a man who was putting on a show. He wanted to kill me, and he would have if Grayson didn't beat the shit out of him."

"That's not … no. Carver wouldn't have done it. He's … he was just angry."

I squeeze his hand, staring into his eyes as I lower my voice to a soft whisper. "He was going to kill me, Cruz. I saw it in his eyes. He wanted to end me just like I ended his father."

Cruz releases me and drops back against the wall, watching me closely as he rests his hands over his knees, his head tilted back against the hard concrete. "They'll put you on trial," he explains, moving on from the topic of his best friend wanting to possibly murder his part-time fuck buddy. "It'll be hard. The eight families who stand against you will make it nearly impossible for you to get a word in. They'll drill you, examine every little word you say, and try to turn it back on you until you're found guilty."

"And the other eight families?"

"They'll advocate for you. To them, you're innocent until proven guilty."

"They all watched me kill him. I *am* guilty."

"Yes, but they will argue that he had it coming. You said so yourself. He boasted about killing your parents and if that's true, which we all already assumed, then it was the rightful punishment, just carried out in the wrong way."

My brows furrow. "How do you mean?"

"Just like in the real world, murder is a crime that cannot go unpunished, and until now, the death of your parents was always considered a tragic accident—it still is. Some believed it was murder, others believed the accidental fire story, so no punishments were handed out. Taking the life of our leader … that's unheard of. It's the worst crime anyone in this world could commit, and once the truth got out, Royston Carver would have been sentenced to death—an eye for an eye as you like to say."

"So, I'm in the clear?"

"Not exactly," he tells me. "The only evidence you have to prove he was guilty is now the words of a dead man. No one heard what he said to you. There's no recording or proof that he did it, just your word, and considering the position you're now in …"

"I'm fucked."

"Exactly."

My head drops and I study the backs of my hands far too closely. "So, what's going to happen after I've said my piece?"

"Same as everything else," he says, giving me another tight smile that doesn't reach his eyes. "They'll put it to a vote and you better hope that one of those eight families are feeling lenient and give you the benefit of the doubt."

"And if they don't?"

"Then it'll be an even split and you'll be thrown back in here until there's a final decision."

Dread sinks heavily into my gut. "I'm screwed," I murmur into the quiet cell. "They'll never agree."

Cruz's eyes drop, feeling the heaviness just as I am. "That's why I'm hoping Carver might come around."

I drop my head into my hands and the room falls into silence once again. If my future is dependent on Carver, then I'm royally fucked. I'll never get out of here. Though a small part of me is glad that I'm here for avenging my parents' murders. At least I can live with myself knowing the man I killed completely deserved it and that the outside world is now better off for it. The same goes for Kurt. Scumbags like that don't deserve to walk the earth, they deserve to rot in hell. If only I could get my hands on Sam. Now that would just be the cherry on top.

A few minutes pass before I glance back up at Cruz to find his concerned stare already locked on my face. "Don't look at me like that," I tell him.

"Like what?"

"Like I'm doomed," I say with a deep sigh, my bottom lip pouting out knowing damn well that I am doomed. "You're supposed to be the inappropriately flirty one. If doom and gloom was the vibe you were hoping for, you should have sent Grayson."

A small smile tugs at the corners of his lips as he raises a brow and slowly pulls himself up off the ground. "And what would you have gotten had I sent King?"

A breathy laugh pulls from deep within me as a cocky grin tugs at the side of my mouth. "A little something to soothe my sore throat."

Cruz rolls his eyes but can't help the laugh that bubbles out of him. "Come here," he says, stepping into the bars and offering me his hands. I take them and he instantly pulls me up to my feet before pulling me flush against the bars and wrapping his warm arms around me.

His hands roam over my back, dropping down to my ass before traveling back up. I try to smoosh my face into the side of his neck where it usually belongs, but the bar makes it impossible. "You're going to be fine. If Dynasty can't agree to let you go, then I'll bust your sweet ass out of here myself."

"Oh, really," I laugh, raising my head to meet his sparkling green eyes. "And how do you suppose you'll do that?"

He scoffs as though the answer is as clear as the bright blue sky. "How do you think?" he smirks. "Just one little flick of my finger and this whole cell would come crumbling down around you."

"Then go right ahead, Hulk. Show me your impressive skills."

Cruz sucks in a horrified gasp. "What do you take me for? I'm only looking out for your safety. I'm not a complete savage."

"Only in the bedroom then?"

"Damn right," he grumbles, his voice low and filled with lust as he grips my chin and raises it, bringing my lips to his. "Now shut up and let me take your mind off it."

I don't even get a chance to respond before his warm lips are pressing down over mine and he kisses me deeply. Cruz's tongue slips inside my mouth and I melt into him, letting him hold my weight as I quickly get lost in his kiss.

My pussy clenches with desire and I wonder just how far things can go with these stupid bars between us when Cruz pulls back and runs his heated gaze down my body. He reads the phrase on the front of my panties before taking my hips and slowly dropping to his knees. "Well, well," he murmurs, his eyes rising to meet mine as he slowly draws my panties down, making heat flood between my legs. "The panties have spoken. Who the hell am I to disappoint?"

Fuck me. I really do deserve to be locked away in a cell.

Cruz licks his lips as a wicked grin stretches across my face. Who the hell said that I can't enjoy myself while I'm down here? And judging from the darkness seeping into Cruz's green eyes, I'd dare say we're on exactly the same page. Even more so when he pulls me hard against the bars and slips my leg through the small gap, hooking it over his shoulder.

He dives in, absolutely no point in waiting, and I instantly curl my fingers into his hair and watch him work. The view of his tongue slipping out of his mouth and flicking over my clit is something I will never tire of. I suck in a breath as he does it again, my fingers tightening in his hair, already on edge.

Cruz works my clit with his skilled tongue and reaches around me and the bar, slipping his hand under my leg until his thick fingers are pushing up into my aching pussy. He gives me exactly what I want until I'm screaming out his name, my cries bouncing off the walls of my cell and echoing far down the hallway. There's nothing quite like being able to scream as loud as you can, knowing that not a damn person can hear you, except for the man whose tongue is flicking against my clit.

My pussy aches, the need to pull Cruz through the metal bars and fuck him until I die is far too strong to handle. I'd give anything to feel him sinking deep inside me, but for now, this will have to do.

My orgasm builds deep within me, each pass of his tongue only making it so much more intense. My fingers pull at his hair as his fingers massage inside of me, finding that spot that drives me wild.

He picks up his pace, and within seconds, I forget where I am as all that exists is the convulsing, violent orgasm that tears through my body. "HOLY FUCK, CRUZ," I cry, tears springing to my eyes from the intensity. My body turns into a quivering mess and the second my orgasm finally eases, I collapse to the ground, Cruz barely saving me before I come to a crash landing.

I just stare at him, taking in the proud smirk that covers his lips, as well as the shine that sits over his mouth like a trophy. I crawl back to the bars and just like that, his lips are back on mine and I taste myself, feeling a thrill rush through me.

Cruz murmurs against my lips. "I'll never get bored of how responsive you are to my touch."

I groan into him. "Trust me, I'm right there with you."

I feel his lips pull into a wide smile. "I still stand by what I said," he tells me. "If King changes his mind and feels like fucking you over, I'm running away with you and keeping you all to myself."

"Assuming you can break me out of this cell with your magical touch."

"Hey," he laughs, pulling back and curling his arm around my waist. "I'm a man of my word."

"I'm counting on it."

His eyes soften and sparkle with something unfamiliar as he

watches me for a quiet second, and as if he flipped a switch, a dorky smile stretches over his full lips. "Did I ever tell you about the time I catfished Gray into thinking I was a hot Swedish chick who wanted to fuck?"

My brows shoot up in interest. "What?"

"Uh-huh," he smirks, getting comfortable. "I even convinced the fucker to record himself jerking off then shout 'YAHTZEE' when he came."

"Bullshit," I laugh. "You didn't."

"I sure fucking did, but man, he was pissed when he found out," he tells me. "Actually, he'll probably fucking kill me if he found out that I told you."

I shake my head, scooching down against his warmth as a real belly laugh takes over me. "I think Yahtzee is going to be his new nickname," I grin. "What else have you done to those sorry fuckers? I want to hear it all."

Cruz grins, and just like that, he tells me every last story he has on the boys—the good, the bad, and the more than ugly. We talk and laugh, my situation completely forgotten until I'm awkwardly falling asleep against his shoulder with a bar pressed against the side of my head.

But even then, with Cruz's warm arms wrapped around my body, it does nothing to keep the monsters at bay. I find myself still desperately wishing for Carver, now more than ever.

3

My head pounds as I wake on the hard ground of my cell to find Cruz shivering beside me and his suit jacket from last night's sham of a party draped over my body.

That idiot. Even while I'm asleep he's still trying to play my knight in shining armor. At least he still has his dress shirt stretched across his strong body, pulling at the seams, so I guess he's not a complete idiot.

My body aches as I pull myself off him, adjusting his jacket over my body and trying to bask in its warmth, but it's got nothing on a good bed and his body wrapped around mine. I could have slept in the hard bed with the blankets from hell, but something told me that sleeping against Cruz's shoulder with a bar pressed against my head was my best option.

Cruz begins to stir, and I keep extra still, wanting him to get all the sleep he possibly can. I kept him up late last night, much later than necessary as I feared closing my eyes. I demanded story after story until neither of us could force our eyes open a second longer.

A throat clears from above us and my head jerks up, my eyes widening in surprise. Cruz wakes, and before I can even make out the face of the man standing before us, we're both on our feet, ready for a threat.

We find Tobias King standing before us, and we both sag in relief, but that doesn't mean we're out of trouble yet—he looks pissed. His eyes—that are just like his son's—rake over Cruz and the guilty expression that crosses Cruz's perfect face almost has me ready to lash out at Tobias. How dare he make Cruz feel like shit for spending the night with me. He was my savior last night and he should be rewarded. In fact, the second I get out of here, I'll be sure to do just that.

"Out," Tobias demands, his cold, hard stare falling against Cruz and silently suggesting that if he doesn't make it quick, he'll regret it.

Cruz glances back at me and the conflict in his eyes is nearly enough to bring me to my knees. He wants to stay. He wants to be the person by my side, holding my hand and telling me that it's all going to be okay. But he can't go against a direct order from a superior—a head of Dynasty for that matter.

"Just go," I tell him, wishing desperately that I could drop to my knees and beg him to stay. "I'll be fine."

"You sure?" he insists, not moving an inch until I give him an encouraging smile, silently telling him that I'm perfectly fine despite the turmoil and fear I feel inside. Reluctance spreads over his face, but without another word, he turns back to Tobias and steps up in front of him. "If anything happens to her in there …"

"She'll be safe," Tobias demands, his voice low as his eyes narrow on his son's best friend, clearly not enjoying his audacity to speak out of line, and probably thinking up a million ways that he could be punished for it.

Cruz just grunts and steps around Tobias before walking back down the hallway and glancing over his shoulder, keeping his blank stare on me, and taking my heart right along with him.

He's gone within seconds, and as soon as I can, I slice my gaze to Tobias. I know I'm supposed to trust him, he's one of the good ones, but in a position like this and a world that is full of corruption, I don't know who the hell I can trust. Carver is proof of that.

Tobias steps closer to the cell door and slips a key into the lock. My whole body shivers at the sound of the door sliding open as I'm thrown back in time to a different cell, standing half-naked before strange men, but I don't let it show as I keep my hard stare on Tobias. Even if he claims to be one of the good ones, he still left me down here, didn't come to offer me dinner, a warm bed, or company.

This man was supposed to be my father's closest friend, and this is the way he treats his daughter. I'm not going to lie, I'm not impressed. If all the guys' parents are like this, it's no wonder they're so much happier when they're all gone.

Tobias' gaze sweeps down my body, taking in my lack of clothing and pressing his lips into an unapproving tight line as he scans over the front of my panties. "Here, put these on," he says, thrusting a pair of distressed jeans and a black tank my way. "These belong to Hunter's younger cousin, but they should fit you just fine."

My brows shoot up as I stare at the clothes. "He has a cousin who lives around here?"

"Plenty," Tobias says as though it's not even close to being a big deal. How the hell didn't I know this? "He has two younger siblings at home. Caitlin and Cody, they just turned six at the beginning of the year."

My mind reels as I take the clothes. Tobias discreetly turns around to offer me some privacy, but it's not as though he hasn't already seen what's on offer. "Do any of the other guys have any siblings that I need to know about?"

"They all have siblings," he grumbles, making my eyes bug out of my head as I pull the jeans up my legs, surprised to find that they fit like a glove. "However, I don't see how that is anything you need to know."

Damn. The respect I had for him plummets. This guy really isn't who I thought he was going to be, but really? I don't know why I expected anything different. I don't know what kind of man my father was or what kind of company he liked to keep. Hell, maybe Tobias is just having a bad day or genuinely believes that I was in the wrong last night. I mean, yeah … I did kill Royston Carver. I'm not hiding that. I did it out in the open for the world to see, but he had it coming. He was practically begging me to make a move, and he learned the hard way that when you try to play games with me, you're going to lose.

Tobias doesn't say another word and I let out a sigh as I finish getting dressed, my mind picturing smaller versions of all the guys, and wondering what kind of people their little brothers and sisters might be. Though something tells me that they're probably all a little more like their parents. Otherwise, I'm sure the guys would have told me all about them. But then again, maybe not. I've always had to squeeze information out of them, and every time I do, they act as though they're doing me a grand favor.

I focus on pulling last night's heels back onto my feet, and while they're not exactly the kind of shoes I'd wear with an outfit like this, it works surprisingly well. I feel like absolute shit. A comfortable bed and a nice warm shower would have done me wonders, but it's going to have to wait. Hell, I wouldn't mind using the bathroom either.

Once I'm ready, Tobias steps out of the open cell door and leads me into the hallway, and while it's still concrete walls and hard, cold floors, I feel as though I can finally breathe. He leads me down the long corridor, not saying a word and making me wonder just how guilty he thinks I am. It's not as though he probably hasn't killed men before. It was my impression that Dynasty shrugged off murder as though it was as common as choosing a paint color for their wives to redecorate their million dollar homes. No one flinched when learning that the guys single-handedly took out twelve hitmen sent for me. Aside from Royston's title, why the hell would they care about this? Besides, I don't want to sound like a cocky asshole or anything, but surely I have a bit of leeway as the leader, right? At least, I hope.

We walk out through the hallway and I have to admit that getting to walk is a million times better than having two random men dragging me by my arms. The walk is longer than I remember, and by the time we break out of the hallway and step into the main reception area of the underground world, my anxiety level has risen far beyond anything that I can handle.

Tobias doesn't seem to notice, or if he does, he doesn't care. I follow behind him, and with every step I take, I keep my eyes focused on his back. His build is nearly identical to his son's, though that's about as far as the similarities go. Personality-wise, they couldn't be more different.

My heels click against the tiles as we walk through the wide-open space of the reception area, and it takes me far too long to realize that he's leading me back toward the council chambers where I'd first met the other sixteen heads of Dynasty.

We make our way to the same hallway that I'd blindly followed Carver down just yesterday morning, and at Tobias' deep sigh, I raise my gaze to find King and Grayson quickly approaching from the other end. Seeing me, they pick up their pace and don't stop until King's barging his father out of the way and taking my shoulders in his warm hands.

King's eyes roam over my face. "Are you alright?" he demands as Grayson hovers in close as though he was protecting me from a threat, only it's just us in this long as fuck hallway.

"Yeah," I say, desperately wishing I could just push up onto my tippy-toes and press my lips against his, only with his brooding, pissed off father glaring at the three of us, now doesn't really seem like the right time. "Cruz came and spent the night with me so I wasn't alone."

"But are you alright?" he questions, his eyes focused heavily on mine.

I press my lips into a hard line and shrug my shoulders because honestly, I have no fucking idea.

"Hurry along," Tobias says. "It is not wise to keep the heads of Dynasty waiting."

Grayson flinches at his tone and shoots a wicked glare sailing up to his friend's father. "She's the fucking leader of Dynasty. If she wants to keep those assholes waiting, then she has every right."

Tobias clenches his jaw. "Where do you get off addressing me like that?"

"Father, don't," King warns. "Gray is right. Winter is our leader, and if she's not ready to walk in there, then you have no place forcing her to. She will make them wait as long as she needs."

Tobias glares at the two boys. "Are you so blinded by her body and what she can offer you that you've forgotten exactly what it is that got her in this mess in the first place?"

"Innocent until proven guilty," Grayson reminds him with a hard growl. "But it seems that you've already made up your mind."

King's eyes narrow on his father as Grayson discreetly steps between us, somehow becoming my protector over the last twelve hours. "I have done no such thing," Tobias insists, his tone strong and unnerved. "Do I need to remind you of the nightmares your little sister had last night after watching a woman she idolized murder a man? I know exactly where my loyalties lie, but that does not mean that I cannot be furious with her reckless actions and careless behavior. I have known Royston for fifty-odd years. We grew up together, we learned to fight together, and then we learned how to rule this great organization in Andrew Ravenwood's wake. While he may have held different values and beliefs, he was still a friend, and I am anxious to get young Elodie into the council chambers and hear exactly what she has to say for herself. Only then, once I have heard her out, will I decide if she deserves my continued loyalty."

The boys don't move, holding their ground for a few long, drawn-out moments before King finally nods and gives his father the benefit of the doubt. He releases my shoulder and raises his chin to his father. "I want to come in."

Tobias shakes his head. "Absolutely not," he says. "It's a closed trial. You know the rules."

King sighs, giving up and making it clear that he had absolutely no shot at getting inside that room in the first place, but I appreciate him trying anyway.

I step around the boys, sliding my hand down King's arm and squeezing his hand, hating the concern that flashes in his eyes. "I'll be fine," I tell him. "Carver's father said plenty of incriminating things last night. They'll see that I was right to finish him."

"Let's hope they see it that way."

Grayson nods in agreement before taking my shoulder and giving it a gentle squeeze, making something flutter deep inside my stomach. He meets my eyes, and before I know it, he turns and continues down the hallway.

"We'll be here waiting," King says, before turning and following Grayson, leaving me alone in the long hallway with his disapproving father.

"Right, let's get this over with."

I nod, and just like that, we pick up our pace and make our way down the long corridor until we're stopping outside the council chamber doors. "Are you ready for this?" he asks, deciding to take pity on me. "They're going to be ruthless and will have absolutely no regard for your feelings."

I clench my jaw. "I can handle it."

He gives a firm nod, not an ounce of emotion over his face. "I know you can," and just like that, he opens the door and ushers me inside.

I take a deep breath, the nerves instantly settling inside my stomach. My gaze quickly flicks around the room, and even though it was only yesterday morning that I was in here, it now feels like a lifetime ago.

I take a hesitant step inside before remembering who the fuck I am and raising my chin. The boys would be seriously pissed if they caught me walking in here already looking like I'd lost. I've suffered through too much to give in like that. No, I'm going to walk in here with my head held high, put these old fuckers in their place, and make sure I can walk straight back out of here with my freedom intact—well, as much freedom as being Andrew Ravenwood's long lost daughter allows.

I make my way around the right-hand side of the table with Tobias following behind me until he reaches his spot and takes his seat. I continue, knowing I can mostly trust this side and raise my gaze at the other eight men who take up the seats across the table.

Their glares all hit me like a freight train, but I keep my composure, only faltering a step when I find Carver's dark, stormy eyes staring back at me.

I suck in a sharp, surprised breath.

Fuck me.

He takes his father's seat, and while technically it makes sense for him to be here, I hadn't expected it, which is my own stupidity. Of course he was going to be here. I should have been more prepared.

He watches me closely, following each step I take until I hit the top of the table.

My heart thunders in my chest as I look around the table. This is so much harder than I thought it was going to be. I know I told Tobias that I was ready, but nothing in the world can prepare someone for this.

This meeting will determine my fate, it will determine if I spend the rest of my life rotting in some shitty cell or if I will get the chance to fly. All my life, I've been the one in charge, I've made the rules, and lived by my own free will. I did what I wanted, when I wanted, and now, my future rests in the hands of these sixteen strange men who don't know a damn thing about me—half of them who have already gone to extreme lengths to try and have me killed.

The odds aren't even close to being in my favor.

I slowly drop to my seat, keeping the mask of confidence stretched across my face despite knowing that Carver can see straight through it.

My ass hits the chair, and as I look out at the sixteen men before me, I let out a silent, shaky breath.

It's showtime.

4

"Alright," I say, addressing the room. "Let's not pretend that we're here for a good time. Let's say what needs to be said and get this over and done with so I can go home."

Carver scoffs from across the table, along with a few other men sitting beside him. "You've got a lot of confidence for a *little girl* who just murdered a man in the middle of a ballroom with hundreds of eyes watching you."

I raise my brow, more than ready to throw myself across this table and wrap my hands around his throat in the same way he'd done to me, but hey, if he wants to be petty, then damn it, I can be petty too.

"You didn't think I was so much of a *little girl* when your hands were all over my body. So, what's it going to be, Carver?" I demand, purring his name, more than happy to call him out in front of these old assholes. "Am I a little girl or just a bitch who your father shouldn't have messed with?"

Carver's eyes harden, his jaw clenching as his hand curls into a ball on the table. "Watch your mouth, Elodie," he spits, using my real name as an insult just because he knows how much I hate it. "You don't get to speak of my father."

"That's the exact reason we're here though, right?" I question, my voice strained with fury as I fight to remain in my seat. "Royston Carver had no issues speaking ill of my father last night. So, how is that fair? One rule for him and another for me because I'm a woman? Fuck you."

"Now, now," Earnest Brooks speaks up from beside me as the room turns into chaos, one side yelling at the other. "Let's not allow this to get out of hand."

Carver scoffs, ignoring Earnest's pleas. "Oh, you're going to play the woman card now? Like you give a shit about that."

I stand, making at least four of the men around the table flinch. "Don't act like you fucking know me, Dante. You don't," I spit at him. "The woman card is the whole reason we got into this fucked up mess in the first place. All of you sorry fuckers couldn't get on board with the fact that my father's firstborn was a female. That's what started this shit and I'm going to fucking end it."

Carver just rolls his eyes as men from all around the table scoff.

No matter what side they're sitting on, no man can handle being called out on their sexist bullshit. "We're not here to discuss what happened eighteen years ago," Carver insists. "We're here to condemn you for killing my father, one of the heads of this grand organization."

"Grand organization?" I laugh. "Oh, we're putting on a show, are we? You want to get some brownie points for talking up Dynasty like you owe your life to it? Well, guess what? Dynasty is the whole fucking reason that I've never had a life. The men sitting around this table are the reason I lost my family, I lost my childhood, I lost everything I know. So don't go pretending that this *grand organization* isn't filled with corruption—a corruption that I can guarantee your father was behind. You fucking hate this world. You don't want to be in that chair just as much as I don't want this one."

Murmurs flow through the room and Carver's stare somehow darkens even more, and I freaking hope that my comment drops his ass in boiling hot water. "Watch your fucking mouth," Carver warns, something sinister flashing in his deep, secretive eyes. "You've been here two fucking seconds. You don't know what the hell you're talking about."

Tobias slams his hand down on the massive table, his glare shooting across to Carver as the room falls into silence. "Alright, that's enough," he demands. "That's Andrew Ravenwood's daughter you're speaking to. Show some respect. We're here to get to the bottom of yesterday's incident, not throw insults across the table like a bunch of children. You are here to advocate for your late father, so do that, and for fuck's sake, can the both of you do it with an ounce of respect for our dead?"

I raise a brow at Tobias in a proud, surprised shock. I didn't know the dickhead had it in him. I'm impressed.

Carver leans back in his chair, his glare now not only focused on me, but on Tobias too, and for a brief moment, I sit here wondering where he finds the nerve to act like such a dick in front of his friends' parents when I remember that these guys weren't brought up to be like the normal kids at school. They were brought up to be men in power, they were raised to be leaders, to take charge, and do what needs to be done. In fact, I don't even think they were raised, *they were trained.*

I take a leaf out of Carver's book and lean back in my chair, glancing around the big table. "Okay," I say. "Let's start over. Where shall we begin?"

A man from the left-hand side of the table raises his chin. "How about the start?" he says with an irritated scoff, clearly trying to be funny and making a mockery of the whole situation.

I eye him for a second, surprised to find him younger than the others; perhaps thirty-five at the most. "Oh, we've got a class clown, huh? How exciting."

His gaze narrows and I don't bother asking his name. His stare makes it obvious he didn't appreciate my comment—but fuck him. I didn't appreciate his either. So instead, I turn to Earnest, knowing he's bound to give me some guidance while hoping that my dismissal grinds against the clown's nerves. "The dance?"

Earnest nods, a blank, hard expression on his face. "Yes, start there."

I let out a breath and face the sixteen men around me while trying to keep a neutral expression as I pass by Carver's hard stare. "As some of you would have seen last night, I was doing the traditional dance with Hunter King after the initiation when Royston Carver stepped in."

"Get on with it," the class clown interrupts, getting glares from all around the room. "Are you going to recap every fucking detail? We're not blind, everyone here is aware that you were dancing with Royston. Get on with it."

A grin pulls at the corner of my lips, and I stand, my eyes unintentionally flicking toward Carver before focusing heavily on the dickhead across the table. I slowly walk around, the tension building with every step I take. He watches me carefully, realizing before I've even got to him just how badly he's fucked up. I may be the one on trial here, but I'm still his fucking leader.

I walk right up to the back of his chair and lean around him. "What's your name?" I question, fixing him with a deadly stare.

He swallows before narrowing his gaze, assuming I'm just some punk kid who he can toss around and make a fool of. "Matthew Montgomery."

"Well, Matthew," I say with a sickly-sweet smile. "Do I need to muzzle you or will you shut the fuck up so I can tell you assholes what the hell went down last night? It's quite a simple task, but if you can't manage, let me know now so I can pull your balls out through your throat."

Matthew's jaw clenches, but I keep the smile plastered across my face, knowing damn well that when it comes time to vote, this bastard won't be on my side. He leans back in his seat and I watch the humiliation wash over his face. Then just to add salt to the injury, I wink and blow him a kiss before slowly walking back to my seat, knowing damn well that he won't be an issue for the rest of the trial.

"Okay," I announce to the table as I take my seat. "Does anybody else have any issues with my storytelling abilities or am I free to continue with my rundown of the night?"

"Just get on with it," Preston Scardoni says. "I have things to do today."

As much as I hate the guy, I ignore the sharp tone in his voice and pick up where I left off. "Royston Carver interrupted my dance with Hunter King, and the first thing he told me was to plaster a smile over my face to express a united front for the people watching. Naturally, I wasn't fond of his demands and tried to leave but he held me tight enough to leave bruises on my arms, refusing to let me walk away."

Carver's stare tightens. "Prove it."

I raise a brow and do just that, knowing damn well that Carver is familiar with every little mark, freckle, and scar on my body, even though he's never touched me in the way he truly wants to. Without skipping a beat, I stand and turn so that he can see the thick purple lines of Royston's fingers that dug into my skin last night.

Shocked gasps come from the right-hand side of the table while scoffs and disbelief come from the other. Anger flashes over Carver's features, and a second later, it's gone, replaced with the same irritating mask he wore when I first walked in here. "That could have been from anything," Preston Scardoni insists. "You're a reckless, violent teen.

You have absolutely no proof that those marks came from Royston."

God, I've never wanted to throat punch someone more in my life.

"I agree," another man says from beside him. "While Royston certainly was a piece of work, that's not sufficient evidence to claim that he deserved to give up his life."

"Elodie never claimed that was why she killed Royston," Earnest throws back across the table. "She was simply recapping her story."

"Exactly," Preston scoffs. "It's nothing more than a story. How are we to ever believe a word this girl says?"

"Because it's the truth," I demand. "And you damn well know it."

Preston growls, slamming his hand on the table, much louder than Tobias had earlier. "I know of nothing," he roars. "I had nothing to do with Royston's misdemeanors."

"So, you agree then? Royston is guilty of misdemeanors?"

His eyes widen. "What? No …"

"Just what I thought."

"That's enough of your twisted mind games," Carver says. "My father wasn't guilty of anything."

I scoff, shaking my head at him, unable to believe the level he'll go just to get at me. "Don't make me destroy you, Carver," I beg of him. "You've told me enough about this world and the families within it to bring you down, and I'd really prefer not to do that to you, but if you keep pushing me, I'll be left with no fucking choice."

Carver's stare tightens. While the boys haven't told me specific things about this world, they've given me enough breadcrumbs to be capable of putting the pieces together. And if it's my freedom on the line, he knows damn well that I'll bring anyone and everyone down around me just to save myself.

"Let's get this trial back on track," Earnest says, looking more frustrated by the second. "You were dancing …"

"Right," I say, slicing my annoyed gaze away from Carver. "He was forcing me to put on a show for the people around us, and as he was, he was busy telling me his big plans for the future."

"What plans?" Carver demands, leaning in and making me wonder if he really doesn't know.

I turn my gaze back to his, somehow still needing him as my comfort within this strange world, despite the way my head is telling me to pull away. "He was planning on taking over leadership. He wanted to rule over you all," I tell them, looking back at Carver. "Why don't you put your bitch of a mother on trial? She's as guilty as they come. I bet she was even the one to put the idea in his head."

"Watch it," Carver demands as gasps and whispers are heard right around the table. "That's my mother you're talking about."

I can't help the scoff that pulls from deep within me. "Fuck off with your theatrics. It's not like I'm saying anything we don't already know. That show she put on for the people last night was embarrassing."

"How the hell did Royston plan on taking over leadership?" Preston demands, getting us back to the point, not bothering with the bullshit nastiness getting thrown between me and Carver. "Sounds a bit far-fetched to me."

"He said that he didn't believe I had what it takes to be the leader of Dynasty, and while that question is still up for debate, it's not the issue at hand. He stated that I was going to be the face of the organization, but I would answer to him."

"And?" Earnest prompts.

"And I told him that he was fucking insane," I spit. "There's no way in hell I was going to answer to a man like him, especially the asshole who killed my parents."

Carver shakes his head as everyone watches on through narrowed eyes. "You don't know that."

I stand, throwing my hands down on the table in frustration. "He admitted it to me," I yell staring Carver down. "He was pissed because I wasn't going to willingly conform to his plan, so he pushed harder and said that I either answer to him or he'll continue in his endeavor to end my life."

Gasps come from the right-hand side of the room as Tobias looks at Carver. "Is this true?" he demands. "Was your father responsible for the attack on Elodie in the woods?"

Carver shakes his head. "No, he wasn't. I would have known. He was a proud man. He would have boasted about it in private."

I scoff. "You mean just how he boasted about killing my parents right after he admitted to trying to kill me?"

Carver stands, the anger pouring out of him in waves. "You have no fucking evidence."

"He told me. He laughed about the way my mother screamed," I yell back at him, the emotion far too high to handle. "He told me how he forced her to watch his sharp blade slice through my father's throat and then did the same to her. So forgive me, but I did what any other red-blooded human would do, and I ended his fucking pathetic existence. Hold it against me for all I care, but I will never live to regret it. Royston Carver deserved to die an excruciating death. I only hate that I didn't get the chance to drag it out."

"What happened, Elodie?" Mr. Danforth says to my right. "What did you do?"

I suck in a shaky breath and look back at Carver, feeling the guilt sweeping through me. "I told him to rot in the deepest pits of hell and stabbed him with the dagger I'd stolen from the initiation, making sure to pierce his lung."

Carver drops back to his seat, silence falling around the room. A beat passes where no one says a damn thing until Carver's tortured stare lands back on mine. "You had no right."

"I had every right."

Cruz's father clears his throat. "Whether you had the right or not, that's beside the point. You murdered one of our heads, one of our brothers. That's not how Dynasty handles things."

"He did it," I insist.

"I'm sorry, Elodie," Mr. Danforth continues. "While I'm compelled to trust your story, you have no hard evidence, just the claim that he said those things to you."

My world crushes and dread settles heavily in my gut. I'm not going to get out of here.

"Let's put it to a vote," Mr. Danforth says, "Then we can move forward from there."

"Wait." My head snaps back to Carver to see a darkness in his eyes that I've never quite seen before, and my nerves instantly stand on edge. "I just have one question before we take our vote," he says, his voice low and filled with regret as he meets my eyes, waiting a beat to make sure that every fucking ear in the room has his undivided attention.

I wait, my heart thundering in my chest, knowing that this is it. Whatever he's about to say is going to destroy me.

"Answer me this," Carver asks, his voice wavering. "Two nights ago, when you first learned the names of the seventeen families of Dynasty. Did you, or did you not suggest taking out the head of each of the eight families that sit to your left, to rid Dynasty of its corruption and replace them with their sons or daughters? The young members of our people who can be easily swayed to vote in your favor?"

Well, fuck.

What the hell is he doing? I know he hates me right now, but this? This is just condemning me to life behind bars. I'll never be free after this. I'll never have their trust.

Gasps sound all around the room, cries of outrage from the left and shocked murmurs from the right. If they didn't think I was guilty before, they sure as hell do now.

I meet Carver's heavy stare with one of my own before letting out a breath and nodding my head. There's no point denying it. I've never been one to lie, and while the comment I made was taken far out of context, I can't deny that I ever said it. "Yes," I tell the room. "Two nights ago, after learning the probability that the men to my left were most likely responsible for the attack in the woods, I suggested taking them out and rebuilding Dynasty without corruption, and in the image my grandfather, Gerald Ravenwood, first dreamed of. It was a comment made in anger, never meant to be taken seriously."

There's silence throughout the room and then finally Earnest takes pity on me and addresses the room. "Let us vote. All in favor that Elodie Ravenwood is guilty of murder and should receive further punishment, raise your hand."

My heart races as I slowly look around the table, one by one, hands begin rise.

One. Two.

Eyes meet mine across the table, narrowed stares, and guilty expressions.

Three. Four.

All hands to the right remain down and I focus on the other remaining four to my left—Scardoni, Beckett, Montgomery, and Carver, and sure enough, hands continue to rise.

Matthew Montgomery raises his hand. That's five. Preston Scardoni joins the party, making it six. Then just when I think I can't take it any longer, Grayson's father, Harlen Beckett slowly draws his hand high above his head.

Seven.

I meet Carver's stare. It's all on him. The final vote to be cast.

Will he save me or condemn me to a lifetime behind bars?

Seven hands raised, nine hands down.

My heart thunders in my chest, the sound loud in my ears as my hands begin to sweat. I keep my gaze trained heavily on Carver as he does the same, and for just a brief moment, I can pretend that it's just the two of us in the room.

He sees the desperation in my eyes just as I see his need to get me the fuck out of here, but it doesn't make sense. Why put me here if he never wanted this for me? He was always supposed to protect me. He told me that I could trust him.

Then ever so slowly, Carver raises his hand and crushes me, his heart on his sleeve as devastation washes through me.

"We have an even vote," Earnest says before looking back at me. "I'm sorry, Elodie, but you must remain down in the cells until we can reach a verdict."

And just like that, two men come storming into the council chamber and curl their hands around my arms, just as they'd done last night, before dragging me away and taking me straight back to hell.

5

The soft *tap, tap, tap* of my bare feet pacing back and forth in my tiny, dark cell is the only noise I hear for hours. My hands ball into fists, only to be released as I let out a frustrated breath.

How the fuck could Carver do this to me? Surely, he knows that his father was guilty. Surely, he knows how badly he deserved to die.

There has to be something more going on here. I know Carver and I had a shaky relationship to start with, but to condemn me to a life behind bars? That's taking it way too far. Even through all of this, through his hand around my throat, through his pissed off glares and nasty comments, I still trusted that he'd have my back.

I've never been so wrong.

God, why is it so hard to hate him?

He was the guy who'd come after me in the middle of the night to make sure I wasn't getting myself in trouble, he's the guy who had the balls to break all the hard truths to me, the only one to ever give it to me straight. He's the guy who'd allow me to sneak into his bed at night to keep the monsters away, he's the one who came after me in that shitty cell that Sam had shoved me in. Time and time again, Carver has been my savior, but now … he feels like the perfect stranger.

I thought something was building between us. It was strained, but it was something big. I could feel it right down in the bottom of my chest. When he touched me … when he kissed me, it was like magic pulsing around us. The electricity would spark, and I'd feel as though I was on cloud nine. Nothing could possibly get better than the times Carver and I were briefly on the same page.

All that's gone now. We'll never get that electricity back. The fire that sparked between us is well and truly dead, just like our fathers.

My fingers bunch into a tight fist and my nails dig into the soft skin of my palms, instantly drawing blood. I try to stop, but I can't. It gives me a release that I can't possibly find anywhere. My body itches to fight. I need to beat the living daylights out of someone, and that someone needs to be Carver, but I'll settle for the next dickhead who walks down this hallway and dares to face me.

I need to fucking scream.

I've never felt so angry. My blood boils and I hate how much I've allowed this to affect me. The boys will get me out of here; I know they will. I shouldn't be stressing about it. I just need to give them time. I'm sure they're working on a plan right now. At least I hope they are.

I'm not so sure about Grayson yet, but I feel as though I can trust King and Cruz, at least for the important things. Can I trust King to resist thinking about getting his dick wet? No, certainly not. Can I trust Cruz not to take off with my Ducati whenever the fuck he wants? Again, no. But when it comes to my safety, my life, I trust them with all that I am.

The frustration burns brightly inside of me and I cross to the small, uncomfortable bed, dropping to my knees and slamming my head down against the pillow. I hold it to my face and scream as loud as I can, letting out every ounce of energy that pulses through my veins.

I scream and scream, tears of anger springing to my eyes until my throat is raw and aching.

How did this even happen? One second I was putting on a show for the sixteen families of Dynasty, doing their bullshit cult initiation, and the next, there was a dead man at my feet with his blood pooling around my heels and a satisfied smirk stretching across my face.

Who the fuck am I?

"WINTER. WHAT THE FUCK ARE YOU DOING?"

My head whips up to find Grayson, King, and Cruz standing on the opposite side of my cell, staring in at me like I'm some kind of sideshow with their faces pressed right up against the metal bars. My breath comes in hard, sharp pants as I look at the three of them, wide-eyed and concerned.

I drop the pillow back to the bed and go crashing down to the hard concrete beneath me, completely out of breath. I didn't realize that screaming into a pillow was such a workout.

I lean back onto my hands and look up at the three guys in defeat. "You have to get me out of here," I beg, my throat raw as my voice comes out with a broken rasp.

"We're working on it," Grayson promises me, the depth of the concern in his eyes really putting me off. Since when did he care so much? He's had my back since the second Carver's hand found my throat.

"I just … I … I can't be in here anymore. I have to get out of here and … fuck. I have to hit something. I don't know. I can't take it anymore."

"You're okay," Cruz murmurs, desperately trying to calm me down. "Just breathe. You're getting yourself all worked up. I know you're angry with the system but hurting yourself like this isn't going to help."

"The system?" I demand, throwing myself to my feet and instantly beginning to pace. "I'm not angry with the system. I'm fucking angry with Carver."

"Carver?" King grunts. "The fuck are you talking about?"

I stop pacing and walk straight up to the metal bars, their closeness somehow making it a little easier to breathe. I meet each of their hardening stares, and the second I get close enough, Cruz reaches through the bar and captures my hand in his, holding it tight and refusing to let me yank it free in his need to give me all his comfort and support.

I take three slow breaths, knowing that if I continue like this, I won't be able to talk for days and that will really fuck up my plans to give Carver a piece of my mind.

I'd give anything for my brass knuckles right now. I'd love to introduce them to Carver's face, but a throat punch and a few knees to the junk will have to suffice.

"Winter," Grayson prompts, his voice low and demanding. "What the fuck did Carver do?"

I meet his heavy stare, our eyes connecting with an intense force that keeps me captivated. "It was going alright. I thought I was about to get out of there, and just before they were going to make their vote, Carver asked 'did you, or did you not suggest taking out the head of each of the eight families that sit to your left, to rid Dynasty of its corruption and replace them with their sons or daughters?' " I say, mimicking Carver's stupid deep voice.

"FUCK," King grunts, pulling himself away from the bars and instantly pacing behind the two boys. He pauses for a beat to look back at me. "You would have looked guilty as shit," he spits as Grayson seems to shake with anger and Cruz's hand tightens in mine to the point of pain, but fuck me, it's a pain that I welcome. "That was just a bullshit comment, one we've all made multiple times over the past few years."

"Tell me you're fucking lying," Grayson demands. "Carver wouldn't do that. He wouldn't use something like that against you. That's not how he handles shit."

"Just like he would never curl his fingers around my throat and squeeze until I couldn't breathe? Yeah, he's a real fucking saint. Open your eyes, Grayson, Carver isn't the guy you thought he was. He's just like his father. He dropped a fucking bomb over me and hung around to watch it explode."

"Don't say that," Cruz murmurs, his heart heavy on his sleeve. "He's just … he's going through some things. He had no choice. He just watched you kill his father and now he has to advocate for his revenge hungry family. You know that."

"No," I say, shaking my head. "This wasn't just advocating for his family, this was more. He fucking dumped me in a pile of shit and made sure that I'd never get out. He's the whole fucking reason I'm in here right now. I should have walked free after that trial, but he fucking made sure that I was to suffer."

Grayson pulls on the bars as though he could tear them free. "What the fuck are you talking about? What did he do?"

"During the vote," I tell them, glancing at each of them to see their heavy, confused stares boring into my eyes, silently begging me not to say what they're already dreading. "Carver had the deciding vote. Everyone else had already raised their hands and it was down to him. All he had to do was keep his fucking hand down and I would have walked free."

"No," Cruz says, shaking his head. "He wouldn't do that to you. It's one thing to put on a fucking show for his family, but he wouldn't condemn you here."

"Well, he fucking did. He looked me right in the eyes and raised his goddamn hand, making it clear that he was the one doing this. He had the power to set me free, but he raised his fucking hand." Angry hot tears spring from my eyes, and I tear my hand out of Cruz's to hastily wipe them away. "He put me in here. It was an even vote. Carver could have saved me."

Grayson pushes away from the bars with an angry grunt as I sink to my knees, feeling more defeated than ever. Carver was the one who put me in here, but he's also the only one I can count on to get me out.

I'm fucked.

Grayson's hands ball into fists and I watch him pacing up and down the narrow hallway, his hands pulsing exactly the same way that mine do when I'm pissed off. "How could he fucking do that?" Grayson demands, not looking at anyone in particular, but openly speaking to us all. "It doesn't make sense. You guys didn't hear the way he'd talk about her in private. That fucking … FUCK."

Just like that, Grayson storms right back the way he came with a look on his face that would have even the strongest of men crumbling. "Shit," Cruz sighs, pulling away and walking after him.

"Where are they going?" I ask, looking up at King who shakes his head, his jaw clenched in anger.

"Grayson is about to beat the living shit out of Carver," he says as though he knows Grayson's exact intention, "and Cruz is going to make sure he doesn't fucking kill him."

"Shit," I groan, dropping my head forward as the fierce jealousy cuts through me like a knife. I'd give anything to go in Grayson's place, to feel my knuckles busting his lip, my foot slamming into the side of his ribs. I've given my all on Carver before and I hardly made a dent. While it felt great at the time, he deserves so much worse than what little damage I could do, so hopefully, Grayson's right swing comes with a little more force than mine ever could.

King takes a few calming breaths before taking a step forward and placing himself right in front of the bars again. He grabs them with both hands, keeping his eyes locked on mine for an intense moment, saying everything he needs to say with that one look—he wants me out of here, he wants me lying in his bed with his arms curled tightly around me where he can keep me safe from the horrors of the world, and fuck it, I want that too.

I want to forget all of this. I want to go back to the shitty life I had jumping from home to home before I found out any of the Dynasty bullshit. It was a hard life full of horrors and the unknown, but I was content with what I had. I was going to finish school and somehow make my way through college. I was going to get a job that paid enough to keep a roof over my head, and I was going to live. I might never have thrived, but I would have lived by my rule and on my own schedule.

How is this the life that my parents had mapped out for me? Surely they would have wanted better for their only daughter.

King dips his head forward against the bars, covering his face in a dark shadow. "I'm going to make this right," he says, his voice so low and filled with a raw honesty that it has my heart racing. "I don't care who I have to betray, who I have to cut, I will get you out of here. I will make this right."

I slowly get to my feet, knowing just how fucking hard that would have been for him to say out loud. I walk across the cell and put myself right in front of him, gripping the bars right below each of his hands, and basking in the feel of his skin pressing against mine. I meet his eyes, hating just how haunted they look. "You can't," I tell him. "No one can fix this, only Carver, and even if he does, I'll never be able to forgive him."

King lets out a sigh and releases the bars before slipping his strong arms through them and wrapping them around me, only just squeezing his strong muscles through. "I hate this," he tells me. "I could fucking kill Carver for putting you in this situation. We all fucking knew Royston was guilty, we just needed the proof. So I can't understand why he's acting all shook."

I shrug my shoulders and do my best to soak up every little bit of his comfort. "Who knows? Maybe he truly believed his father was innocent."

"Nah," he says, shaking his head. "Out of us all, Carver was the most suspicious of his father. This is something else. He knows he was guilty, and he was waiting for the day where he got to kill him himself."

Guilt drops into my stomach and makes me feel sick. "I'm so sorry," I whisper, my voice traveling through the silence. "I promised you at the beginning that I'd never come between you guys, and now look at us. You guys are trying to kill your best friend and visiting me in a fucking cell."

King's fingers run down my back before he curls my long hair around his hand and forces my head to tilt up and meet his eyes. "To be fair," he says, leaning in and softly brushing his lips over mine. "None of us could have foreseen that you were going to steal a fucking antique dagger and kill the fucker in the middle of the dance floor."

"Good point," I say. "But taking my track record into consideration, you probably should have prepared for something like this."

"Yeah," he scoffs. "Trust me, we'll be much better prepared in the future."

"Future?" I laugh. "You're assuming that I'm going to have one of those."

King's lips press into a tight line, his eyes hardening as he watches me. "You'll have a fucking future, a grand one if I have anything to do with it. We'll get past this. It's just a matter of time until I'm fucking you up against the side of a random house and stealing even more of that innocence away from you."

I can't help but laugh. "Who the fuck have you been screwing this past month? There's not an ounce of innocence about me. I was well and truly corrupted before I got here."

King's eyes soften and the appreciation that filters through his gaze has the butterflies soaring around my stomach and making me feel an equal mix of hope and regret. "Nah, babe. You're filled with innocence, you just don't see it."

"Well," I scoff. "There were sixteen men who sat around a table this morning, and they sure as hell had a hard time pinpointing my innocence, and eight of them didn't even bother to look."

King sighs and pulls me back in, doing his best to curl me into his chest despite the bars between us. "You don't need them to see your innocence," he says, his tone dropping as his hand slowly moves up and down my back. "You just need one of them to change their vote."

My brow shoots up as I gently pull back and raise my chin to look into his eyes. "And how the hell am I going to do that?"

"Don't you worry about it, babe. You just focus on not going insane inside this little box."

"I don't think that's possible," I say. "But why do I get the feeling that one of those eight men are about to get seriously screwed over, and why am I secretly hoping that it's Carver?"

King just laughs before indicating across the room to my tiny little bed. "Are you sleeping?"

I scoff, hating the topic change, but I let it slide for now. I doubt he was going to share much more than that anyway. "What do you think? I forced Cruz to stay up all night telling me stupid stories about you guys just so I could avoid closing my eyes."

"Is it that bad?"

I nod, not wanting to admit just how bad it is out loud. "I'll be fine," I tell him. "I have the mental image of Grayson jerking off and screaming 'YAHTZEE' to keep me company."

"Fuck me, that was a good one," King laughs, before shaking his head in horror. "I'd hate to find out what little secrets Cruz has spilled about me."

"Oh, trust me," I say, my eyes lighting up. "You really don't want to know."

6

I shiver against the small bed as my body aches from an uncomfortable night. Dynasty must have billions of dollars. Is it really too much to ask them for a comfortable bed in their cells? They have a fancy as shit security system keeping me locked in here, which would have cost them a bomb, plus the underground cell itself, which I'm sure wasn't cheap, but they decided to go stingy on the bed? Fuck them.

If they're going to keep me locked in here much longer, then the least they could do is offer me some nice blankets, a pair of cute pajamas, and maybe a robe. I wouldn't mind a hairbrush and a mirror—perhaps a toothbrush if it's not too much to ask.

I peel my eyes open and stare at the ugly grey concrete wall in front of my face.

I hate this place. I wonder how slowly today is going to drag by or if the boys are going to hang out with me again. Cruz and Grayson came back a few hours after they'd left, both looking worse for wear and the three of them stayed for most of the night until I sent their asses back up into the real world.

They looked like shit. There was nowhere for them to get comfortable down here and for the most part, Grayson looked like he needed to go put his hand in the freezer. He must have done a good job rearranging Carver's face. Cruz, on the other hand, looked like he'd accidentally gotten an elbow to the face.

They were reluctant to leave, and in hindsight, I probably should have kept them around. Who knows who could have snuck down here in the night to finish me off, but as it is, I'm still breathing, at least for now. I'm sure it won't be long until the culprit behind the hitmen in the woods strikes again, and I'm sure whoever it is, will be a little sneakier about his next attempt.

I let out a sigh and roll over to stare up at the roof, but a shadow across my cell catches my attention. I fly off my shitty little bed within the same second, nearly wetting my pants in the process. What is it about that first morning wee that sends a girl insane?

My gaze snaps to the shadow, my heart thundering in my ears, making it nearly impossible to rely on my other senses. The shadow stretches far across my cell and I follow it back to the man standing on the other side of the metal bars.

Dante. Fucking. Carver.

He looks like death warmed up. His face is covered in black and blue bruising, a cut above his eyebrow, and a swollen lip. My gaze shifts down his body, taking in the bruising over his arm and following it right down to his knuckles where I expect to see the signs of a fight, only his knuckles are clear, speaking volumes.

He didn't fight back. He sat there and let Grayson beat the shit out of him for putting me in here, and while a part of me wants to celebrate that he must feel like shit for doing this to me, the rest of me is just pissed. He doesn't get to feel like shit. He made a conscious decision to keep me locked up, he looked me in the fucking eyes and raised his goddamn hand.

He ruined me, and I'll never forgive him.

Anger pulses through me at just the sight of his broken face, yet somehow while broken and bloodied, he still looks like the most dangerous person I'll ever meet. "What the hell do you want?" I growl, throwing myself at the bars and gripping them as though I could run straight through them to finish his ass off.

He leans casually against the far wall, right out of my reach, not moving an inch as he silently watches me. It's like a taunt, as though he's come to bask in my humiliation, come to laugh at the bitch who got screwed over.

His silence only serves to infuriate me further and I slam my hands against the bars again. "What do you want?" I demand, hating that I'm having to repeat myself to this asshole, the night having absolutely no success in calming the wild rage pulsing within me. "Have you come to laugh at me? Or just get a good look at the pathetic bitch you locked up?"

His eyes harden, but his silence only makes me yell louder. "Where's your sense of loyalty? You fucking betrayed me, Carver. I thought I meant something to you. I thought … Fuck, I don't even know what I thought, but it's not this. You're a liar. All this time I thought you were the one I could trust, the one who would give it to me straight, but you were just weaving a fucking web, earning my trust so that you could crush me the second you got a chance."

Carver clenches his jaw as my already sore throat screams in agony. His silence kills me, and I tighten my hold on the iron bars, wishing I could reach through and strangle his bitch-ass. "Just because I'm locked in this fucking cell, doesn't mean I won't ram you with a huge fucking dildo," I roar at him, knowing damn well that I'm provoking him, but what the fuck can he do to me in this cell? It's not like he can magically break through the bars to finish what he started. "Why. The. Fuck. Are. You. Here?"

He pushes off the wall and steps right into me, so close that I could easily slip my knee through the bars and slam it right into his junk, showing an incredible amount of bravery for his balls. Though, a guy like Carver could dodge out of the way and have me in a headlock before my knee has even made it past his thigh, yet he still doesn't say a damn word, just stands there looking all sorts of pissed off.

"I swear, Dante," I spit, his real name on my lips giving me far too much power. "Fucking say what you came to say and get the fuck out of here. I can't stand to look at you a second longer than necessary."

Hurt seeps through his stare, but before I get a chance to call him out on it, he dips his hand into his pocket and pulls out a key. I watch him closely, my heart beginning to race.

What the fuck is he doing with a key?

His eyes tighten and I watch as he reaches across to the lock on my cell and slips the key straight in. His stare never leaves mine, and I watch the exact moment that he realizes I'm fucking terrified of what he might do.

My heart thunders, racing with fear. The last time he got close enough, he tried to kill me, and right now, I don't have the security of the boys and the rest of the organization standing at my back. If he were any other person, I could take him. At least, I'd try, but Dante Carver … no. Even if he was trying to take my life, I don't know if I have what it takes to end his first.

I watch him as he slowly twists the key, unlocking the door, and then slides the heavy lock out of place.

A new, louder silence falls around us as my heart hammers, my fear doubling by the second. The heavy lock falls back with a loud bang that makes me flinch, and I watch his every movement as his skilled fingers curl around the iron bars and slide the door out of his way.

I back up a step, hating that I'm showing my fear, but in this case, my fear is all I have left. Even though a part of me, deep, deep down is trying to tell me that I can still trust him, *that I should trust him.*

Carver takes a step forward and I notice how he keeps himself perfectly positioned so that I can't run past him and free myself from his twisted game. "What are you doing?" I question, my voice wavering and instantly making me feel pathetic. I've always prided myself on my strength when facing impossible situations, but right now, I sound like a little bitch who's about to beg on her hands and knees. That's not me. I don't let men get away with this kind of bullshit, but Carver is different. All four of them are different.

He stalks me, slowly walking toward me with his eyes locked on mine. Once upon a time, I used to love the feel of his eyes boring into mine. It was wild and unexpected, and the sexual tension was through the roof, but now … while it's still intense and raw, it's also full of secrets, lies, and uncertainty.

I back up another step and he continues to stalk me like a hungry lion chasing a mouse. He's going to kill me. He's going to finish what he started and then destroy the evidence. So why the fuck is my gut urging me to trust him?

Tears threaten to spring from my eyes, but I hold them back as I quickly run out of space. I will not let him see how weak he's made me. I raise my chin. If this is it, if today is my last day on earth, then I'll be going down with my head held high. "Just make it quick," I tell him, my heart thundering so fast that it couldn't possibly be healthy, but what does it matter?

Carver narrows his gaze and steps right into my personal space. His natural, manly scent wraps around me and I instantly long for the connection that pulsed between us every time he was near. My body craves his touch as my mind silently begs for him to hold me. Maybe if I'm a dead woman, I might be able to talk him into kissing me just one last time.

"I'm not here to kill you," he says so naturally, as though talking about my death is a normal occurrence between us, though lately it really has been.

My brows furrow as I meet his dark stormy eyes. He looks so angry, so worn down and tired. It's almost as though he's the one who hasn't been sleeping. "I don't believe you," I tell him, noticing how his hand flinches at his side, trying hard not to reach out and take my waist just as he always does, but at this point, he'll be damn lucky if he ever gets this close to me again. "You've already tried to kill me twice. Third time's a charm."

"What the fuck are you talking about? I've never attempted to take your life."

I sputter, unable to believe what I'm hearing as I tilt my head back further and point out the dark bruising around my throat. "What the hell do you call this, Carver? Because it sure as fuck didn't feel like an accident."

"You had just murdered my father. You don't know this fucking world, Winter, not like I do. I had to do it. I had no fucking choice."

I scoff. "Just like you had no choice to send those twelve hitmen against me in the woods."

His brows shoot straight up. "Are you fucking insane? Or don't you remember that I was the fucking idiot who was standing at your back, making sure that your ass got out of there alive?"

"You can't deny how convenient it was," I spit.

"What's that supposed to mean?"

"You're one of the eight, Carver. How am I supposed to believe that you didn't drag me into the woods to set me up? You got me alone in there, fucked with my head, and then left me to fend for myself. You've been a shady fucker since the moment I met you. Who knows, maybe you're playing the guys too. It was certainly a good show you put on, racing back for me and playing the hero to claim you saved my ass. It sure makes you look pretty fucking innocent."

He shakes his head, his eyes blazing with anger as the insistent feeling in my gut demands that I trust him. "You don't know what you're talking about."

I scoff, more pissed than anything. Hell, even if he didn't have anything to do with the attack in the woods, I'm still not going to back down because I'm a stubborn ass and he deserves every bit of my fury. "I am so fucking over you assholes telling me I don't know what I'm talking about, because from where I'm standing, I'm the only bitch who has the story straight."

His jaw clenches and his eyes burn with anger. "If I wanted to kill you, you'd have been dead a long fucking time ago, Winter. I've had you alone, sleeping in my bed night after night. It would be as easy as waiting for you to fall asleep before snapping your fragile little neck. Don't fool yourself."

I step into him, cutting straight into his personal space just as he'd done to me, and force him back a step. "Then why the hell are you here?"

He silently watches me for a moment, thinking harder than any one person has the right to before his eyes tighten. "Tell me what my father said to you that was so bad you had to fucking kill him."

I scoff, my disbelief forcing me back a few steps as I stare at the guy who could have meant the world to me. "Are you fucking kidding me? After everything we've been through, you don't trust what I said in that fucking council chamber was true?"

Carver shakes his head. "It's not," he states as though it's a cold, hard fact. "You're fucking lying. I know you are. My father would never try to overthrow the whole council like that. Why the fuck would he? You've been gone for eighteen years. If that were his plan, he would have carried it out way before you got here."

I scoff, unable to believe what I'm hearing. "I don't give a shit what that man could have done before I got here. All I know is that he stood before me and demanded that I be his fucking yes man. But what would you know anyway?" My eyes harden and I step back into him. "When was the last time you spoke to him? You're fucking best friends with Cruz and King, and not to mention, already a full member of the organization. Your father probably didn't trust you for a fucking second. Especially when he realized that I knew exactly what happened to my parents. Who do you think he assumed told me, huh? Who would he have thought was the weakest link?"

I watch him, knowing damn well that I'm playing mind games, but it's the truth. A man like Royston Carver would never trust his heir, especially one that usually has a good heart. I wouldn't be surprised if that's the reason he stayed away from Carver for so long. He was probably hoping for a son who would inherit his sick, twisted mind, and want to follow in his footsteps, but Carver is better than that, and despite how much it pains me to admit that—it's true.

Carver lets out a sigh, his frustration increasing by the second and only reminding me how far apart we're drifting. "You don't think I know that? You don't think that I spent years by my father's side as a kid, fucking wishing that he could love me, wishing he would think that I was strong enough to one day take his seat at the table?" Carver bears down on me, the emotion pouring out of him in waves. "I was never enough, but I came to fucking terms with that. It's no secret that he didn't trust me, but that doesn't mean that I didn't know the bastard. I made it my fucking business to know every last thing about him. Now, tell me what the fuck he said to you."

I step into him, a smirk pulling at my lips as I raise my chin and meet his hard stare. "Well," I say, hating to be the bearer of bad news. "It looks like you failed because every last word I said is true. Your father was planning to rule and corrupt Dynasty, *and you missed it."*

Guilt flashes in his eyes and I see the exact second that he decides to trust my word, but after the shit that's gone down between us over the last few days, neither of us is ready to back down. "You killed my father, Winter," he says, his voice dropping low as he stares into my eyes. "I couldn't ignore that."

My stare doesn't waver as I raise my chin, letting him see just how far he's pushed me. "And he killed mine," I state before pressing my hand into his chest and pushing him backward. "I couldn't ignore that."

I take three long strides until Carver steps out of my cell, and keeping my eyes trained heavily on his, I pull the cell door closed between us before reaching through the bars and sliding the lock back into place, letting him see just how much he's hurt me. I twist the key and pull it out before tossing it far down the hallway and silently watching him.

Pain and regret twist across his handsome features for the slightest second before he rights himself and takes a step back. My heart races, the pain stinging my chest like a hot knife through butter.

Carver watches me for a silent moment, receiving my 'fuck you to the ends of the earth' message loud and clear. Things will never get better between us. That connection we once had is gone, the fire quickly sizzling out and leaving us both in ruins.

Then finally releasing me from the intensity of his stare, he drops his gaze and walks away, leaving nothing but a broken and shattered mess behind.

7

Four days. Four nights.

I don't know how much more of this I can take. I think I've slept a total of eight hours since first being locked up and my brain is beginning to sizzle. I can't deny that the conditions are much better than the ones in Sam's cell, but if I have to stay any longer, I'm going to start questioning myself.

Sam's cell put me through physical torture. The constant sound of dripping water and the cold, damp floors mixed with the sound of girls screaming. Dynasty's cells are different. This is mental torture. I'm alone with nothing but my own demons to keep me company, and trust me, they're not friendly. Right now, I'm starting to think this is much, much worse.

I walk up and down my cell, my body itching to get out of here, itching to walk further than five steps at a time. I'd do anything just to be able to run, to go back up to the normal world above and ride my Ducati through the streets for hours on end.

I hate it here, but maybe I truly deserve this. Maybe after killing Kurt and Royston, this is exactly where I'm supposed to be. This is karma catching up to me.

My ass drops heavily onto the small bed and I pull my knees up into my chest as my back leans against the cold concrete wall. I've never felt so hopeless in my life. I'd give anything just to feel the warmth of the sun brushing against my skin and the soft breeze blowing through my hair. I want to be able to feel the boys' touch on my body with the softness of a big bed beneath me, not these stupid metal bars holding me back. But most of all, I want to feel Carver's skin underneath my fist as I beat the living shit out of him. That'll never happen. Dynasty will never let me out of here.

Is this what depression feels like? I don't think I've ever felt so dejected.

The familiar sound of someone walking down the hallway fills my cell and a small victory pulses through me. I love when the guys come to sit with me; it's my favorite part of the day. They've been amazing through all of this, always staying as long as they can so I'm not suffering here by myself. Cruz even brought me a ball to keep me occupied. I'm pretty sure his intentions were for me to throw it against the wall and catch it on the rebound then repeat the process a million times more, but I can't say that I've done that once. Instead, I tore the little ball to shreds and used it to funnel my anger. It was therapeutic, but like most good things, they always come to an end. The ball lasted for two hours and my fingers were aching afterward, but it left me feeling accomplished—plus it was a good time waster.

I hear the person coming closer and I raise my head, a smile pulling at the corners of my lips. I bet it's Cruz. The footfalls are too quick for King. He likes to take his time, where if it were Grayson, I wouldn't be able to hear anything until he was already standing right in front of me. He's a lot like Carver in that way. They're both silently lethal, and though it's scary as hell, it's also one of the most attractive things I've ever witnessed.

I turn to face the hallway just as I expect Cruz to walk out in front of my cell. "Where the hell have you been all of my life?" I say, a smirk kicking up the corners of my mouth just in time to see the older version of Cruz step out before me.

My eyes widen as I take in Mr. Danforth, desperately wishing those cringey words hadn't slipped out of my mouth. I get to my feet and cautiously watch as he walks straight to the door of the cell. He slowly raises his gaze to meet mine. "Congratulations, Miss Ravenwood. You're free to go home."

I've pictured this moment a million times over the past few days. In my head, I'd run to the door and fly out of it faster than humanly possible. I'd run, I'd cheer, I'd tell everyone I pass that they can go and suck my big dick because I was free. So why the hell am I just standing here gaping at the guy?

"Um … what?" I ask, my face twisting in confusion. "What do you mean I'm free? I thought I was going to be stuck here for months before someone pulled their head out of their ass and changed the vote."

"It seems that the vote has been changed in your favor," he tells me, slipping the key into the lock and opening my cell to stand before me. "What are you waiting for? Would you prefer to stay?"

My eyes bug out of my head and I get my feet moving. "Fuck no."

"That's what I thought."

I dart out of the cell, and Mr. Danforth closes the door behind me, causing me to jump at the sharp bang of the metal sliding back into place. It's a noise that I will never be okay with; it grinds on my nerves and gives me the worst kind of anxiety that, hopefully, I'll be able to conquer one day. Though, I could save myself a lot of trouble and try not to end up in someone's shitty cell ever again.

Good plan.

Mr. Danforth silently walks beside me, leading me out of the long hallway, and with each step I take, I pick up my pace. My muscles ache from being so cramped and not being able to really move. My back has been screaming since the first night sleeping on the cold ground beside Cruz, and my neck hates me after attempting to spend the next three nights sleeping on the hard bed.

I can't wait to get back to my place. I think I'll lock myself in the bathroom and set up a bath fit for a queen. I'm thinking rose petals, a glass of champagne, I might even pretend to read a book, and then afterward, put on a silk robe that makes me feel like the most exotic creature who ever walked the planet. I'm going to live it up. I'm going to enjoy my freedom and remind myself why the hell I valued life in the first place.

But I just have to make one little stop first.

We walk for what feels like forever until we finally break out into the massive reception room and I find three no-good, deathly enticing men standing at the opposite end. Everything clenches inside me and a wicked smile pulls at my lips.

Fuck, that's why I love freedom. I think after I spend the rest of the day pampering myself, I'm going to spend the night with King and Cruz buried deep inside of me, and hell, if Grayson is down, then he can join in the party too.

"My son seems quite taken by you," Mr. Danforth comments beside me, his voice a whisper, yet somehow still traveling the distance of the room and making Cruz straighten and narrow his gaze at his father.

I glance across at Mr. Danforth, my brows furrowed as I try to get a good read on him. "Why do I get the feeling that you don't approve?"

He slices his eyes forward, keeping them trained on the three guys at the other end of the room. "It's not that I don't approve, though don't get me wrong, I'm not exactly thrilled that the woman he's choosing to spend his time with is someone who's just been locked away for four days on murder charges. You are the leader of Dynasty, there's no one better suited for my son. However, it's not how we do things."

My brows somehow pull down further as I glance back at the guys in confusion. "How do you mean?" I question, dropping my voice lower to keep as much of this conversation private as possible, but something tells me the boys can hear every little word.

"Our young are encouraged to find a suitable partner who comes from wealth or who already has made a name for themselves in the outside world. We do not encourage dating within our ranks. Our children must first marry and then create heirs of their own to continue our traditions."

I shake my head. "I must be missing something here," I tell him. "Correct me if I'm wrong, but I'm a woman, right? I mean, I'm not exactly interested in marriage or babies right now, but maybe one day in the distant future. So, what's the problem?"

Mr. Danforth stops before we get too close to the boys and I pull myself up to meet his stare. "I'm sure you will birth many heirs to continue your family name. The issue is that you are the leader of this fine organization and Cruz is my heir. If you were to marry, Cruz would be made to take on the Ravenwood name and stand behind you at the table as your spouse, leaving the Danforth seat empty."

I shake my head, not quite understanding, so he gives me a little more to go on. "Your children would carry the Ravenwood name. If you were with Cruz—or any of the other heirs for that matter—your firstborn child would stand as a Ravenwood. Your husbands family will no longer hold a voice or value at our table."

"But you have other children. Cruz has siblings. If something were to ever happen between us, couldn't they just step into his place?"

Mr. Danforth shakes his head. "Firstborn children only."

I rock back on my feet, thinking way too hard about this. "So, technically what you're saying is that Cruz, or any of the other heirs, could knock up some other chick, and then be with me, as long as their firstborns aren't mine?"

Mr. Danforth lets out a heavy sigh and rolls his eyes before picking up his pace again. "Technically," he confirms with an unimpressed scowl. "However, that is certainly not encouraged. Dynasty upholds the values and importance of marriage vows." I follow him as he continues. "Besides, we encourage all of our children to marry outside of Dynasty so that our organization is always flourishing and growing."

"Sounds like a load of shit to me," I grumble under my breath, getting a side-eye from Mr. Danforth.

"It is not my position to offer you advice," he says as we approach the boys. "But considering that your parents are not here to do so and you are still new to this role, learning what your position entails, I will say this. You are not invincible. Yes, you have the title of being the leader of our people, but you are only human. You are not untouchable, and because of that, you need to watch yourself. I understand your sarcasm and need to rebel against everything that comes your way, but others will not appreciate that. So, understand this, young Elodie, you need to be careful. Dynasty and its traditions is not something that should be messed with."

I meet his heavy stare and attempt to bite my tongue. The last thing I need after being locked up for four days is some old guy telling me that I can't marry or have kids with his son or telling me how to handle myself within the same organization that ensured my parents' murder. What the hell is his deal anyway? Marriage and kids are the furthest things from my mind. In fact, I don't even think having little devil spawn versions of myself is something that's going to be on my agenda … like ever. I had a shitty upbringing and I doubt that I'll make a good mother, or even a good role model for a child. That's just asking for trouble.

But then … maybe ten or twenty years down the track, I might change my mind, but at the rate I'm going, I probably won't live to see my nineteenth birthday.

"You know what?" I tell Mr. Danforth, hating the authoritative tone I'm taking with him. "You were right. It really isn't your position to be offering advice."

He watches me for a drawn-out moment, his lips pressing into a hard line as his eyes narrow. Then without another word he simply nods and walks away, leaving me staring after him.

"Uhhhh … what the fuck was that?" Cruz asks from his position by the entrance of the massive open room.

I turn my gaze to the three boys, and just like that, a wide smile stretches across my face and I beam at them. "I'M FREE."

I bolt toward them and move my feet faster than they've ever moved before. A high-pitched squeal tears out of me, and before I know it, I launch myself into the air and come crashing down into King's arms. He holds me tight, spinning me around as Grayson and Cruz watch on with wide smiles.

"I fucking knew you'd get out," King tells me before giving me a bruising kiss.

My legs unhook from his waist, and the second my feet hit the ground, Cruz is there, pulling me into his arms, one hand against my back, the other squeezing my ass. He kisses me briefly before giving me a beaming grin. "Come on," he says. "We have to go and celebrate."

I nod, quickly meeting Grayson's eyes before looking back at the other two. "Deal, but before we do that, I have a score to settle with Carver."

Cruz cringes as King presses his lips into a tight line. Grayson, on the other hand, is all in.

We walk for the exit, and as we break out into the parking garage, it takes me far too long to realize that the garage is empty and the boys had to have walked here.

"Umm … where's the car?" I ask, glancing around to find it completely empty. I'm not going to lie, I'd prefer to be hand-delivered right to Carver's door.

Cruz cautiously glances away. "We kinda thought you'd want to go straight to Carver, so we figured that if we walked … we'd get a chance to tell you everything that's been going on over the past few days."

I let out a frustrated sigh. "Assholes," I mutter under my breath.

Grayson scoffs and I glance his way to find his unwavering stare straight forward, and I can't help but feel like he's making a point of not looking my way, but why? He's been acting weird over the last few days. He's been a surprising protector since the second Carver's hand found my throat and I don't know what to think about it. It's weird and it's making me feel things I wasn't quite ready to feel.

I try to put it to the back of my mind as we step into the massive car elevator that we were just in a few days ago, only now, it feels like a lifetime ago.

The door closes, locking us in, and as Cruz presses the button to send us up, I can't help but feel the tension in the little dark room growing by the second. I'm boxed in with three of the most intense guys I've ever met, and I can't see a damn thing.

The elevator rises and a body steps in behind me. My back straightens, and before I can ask which of the guys it is, a hand gently presses down over my mouth. His other hand curls around my body as his lips drop to my neck and my knees instantly go weak.

He holds me up as I sink into his touch, and at this point, I don't even care which of the guys it is. Though if I'm honest with myself, I'm kinda hoping that it's Grayson. Maybe then he'll climb aboard the sharing train and come home with me and the boys. Either way, I'm not about to let this opportunity go to waste. There's something exciting about the idea of getting caught.

His hand on my waist starts gliding further down my body until he's cupping my aching pussy and I long for my jeans to be torn away, but we only have a few seconds before we reach the top and the door opens wide, giving me my first glimpse of sunlight in over four days.

Not wanting to waste a single second, I turn in his hold and push up onto my tippy-toes, collecting his lips with mine. He kisses me deeply and his taste is intoxicating. There's something familiar about it though, but I know Cruz and King all too well and it's not them.

A thrill burns through me as my hand falls upon his chest, but as I travel it up and hook it around the back of his neck, it hits me.

It's not fucking Grayson either.

I suck in a gasp just as the elevator reaches the top, and just like that, his lips are torn away from mine and I feel a slight gust of wind as he rushes away. The elevator door begins to open and the second the light seeps through, I quickly glance around to find King and Cruz to my right and Grayson minding his own damn business to my left. None of them looking my way or even remotely aware that we're not alone in here.

I look at the shadows, knowing damn well that Carver is in here somewhere. I know his body almost better than I know my own, but that taste on my tongue … that's something I could never forget. I know the way he kisses me; he's so forceful and demanding. I know the way his hands feel on my body, gliding across my skin as though he owns it.

So why the fuck does he think he has the right to touch me after all the bullshit he's put me through? Fuck him.

My jaw clenches as the door fully opens and Cruz looks back at me as the guys start making their way out. "You coming?"

I pause a beat, still looking into the shadows and feeling Carver's silent, deadly stare on me, wishing more than anything I could find him just so I could make him feel even an ounce of the pain I've been suffering through over the past four days.

Not able to figure out where the fuck he is in this big elevator, I reluctantly turn back and walk out with the guys. Feeling the first rays of sunshine to hit my skin in days, I'm instantly pissed off that I can't enjoy it right now.

"What's wrong?" King murmurs, making the other two glance my way with concern marring their devilishly handsome faces.

I look back at the elevator, but just like everything else that's gone down between me and Carver, I keep it to myself. I don't know why I do it. It's not like Carver has ever asked me not to say anything, and King and Cruz have already expressed that they'd be cool with Carver sharing too. So why do I find it so hard to talk about?

There's always been something deeper with Carver. It was a different kind of intensity than what I experienced with the others, but he made sure to destroy that. There will never be anything like that between us again, despite how fucking magical it felt having his lips against mine.

"It's nothing," I tell them, continuing down the long path that leads to the main entrance of our crazy little world. "Now, get me home. I want to shower and feel human, and then you assholes need to tell me exactly what's been going on around here."

8

The hot water rushes down my skin as the soapy loofah roams over my body and helps me feel human again. I tip my head back and close my eyes, groaning as the shampoo rinses from my hair.

"Fuck me," a low groan sounds from the bathroom door.

A sultry smile cuts across my face and I don't bother opening my eyes. I'd know that low, raspy tone anywhere. "Are you coming in?"

Within seconds, Cruz's clothes are lying scattered around my bathroom floor and he steps into the warm shower, his hands instantly taking my body. "You're so fucking beautiful," he tells me, his voice soft and filled with lust. "I don't know if you've worked this out yet, but I'm so fucking happy that you're out."

I step closer into Cruz and open my eyes. "Careful," I tell him. "It sounds like you're dangerously close to falling."

His eyes become hooded as he watches me, his thumb gently moving up and down on my waist. "Would that be such a bad thing?"

My heart swells, his words sending butterflies soaring through my stomach and making me feel things that I don't think I'm ready for. I place my hand against his chest, feeling the rapid beat of his heart beneath. "Maybe," I murmur, watching as his brows slowly draw down. "Your father seems to think it'd be the end of the world."

"My father doesn't know what the fuck he's talking about," he tells me before letting out a sigh and bringing his hand to my chin. He runs his thumb across my bottom lip. "I heard what he said to you, but I have to admit, I didn't think you were the type to get pulled into the bullshit traditions."

"I'm not," I whisper, moving in a little closer and feeling his body pressed right up against mine. "I don't give a shit about their stupid rules of having babies and creating an heir, but despite how much you play it down, it means something to you."

Cruz's gaze drops from my eyes and I can practically see the thoughts filtering through his mind. He lets out a soft sigh and leans against the cool tiles of the shower before pulling me with him. "You're right," he murmurs. "I do. I've been raised with these values and it's always been drilled into me that producing an heir to carry on the Danforth name is the most important thing in the world."

"So, why'd you let yourself get so close to me?"

He shrugs his shoulders. "To be perfectly honest with you, I didn't even realize it was happening until it was already too late. It was just innocent flirting. It was fun and we both fucking loved it, but now you're making me question everything."

"How so?"

His tongue slips out and runs over his bottom lip, and I realize he's trying to give himself a second to consider his response before accidentally saying the wrong thing. "I've told you before, Winter. I'd fucking do anything for you," he tells me, pausing a moment to let that sink in. "Even if it means giving up my seat at the table."

My jaw drops as I stare at his heated expression. "You don't really mean that," I whisper, silently begging him to tell me that he's not that serious about me.

Cruz pulls against my waist and draws me back into him until my face is curled into his chest and his chin is gently resting over my head. "I'm sorry, Winter, but yeah, I fucking mean every word."

"I'm not going to let you give up your seat like that."

"Tough shit, babe. Because I'm not going to let you walk away from me. I want you any way I can get you, even if that means sharing you with every single one of my friends."

I try to wriggle away to meet his eyes, but he just holds me tighter, keeping me locked in the safety of his arms. "But—"

"No," he tells me. "I'm sorry, I know you weren't ready to hear that, but I also don't want you worrying about the bullshit my father hit you with. It doesn't matter to me—not anymore. I know what I want. Besides, something tells me you're not about to go and agree to any marriage proposals, so what does it matter? No one here is getting married and changing names, so no one is losing their seats."

"But isn't the whole baby thing sort of … I don't know, encouraged?"

"It is," he tells me. "But encouraged is very different from forced. No one is going to tell you that you have to pop out a kid unless that's what you want for yourself. Besides, having a child out of wedlock is extremely frowned upon, so if you never tie the knot …"

A smile pulls at my lips and he finally lets me pull back to look up at him. "… then nothing has to change."

"Exactly," he tells me. "And I don't know about you, but this little thing we've got going on is far too interesting to stop now."

"Are you sure?" I ask. "I don't want you coming at me in a year or two and demanding that I wear your ring on my finger, especially if King is still down with sharing."

"Trust me, babe," he says, a wicked grin stretching across his face and sending a thrill shooting through me. "You have nothing to worry about, not that I wouldn't love being hitched to a fucking bomb ass chick like you, but the more I adjust to sharing you, the more I like it."

"You know what I like?" I ask as my hand slides down between us. My eyes grow hooded and I watch the way his roll with pleasure as a low growl rumbles through his chest. I think he knows exactly what I like.

Cruz's fingers tighten on my waist and before I get a chance to say another word, his lips are pressing down on mine as my hand curls around his hard cock.

"Okay," I say, dropping down on my parents' large couch between King and Cruz as I watch Grayson awkwardly pace in front of the magnificent fireplace. "Someone start talking and tell me how the hell I got out of that cell."

The three guys glance around at each other, either trying to work out who's going to be the one to talk or figuring out how they're going to twist the story to make them all sound like the hero. Though, if twisting the story was what they wanted to do, they could have done that before showing up to walk me home.

Grayson lets out a sigh and stops pacing before turning to face me, his eyes boring into mine and silently telling me to prepare myself. "Carver called for a private meeting with the heads of Dynasty to discuss your … situation, and at the end, called for another vote."

"Okay," I say as he pauses and presses his lips into a tight line, making my patience wear thin. "And?"

King turns to face me, and I catch his eyes, only to see confusion and pity. "None of the other seven families changed their mind, so Carver had no choice but to stand against his family to get you out of there."

"No," I say, shaking my head, my brows drawn in confusion. "That doesn't make sense. He wouldn't do that. Carver was so sure that I was lying. He came and told me himself. We fought and I kicked him out of my cell."

"Out of your cell?" Grayson confirms.

I nod. "Yeah, he had a key and welcomed himself in. I thought he was coming to finish what he started. It turns out that he just wanted to yell at me some more and prove that after everything we've been through this past month, he couldn't trust me. I kicked him out and locked my ass back in there."

Grayson takes a step toward me, only stopping because of the coffee table between us. "He had a key?" he asks, getting hung up on the least important part of what I just said.

I let out a groan. Am I speaking another language? "Yeah," I say, glancing at both King and Cruz, the confusion starting to piss me off. I must be missing something here. Call me a spoiled brat, but I want my answers and I want them now. Who cares about the stupid key? How's that any different from Cruz getting the code? "What's the big deal? He's one of the seventeen heads of Dynasty now. I figured all the top-dogs around here had access to the cell keys and codes."

Cruz lets out a surprised breath before meeting my stare and shaking his head. "No, babe. Not even close. He made a fucking show that he was going to kill you at your initiation, so only my dad and Tobias had access to the keys. The only way Carver would have been able to get them is if he'd somehow stolen them from their personal safes … or if he had some sort of agreement with them to gain access to you, and after how determined he's been to end you, I could only imagine what kind of agreement that would have been."

"What the hell are you saying?" I demand, flying to my feet and instantly pacing, just as Grayson had been doing. I look at the two boys left on the couch. "The good guys want me dead too? Is it not enough that I've had to deal with Royston, hitmen, and fucking sex traffickers? Now your parents want me dead as well?"

"No," King says, throwing himself to his feet. "That's ridiculous. My father would never. He was Andrew's closest friend. He's always said that despite you being away from all of this, he's always thought of you as an adopted daughter. You can trust him. He's loyal to you, Winter."

I turn my gaze on Cruz as Grayson huffs from behind me. We all ignore him as I keep my stare on Cruz, desperately needing his response. "My father wouldn't," he tells me. "He might not want me getting close to you, and he may be an ass with questionable morals, but he'd never hurt you like that."

I drop down onto the coffee table as Grayson loses his patience. "Are you guys fucking kidding me?" he demands. "You're seriously questioning Carver right now? We've been best friends since we were all fucking born. You know damn well that he would have stolen that key, and it would have been right out of Tobias' safe. He hasn't changed the passcode to that thing for twelve fucking years."

Guilty expressions twist over the guys' faces, and as they quickly glance at one another, I see the exact moment they realize Grayson is right. I meet his furious stare. "How sure are you?"

"Sure enough that I'd happily leave you and Carver in a room with a knife and know that you'd be the one to walk away. He'd never fucking hurt you, Elodie, and the fact that you think otherwise really fucking pisses me off."

"No," I say, getting back to my feet and stepping straight into him. "You don't get to guilt trip me like that. You weren't the one who couldn't breathe while his hands were wrapped around your throat."

I feel Cruz at my back, pulling me away from Grayson, but as I move back a step, Grayson comes with me. "It was a fucking show for his family and the other members of Dynasty. All of it has been a show, and if you'd have just controlled yourself and not been so reckless with that fucking dagger, you could have come to us and the whole thing would have been avoided. We would have taken Royston out and it would have been done without your ass ending up in a cell."

My eyes bug out of my head. "Are you serious? You're blaming me in all of this? He taunted me about murdering my parents. He deserved to die."

"I'm not saying he didn't, but you retaliated by dropping to his goddamn level. You're better than that."

"Fuck you."

"Yeah," Grayson scoffs, rolling his eyes as though I'm so far below him. "Fuck you too, babe."

"Okay," King says, stepping in between us and pushing Grayson toward the fireplace as Cruz drags me back to the couch and all but throws me down to it. "Both of you take a fucking breather. Getting into bullshit arguments like this isn't getting us anywhere. We need to work out where to go from here."

"What do you mean where to go from here?" Grayson questions, his frustration still getting the best of him. "There is nowhere to go.

It's over. Winter is out and Carver is fucking screwed."

My brows furrow. "How is he screwed? He's the head of his family. He has the freedom to make any call he wants."

Cruz shakes his head. "He really doesn't," he explains. "Being the head of a family … it's not just being the boss man, it's so much more. He has to advocate for them, be the voice at the table, and I can guarantee they would have been gunning for your execution."

My eyes widen. "They would have really done that?"

King nods. "Mmhmm, and he would have had no choice but to advocate for that, but he stood against it, and because he did that, you got to walk free."

"Don't do that," I warn him. "You're making him out to be a hero, but I can't just forgive and forget. I was in a cell for four fucking days. Have you ever been locked up? Do you have any idea what it's actually like? The loneliness, the fear?"

"No one is trying to belittle what you went through or force you to forgive him. I get it, it's going to be a long fucking road before either of you can trust one another again, but you're not understanding what it actually means to stand against your family like that."

Exhaustion filters through me and I sink back against the couch, looking up at the three boys. "Then explain it to me."

Cruz takes pity on me and drops down onto the coffee table, right where I was sitting just a minute ago. "He betrayed his whole fucking family for a girl he met a month ago, a girl who killed his father in front of his little sisters, his mother, and his whole extended family. In our world, that's worse than any crime any of us have ever committed.

Family is a sacred bond, and no matter what, you never betray that," he explains. "And when someone does, the family has every fucking right to walk away."

A heaviness sinks into my stomach. "Wait," I say, my gaze flicking between them all. "What do you mean walk away?"

King sighs. "They packed up their shit and left Carver behind first thing this morning," he says. "Do you see it now? He chose to save you over ever seeing his mother again, and unless she decides to forgive him and come home, he'll never get to see his little sisters grow up."

Fat tears form in my eyes and slowly run down my face. "But I … I didn't know. I didn't ask him to do that. He could have—"

"Could have what?" Grayson asks. "He could have condemned you to death? Left you to rot in that cell for the rest of your life? No, you know him better than that. He'd never be able to do that to you. By killing his father, you forced his hand. He had no choice but to put you in that cell. Do you think he enjoyed that?"

I look around the room, my mind an absolute mess. "But you … when I told you what happened during the trial, you got angry and went and beat him up."

"I did," Grayson says. "But it wasn't out of anger. It's what he needed to be able to live with himself."

I nod, letting the weight of his words hit me as the tears continue falling from my eyes and splashing onto my black jeans.

I would do absolutely anything for the chance to see my family again, but Carver just gave that all up to save my life. Grayson is right; had I controlled myself on that dance floor, this all could have been avoided. I could have spoken privately with Carver afterward and we could have worked out a plan that would have given us all what we wanted, but I was reckless. I was thinking only of myself, and because of that, I forced Carver's hand. I took his choice away.

Seeing that I need some time to process, the boys slip out of my living room and I listen as the three of them walk straight through the massive house and out the front door.

When the hell did my life get so complicated? What happened to the good old days where my only worry was what kind of reaction I'd get from the kids at a new school, and just how long I'd have to stay in each new home?

I sit on the big couch for an hour, staring at the fireplace and trying to figure out what the hell I'm supposed to do. I have so much anger built up inside me and now I'm drowning in guilt. I don't want to forgive him. I can't forget the lonely nights in that cell where the faceless men would come and visit me in my dreams, but he gave up his whole fucking family.

I killed his father.

Fuck. He should never have done it. He should have let me go.

I pull myself off the couch and wipe the tears on the back of my arm before walking straight out of the house. I don't stop until I'm standing in front of the one door that I could always trust to keep the monsters at bay.

Not wanting to barge right in, I bring my hand up and gently knock against the hardwood, sending my heart into overdrive.

I feel fucking sick. Why does this have to be so hard, and what the hell am I even supposed to say to him? So much has gone down between us and not a damn thing of it has been good.

I wait a moment, my gaze flicking back toward the stairs. I should just leave; I'm only asking for trouble.

I never should have come here.

Before I can walk away, the door opens and I find myself staring up at a broken man, his usual dark stormy eyes completely shattered. My bottom lip trembles as everything breaks inside of me. "I—"

"You know, don't you?" he asks, cutting me off before I get the chance to really say what needs to be said. Though, I really don't know what that is. 'Thank you' doesn't seem like enough, while 'sorry' sounds so utterly pathetic after everything that's already been said and done.

I nod, swallowing over the lump in my throat as I briefly remember his kiss in the dark elevator, a goodbye kiss, nothing more. But as I look into the hollow depths of his stormy gaze, it becomes all too obvious; Dante Carver is in love with me.

Then just like that, Carver takes a step back and closes the door between us. The soft click of the lock falls into place, splitting my heart right down the center—the final nail in the coffin.

9

School just seems so trivial after everything that's gone down over the past few days. What the fuck are we even doing here? Is there a purpose now knowing that my whole future is already planned out for the rest of my life, knowing that I'll never want for anything, never have a chance to go to college and get a real career? What's the point in suffering through the last few months of exams, hormonal teenagers, and demanding teachers?

I look up at the big school. Maybe the whole point is to give me just a sliver of normalcy before I dive headfirst into the world of Dynasty. Though, it's not like I haven't already experienced my fair share of it, and damn it, it left an awful taste in my mouth. I don't know how they expect me to last until my dying days in that world, but if I have my way, Dynasty will cease to exist.

Though I can't deny how intriguing the idea of flushing out all the corrupted assholes sounds and starting fresh with the heirs. Maybe if we start them young, they can be easily swayed to not be dickheads like their fathers before them, but then I'm stuck with guys like Grayson, Carver, and King, and it's no secret that they're the biggest dickheads of them all. Not Cruz though, he's as sweet as candy … and just as delicious too.

As I pull my helmet off, I glance down at my Ducati and let out a sigh. After finding out exactly what Carver did for me yesterday, I've been in a slump. I can't focus, I can't smile, I couldn't even ride in a straight fucking line without nearly causing an accident. Carver hasn't left my thoughts, and the way my chest constantly aches is seriously starting to mess with my head.

I hate that he did that for me, and I hate even more that it's because there's something between us—at least there was. I think … I don't fucking know anymore. But if he didn't care for me, why the hell would he go to those lengths to protect me?

Fuck him. Why did he have to go and complicate this so much more? The world is already hard enough as it is. The guilt I feel for what he did for me, but also the anger at the whole situation … shit. I don't know how we're ever going to build a relationship again—not that we really had one.

I can't imagine what he's feeling right now.

The familiar black Escalade pulls into the student parking lot and I watch it as it pulls into the space next to my Ducati. I feel all four of the guys' intense stares on me and the second the four doors open, it only gets worse.

Grayson gets out first and takes two steps toward me as Carver cuts in front of us, his stare boring into mine and holding me captive. His natural manly scent hits me as he passes, and my chest begins to ache all over again. The second he slices his stare away from mine, everything goes weak. It's not until Grayson's big hand curls tightly around my elbow, holding me up, that I realize I'm falling.

I quickly right myself and catch my breath, only to realize that Grayson still stands behind me, his hand at my elbow. My heart races. The last time we spoke without our emotions running wild was in the kitchen of King's cabin in the woods when I discovered the raven tattoo stretching over his chest. I couldn't help but feel like it had something to do with me, and even now, after everything that's gone down the last few days and the way he protected me, I'm questioning everything.

I pull my elbow free and give him a tight smile. "Thanks," I murmur. "I'm good now."

Grayson nods and takes the helmet out of my hands as King and Cruz step out from behind the Escalade. They both watch us standing so close together, glancing between us with a strange curiosity that has me fighting a smile and rolling my eyes. There's not a doubt in my mind that they're wondering if our little threesome just became a party of four.

Not wanting to hang around for their interrogation, I make my way to the main entrance of Ravenwood Heights Academy with the three guys following behind, my helmet still tucked safely under Grayson's arms.

We walk into the school together and I get all of three steps before Ember comes crashing into me. "What the actual fuck, girl? Where the hell have you been? You know it's been like … fuck … days since I saw you last. What happened to you?" she demands, grabbing hold of my shoulder and scanning her gaze over my body. "I swear, I thought you must have picked a fight with the wrong guy, been roofied, and then woke up in a random Mexican hospital. I've been so worried about you. I mean, is it that hard to answer your phone or send a text? Sheesh, girl."

My face twists into a cringe and I give her an awkward shitty smile. "Sorry," I say, knowing that's not going to cut it. "I haven't seen my phone since … crap. I don't even know when I last saw my phone, but it's been a while."

Ember gives me a blank, unimpressed stare as the students walking in through the main entrance have to shoulder charge me to get past. "Seriously?" she grumbles. "Four fucking days, babe. What happened to you? I'm going to need something a little better than 'I lost my phone.' I mean, I thought maybe you'd been put with a new family and I didn't get a chance to say goodbye."

My heart breaks for my friend, and once again, I'm left feeling like the shittiest person on earth.

I pull Ember in and wrap my arms around her small frame. "I'm sorry," I tell her, trying to keep the ache out of my tone, but failing miserably. "I didn't mean to disappear like that, I just had … a lot going on and then all this shit went down with Carver and I just … I'm sorry."

Ember pulls back and gives me a tight smile. "I guess you're not about to tell me what happened with Carver?"

A smile cuts across my face and I shake my head, which only makes her sigh. "Damn, it was worth a try," she tells me. "I still don't think I really understand how you ended up living there, but I'm not going to lie, I'm jealous as fuck. Those guys are … wow. They're just wow. There's no other word to describe them."

"Trust me," I grumble under my breath as I loop my arm through hers and lead her down the hallway toward my locker. "I have plenty of descriptive words for those guys, but right now, I need you to keep my mind off them. What's been going on with you?"

"Really?" she groans. "You're not going to give me anything? Not even a little hint at what went down between you and Cruz after your party? Because I haven't forgotten that you were supposed to tell me what's going on between the two of you, and don't think I didn't notice how you skipped out early. You were fucking him, weren't you?"

A wicked smile cuts across my face. "So, you and Jacob, hey? How's that going?"

She gives me a blank stare. "Really? You're going to avoid it altogether?"

"Damn right, I am," I laugh as I drag her to my locker and momentarily forget which one is mine. I swear, at this stage, I think I've actually spent more days away from school than actually being here. "Now, tell me everything that's been going on with you. I've missed your hourly updates on your life."

Ember rolls her eyes as we come to a stop outside a locker with a familiar combo lock attached to it. I fumble with the code as Ember drops her shoulder against the neighboring locker before going all girly on me and letting out a deep sigh. She meets my stare as a beaming smile stretches across her face. "Do you really want to know?"

"Umm … yeah," I laugh. "Tell me everything. Besides, it'll hopefully work wonders in getting my mind off the four assholes who know nothing about personal boundaries."

Ember narrows her eyes and I see the desperation pulsing through her. She wants to push me for information, but she knows that if I were going to tell her something, I would have already done it. "Fine," she says with a sigh, giving up on the hope of learning exactly how devilish Cruz Danforth really is. "Where should I start?"

I shrug my shoulders. "Tell me everything you know about the guy," I say, feeling my stomach twist with guilt. If only she knew that the guy she's seeing is a member of Dynasty, and also the guy who managed to place himself right at the top of my shit list—right under Carver of course.

Jacob Scardoni was at the party in the woods and after Carver let me know what he thought of my theory that he was being a double agent and had something to do with it, my suspicions fell on Jacob. If I'm completely honest, I think I've always suspected Jacob. He seems far too shady to me.

Ember told me she had a crush on him for ages, and now suddenly, he wants to be with her. It's too convenient, plus the fact that he just happened to be at that party right before the hitmen were sent after me. Who else would have known that Carver had me alone in the woods?

Jacob is using her as a pawn to keep an eye on me. At least, that's what I think. I really hope for Ember's sake that he's genuine because if he breaks her heart, I'm going to break his face, and I'm going to enjoy every last second of it.

She starts going on and on about their date over the weekend, and the longer she talks, the harder it is for me to smile. This bitch was out getting wined and dined while I was pacing the small concrete floor of my cell. But I'm not here to bring her down.

I don't know why I've been holding back from Ember. I want my world and hers to stay completely separate. She's my light at the end of the tunnel. Maybe it's her innocence that draws me in. The last thing I want is to corrupt her precious soul and expose her to the real ugliness of what my life has been like over the past month. Besides, if she knew just how easily I shoved that blade through Royston Carver, she'd be horrified. She'd never talk to me again, and I couldn't possibly handle that.

I need Ember in my life; I need her to keep me grounded and remind me of the important things.

Ember goes on about her date and tells me in fine detail about the extra special activities they participated in afterward. As she does, I find myself comparing Jacob to King and Cruz, and I come to the conclusion that Jacob Scardoni doesn't have a clue what he's doing. It looks like poor Ember got the consolation prize while I took home the gold.

As she talks, I look back over my shoulder just as Grayson slips my helmet inside his locker and my lips press into a hard line. I know he's just trying to be helpful by holding it for me, but in reality, he's taking my freedom without even realizing it. Though, how could he? Normal people wouldn't have an issue with it, but I'm not normal people.

I never ride my bike without my helmet. I've heard way too many horror stories and it makes me cringe every time I see Cruz taking off without one. But not having it close by means that I can't just run out of here and escape in the blink of an eye. I'm trapped here until Grayson decides to walk his toned ass back down the hallway and unlock his damn locker. Though, I could always go and ask for it, but that would mean admitting that my helmet is a security blanket, and I'm not about to lower myself to those standards in front of a guy like Grayson, who would no doubt use it against me.

Letting out a sigh, I turn back to my locker to close the door, but as I go, I catch Carver's pained stare and a heaviness instantly drops into my stomach. I hold his stare for a second longer, and as I do, a million messages seem to pass between us, but like two people who struggle to communicate, I can't understand a damn thing that he's trying to tell me. All I know is that whatever he's trying to say, it's going to hurt.

Fuck him. Why does this have to suck so bad?

Not being able to handle his intensity, I tear my gaze away and focus on what I'm doing, and before I know it, the bell sounds through the school and Ember drags me away. We step into our homeroom class and watch as Mr. Bennett makes a point of ignoring the students piling through his door.

I take my seat beside Ember and we talk quietly between ourselves until Mr. Bennett is striding across the room and closing the heavy door. He goes through the attendance, and by the time he's taking his seat again and putting his feet up on his desk, the classroom door flies open.

All eyes fly toward King in the doorway as his eyes come to mine. "Let's go," he grunts as though stealing a student right out of homeroom is completely acceptable.

"What? No," I say, glancing back at Mr. Bennett, who watches on with a scowl across his face.

"Don't make me come in there and throw your ass over my shoulder," he warns me. "You fucking know that I will."

I let out a loud sigh, hating how he uses that authoritative tone on me, but screw him. If he can use it on me, then I'll sure as hell use it right back on him. "Why? What is so freaking important that it couldn't wait until break? Hell, I just stood in the fucking hallway for the past ten minutes. You could have talked to me then."

King's eyes narrow. "Now, Winter."

I groan and stare at him a second longer, but it's clear as day that he has absolutely no intention of walking away. I quickly glance at Mr. Bennett who instantly drops his gaze in dismissal, and just like that, I push my chair back, letting it scrape across the classroom floor.

I make a show of my irritation by slowly getting up and grabbing my things off the desk in front of me, more than aware of Ember's curious gaze burning into the side of my face.

I make my way toward King and hold his stare, and with every step I take, I see him trying to get inside my head. "What?" I demand, stepping right in front of him.

King rolls his eyes and grabs my wrist before pulling me out of the classroom and closing the door behind him. He walks down the hall and I have to jog a few steps to keep up with his long strides. "What do you want?" I ask. "You can't just drag me out of homeroom whenever the hell you like, you know. You may be bigger and stronger than me, but I'll tear your ass up, Hunter King."

We storm down the empty hallway until we finally reach my locker and only then does he stop. King takes my waist and pushes me up against my locker. "What the hell is going on with you?"

"The fuck are you talking about? You know exactly what's going on with me."

"No," he says, leaning into me and narrowing his gaze on mine. "It's something more. I can see it in your eyes. You've been different this morning. What happened?"

My heart races as I bite down on my bottom lip and glance away, not ready to discuss it, yet my hands come to his shirt and I pull him in closer, desperately needing his comfort. "It's nothing," I tell him, sinking into the feel of his arm curling around my body. "Just bullshit with Carver."

"What happened?" he urges, his tone deep and demanding.

I let out a sigh. "Nothing that I shouldn't have expected," I tell him, feeling the weight of Carver's rejection sitting heavily against my chest. "After you guys left my place yesterday, I went to see Carver to talk and he just … he wanted nothing to do with me. It's as though he couldn't even stand to look at my face, and I don't know it just—"

"It hurt," he finishes for me.

I nod into his chest and he lets out a deep sigh, almost as though my pain hurts him just as much. We stand together for a long moment with nothing but silence between us as he allows me to soak up every little bit of his comfort. When I finally feel strong enough, I push him back just a step so that I can see his face. "Did you really drag me out of homeroom just to see how I was doing?"

A guilty smirk cuts across his face as his eyes shine with a devilish sparkle that has everything inside me clenching. "Well, to be perfectly honest," he says, quickly glancing up and down the hallway, "I pulled you out here so I could fuck you up against your locker."

I suck in a gasp, my eyes wide as I quickly glance around, making sure we're still alone. "Are you insane? You can't fuck me here in the middle of the hallway. Someone could see. Not to mention, that sounds like an indecent exposure to minors charge heading right your way."

"Who's going to see? We're all alone. Everyone is in homeroom. Besides, I bet it'll get your mind off Carver pretty damn fast."

"But—"

King raises a brow, his lips pulling up at the corners with his cocky confidence. "Wow, you're surprising me, Winter. I never took you for the chick to be scared of a challenge."

My jaw drops at his audacity. "That's a low blow," I tell him. "You know I'm not scared, but there's only five minutes left in homeroom and then this hallway will be packed with bodies, and I don't know about you, but this whole school has already seen me sucking a dick, they don't need to watch me riding one too."

King dips his head, his lips skimming over my shoulder as he grinds against me, making me groan with desire. "I know your body better than I know my own, Winter," he murmurs, his hand slipping down between us and cupping my needy pussy. "I could have you thoroughly fucked and satisfied before you even have time to scream my name, and you damn well know it."

"Fuck," I grunt, glancing up and down the long hallway. "If we get caught, I'm going to fuck Cruz every hour on the hour and make you watch."

A wicked, excited grin stretches across his face, and not a second later, those lips are crushing down on mine with his hands working the fly of my ripped jeans. He tears them down my body as I free his heavy cock from the confines of his pants, and just like that, he buries himself deep inside of me.

We both groan, and as he really starts to move, I'm forced to bite down on his shoulder to keep from screaming out. He fucks me hard and fast, and just as he said, all thoughts of Carver fly from my mind.

He picks up his pace, his lips against my neck as I glance down the hallway, making sure that we're not about to get caught. My nails dig into his back and he groans in pleasure, the sound like an electric current shooting straight for my pussy.

My orgasm sneaks up on me, and I clench down around him as I come hard, closing my eyes as the pleasure rocks through me. "Fuck,

King," I groan, loving the feel of his fingers tightening on my waist.

He rocks into me two more times before he comes hard, sending hot spurts of cum shooting up into me, and just as I come down from my high, he pulls out of me, both of us panting, desperate to catch our breath.

King quickly adjusts himself and tucks his big cock back into his pants as his lips crush against mine. "Tell me that you didn't need that," he says, his lips pulling into a cocky grin.

I can't help but laugh as I push him back and grab my jeans. "You're way too confident for your own good," I tell him, finding my jeans on the floor and quickly stepping into them before his cum has the chance to run down my leg.

I get the zipper up just as the bell sounds through the school, and not a second later, the hallways are flooded with clueless students. King's hand slaps down on my ass as I scurry away, desperately seeking out the bathroom, while the only sound I hear is his deep, roaring laugh, more than proud of his achievement.

10

The soft afternoon rain falls against the roof of Carver's home as Cruz drags me through the living room. We crash down onto the couch, his lips pressing against mine and his arm locked securely around my waist. His hand slides down my back until it's cupped securely over my ass.

His tongue dives into my mouth, exploring and taking whatever the fuck it wants. I adjust myself on top of him, straddling his waist and looking down at him. My tongue glides across my bottom lip as I grab the hem of my cropped tank and peel it over my head.

Cruz's eyes become hooded as he watches me, the need and desire pulsing through his gaze like an electrical current that speaks right to my soul. Cruz sits up, and keeping one hand on my waist, the other reaches around my back and unhooks my bra.

I let the red material fall down my arms until it drops between us, and just as Cruz leans in and sucks my pebbled nipple into his mouth, I spy King and Grayson over the back of the couch, walking through the massive kitchen.

King instantly stops, his gaze sweeping to mine as though he knew exactly where to find me in this big room. His brow raises with interest and I watch the way he watches me back, silently asking for an invitation, but he got his turn this morning, and damn, the risk of getting caught was definitely worth the reward. King moves forward, propping his shoulder against the wall, more than happy to sit back and watch the show.

Grayson on the other hand, makes his way through the kitchen, collecting everything he needs for a killer sandwich, and for a guy that could kill a man with his bare hands, he's extremely unobservant, at least right now he is. It isn't until Cruz's tongue flicks over my nipple and a soft, needy groan pulls from deep within me that he realizes something is going on just behind him.

He spins around, and as my head tilts back with pleasure, I thrust my chest into Cruz, silently begging for more. He locks eyes with me, his interest instantly filtering through his gaze as it swoops over my half-naked body.

Grayson steps in beside King and while there's certainly interest in his eyes, there's also a shitload of hesitation. He's not sure about this little deal that King, Cruz, and I have going on. He wants in, but he also wants nothing to do with it.

"What are you waiting for?" Cruz murmurs, not taking his hands off my body as he speaks to the guys behind him. "After four days in that cell, I think this little she-devil is going to need all the attention she can get."

An excited thrill shoots through me and I look back at the two boys by the kitchen. They glance at each other—a cocky smirk on King's face while an apprehensive expression crosses Grayson's. "Trust me," King murmurs to his friend. "You don't want to miss this. The way her body … fuck, man. You can deal with the 'what does this mean?' questions afterward."

Grayson's gaze slices back to mine as King pushes off the wall and walks deeper into the living room. My eyes heat as I meet Grayson's intrigued stare. My bottom lip gets captured between my teeth and I don't doubt that he sees a hungry lioness silently calling his name.

A soft moan slips from between my lips as King steps in behind me and brushes his fingertips across my skin, and as if the sound was a calling card that spoke right to the deepest parts of him, Grayson slowly pushes off the wall and steps through to the living room.

My back straightens with interest as my heart thunders in my chest. Is he really down for this?

I feel Cruz's smile against my skin, and I can't help but look down and meet his gaze. He's just as excited as I am. King grabs me from behind and pulls me off the couch, putting me down on my feet in front of him just as Grayson steps into his side.

Cruz stands, and the three of them circle me, and as I glance up at all of their hungry stares, a nervousness creeps through me. I've proven to myself that I can handle two, but can I satisfy all three of them at once? I guess I'm about to find out.

After weeks of wondering what Grayson's lips would taste like on mine, I can't resist turning to him first. Nobody touches me, they let me take my time.

I step closer to him, meeting his hungry stare. My hand instantly falls to his wide chest and the nerves triple. Why am I so anxious about this? My fingers glide down his body until they find the hem of his shirt and I slip them underneath, feeling the warmth of his skin below.

I raise it back up to his chest, right where his raven tattoo would be, and I watch as he sucks in a slight breath. His hand comes to my waist and the fire that burns between us is like nothing I've ever felt before, and for just a second, King and Cruz fade away, leaving nothing but the intense connection I have with Grayson.

He pulls me in, and as he does, I rise onto my tippy-toes, needing to be closer. His hand drops over my body, getting a good feel of my ass and as I raise my chin to finally feel his lips on mine, King steps in behind me, placing his hand on my other hip.

The excitement burns through me like fire and lightning, and just as Grayson brings his lips down to meet mine, an irritated scoff comes from the kitchen. I whip my gaze around to meet Carver's very pissed off one, just the sight of him making all the bullshit emotions well up inside of me. "Really?" he questions, but it's impossible to tell if he's talking to me or the boys. "Out of all the places you could have done this, you choose to fuck in my living room?"

Embarrassment instantly seeps through me and as his stare bores into mine and his anger pulses through, my need to get fucked within an inch of my life drains away. My hand falls from Grayson's chest and the smirk that cuts over Carver's face is like having a bucket of ice water tipped over my head. He knows what he's done, and the bastard is fucking proud of himself.

An irritated groan pulls from between my lips. "What's the matter, princess? Jealous it's not your dick I'll be sucking?" I grumble, snatching my tank off the ground and quickly pulling it over my head, not wanting him to see my body unless it's him that I'm about to give it to.

"You fucking wish, *Elodie,*" he spits.

Cruz falls back to the couch with disappointment flying across his handsome features. "Fucking cock block," he grumbles under his breath as King steps back out of my personal space.

Carver just smirks as though he's a hero, but I don't miss the jealousy pulsing through his sharp gaze. I was fucking right, he's as jealous as they come, but just because he saved my ass and is not being a stubborn asshole, doesn't mean that he gets to have me.

Carver turns and walks out of the room, leaving nothing but a heaviness behind. The mood is completely gone, and Grayson quickly backs away, almost as though he's embarrassed to have been caught dipping his fingers into the honey pot. "I, uhh … I've got shit to get done anyway."

I roll my eyes. "I don't need your excuses," I tell him. "Just go."

Without another word, Grayson turns his back and strides right out of the living room and back through the kitchen. I watch him for a second and can't help but notice how he makes a left and takes himself toward the gym, probably hoping to work me out of his system.

I fall into the couch beside Cruz and his hand instantly comes down on my thigh. "You okay?" he grumbles just moments before a throat clears in the room behind us.

The three of us whip around to find Tobias King standing in the main entrance of the living room and I gape at him, my heart racing. Fuck me, had Carver not interrupted us, my father's closest friend would have walked in on me mid gang bang.

What are the fucking chances?

King instantly flies to his feet. "Dad," he grunts, the relief in his tone screaming louder than anything I've ever heard. "What's going on? Is everything okay?"

"Hunter," he says, nodding all too formally toward his son, making me wonder when the last time they actually spoke was. That's not exactly the way a father would greet a son who he sees every day at home, but then, this world isn't exactly classified as normal. "Nothing is the matter. I have a few spare hours and thought now is a suitable time to take Elodie for her induction. There is a lot she has to learn, and had she not wasted her last few days in our cells, she would have already been properly trained in her role."

My brows shoot up as I get to my feet beside his devilishly attractive son. "Oh, umm … are you sure? I wouldn't want to be a nuisance."

"Positive, he says. "Have you completed all of your schoolwork?"

"I—" I pause. I don't think I've ever had an adult ask me if I'd completed my homework before. I nod. "Everything is up to date."

"Good. Hurry along then, we have a lot to cover."

I glance back at King and he nods, silently reminding me that I can trust him, and after receiving a proud smile from Cruz, who adjusts the front of his jeans with a cringe, I hurry around the side of the couch to meet with Tobias King.

The second I stand at his side, he turns, and I follow him out of the living room as I hear Cruz burst into howling laughter behind us. "Fuck dude, that was far too close for my liking."

"You're telling me," King responds in a hushed tone, followed by the sound of him dropping down onto the couch, most likely in his favorite spot with his feet up on the coffee table. "Can you imagine if he'd walked in to see that shit?"

Cruz snickers at the thought, and as Tobias looks down at me, my cheeks flush the brightest shade of red, but I don't dare meet his stare. How could I, knowing that not two minutes ago, I was about to let his son rail me until I was unconscious?

Fuck me. That really was a close call.

I keep my mouth shut and just keep walking, acting as though I haven't got a clue what the boys are talking about until Tobias' curious stare finally slides back to the front door.

We walk in silence until the soft afternoon rain is falling around me. Tobias offers me his elbow as we descend the grand stairs, and despite being more than capable of handling the stairs on my own, I find my hand slipping around his arm.

It's probably just an age thing. Tobias would have been raised in wealth as the perfect gentleman, and despite being anything but a lady,

I appreciate the gesture. Though, I don't know where he went wrong with his son, because Hunter King is anything but a gentleman.

We reach his car at the bottom of the drive, and as he holds the door open, it hits me. Carver would have received notification of him coming through the gate.

That fucker. He knew Tobias was coming and he came to break up the party so his friends didn't get caught fucking the same chick.

Screw him. Why does he keep trying to save me? I clearly don't deserve it, but on top of that, there's a massive part of him that can't stand to be around me. It doesn't make sense.

I've never been so confused by someone in my life.

I shake off the thoughts as Tobias drops down into the driver's seat. We sit in silence and I look out the window at the happy families playing in their yards and try to remember whose house is whose. Though, it's not like it's going to matter. The majority of the men who have been trying to take me out haven't exactly been showing their faces. They're keeping a low profile just as I should be doing.

We get to the end of the road, and just as Carver had done the first time he brought me here, Tobias turns right and we take the skinny private road to the concealed car elevator until we're dropping down into darkness.

Tobias leads me out into the underground world, and we walk through the main entrance. "So, what exactly does this induction thing entail?"

He shrugs his shoulders. "To be completely honest with you, Elodie, I have no idea. I'm making it up as I go. Your father didn't exactly leave a handbook of how to do things in case he was brutally murdered and his only child would have to rule at a young age. In a perfect world, your father would be here, and he would have taught you everything you needed to know as you grew."

"Okay," I say, taking a deep breath. "So, where do we start?"

"I suppose we take you on the grand tour and then we head for your father's main office."

"Main office?" I ask, my brows furrowed as Tobias leads me toward the right, far away from the hallway that ends with the holding cells. In fact, I might ask Tobias to leave that part out of my grand tour. I think I've seen enough of those cells to last a lifetime.

We take a few steps and stop at a door. Tobias leans in and opens it for me before ushering me in. "Yes, your father had four offices in total, one in your home that I assume you've already discovered."

I nod. "Yeah, I had a peek, but it felt too personal, so I backed out and closed the door before I got the chance to take a proper look."

"Well, you should," he tells me. "Knowledge is the key to success. Your father kept a lot of paperwork in his home office. It will do you well to go home tonight and get familiar with the documents he felt important enough to keep. Imagine the wealth of knowledge you could learn about the people around you just from a little light reading."

"Light?" I scoff. "There's nothing light about it. There were bookcases upon bookcases in that office."

"Then I suggest you get started."

My lips press into a tight line and I drop the conversation. The last thing I want is to spend my time reading over old documents and books, but I can't deny that he has a very valid point. There could be all sorts of information in those documents about the people I'm supposed to lead, and if it was worthy enough for my father to hold onto, then who the hell knows what kind of advantage I'll be giving myself in this twisted game.

"Follow me through here," Tobias says, stepping through to another room.

I go straight after him and pause at the door as I find the wide room covered from wall to wall in the kind of technology that one only sees in movies. "What is this?" I ask, taking in all the screens and monitors.

"This is our state-of-the-art tech room, where all the magic happens," he says, sounding like a proud father, much prouder than when he was speaking to his son. "Any computer or system can be hacked from this very room. No matter how secure their systems are, Dynasty will always be better. This is how we function, how we thrive. This right here is the heart of Dynasty. Without this, we hold no power. From here, we're able to control every missile launcher across the globe, we can control governments, the stock market, everything is ours with just the touch of a button. This right here is where your criminal record vanished into thin air."

I gape at it all, my mind reeling with the information. This room is an accident waiting to happen. More than that, it's a fucking cyber weapon, and under the control of someone with less than pure intentions, this equipment could mean disaster. "But … why? Why does anybody want that kind of power? What if leadership fell into the wrong hands? The whole world could be destroyed with just the click of a button."

"That is exactly the reason why we have a council. Your role is not to be taken lightly. There are members of Dynasty who are only looking out for themselves. They want to see their own success, want to see how far they can push the limits—"

"People like Royston Carver."

"Exactly," he says with a firm nod. "If leadership was to fall into the hands of someone like that ... Christ be with us."

"It's really that bad?" I ask, looking up at him. "Dynasty really holds all that power?"

"It does. It wasn't like this at first," he tells me, ushering me back toward the door and locking it behind him. "Your grandfather, Gerald Ravenwood, built the foundations of Dynasty, but it was your father in his younger years who truly made it what it is today, and once he was satisfied with it, he took a step back to watch it flourish."

"But that wasn't enough for others," I commented. "They wanted more."

Tobias gives me a tight smile. "Sometimes perfect just isn't enough."

Damn. Why does that one little comment speak right to my soul?

We continue our tour and Tobias leads me to another room filled with filing cabinets. "This room is self-explanatory. Everything you will ever need to find is in here, filed in alphabetical order," he tells me. "But don't be fooled, it's a lot bigger than you think. This room goes on for nearly a mile. What you're seeing here is just the 'A's'. There's a false wall between each letter just to make things a little easier."

My mouth drops as I stare at the massive filing room. "Who the hell is responsible for doing the filing?" I ask, instantly wondering if I have the power to give the poor fucker a pay raise. I mean, what kind of bullshit crime would someone have to commit to be dumped with that job?

"Some of the children like to volunteer," Tobias tells me. "It's their way of earning a bit of pocket money, not that they really need it. For the most part, we like to play it smart and keep it for those who require a bit of … downtime."

"In other words, it's used as a punishment."

Tobias gives me a weak smile. "I guess you could put it that way."

I scoff. "I bet King, Cruz, Grayson, and Carver have spent many hours down here."

A real belly laugh comes tearing out of Tobias as he steps back and pulls the door closed. "Oh, believe me, by now, those boys would know every little square inch of the filing rooms. I bet they could tell you exactly how many bricks make up each room." I can't help but laugh and find myself looking up at him as a fond smile settles across his face. "You know, your father and I used to spend a lot of time down here too."

"Oh, really?" I smile.

"Sure did, we were known to get into a bit of mischief ourselves as young ones," he tells me, the fondness in his tone unmistakable. "It's a real shame he's gone. I had many great years with him."

"I bet. I'm just sad that I never got a chance to know him. I bet he would have made a great father," I murmur, wondering why the hell I chose now to be so vulnerable. Yet the second I started, I couldn't stop. "The life I could have had here … it would have been amazing. I would have grown up alongside the boys and I wouldn't have felt lost like this. I would have had a real home … a real family."

"Your parents would be proud of the young woman you've become," he says, letting out a heavy sigh. "You know, I never suspected that fire was an accident," he explains. "Your parents were vacationing up in the mountains when I received your father's distress call. When I got there, I found that both of your parents had perished in the fire, but the fire and rescue team managed to get you out just in time. Of the sixteen remaining heads of Dynasty, I was the first to arrive on the scene, and when I saw the blood on your clothes, I knew instantly there had been foul play. I just couldn't figure out who was responsible."

My gaze drops to the marble tiles of the hallway as my voice lowers, too afraid that it will break. "What happened after that?"

"My wife and I hid you away for a few months. You were only a newborn, just a sweet, innocent little girl. Hunter was growing out of his bassinet, so you slept in there until we came to the decision to put you in foster care."

I stop walking, staring up at the man who made the decision to abandon me to an awful life for the past eighteen years. "That was you?" I breathe. "You abandoned me to the system?"

A softness spreads over his face. "I'm sorry, Elodie. Not a day goes by that I haven't hated myself for making that call. I watched you grow, watched you bounce from home to home, but you were not safe here. You were only three when the other members of Dynasty discovered your existence, and only three days later, the car you were in was driven off the road. Ever since then, we knew we had to keep on top of it and we've been one step ahead this whole time."

"Up until the attack in the woods," I scoff.

"Yes," he says with a regretful sigh. "As you grew closer to your eighteenth birthday, they were finding you quicker each time, and even after all these years, we still couldn't pinpoint who was behind the attacks, but now we finally know, and Dynasty can now rise up to what it once was."

Not really knowing how to respond to that, I remain silent, just letting it all sink in.

Tobias gets the hint that I need time and continues with his tour. It takes him nearly two hours to come full circle, and by the time we're done, I'm completely exhausted. My legs are sore from walking and my mind is reeling from all the information.

Tobias delivers me right to my front door, and after thanking him for everything he's shared with me tonight, I fall through the doors and dive for the stairs. He went over a million things all to do with my role and what it actually means to be a leader here, but after the whole cyber weapon thing and the putting me in foster care decision, I blanked out a bit. I'm pretty sure I only caught every other word after that.

I take myself upstairs, and after showering and getting into my pajamas, I find myself staring at my bed. It would be so simple to slip in between the sheets and take myself off to sleep. At least, try to sleep while I pretend the monsters inside my head aren't terrifying.

Knowing sleep won't come, I slip back out of my bedroom and find myself in my father's home office. I've avoided this room for the most part. It seems too personal, but then what does that matter? I've spent hours sitting on the floor of their massive closet. What's more personal than that?

I drop down into the big couch that lines his office and wonder what his time in here would have been like. Was it an escape from the craziness of the world he ruled? Was this where he got his peace and quiet, or was this where he would go to get shit done?

I grab the throw blanket off the back of the couch and pull it over me. It smells like it's been sitting here for twenty years, and because of that, this blanket just became my favorite thing in the world. The rest of the house has been looked after. Modern furniture fills the rooms, but this room looks as though it's never been touched.

My eyes grow heavy and I scoot down on the couch, imagining that my parents are still here. I wonder what they'd be like, where their lives would have taken them, and just like that, I close my eyes, and for the first time since being locked in Sam's dark cell without Carver's arms around me, I sleep peacefully, the monsters kept at bay.

11

Grayson leans back in his chair, his eyes roaming over my body as though he doesn't even realize that he's doing it. The confusion seeps out of him, but it's clouded by intrigue. I watch him back, wondering just what he'd do if I was to cross the room and straddle his lap. Would he push me away or pull me in? All I know is that three nights ago, his lips were only an inch from mine, and kissing him is all I've been able to think about. You know—when Carver isn't taking up all the space inside my head.

Cruz's scoff from the dining table breaks our trance and I look his way, watching as he rolls his eyes at Grayson. "Get in line, bro," he tells him. "I've been trying to seal the deal for three days, but Carver keeps cock blocking me."

"You're more than welcome to go and fuck in your own house," Carver calls from the living room.

"With my parents and my little brothers knocking at the door? Yeah fucking right."

Carver grumbles under his breath. "At least you've got your brothers."

Cruz's face twists with a cringe just as I feel like I've been shot straight through the heart. That one stung. Both Cruz and King glance my way and I shake my head, not wanting to see their pity. Every time I'm reminded of what Carver lost to save me, a little piece of me dies inside. I still can't believe that he sacrificed his family for me. He gave up the one thing I've always wanted, and it's killing me that he won't just give me two seconds to talk to him about it. I don't know if he's too hurt to even think about it, or just being a stubborn asshole, but I need to fix this. I just don't know how.

Letting out a sigh, I get up from the table and make my way into the living room, feeling the guys' eyes on me, carefully watching my every step, but I don't care. I'm determined to fix this. If only I could get him to loosen up. Maybe then he'll be happy to talk it through.

Carver sits back on the couch, his feet up and looking like the best kind of meal in his white long-sleeved shirt with his sleeves pushed up to his elbows and showing off his strong forearms. My mouth waters just looking at him, but when he raises those dark stormy eyes to meet mine, my heart shatters.

He raises off the couch and walks toward me. His heavy stare remains locked on mine, and with each passing step, the tension in the room intensifies until he's right before me. He passes so closely that the soft material of his shirt gently grazes my arm, and as he goes, that manly scent teases my senses.

I spin around, watching as he goes. "Seriously?" I demand. "That's it? That's all I'm going to get from you?"

Carver scoffs and turns on his heel, stepping back into me. "What do you want me to say, Winter? You want me to wrap my arms around you and tell you that it's all going to be okay? You want me to just forget that you killed my father on a fucking dance floor in front of every member of Dynasty? You want me to pretend that you didn't fuck everything up for me?"

"I—"

"No. It ain't going to happen. You can't just wave your magical little pussy around and make everything go away. That's not how the real world works, babe. You forced my hand, and yet somehow, you come out of this looking like the innocent little victim."

"Carver, just—"

He grabs me, pushing me up against the wall and stepping right into me, so close that I can feel the rapid beat of his chest under my hand. "Every time I see your fucking face all I can think about is my hand wrapped around your throat, squeezing it until you couldn't fucking breathe. That's what you did to me."

He stares right into my eyes, both of us breathing hard until Grayson steps in behind him. "Come on, bro. Take a walk. You both need to cool off."

Carver clenches his jaw, absolutely hating when one of the guys tells him when to back off, but right now, I'm grateful for it. My fingers curl into a fist, capturing his shirt in my hand, knowing that it's only seconds before he pulls away, but I'm not done with him yet. I need to get him back in the gym where I can work out all this anger. Maybe we both need to take our frustrations out on one another.

Carver's gaze drops to my hand tangled in his shirt and the corner of his mouth kicks up into an amused smirk, and just like that, he knows that he's gotten under my skin. His eyes slice back to mine, seeing just how desperate I am for my pound of flesh, and the way he scoffs tells me that no matter what, he'll never give it to me.

He tears away from me, and my fingers instantly come loose from his shirt as I stare after him, the anger raging inside me. I watch as he walks away and just a moment before I storm his back, intent on ramming my fist straight up his toned ass, Grayson adjusts himself, obscuring my view of his friend. "Go walk it off," he tells me. "Why don't you take that bike of yours for a ride. It's been a while since she's had a good run."

My fists pulse at my sides as I watch Carver over Grayson's shoulder disappearing down the hall. "She can ride that thing all she wants, but when she fucks it up, I'm not buying her another one."

The fuck? *Another one?*

"What the hell is that supposed to mean?" I demand, stepping out from around Grayson and storming after Carver as I hear both King and Cruz sigh at the table, each of them slowly getting to their feet and stepping toward us, more than ready to hold me hostage when I decide to annihilate Carver.

Carver stops and slowly turns to face me, a cocky as fuck smirk pulling at the corner of his mouth. "You fucking heard me, babe. What do you think it means?"

My jaw clenches as I desperately try to keep myself from shoving my hand right through his ribcage and squeezing his fragile little heart just like they do in '*The Vampire Diaries.*' I step into him and shove my hands against his chest, only doing more harm to myself than to him. "I won that bike fair and square," I tell him, my fury rippling beneath the surface. "You've already taken my freedom away from me, you're not taking my fucking bike too."

"Won it in a bet?" he laughs. "That's fucking rich coming from you. Do you honestly think some guy is going to bet you his bike and let you ride away with it into the sunset? Come on, Winter. You're not that fucking daft. That's a twenty-thousand-dollar bike and the helmet just happens to fit you perfectly."

I shake my head. "You're wrong. I won it."

Carver just laughs as Cruz steps into my back, taking my waist as he looks over my head at his friend. "Give it a rest," he tells him. "We fucking agreed not to do this. That bike was all she had."

Heaviness sinks into my stomach and I slowly turn to look up into Cruz's honest stare. "Please," I beg him. "Tell me that he's just trying to fuck with me."

"I'm sorry, babe," he sighs, quickly glancing up and fixing Carver with a lethal stare. "We didn't intend for you to find out like this."

"Cruz," I snap, prompting him to get on with it.

Grayson takes a step closer, raising his regretful stare to mine and being the one to put me out of my misery. "We've been watching you closer this past year, keeping tabs and making sure that you were okay. It was pretty fucking obvious that you were screaming for an escape, so Carver bought the bike. We knew you weren't just going to take some bullshit handout, so we paid some dickhead at the bar to lose it in a bet. Cruz gave him a crash course on how to ride it and we had him teach you for safety."

My whole world burns to ashes around me, and I look up at Cruz, silently begging for him to tell me that it's all a lie, that they're fucking with me just to see my pain. "I'm sorry, babe," he says, pressing his lips into a tight line and slowly shaking his head. "That bike … fuck, I could see how much it meant to you."

I quickly glance at King but the regret shining in his bright blue eyes is too much for me to bear, so I turn back to face Carver. "And just like that, you take away the one thing I had left."

The silence burns between us, and as I look into his dark eyes, I finally figure it out. My actions took his family from him, and now he's doing the same to me, but judging by the hurt in his eyes, it fucking killed him to do it.

Against my better judgment, I take a small step toward him, desperately needing to ease his pain. My hand falls to the front of his shirt, falling until my fingertips catch on the lip of his belt and we just stand, staring at one another, our hurt coming through loud and clear for the world to see, and for just a minute, it's as though no one else exists.

A sharp ringing cuts through the room and our trance is broken. I quickly shuffle back until I'm pressed right up against Cruz, and as King answers his phone, I take in the way Carver watches me in Cruz's arms. The jealousy is strong. He wants to be the one that gets to comfort me, the one who gets to curl his arms around me at night, the one who makes me feel alive, but with every passing minute, he makes sure that will never happen.

King grunts a few times into his phone, and the second he ends the call, his gaze raises to mine. "This conversation is going to have to wait," he informs me. "You're needed in the council chambers for a meeting with the heads of Dynasty."

Carver's brows drop just as fast as mine. "Why?" he snaps, probably just as curious as to where the fuck his phone call was.

King shakes his head. "No idea," he says, indicating to his phone. "That was my father. He just said to get your asses down there."

Without another word, Carver turns on his heel and stalks toward the front door. I let out a sigh and follow behind him, leaving the guys watching after me.

Carver and I break out into the fresh air and he doesn't wait for me to catch up, just storms down the stairs toward his Escalade. He gets in at the speed of light, and within seconds, his engine is roaring to life. He watches me through his windshield, and I don't doubt that he's waiting for me to get in. So just to be an ass, I climb straight on my Ducati—*his* Ducati.

Without missing a beat, Carver takes off, his Escalade flying up his long driveway. I quickly pull my helmet over my head, and within seconds, the Ducati is right on his tail. We stop and I wait impatiently as he enters the code at his gate—my birthday. It peels back slowly and the second we can, we race out of it.

Hitting the main road, I follow him until we're pulling into the dark elevator, and as the door closes behind us, I can't help but remember the last time we were here. His lips sat upon mine and his kiss was filled with desperation.

I feel his stare on me.

The butterflies swarm in my stomach. It would be so easy in this dark, private elevator. I could get straight off my bike and climb into the Escalade and I know without a doubt that he'd cave and finally allow us to give in to our most basic urges, but I'm way too fucking stubborn for that.

The second the elevator door creeps open, his stare falls away, and the butterflies vanish as though they never existed in the first place. I hit the throttle and the Ducati roars through the underground parking lot. I see Carver in my mirrors, pulling out behind me and parking in what used to be his father's designated spot, only I'm not here to play by someone else's rules.

I ride the Ducati right up to the doors of Dynasty, and as they open, I go straight through.

It's nearly a ten-minute walk getting from the door to the council chambers and I'm not about that shit. With the Ducati, I'm about to be there in thirty seconds, but it's going to be even better watching Carver get left behind. I wonder if I could start this meeting without him.

As the Ducati enters the hallway that leads right down to the council chambers, the roaring sound of the engine becomes deafening. I laugh as I imagine the old fuckers in that room at the end of the hallway, wondering what kind of insane fuckery is heading their way.

I get halfway down the hallway before I see the door ahead open and three men step out to see what's going on—Preston Scardoni, Harlen Beckett, and Matthew Montgomery, the asshole who insists on talking shit.

Scowls cross all their faces, and seeing as though these three men are part of the eight who stand against everything good in the world, I wonder just how easy it would be to knock them down like bowling pins.

As my bike comes to a stop, the men disappear back inside the room and I don't waste time following them in.

There's nearly a body at every seat, and apart from me, it looks like we're just waiting on Carver and the old dude who sits directly across from him that never really says much.

"Elodie," Sebastian Whitman says, standing from his seat and leaning forward over the table, bracing himself on his knuckles. "Must I remind you of the high standard we hold here at Dynasty?"

I groan to myself, desperately trying not to show just how infuriating his comment was. He sounds like some hoity-toity CEO speaking down to the new intern. "I was under the impression that this meeting was urgent, seeing as though you've called me here on a Sunday afternoon."

"It is," he insists.

"Good, then we agree. I took the best form of transport to get me here in a timely manner. Now, what's so important that it needs my attention right away?"

Earnest Brooks clears his throat from beside me. "Excuse me, Miss Elodie. We are still waiting on two members of our group. We must not commence without them."

I let out a sigh and lean back into my chair. As we wait for Carver and the other guy, I glance around the room. Everyone sits in awkward silence, and not a single conversation flutters around the table. Someone could let one rip and you'd hear it from a mile away.

The thought has a ridiculous grin stretching across my face, but when the door opens and Carver walks through, I instantly straighten. I watch as he leisurely walks around the table, making a mockery of wasting everyone's time.

The seven men on the left side of the table stare at him as though he's some kind of traitor, while the right-hand side watches him with curious stares, wondering if things are finally going to change. Did Carver switch sides momentarily to get me out of that cell, or is he jumping ship and finally making the change that Dynasty so desperately needs to see?

By the time he takes his seat, the other guy is rushing through the door looking frazzled for being the last to enter. "I apologize," he says, hurrying toward his seat. "Let's get this started."

"Yes, let's," Preston Scardoni says from across the table. "We must discuss your plans for the future of Dynasty."

"My plans?" I ask, my brows raising, more than aware that these dickheads aren't ready to hear the real plans that I have for Dynasty.

Though I'm also wondering why they consider this urgent. This could have waited til tomorrow. "Apart from finding out who was behind the attack in the woods, discovering who helped Royston Carver cover up my parents' murders, and taking down Sam Delacourt, I have no plans."

"No," Preston says. "That is not good enough. You are our leader, you must lead."

"Oh, so this billion-dollar corporation falls all on me?" I question, my stare boring into his. "Correct me if I'm wrong, but I thought this was a council. We work together for the greater good of Dynasty. Put your ideas forward and we'll vote on them as a group. Was that not the intention of this group, or am I here solely to carry the load of sixteen grown men? Now, I've told you what my plans are, and I'm not here seeking approval. You're either with me or against me."

Grayson's father narrows his eyes. "That's not how we do things around here," he tells me in a tone that his son is all too good at replicating. "You have no proof that Royston had help, and the same goes for the attack in the woods. Who's to say that wasn't an outside force? You've made plenty of enemies in your short eighteen years."

"Who do you take me for?" I ask him. "I'm no fool, and I know when someone is conspiring against me. I will get to the bottom of this. The Royston threat may be gone, but I'm not some stupid girl who's just going to assume that all of my issues died with him."

"And what if they did?" Mr. Danforth comments. "What if Royston was behind the attack?"

"Then nobody in this room should have anything to fear. If you're all innocent, then I won't find any evidence to suggest otherwise. So, in that case, what does it matter if I look into it?"

I see heads nodding to my right while there's nothing but blank masks coming from the left. "Do what you need to do," Earnest says beside me. "You will have our full support and cooperation. Dynasty has been filled with corruption for far too long, and it's time to weed out the weak. If someone in this room is guilty of an attack against our leader then we need to know. However, the matter of Sam Delacourt is out of our hands. We do not get involved in criminal matters or revenge plots. That is not what we are about. We stepped in solely to keep you safe, but now the matter has closed, and we will have no part."

My mouth drops as I stare at him, and as I slowly glance around the room, I find sixteen faces staring back at me, all in agreement. "Are you serious?" I ask the room as I watch Carver clench his jaw and subtly shake his head. "Do you have any idea what kind of bullshit I went through at Sam Delacourt's hands? I won't just sit back and let him do this. Every day, he's finding new girls to take off the streets, away from their homes. What if this was one of your daughters?"

A few of the men flinch at the thought, but not a damn one speaks up to make a change, or to be the difference that Dynasty so desperately needs. We have the technical power to change the world at our fingertips, and these fuckers are saying bullshit like 'that's not what we're about.'

Fuck that.

The desperation pulses through me and my control is quickly

slipping. I glance back at Carver, needing his guidance despite how ashamed I am of myself for having to ask.

He discreetly nods his head toward the door, and just like that, I stand, looking out at the men before me. "Like I said, I'm not here seeking your approval. I'm going after Sam Delacourt, and anyone who stands in my way is going to feel my wrath."

Then without another word, I walk out of the council chamber with Carver right on my heels.

He straddles my bike, and not a second later, I climb on behind him, my hands gripping his waist as he takes off like lightning in a deadly storm.

My hand slams down on the table as Carver, Grayson, Cruz, and King stare up, finally watching me as though I'm an equal, not that bitch-ass girl they would constantly pull their armor on for. "I'm done waiting. Sam has gotten away with this for too long. We have to do something about it. I won't stand by any longer."

Grayson leans forward, catching my gaze. "What happened in that meeting?" he demands. "This issue has been there all along, why come to us now?"

I flick my gaze toward Carver, and I see the explanation on the tip of his tongue, but I beat him to it, knowing damn well that he's going to sugarcoat Dynasty's bullshit, just as they've always been trained to do—but not me. "Those dumb fuckers back there aren't going to let me go after Sam. They won't support me, and I'm sure as hell that means they won't lend me those fucking big-ass computers to find him either. But I'm not backing down on this. I won't stand by and let Sam continue to get away with it when we can do something to stop him."

Cruz stands and meets my pissed off gaze, the anger I already hold for him from keeping the truth about the Ducati from me only making matters worse. In fact, it makes it worse for all of them. They should never have kept that from me, but now is not the time to pull apart the reasons for their deceit. "I know how much this means to you, but Dynasty has never done this before. They don't get involved in criminal matters. That's just always been the way we've operated. If we get involved with this, what's to stop others from asking us to do the same with their issues? Before you know it, Preston Scardoni is going to be demanding that we fuck up the drug dealer who sold meth to his son last summer. It won't end well. It's an endless cycle, and eventually, Dynasty will get caught."

I roll my eyes. "Quit advocating for them," I say with a groan. "Dynasty and the men who have held it hostage for the past eighteen years are all assholes. Tobias showed me what kind of power Dynasty truly holds, and the fact they haven't intervened to get rid of people like Sam Delacourt completely baffles my head. If I'm running this fucking show, then I'll be making some changes."

"Woah," Cruz says, walking around the table to drop down next to me. "I'm not advocating for anyone. I'm just saying how it is. If you want me to fucking go balls to the wall to take down Sam Delacourt then I'm all in. But you need to know that if you do this, Dynasty is going to have something to say about it."

"There wasn't an actual vote," Carver says. "It was just implied, so technically she has every right to go after Sam. Dynasty can't fucking stop her."

"But they won't help her either," Grayson says.

I lean into the table, scanning my gaze over all the boys. "Who said we need Dynasty?"

King narrows his eyes. "Babe, I'd hate to be the bearer of bad news, but Dynasty is fucking everywhere. They'll know what you're doing."

"I don't give a shit if they know or not, all I'm saying is that we don't need them to do this."

Grayson leans back, watching me through a narrowed stare. "Do what exactly?"

A determined, wild grin stretches across my face as I turn to Carver. "We're going to fuck up his whole operation and you're going to put it in motion."

Carver scoffs, shaking his head. "No offense," he says, his words a contradiction to the tone of voice he's using. "I'm still dealing with the last bullshit favor I did for you. I'm not about to go and put my neck on the line for another."

King scoffs and shakes his head as I walk around the table and stand right behind Carver. A strange nervousness comes over me at being so close to him, but it's a feeling that I'm slowly becoming familiar with. Hell, half the time it gives me a thrill while the other half is nothing but dread. It's always a mystery when it comes to Dante Carver.

"Because of you, I spent four days in a cell. My throat was bruised, and I was forced to sleep alone. You owe it to me."

Carver flies out of his seat, throwing himself to his feet and backing me into the wall. "I don't owe you shit. I gave up my fucking family to save your ass after you murdered my father. Consider the debt already paid, not that there was ever a debt to be paid."

Grayson rushes between us, pushing Carver away from me, but deep down, he and I both know that I like it when he's rough like this. This dominating, angry version of himself is scary as hell, but damn it, it speaks right to the devil that lives inside me. He's dangerous and I love it.

I push back against Grayson's hold and seeing that I can handle Carver, he falls back. "Then don't do it for me," I tell him, more than ready to call his ass out. "Do it for the girls who are getting raped day in and day out, do it for the parents whose children are getting taken off the street, but most of all, do it for yourself because fuck knows that if you don't, you're going to live with the regret of letting me down for the rest of your life, and it's going to eat at you every fucking day."

Carver scoffs as the boys watch us closely, desperate to hear what he has to say. "You really think you have so much hold over me?"

I laugh and while the sound might wrap right around a few of the guys in this room, all it does to Carver is grind on his nerves. I move into him, rolling my tongue over my bottom lip and watching how he instantly becomes captivated. "I don't think, Carver. *I know.* So, what's it going to be? Are you going to step up for all the girls that have been victim to Sam's horrors, or are you going to let them down too?"

His jaw clenches and he holds my stare for a moment too long before letting out a defeated sigh. He steps back from me before turning and walking away. Silence filters through the room as we all listen to Carver as he walks to the living room.

"Sam," he demands, his tone darker and harsher than anything I've ever heard. Fuck, it's a tone that not even I would fuck with. It sends chills sweeping through my body, and I realize that all this time, whenever Carver comes at me, whenever I think he's giving his all, he's been holding back, every fucking time. "You sold me a fucking brat. What kind of business are you running?"

There's a short pause and I find myself holding my breath. "I DON'T GIVE A FUCK," Carver roars down the line. "The bitch already has a bullet between her eyes, so you can either refund me my five mil, or you can get me a new girl."

Cruz's hands fall to my shoulders as I notice Grayson discreetly stepping into my side, but I'm far too caught up in Carver's conversation to work that mystery out. "Do you think I give a shit that you're at your brother's funeral? You have two fucking days to get me a new girl or I'm taking my business elsewhere."

And just like that, Carver ends the call and walks back out of the living room, knowing damn well that he has four sets of eyes tracking his every movement. His stare comes back to mine, and a furious scowl sits upon his delicious lips. "Two fucking days," he tells me. "You better have a solid plan put in place, otherwise, I'm out."

I nod, and before another word can come flying out of my mouth, Carver takes off toward the home gym. No doubt in a desperate bid to work me out of his system.

13

I toss and turn, throwing the blankets off before instantly scrambling for them and pulling them back up. I groan, grunt, and sigh. Tonight fucking sucks. I'd do anything to just fall into a peaceful sleep but all I can seem to think about is what's going to happen when I face Sam Delacourt again.

I'm not ready.

Fuck it, I *am* ready.

Shit.

I've been going back and forth for hours, trying to figure out how the fuck I'm going to pull this off. I don't even know where he's going to be or if I'll have the strength to go through with it. He's the man who was responsible for locking me in a dark, cold cell, and I won't stop until he's had what's coming to him, but when it actually comes to facing him, I'm terrified that I'm going to crumble. My only saving grace is that the boys are going to have my back.

What if Sam's men outnumber us? I know the guys have ridiculously impossible skills that are equally as deadly as they are impressively sexy, but at the end of the day, they're only human like me. They're not superheroes no matter how many times they defy the odds. They're just like me which means they can bleed, and when you can bleed, you can die, and if anything were to happen to them, I'd never forgive myself.

"You're thinking too hard," King murmurs, curling his arm around me and pulling me in tighter against his chest, making me feel like complete shit for disturbing his sleep, but on the other hand, watching the hard lines of his handsome face soften with sleep is one of the best things I will ever experience. "Just relax. It's going to be alright."

"Sorry," I grumble, snuggling my face into the pillow. "I didn't mean to wake you. It's just … I can't—"

"Sleep," he finishes for me, pulling his arm back and rolling us until he's hovering above me, his body weight braced against his elbow as he stares down at me. He dips his head, gently brushing his lips over mine in a rare show of emotion. "I hate that I can't help you. I'd do anything to be able to ease your mind."

"I know," I whisper, twining my arms up around his neck as my legs hook around his waist, holding him to me as close as possible. "I'd give anything for you to be able to do it too. I hate that Carver was the one who came fully equipped with the magical touch. Why'd it have to be him?"

"You're asking the wrong guy," he murmurs as I feel him hardening against my pussy.

I slip my hand down between us and curl my fingers around his large cock. He's already satisfied me more than enough tonight, but who am I to say no to a perfectly good opportunity like this? Our clothes are already long gone, my shirt dangling from the corner of the dresser as his pants lay strewn across the bedroom floor.

I start pumping my hand up and down his heavy cock, loving the feel of the thick veins beneath my fingers, and just as it always does whenever I touch him, my pussy floods with need. King adjusts himself above me and just how I like it, he pulls himself free from my hand and slides his thick cock deep inside my aching pussy.

He fills me, stretching my walls and making me groan as he pushes all the way in, hitting me right at my deepest point. King pauses there, allowing both of us a heated second to get used to the feel of him deep inside me. My arms tighten around his neck, drawing him down to me just as his lips press against mine, his cock flinches and I moan into his mouth.

He slowly draws out of me and I hold on tight, groaning with the need that pulses through me. I don't know how he does it. Every time with him is so good, so full of power and domination. He commands my body, his touch setting me on fire and demanding the same in return.

King pushes back in and I gasp against his mouth, my eyes rolling into the back of my head. He's so forceful, yet so slow. It's like having the best of both worlds. He's usually the one I can count on for a hard, quick fuck that makes me scream. When I need something a little more sensual, someone to slow it down and make my body burn, I'd crawl into Cruz's bed, but King is bringing out all the stops tonight and proving that he's so much more than the broody, demanding asshole who snuck through my bedroom window over a month ago.

I can't believe how far we've come since that night, but something tells me that we have so much further to go.

King continues moving, driving up inside me and hitting every fucking spot that sends me wild with pleasure. My eyes clench and his hand slides into mine, interlocking our fingers. It's so much more personal than what we've ever experienced before. The connection burns between us and I feel that for the first time since meeting Hunter King, I could never live without him.

As if reading my mind, his lips come down on mine and he kisses me deeply. Every thought, every worry, every fear fades away until all that exists is him. It's like a light between us, constantly growing, constantly burning brighter until it completely consumes us.

My body begs for a release, but he holds back, slowly building it until the intensity is nearly too much for me to bear. My pussy clenches around his thick cock, squeezing tight as my legs lock around him, forcing him deeper.

In. Out. In. Out.

It's the most delicious form of torture and I'll never get enough of him.

His cock scrapes along my walls, nearly too thick to fit inside of me. I squeeze my hand down between us, bypassing my aching clit and feeling where he thrusts into me. My fingers circle around him, squeezing tighter, my wetness instantly soaking my skin.

He draws back and forth as he swallows my loud moans, and only when my body is completely on edge does he push me harder. King picks up his pace and hits that magical little spot over and over again until I cry out, my orgasm exploding through me as my pussy convulses around him.

His hand tightens in mine, almost to the point of pain, and then finally, I feel as he comes hard, groaning my name as hot spurts of cum shoot deep inside me. I smile against his lips. There's nothing quite like knowing my body can make him feel so damn good.

King pants, his muscles bulging from holding himself above me, and just when I think he's about to pull out of me and collapse to the bed beside me, he grabs my waist and rolls us until I'm sitting over him, his cock still buried deep inside my pussy.

He gazes up at my naked body, his eyes roaming over my skin. "I could look at this all day," he tells me, bringing his hand up and gently brushing his knuckles over the curve of my breast and making my nipples harden and crave his touch.

"I could be *with you* all day," I murmur, letting my fingertip roam over the tight ridges of his abs and loving the way his eyes soften at my touch.

A smile pulls at his lips and he tugs on my waist, bringing me down to him. "What would help you sleep? A hot shower? Warm milk?" he questions, raising a brow. "I could fuck you into exhaustion if you think it would help."

"Wow, your selflessness just blows me away."

"What can I say?" he smirks before sending me a wink that has my heart racing. "I'm just an honest guy trying to make the world a happier place, one woman at a time."

"One at a time? Hey," I say, sucking in a sharp breath. "I have to admit, I'm disappointed. You need to step up your game. I've raised the bar to two at a time. Three if you count what nearly happened with Grayson."

His lips press into a tight line. "What exactly is going on with Grayson? Are you guys hooking up?"

I shake my head. "Not that I'm aware of. That four way in the living room would have been the first, and since then, I get the distinct feeling that he's trying to avoid me."

"Except when anything's going down," he comments. "He's certainly been taking over the role of your white knight."

"Ooooh," I tease. "Has Grayson touched a nerve? Would you prefer to be the hero?"

"Hardly," he scoffs. "If that idiot wants to be the guy who steps between Carver and his target, then he can be my fucking guest. Carver won't hold back with Gray. If he keeps getting in his way and telling him to back off, Carver will eventually snap, and when he does, you better run. Otherwise, you'll end up with an elbow to the eye."

I cringe. "Is it really that bad?"

"Yup. Gray and Carver have a history of butting heads. They're their own worst enemies, but it works out well for me and Cruz because we rarely have to step in. All I'm saying is that Cruz and I have noticed him paying a little more attention."

"I'm not going to lie," I murmur. "So have I." He gives me a blank stare and I narrow my eyes as I watch him a beat longer. "If Grayson and I … you know, would that be a problem?"

King shakes his head. "Nope, as long as he treats you like a fucking queen, then I'm down. But it's you I'm worried about."

"Me?"

"Mmhmm," he says, a grin cutting across his face. "That's a lot of dick for one chick to handle. I'm not sure that you're down for the challenge."

I can't help but laugh as I pull myself off him and scramble to the side of the bed, knowing damn well that I'm making a mess of his bedsheets. "Trust me," I tell him, grinning back at him lying gloriously naked in his bed. "I can more than handle it, but if you want to make it a challenge then you better be prepared to lose."

"Baby, I never lose."

"Uh-huh."

I prance across his bedroom and dive into the bathroom before quickly cleaning myself up and splashing water over my face. It's well into the middle of the night and after the disastrous few hours of trying to fall asleep, I know better than to try again.

I make my way out into King's bedroom to search for my clothes in the dark, and when I finally pull my pants on, King's face falls. "Where are you going?"

I let out a breath. "I think I'll go for a walk," I tell him, looking back and shrugging my shoulders. "I don't know, is that weird? It used to help when I was a kid and couldn't sleep so I figured that I'd give it a try."

"Okay," he says, pulling himself out of bed and grabbing his shirt. "Let's do this shit."

He starts dressing and I stop and stare at him. "What are you doing? Go back to bed."

"And have the boys tear me a new asshole when something happens to you out there? No thanks. You're surrounded by the homes of the men who have sent hitmen against you. I'm not about to risk your life. Besides, I have a challenge to win, and I'll be damned if you get taken out before I get to see you handle three dicks flying around your face."

I give King a beaming, innocent smile. "Have I ever told you that you have a way with words?"

He rolls his eyes and presses his hand to my lower back. "Come on," he says, grabbing one of his massive hoodies and shoving it into my hands. "Let's get this over and done with."

I smile to myself as I pull his hoodie over my head. He leads me out the door and we take three steps before he comes to a stop outside Carver's bedroom. "Are you sure?" he asks. "There's a simple solution here."

I shake my head. "No, I'm not going in there," I tell him. "He's just going to send me away. It's not worth the rejection."

He silently nods and continues down the hallway toward the stairs.

"Does it bother you that much?" he asks. "When he pushes you away like that?"

"Sometimes," I admit, hating the vulnerability. "Before everything happened, I thought something real was building between us and that all just seems to have vanished, but all the feelings are still there. It kinda hurts, which sucks because I didn't even realize that I was starting to feel something for him."

"He's a fucking idiot," he tells me. "Both Grayson and Carver are. They both want you. I see it all over them, but they're too fucking stubborn to admit it. Carver though, he's an extra special dose of fucked up. He's just sore about what happened and is pushing you away to punish himself. I've never seen him like this before, but he'll come around. He just needs a bit of time to act like a fucking bitch."

I laugh under my breath because thinking about it too seriously is bound to put me in a mood, and I don't want that for King. Our lives already revolve around Carver's bullshit, so when it's just us, I want it to be all about him.

He leads me down the stairs, and within a second, we break out into the cool night air. The breeze is chilly, and I snuggle deeper into King's hoodie. "So, what's the deal with your dad?" I ask him as we start making our way down the grand stairs. "You guys seem to have a really strained relationship. Don't take this in the wrong way, but it sounded like he kinda likes me more than you."

King scoffs, keeping his hand at my lower back as he leads me down the stairs. "That's the understatement of the year," he laughs. "I don't know how much he shared with you, but there were a few months when you were just a baby that you stayed with my family. Apparently, you and I even shared a bed."

"Ironic that eighteen years later, I still found my way between your sheets."

A cocky smile kicks up the side of his lips and I try to focus on what he's saying rather than just how fucking gorgeous he is. "Concentrate," he warns me with a devilish excitement lighting his eyes. "I don't give out bedtime stories often."

"Go ahead," I tell him as we hit the bottom of the stairs. "You have my undivided attention."

King rolls his eyes before hooking his arm over my shoulder and pulling me right into his side. "So, you were just a newborn and I think I was maybe one or something like that. I don't really know, but I was a shit of a baby, and you were the perfect little angel, and my parents fell in love with you. You were apparently a daughter to them, and they wanted to raise you as their own. So when you were sent away into the foster system, it was like losing the one child they actually wanted."

I shake my head. "No, it couldn't have been like that. You're being too hard on yourself."

"I wish," he tells me. "I was the firstborn son. I was the one who was put here to be a carbon copy of my father. My mother never wanted a son and was forced by Dynasty to abort three pregnancies before mine because they were all girls. My parents resent me, just as I do them, and as I grew and heard all the stories about the precious little heir that my parents got to love for those few short months, I guess I kinda resented you too."

I look up at him, meeting his dark stare. "Are you serious?"

"Unfortunately, and if I'm completely honest with you, I think I resented you right up until I threw you against the wall of that shitty foster house and fucked it out of my system."

"Well for what it's worth," I tell him, "I apologize for being such an awesome baby. Not all babies could have been as cool as me, and unfortunately, you were the prime example of that."

King knocks my hips as we're walking and I fumble over my next step, but he's right there to catch me. "Knock it off," he tells me. "The shitty babies are the ones who grow up to be fucking geniuses."

"Uh-huh," I laugh before glancing up at him again. "So, how are things with your father now? You don't seem like you want to kill each other, so I guess that's a bonus."

"You just caught us on a good day," he jokes. "But for the most part, it's fine. We butt heads a lot, but I'm his heir so it was always going to be strained. It's the same with all the guys and their fathers. I have a little brother and sister, Cody and Caitlin. They're fraternal twins and I guess were Mom's miracle babies. She didn't think she could have any more and then seven years ago, she found out she was pregnant. They've thawed out a lot since they were born."

"Really?" I ask, my eyes brimming with happiness. "I don't know why I always seem so shocked when I learn something about all of your siblings. I guess it's hard to picture such brute assholes like you with little kids running around."

King laughs as we reach the top of Carver's driveway, and just before something can come flying out of my mouth, his hand over my shoulder shoots up and presses down against my lips. He nearly picks me up and drags me toward the bushes by the front gate. "Shhhhh," he whispers, putting me right in front of him and staring down into my eyes, watching me closely to make sure I'm not about to give us away.

I search his eyes, desperately listening for whatever it is he hears, when I finally hear the faint, hushed voices on the other side of the gate. "Two o'clock," a woman murmurs, a strange familiarity to her tone but nothing that I can place in the dead of night.

"Consider it done," the person with her responds, this voice even softer, yet somehow has a chill sweeping through my body. "When do I get paid?"

"When you come through with the goods," she says. "Now get out of here. It's too risky."

My brows furrow as King stands impossibly still, and then all too soon, the voices fade away, leaving us with questions that we didn't know we wanted to ask. I capture his gaze, and after a beat, he deems it safe to step out of the bushes, but he leads me straight back to Carver's front door, deciding that our midnight stroll has already been exciting enough.

14

The sun burns against my skin and I let out a deep sigh. It's been far too long since I've been able to relax by the pool with a friend by myself. It's early April, and while the weather is usually a cold and unpredictable pain in the ass this time of year, today the sun decided to shine. There's still a chill in the air, but when the breeze slows, the glorious warmth of the sun gets to do its thing.

Ember moans beside me, soaking it up just as much as I am. "So, this is really your parents' place?" she asks me, glancing across at me as she lays on the sunbed in her tiny black bikini with her head tilted up toward the sky.

"Apparently," I say with an awkward shrug of my shoulders. When the sun decided to come out and play, I couldn't resist inviting her over, but when the questions came about why I was still hanging out at this place and not at Carver's, a few minor truths had to come out. I figured telling her that this was my parents' home was the easiest one to go with.

"You're telling me that Ravenwood Manor, the house that the whole town was named after, was your parents' place?"

"Yep," I say, refusing to look her way in fear that she'll be able to tell that I'm only just touching the surface. "At least, that's the story the boys told me."

"The boys?" she scoffs. "And how the hell would they know?"

"Beats me," I say, my shoulders bouncing with a quick shrug. "It's probably all bullshit, but I haven't seen anyone else coming to claim the place, so why not reap all the rewards while I wait for the truth to come out?"

Ember laughs and slides down further on the sunbed. "Damn girl, I like the way you think, but seriously, what if they're not lying? Don't get me wrong, I don't know these guys as well as you do, but they don't strike me as the kind to keep a pet if she didn't belong."

"I've never heard truer words," I tell her. "They're really not. They're super intense, and while they can be complete assholes, they're not liars and … I don't know. Maybe I need to take their word for it. Maybe this place really did belong to my parents."

"But they're dead?"

"Yup."

"Sooooo," she says, her brows raising as she draws out her

conclusion. "Technically this place is yours?"

I shrug my shoulders, hating how blasé I have to be with her. "I mean, I haven't exactly read a copy of the will, but that's generally how this shit works, right?"

"Fuck," Ember laughs, sitting up on the sunbed and letting her feet fall to either side as she gapes at me. "Then you're fucking rich. Why the hell aren't we partying yet? Hold up. Rewind. Why the hell am I only hearing about this now? When did you first find out?"

Ahh, crap.

My face twists into a cringe. "The weekend."

Ember's face drops and she gapes at me as though she can hardly believe what she's hearing. "You've known about this for like … a week and you're only just telling me now? Holy shit, Winter. We could have been partying it up all week. Just imagine the awesome movie nights and keggers we could have here. Oh, OH," her eyes bug out of her head. "Can we do something like that party you had at King's cabin in the woods? That would be fucking awesome."

"Hell to the freakin' no," I say. I don't think I've ever heard such an awful idea. "This is the only home I've got, the only thing that's ever truly been mine, and I'm not about to let a whole bunch of drunk high school bitches come in and destroy it. Besides, this is the only thing I have of my parents. I need to take care of it. I can't imagine what they'd think of me if I destroyed the home they built."

"Weeeeeeeak," she groans, falling back to her sunbed with a loud huff.

I laugh to myself. She can hate on my plan all she wants because she'll never truly understand. Ember grew up in a fancy neighborhood with the biggest house on her street. She's never wanted for anything, so things like furniture and sentimental crap are all replaceable, but not to me. It all means something so much more to me.

I bring my frozen daiquiri to my lips and take a long sip. This is the fucking life. While finding the answers I needed about my parents was a long and painful journey, it's also opened me up to this amazing life. Though I have to admit, finding things like a machine that mixes daiquiris are the real hidden treasures, and it makes me wish that I could have met my mother. From her closet, her jewelry, her taste in art, and the surprising little knick-knacks I come across every day, she seems like the kind of woman I would have loved to live my life beside.

I have it all here, you know, considering I pretend that Dynasty doesn't exist. How lucky does one kid have to be to not only discover that she has a home left to her, but one as incredible as this? I just hate that all of this is clouded by the reality of murder, sex trafficking, and corruption.

I'm not going to lie; I have four boys keeping me distracted from that reality. Some in a good way, and some in an infuriatingly disastrous way that makes me want to gouge out their eyeballs with plastic spoons and then feed it to them, but then not seeing those eyes everyday would be devastating.

Ember finishes her daiquiri and sits up with a pout, holding up her glass. "I'm out. Do you want a refill?" she asks, getting to her feet and scooping my glass right out of my hand, not bothering to wait for my response.

"Hey," I argue. "I wasn't finished with that."

"Tough shit."

She goes to walk away when a high-pitched squeal is torn out of her. My head whips around just in time to see a strange man barreling toward her at the speed of light. My eyes bug out of my head and before I even get to my feet, the man is on Ember, his fist flying toward her temple.

"EMBER!" I scream her name, my eyes wide with fear as I watch his big fist slam straight into the side of her head. The force spins her, and I watch in horror as she crumbles to the ground with a hard thud. But it's not even close to being over.

The man runs at me and I bolt from the sunbed, sheer terror pulsing through my veins. He's fast and his muscles bulge from his arms. This guy means fucking business. This isn't just fending off some dipshit pervert outside of a whorehouse. This is a fucking hitman and he's coming right for me.

Not today, motherfucker.

I dart around the pool, feeling more alone than ever. I know my fucking place, and I know my odds of getting out of this alive. They fucking suck.

I wasn't prepared for this. My home was supposed to be safe. I foolishly thought that if I remained within the boundary of my parents' home, that I was free from the hitmen and death threats. How fucking naive was that? I should have been better prepared, and now my best friend is lying on the ground beside my pool, and I have no idea if she's alive or dead.

What was I thinking sitting out by the pool? I was a sitting duck, just asking for the big bad wolf to come and end me.

Fucking stupid. Stupid, stupid, stupid.

I'm not even going to get a chance to say goodbye to the boys. They're going to come racing in here to find my dead body and be heartbroken. Poor Cruz. The other three will hide their emotions, but Cruz … he'll be a fucking mess.

I didn't even get a chance to make it right with Carver, or to feel Grayson's lips pressing against mine. I'm only eighteen; I haven't even had a chance to live yet.

My panic races through my veins, pushing me faster, but he's quickly gaining on me, making it clear that this guy isn't just some bullshit guy with a gun hiding in the woods. This is the kind of man that comes fully equipped with years of training.

I push my legs to the point of pain, stretching my strides and desperately wishing that I had something more than just a red bikini to defend myself with, but what's the point of fighting back? All I'll be doing is delaying the inevitable.

I'm a dead woman.

My feet thunder against the pavement and I get halfway around the pool before his thick arm curls around my waist and I'm hauled back. A loud, high-pitched squeal tears from my throat as I'm dragged back toward the edge of the pool.

I dig my nails into his arm, drawing blood as I fight to get out of his hold. "LET ME GO," I yell, hot tears springing to my eyes as I kick my legs out, desperately trying to find purchase and get myself free.

I'm too young; I have so much left to do in life. I'm not ready to die. I don't want to go yet.

Blood stains my fingers but I keep digging my nails in, fighting, and screaming for freedom.

The guy grunts as he desperately tries to maintain his hold on me, tightening his arm around my waist until it's nearly impossible to breathe.

The edge of the pool comes closer and closer and my heart races faster than it's ever raced before. He leans back and my feet are instantly pulled off the ground.

I try to reach for something, anything to hold onto that could save me from going in that pool. I'm not a strong swimmer, never have been, and against an asshole like this, I haven't got a snowball's chance in hell.

I reach around me, and just like I wanted to do to Carver, I shove my thumb straight into his eye, pressing hard and hoping to whoever exists above that it's enough to at least loosen his hold on me.

I'm at a fucking loss. I've been in all sorts of shitty positions, but never has it been this bad.

The guy roars in pain and instead of throwing me down to put an end to his agony, my body is launched toward the pool.

I crash down into the water, my shoulder slamming against the edge and sending pain shooting through my arm. The force of his throw has me quickly falling deeper into the water and within seconds, my head slams against the bottom of the pool, hard enough for me to see stars.

I push off the ground, desperate to get to the surface and suck in a breath of air yet he comes down on top of me, the blood on his arms clouding the water. The guy grabs my elbow and pulls me in closer before curling his hand around my throat and forcing me under.

I flail about, my arms and legs kicking out as I stare up through the water and he looks down at me, blood dripping down the side of his face. My lungs instantly begin to scream, and I fight harder despite knowing that the more I fight, the more energy I'm using to actually survive this.

But no one is coming for me. No one even knows. My only hope is Ember regaining consciousness and putting a bullet through his head in the next two seconds. That's assuming she isn't already dead.

As the seconds tick by, my lungs begin to give out and my rapid kicking starts to ease. The water becomes calmer and it sparkles against the afternoon sunlight. If it wasn't the last thing I was going to see before death, I would say that it's almost beautiful.

I keep my stare on my attacker as I claw at his hand, and with the calming waters, I'm able to make out the finer features of his face. I don't know him, but why would I? The last time I was attacked, it was a bunch of hitmen, so why would this be any different?

He's by no means a pretty guy, especially with the way I destroyed his right eye. At least I'll get to die peacefully knowing I fucked it up. Call me a petty bitch, but I hope he has to wear an eye patch and his bullshit, douchey friends make him feel like shit about it for the rest of his pathetic life. Then he'll always be reminded about how just for a moment, this bitch got the best of him.

My lungs start to ache as my body screams for oxygen.

It's only going to be a few more seconds.

My energy falters and my hands fall away from his fingers on my throat as four beyond handsome faces filter through my mind. I didn't get enough time with them.

Cruz. King. Grayson. Carver.

I hope they can forgive me. I wasn't strong enough to survive, but they'll move on. King and Cruz will find someone else and Grayson will eventually deliver that first kiss to another's lips. Never mine.

The images quickly morph into the photograph I'd seen of my parents and as I picture the soft lines of my mother's face and the sparkle that was captured in my father's eyes, peace settles through me.

I'm finally going to meet my parents.

My eyes close and then finally, the darkness claims me.

15

Water is forced out of my lungs as a heavy weight presses down over me, crushing my chest and sending pain soaring through me.

"Come on," I hear Grayson's deep, demanding growl as he hovers over me. "You're not fucking dying on me yet."

I hear curses and scuffles in the background, and he presses against my chest again. My eyes spring open and more water comes rapidly soaring up my throat.

"Fuck," Grayson sighs, grabbing me and rolling me onto my side as more water pours from my lungs while I fight to suck in a deep breath of welcomed oxygen.

He slams his hand against my back, getting all the water out, and as he does, I look across my backyard to where Cruz sits on the top step of the pool, completely drenched, watching me with fear in his eyes. Seeing the water come up and the life in my eyes, his head drops into his hands and I watch as he takes slow, calming breaths.

King and Carver are on the opposite side of the pool. Carver straddled over my attacker, beating the ever-loving shit out of him while King grabs his head and slams it down over the concrete. The sound is like music to my ears, and I watch intently as he does it again.

I take a deep breath with Grayson hovering over me, and as my hand finds his on my hip, I silently let him know that I'm okay. His body sags as he finally begins to relax. "Fuck, babe," he sighs, falling back onto his ass and closing his eyes, but keeping his hand tightly in mine. "I thought we lost you."

My head lolls against the wet ground and I focus on the air traveling in and out of my burning lungs. Being drowned wasn't exactly my favorite experience to date, and if I had to give it a star rating, it would definitely receive one star. I do not recommend.

No one tells you how bad it burns, but then no one tells you about the peace right at the end. But I guess, who would be around to warn me? The people who have drowned before me are probably all dead, not lucky enough to have four overprotective asshats coming just in time to save the day.

I guess I can add thorough ass kickers and life savers to their resumes now. Is there anything these guys can't do?

Grayson's thumb moves back and forth across the top of my

hand as I let the familiar sounds of Carver's punches soothe and relax me. Cruz stands and climbs the final step of the pool before striding toward me and dropping down by my head.

He grabs me and pulls me into the space between his legs while Grayson still refuses to release my hand, even though he has to stretch to reach it now. I'm not complaining though. After he saved my life, he could be holding my fucking pussy hostage and I wouldn't give a shit.

Cruz's arms curl around me as he leans me back, letting me rest. "How are you feeling?" he murmurs, pushing the wet hair off my face and meeting my eyes with his blazing green ones.

I shrug my shoulders and press my lips into a tight line. "I feel like I just died," I tell him, feeling both Grayson and Cruz flinch at my words.

"I hope you're not fond of swimming," Cruz tells me. "Because I'll be damned if I ever let you near a pool again. Do you have any idea what it's like to run back here to find you lifeless under the fucking water?"

My heart aches for him, hating that he had to see that. It's probably one of those things that will always stay with him, but at least this time there was a happy ending. Today could have easily ended a different way. "It's not like I fell in there on purpose," I tell him, each word burning my throat, but I put my pain aside, desperate to ease his.

"I know," he tells me with a broken sigh. "I promise, you'll never have to worry about that fucking bastard ever again."

I raise my head, watching as Carver and King continue to let loose on him, using his body to release every single one of their frustrations.

Though if I were to walk across there and search for a pulse, I'd bet that he was already rotting in hell, making friends with Kurt and Royston.

They both step back from him and stare down at their handiwork. Carver's knuckles are stained with blood and the same goes for his clothes. He looks back over his shoulder and our eyes meet for an intense moment. His face is a hard mask, and I can't get a read on him, but my gut is screaming that maybe I don't want to hear what he has to say.

Carver turns and starts walking back toward us, leaving my attacker lying helpless on the ground as King walks the other way around the pool. He bypasses Ember lying sprawled on the ground with the remains of my daiquiri spilled across her face and chest.

I sit up straighter as King stops to check on her. "It's okay," Cruz murmurs as I watch King pick her up and lay her down on one of the shaded sunbeds. "She's fine, just knocked out. She'll have a killer headache when she wakes and a shitload of questions."

I nod, the relief pouring through me as Carver detours by the outdoor kitchen and grabs a bottle of water out of the fridge. He makes his way back to me and hands me the cold water. "Drink this," he murmurs, avoiding my eyes. "It'll help your throat."

"Small sips," Cruz adds.

I take the bottle from Carver and nod, a silent thanks sitting between us as he takes a step behind Cruz and sits on the edge of the sunbed that I'd only been lying in less than five minutes ago. He's close enough that I could reach out and touch, but I wouldn't dare because doing that means pulling away from Grayson.

King makes his way over as Cruz opens the bottle of water for me and presses it to my lips, forcing me to collect it and get on with taking a sip. Knowing that he won't back off until I've at least tried, I take hold of the bottle, hating that I have to release Grayson's hand. I tip the bottle up and just as I knew it would, the cold water burns down my throat, but I can't deny that it makes it feel a million times better.

I take a few more sips, and despite not being able to see him behind me, I can sense the cocky pride rolling off Carver in waves.

King sits on the end of the other sunbed behind Grayson and Cruz slowly spins us around so that we face the guys, being careful not to jostle me too much. My new position puts me right in front of Carver, my head level with his knee, and the way he sits forward with his elbows on his knees, puts his bloodied knuckles right in front of my face.

I suck in a gasp and instantly regret it. My gaze sweeps up to Carver's to find him looking down at me, and without thinking, I reach up and take his hand in mine before slowly tipping the cold water over his bloodied knuckles and cleaning them the best I can.

I feel his stare on me, but I refuse to look up, knowing that what I might see in his eyes is bound to hurt or confuse me, but he doesn't pull his hand away and that speaks volumes.

Once the blood is gone, I lift his hand to my lips and gently place a kiss over his broken knuckles while feeling the stares of all four of the guys on me. Three of them in understanding, one with an intense confusion and desire that tears at my chest.

I hold onto his hand a second longer than necessary before finally releasing it and glancing up at the boys. "I thought I was safe here."

Grayson shakes his head. "You're not safe anywhere," he murmurs. "We shouldn't have left you here alone. Your life is in our hands and we let you down."

"I fucking let her down," King says, his tone completely broken as he hangs his head, his devastation speaking loud and clear.

My brows furrow as I watch him, but his despair has me crawling through the guys until I'm seated right in front of him, looking up as he sits on the sunbed before me. "What are you talking about?" I whisper, taking his hands in mine and squeezing tight. "The four of you just saved my ass. Literally saved it. No one here has let me down, especially not you."

"Don't you get it?" he questions, raising his gaze to meet mine. "It's exactly two in the afternoon. The conversation we overheard last night was that fucking bitch arranging this, and instead of beating his ass then and finding out who's behind this shit I hid you in the fucking bushes."

"I … no. Are you sure it's the same thing? They could have been discussing anything."

"Babe, come on. The only reason two people would meet in the middle of the night would be if they were fucking, or about to fuck someone over," he spits, shaking his head. "I knew it the second that asshole tripped the silent alarm. I could have put a fucking stop to this last night. You nearly fucking died today. Fuck, you *did* die."

Desperation pours through me as I look at the guys for help, but they're all just as perplexed as I am. I climb up off the ground and straddle his lap, curling both my legs and arms around him. "Don't do that," I warn him. "You couldn't have known, just as I didn't know. You're not a mind reader. They said absolutely nothing to have made either of us suspicious of an attack against me. I actually thought that it might have been a drug deal."

He rests the top of his head into the curve of my neck, his arms circling me as the guys remain quiet behind us. "If I'd have lost you today …"

"Don't think like that," I whisper. "I'm still here to bust your balls, and now all that's left for us to do is settle the score."

"This bastard was here all fucking night," King grumbles, glancing up at the motionless body across the pool. "He would have been hiding out, just waiting for the right time to strike and I missed it. He would have had access to all of our homes, our families, our little fucking brothers and sisters."

Cruz grumbles behind me. "Did you recognize their voices?"

King shakes his head, looking up over my shoulder at his friends. "Nah, it was a chick, but it's not a voice I've heard before."

"I have," I say, swiveling on King's lap to see them all. "At least, I think I have, I just don't know where. When I heard it, it was like something was pulling at an old memory, but I couldn't figure out where or when I'd heard it."

"Why didn't you say something?" King asks, bringing his hand up and running his knuckles over my cheek, almost as though he's double checking that I'm actually alive and sitting here on his lap.

I shrug my shoulders. "I don't know," I murmured. "I wasn't really sure, and I didn't think it was important."

"It is," Carver grumbles, forcing my gaze to slice across to meet his. "Anyone from your past that has access to our street means trouble, but the bigger question is, how did she get in?"

Grayson scoffs. "More like who the fuck let her in," he spits. "The gate codes aren't available to anyone. Someone let her through that fucking gate, and I'd bet that person had something to do with the attack in the woods and helping Royston cover up your parents' murders."

Chills shoot down my spine as the heaviness sits between us. He has a good fucking point and I don't like it one bit. There are seventeen houses on his street, and in one of them lies the culprit, anxiously waiting for the hitman to return and confirm that I'm dead.

I should raid every one of these houses and interrogate every last asshole I come across. "So, what do we do?" I ask. "Because I have a feeling that the ideas going through my head right now are going to be a little … frowned upon."

Cruz shakes his head, deep in thought. "There's really not a lot we can do," he says. "At least, nothing that's not going to cross the line with the heads of Dynasty. Apart from checking over the surveillance footage and getting the codes that were used on the main gate, we've got nothing."

"But it was a deliberate attack on me," I argue, my voice getting louder and my throat burning in agony. "Those old assholes can kiss my ass. They already said that they'd support me in trying to find the other person responsible for the attack in the woods. How would this be any different? They can't argue that Royston was responsible for this too. They'll have no choice."

Carver raises his chin. "You're forgetting that it's a vote," he reminds me. "They have every right to voice their opinion and say no."

I narrow my eyes at him. "But I shouldn't have an issue with that either, should I?" I ask. "I mean, you're on my side, right?"

He clenches his jaw as his eyes harden, but without his family to force his hand, there shouldn't be anything stopping him from supporting me on this, or anything really.

Carver leans back, his hands bracing him against the sunbed as his eyes bore into mine. "If I openly support you, and it tips the scales your way, you need to be prepared, because the people who are coming after you now are only going to get more desperate. The attacks will come harder and faster, and you'll never be safe. Are you ready for that?"

I glance at the guys, all of them watching me closely, but after only just surviving an attack, I don't know how ready I am to have more coming my way. "I …"

I let my words fall away as I peer back to Carver, needing to know what's going through his mind. His eyes bore into mine for a second before he finally takes pity on me. "Despite our differences," he starts, "you know I have your back. Every fucking time I've been there to make sure you live to see another day and I'm not about to change that. For some fucked up reason that I can't begin to explain, you're important to all of us, but in that council chamber, I can't be who you need me to be. There's no reason why I should openly show my support yet, and if anything, I'll be able to gain the trust of those who don't."

"Speaking of those who don't," I mutter under my breath, turning my attention on Grayson. "What's going on with your family? Do you think there's a chance your dad might jump ship?"

He presses his lips into a hard line. "I'm sorry, babe, but there's no fucking chance in hell. My father is a fucking bastard. The only thing I have in common with him is my name. I've been trying to get in his head, but he's a stubborn fuck, and my mom is just as bad. Fuck, I wouldn't be surprised if after hearing Royston's plan to take over, that she'd pressure my dad to do the same."

My eyes bug out of my head. "Shit, really?"

"Yeah, but you don't need to worry about them just yet. They don't strike while the iron is hot. They're the type to wait out all the bullshit and just when you think you've won, when all the other fuckers have been knocked out of the game, they'll come and fuck shit up and claim all the credit. They'll want everyone to see them as the heroes who could do what they couldn't."

I gape at him, feeling as though I understand him just a little bit better. At least, the chip on his shoulder and the frustrated, conflicted attitude make sense. "You don't think they have anything to do with this?" I question, glancing at the guy across the pool.

"Nah, they don't play well with others. This is someone who wouldn't have the balls to step out on his own."

I let out a sigh. At least he was able to narrow down the list of suspects, but now I have to watch my back. Just fucking perfect.

I turn back to Carver. "So, you want to play double agent?" I ask, eyeing him carefully, and knowing that despite how desperately I want to give him hell, I will always trust him. He's proven himself time and time again, and one of these days, I'm going to have to stop questioning that.

"I think it's the easiest way and our best option," he tells me. "The only way for us to win this is to get ahead of the game."

Cruz's sharp glare snaps to Carver's. "Winter's life isn't a fucking game."

"I fucking know that," Carver fires back at him. "But that's not how they think. She's just a chess piece they want to play, but we need to make sure that when they do, we're already in front. There's no prize for second place. You either win or you lose."

I nod. "So, what now?"

"Now," he says, a grin kicking up the side of his lips as he glances across at the hitman who is more than likely dead, "we take out the trash."

"Are you sure this is really a good idea?" I ask, studying the grins that stretch wide over all four of the boys' faces.

"How are you possibly questioning this?" King laughs, kicking his foot out and connecting with the dead guy's hip. "This is the best idea Carver's ever had."

"I hate to say it," Cruz says, flashing me that perfect grin and smoldering green eyes, making me forget why I was even questioning this bullshit in the first place. "But you need to make a stand. What better way to show these dickheads that you're untouchable? Besides, why not let your crazy run free every now and then? Nobody wants to fuck with a crazy chick."

My face twists into an unsure cringe as I glance down at the body chained to the back of my Ducati. "You sure?"

Grayson nods, a wicked, sinister smirk on his lips. "Three laps should do it."

Carver scoffs. "Four. Three to prove your point, one for good luck."

I roll my eyes and go to grab my helmet but Cruz steps into me and takes it out of my hands. "Sorry, not today," he says, propping my helmet against his hip. "You know I'd usually never tell you to ride without it, but I want them to see your face, see that they couldn't touch you."

"But they did touch me. I *died* in that pool."

"I know you did, and so do the fucking boys, but they don't need to know that. Just race down the fucking street with your head held high and give them that same hard stare that you usually give Carver when you think that he's fucked you over."

At the mention of his name, I can't help but slice that same hard stare back to him only to find a smug grin playing on his lips. That fucking asshole. He's such a cocky fuck. Not wanting to linger on Carver, I turn to King. "Ember?"

"Out like a fucking light," he tells me. "I put her in the bedroom beside yours at the back of the house so even if she does wake up, she won't hear shit, and I doubt she's going to come all the way out here to find you. She won't feel like walking around for a day or two. He got her pretty hard."

"Shit, the poor thing. I hate that she got dragged into this. I've been going out of my way to keep her away from Dynasty for this very reason. But do you know how freaking hard it is? She's heard the rumors about it just like everyone else has and she's more curious about you four than ever before."

"Babe," Cruz says with that signature cocky grin. "She's not curious about Dynasty, she's curious about how we fuck." I roll my eyes, but I can't help the way my cheeks flame the brightest shade of red at the casual, blunt way he talks about it. He laughs before continuing. "Come on. Get on with it. I want to see this motherfucker smeared all over the road."

Wanting to get it over and done with, I straddle my bike and let the engine roar. The sound instantly reminds me that Carver actually owns it, and the fury at the boys' deceit makes me rev it louder.

King steps around my bike as we stand at the top of my long driveway. He walks over to the keypad and starts entering the code and as it slowly peels open, I look back at the guys behind me, each of them wearing a hungry expression as they gawk at my ass in my leather pants, straddling the bike.

The gate slides open and just to be an asshole to the neighbors, I hit the throttle and take off, leaving a thick black line across the road as the dead man's body drags after me. I shoot down the center of the road, being as obnoxious as possible as I drag my trophy around the street. I fly all the way down to the main gate and then turn, but on the way back up, I ride straight over the sidewalk and start making my way back to the end of the road.

By the time I hit my gate again and circle back around with the guys watching closely, people are starting to come out of their homes, wondering what all the noise is about. I quickly glance back to notice my attacker's clothes are tearing to shreds but I really couldn't care less.

Cruz cheers for me as I pass, and Carver puts on a show of disapproval for the people in the houses nearby.

I bet this isn't a sight they get to witness every day, and as I notice that it's not only Dynasty heads walking out to see, but their families, guilt tears through me. I'm sure even the children have seen their fair share of dead bodies. Hell, most of them saw me kill Royston Carver right in the middle of their precious ballroom, but this isn't exactly my finest hour.

I keep on the throttle and stand as I ride, my hair whipping out behind me as I fly back down toward the main gate, keeping on the sidewalk. My bike howls, the sound echoing down the road and getting the attention of every last fucker here.

I see people standing out on their top balconies watching the show with their mouths hanging open, some people seem pissed, while others put the puzzle pieces together and cheer right alongside Cruz.

By the time I get to my third lap, there's more than just black tire marks staining the sidewalk, but I keep going, a little blood and guts never slowed me down.

As I ride, I try to pinpoint all the homes of the assholes I need to be watching for. I really should have asked the boys who lives where, but I figured that it really didn't matter. I was so fucking wrong. From now on, I'm going to make it my business to get to know my enemies.

I'm going to know their names, their wives' names, where their children go to school. I'm going to know who their pool man is by the time I'm done. But most of all, I'm going to get inside their heads and find out exactly what makes them tick.

As I approach Matthew Montgomery's house, the third on the left, I can't help but notice the pissed off scowl stretched across his face. He's such a little bitch. I wouldn't be surprised if he had something to do with this, but he's definitely not the ringleader. He's the kind of man to follow someone's lead and fall in line. When they say jump, he says 'yes master, can I also offer you some round-the-clock ass-wiping services too?' He's a sheep, and because of that, I find myself bringing my bike to a stop right in the center of his driveway outside of his gate.

I grin up at the dickhead watching me from his front steps. "I think this might belong to you," I call, my throat instantly hating me as I step off my bike and pull out the keys. Matthew just gapes at me, too shocked with what I've done to even argue. So, without another word, I walk away, leaving the gory, messed up body behind and laughing as the blood slowly seeps out, staining his polished concrete drive.

I start walking back down the street with a skip in my step. I've never been so proud of myself. Sure, it was probably the most messed up thing I've ever done, and that point is proven as I have to step over the bloodstains left on the sidewalk. I hate that children bore witness to my antics, but I can't find it in myself to regret it.

I stuck it to the assholes who did this to me and because of that, I feel more alive than ever before.

Up ahead of me, I see Cruz coming down the sidewalk and I

pick up my pace, not going too fast as I can't risk exerting myself and breathing too deeply, otherwise my lungs are going to curse me out for the rest of the day.

Cruz meets me in the middle, and before I can say a damn word, he grabs my hand and pulls me toward the massive gates of the house right beside us. He quickly hashes in a code and before the gate has even fully opened, he's pulling me through.

"What are you doing?" I laugh as he drags me right around the corner of the gate and all but throws me into the bushes beside it, keeping me hidden. I realize that this is the second time in as many days that I've been in the bushes with one of the guys, hiding just inside the gates.

"I've got to have you," he rumbles, his voice thick with desire as his eyes roam over my face. "Do you have any fucking idea how hot it was watching you riding up and down the road in these tight as fuck leather pants, owning those motherfuckers? I have to fuck, and this time, I'm not sharing."

A grin pulls across my face as I grab hold of him and pull him even closer, slamming my back up against the inside pillar of the gate, making sure that the bushes keep us hidden from the rest of the world. "You, Cruz Danforth, can have me anyway you want me."

Cruz groans low with need as his hands find the front of my pants and begin undoing the fly. As my pants make their way down my legs, I can't help but peer around to figure out whose gate we're about to fuck against.

I suck in a breath. "This is your place."

"Mmhmm," he rumbles, pressing his body hard against mine and letting me feel just how desperate he is for my body. "I'll take you for a tour later if you'd like, but for now, I need to worship your body."

A soft groan purrs from within my chest and Cruz instantly raises his head to meet my heated gaze. "Don't worry, I'll be careful with you. I know you're hurting."

I shake my head. "You be as fucking rough as you need to. I'll deal with the fall out after, you hear me?" I demand. "Give me what I need."

He winks. "You got it, babe. Right after I spread those pretty thighs and taste your sweet cunt on my tongue."

A thrill shoots through me and just like that, my pants disappear from my legs and Cruz's hands find my waist. He lifts me up onto a ledge beside the pillar, and it puts my pussy directly in line with his face. His eyes flame with desire and I hold onto the ledge with both hands, watching intently as he slowly spreads my legs, putting me on display.

My tongue rolls along my lips and I run my fingers around the back of his head, more than ready to pull him in if he doesn't get on with it and do it himself. But I can always count on Cruz to give me exactly what I need, right when I need it.

He licks his lips as excitement bubbles in his eyes, and not a second later, his tongue rolls over my clit and I suck in a breath, my eyes glued to the scene below. What is it about watching a man's tongue teasing my clit that gets me so hot?

He slips his fingers in and my legs instantly wrap around his head, squeezing him in and holding him close. I feel his smile against my pussy, and it spurs me on. "Fuck, Cruz. Yes," I pant, desperately wishing that I could scream his name.

His tongue works like he'll never get to taste my pussy again, bringing me to the edge and then pushing me further. His fingers massage deep inside me and I have no choice but to clench my eyes and groan as my fingers knot into his hair.

God, I'd give anything to drop to my knees before him and curl my lips around his hard, thick cock and be his little whore.

Cruz pushes me further until I feel that familiar pull building deep inside me. My pussy clenches in anticipation and he picks up his pace, reading my body like a fucking book. His tongue is like magic, giving me exactly what I didn't know I needed, working me as I pull tighter on his hair, holding him closer to my aching cunt. "Ooooh, God," I groan, feeling it building tighter and tighter, my pants coming in short, sharp breaths. "Yes, Cruz. FUCK, YES!"

He presses harder against my clit and then finally, my orgasm tears through me and my pussy instantly starts convulsing, squeezing tight, and spasming around his thick, skilled fingers.

I feel his cocky grin against my pussy, but he doesn't let up. He keeps working me as I ride out my orgasm, only making me sensitive to his intense touch, but fuck it, it's so damn good.

My body finally calms down from its high and I look down to see Cruz's hungry stare and his lips glistening with my excitement. He slowly makes a show of licking them clean and only then does he take my waist and help me down off the ledge.

My hand instantly dips into the front of his jeans that are still damp from fishing me out of the water. I curl my fingers around his hard cock, and he buries his face into my neck, his lips running along my sensitive skin as I work my hand up and down.

Using my other, I push his jeans down over his narrow hips and put that beautiful cock on display, just as it should be. I tilt my head, forcing his back up and meeting his hungry stare. "What do you want?" I murmur, just about ready to give him anything he could ever ask for.

His arm slips around my waist and he lifts me up, pressing me back against the pillar and keeping me pinned and with one, hard thrust, he buries his cock deep inside of me.

The rumble in his throat sets my body on fire and he fucks me hard and fast, his deep thrusts hitting me with a desperate need as his lips come down on mine. My hands curl around his neck and I hold on for dear life as he stretches me wide, filling me nearly to the point of pain.

Not wanting to draw it out, he makes it quick, working my body up, and as I come on his dick, tightening around him and digging my nails into his strong back, he comes hard, sending hot spurts shooting up into me.

We pause, his cock still seated deep within me, both of us breathing hard. "I shouldn't have done that," he admits in a whisper, his lips gently brushing over my lips again, a stark contrast to the bruising, forceful kisses he was just giving me. "I should have taken you home and let you sleep it off."

I laugh and try to shrug off the pain, not wanting him to see just how much our quick fuck has my lungs and throat aching for relief. "Whether you took me home to my bed or kept me hidden in these bushes, I still would have ended up riding your cock until I screamed."

Cruz laughs. "Yeah, you're probably right," he says, leaning down and scooping up my pants. He hands them to me and I groan, finding them completely inside out. There's nothing worse than getting a slim pair of leather pants back in the right way. Pulling them up sweaty legs though is a whole other issue, one that has me thinking back to one of my favorite episodes of *'Friends.'*

Shit. Maybe I watch too much TV, but in the foster system, apart from sneaking out and getting up to no good, there's really not a lot to do.

After way too long, I get myself redressed and cringe as I feel Cruz dripping into my underwear. If I were still naked, it would make me feel like a sexy as fuck queen, but when I'm wearing clothes, I just feel gross.

Cruz takes my hand and leads me back out onto the driveway, leading me toward his home, and with each step I take, I cringe just a little bit more.

Cruz glances my way with a knowing smirk playing on his lips. "What's the matter, babe? Feeling a little … slimy?"

"Ughhhh," I groan, shoving his shoulder and cheering when I manage to get him a whole two feet away. "Don't be gross. Just get me to a bathroom where I can clean up and ditch these panties."

Cruz laughs the whole way to his house and as we walk up the stairs, nerves begin creeping into my stomach. I've already met his father, but haven't officially met his mom or siblings, and fuck, that really shouldn't faze me, yet here I am.

He pushes straight through the door and I go to release his hand, but he refuses to let me go, despite knowing what his father thinks of our relationship.

We walk through the massive house and I look around in awe. I've been around places like this for a while now, but every new one I walk through always manages to catch me off guard.

It's just as big as Carver's place but this one seems a little less homey. It's almost as though his parents were going for a minimalist style, or maybe they just didn't bother to finish furnishing it because they're rarely here.

We walk through to the kitchen and we find Cruz's mom sitting up at the counter going over some paperwork. She doesn't see us, and Cruz can't resist sneaking up behind her and scaring the absolute shit out of her with a loud, roaring "RAAHHHHH."

She shrieks and spins around, only to playfully swipe at her son, her hand against her chest as she desperately tries to calm her racing heart. "I swear to God, Cruz, if you weren't my son, and I didn't love you so much, I would have packaged you up in a box and sent you to live with my sister in Germany years ago."

Cruz laughs and glances back at me. "She says that now, but she wouldn't be able to live with herself when she realized that her sister was trying to force me into an all-natural lifestyle."

I hold back a laugh as Cruz's mother eyes me with caution, probably wondering what the fuck I'm doing standing in her kitchen, but if she has a good relationship with her husband and they actually talk, then I have no doubt that she already knows.

"Elodie," she says, bowing her head in an awkward little gesture. "Welcome to my home. Is there anything I can help you with? Are you looking for my husband?"

Cruz laughs at his mother. "Knock it off," he says. "She's not the queen of England. She didn't come for business, she just came to chill. I promised I'd introduce her to you and give her a tour of the place."

Her eyes bug out of her head for a quick second before she controls her features. "Oh, well in that case, welcome to my home. I'm surprised, have you not been through here before? I'd love to take you on a proper tour. Unfortunately, Cruz's idea of a tour is just pointing toward things. We've only just finished remodeling. We're lacking in furniture, but you're the first person through, so I'd love to show you."

"Of course," I say, warmth spreading through my chest at the fond way she speaks of her son, something I wish I could have experienced with my own mother. "I'd love that."

She starts to walk toward me when she stops. "Oh, how terribly rude of me. I'm getting all excited about the tour that I forgot to offer you a drink. What can I get you, love? Water? A soda?"

Cruz grunts. "Water," he says, his voice filled with authority. "She can't drink anything else just yet."

His mother's brows drop as she meets his stare. "Excuse yourself," she demands, putting the asshat in place. "Since when do you have the right to tell a lady what she can and cannot drink? If Elodie, *the leader of our people,* decided she would like a chocolate fudge ice-cream sundae, mixed into a milkshake by Italian gangsters and served through a twenty-four-carat gold straw, then you better go to the ends of the earth to make that happen for her."

I blink a few times, staring at the way she so effortlessly put him in his place, only in this instance, it's not called for. "It's more than alright," I tell her, stepping forward to stand by Cruz's side. "He's right. I should only be drinking water. I'm sure you just caught my little display going up and down the street on my bike."

"Ahh, yes," she says, her eyes flicking between me and her son. "I certainly did catch that, but I wasn't sure that it was my place to ask."

I shrug my shoulders, not really knowing what I can and can't share with her—but screw it. I like her and I'm in a sharing mood. "I just had a little run in with another hitman and the bottom of my pool."

She sucks in a sharp gasp as she races forward and takes my hands. "Oh, you poor, sweet, sweet girl. What happened? Are you okay? I heard about the attack in the woods. I can't understand how these awful men could do that to such a young lady. You're barely even an adult with so much already on your shoulders."

I give her a warm smile, never having experienced an older woman showing me this kind of motherly love and getting emotional over my well-being. "Thank you," I murmur, instantly deciding that this woman before me is now my favorite adult … ever. "That means a lot to me, but for the most part, I'm fine. He had me under the water until everything went black, and the next thing I knew, Grayson was above me forcing the water out of my lungs and he was dead on the other side of the pool."

She gasps, and in the blink of an eye, her arms are wrapped tightly around me with tears sitting heavily in her eyes. "Oh, Elodie. Your mother would have been sick to hear the awful things that have been happening to you. How are you holding up?"

"Surviving," I tell her, not expecting the raw emotion welling up inside of me.

"If you ever need to talk or just want to get something off your chest, even if it's to complain about the ridiculousness of my son, I'm here. No matter what, you can always count on me."

"Thank you," I whisper. "That means a lot. I've never had someone that I could talk to like that."

She takes me by the shoulders and holds me back to look me in the eyes. "Consider yourself my new adopted daughter," she tells me proudly before looking across at her son. "Cruz, meet your brand-new sister."

I bite my tongue at the horror that stretches across his face. "No," he says, shaking his head and grabbing my arm. He steps into me and murmurs, keeping it loud enough for his mother to hear. "Back away slowly. Girlfriend, fuck buddy, even enemies I'm okay with, but I draw the line at siblings. It ain't gonna happen."

His mother laughs, but before I can say anything else, he's pulling me back the way we came. "Where's dumb and dumber?" he asks her.

She shakes her head and shrugs her shoulder. "Who would know? You know how your brothers get when we come back home. They're probably over with the Winston boys again. Who knows? But if you happen to see them, send their butts home. Their bedrooms are a mess and they've tracked dirt all through my living room."

"Will do," he says, pulling me out before I even get a chance to say goodbye.

Cruz drags me through his home, getting faster and faster by the second. "Where are we going?" I ask as he makes it far too obvious that he has a destination in mind.

His eyes light up like New Year's fireworks as he beams back at me. "I've been dying to show you this."

I groan as he doesn't give away a damn thing. He stops by a door, and without giving me a second to catch myself, he pushes straight through to his massive garage, and I gape at the collection of bikes that take up the far side.

He hurries through the garage still holding onto me, but this time he doesn't need to drag me because I think I might even be going faster than he is. "What the hell, Cruz? You've been hiding all of this in here this whole time? Fuck me."

My greedy gaze sweeps over his impressive collection, and I watch as he walks straight to the Harley Davidson that sits front and center, matte black just like my Ducati. "Check her out," he says, running his fingers over the sleek curves and practically drooling. "Isn't she beautiful?"

Damn. Is it possible to be jealous of a bike?

He looks at it with such adoration that I can't help getting a little closer. He straddles it and I instantly climb onto his lap. He reaches around me, and I feel the vibration of the bike shoot straight through to my core. "Wanna ride?"

"Don't I always?"

A grin kicks up the side of his mouth and he holds me tight as the garage door slowly peels open. I go to twist around him to sit behind, but he doesn't let me go. "Stay," he dares, knowing damn well that I wouldn't be able to resist.

And just like that, Cruz goes flying out of the garage with me sitting in front of him, and my legs wrapped securely around his waist. The wind hits the back of my head and whips my hair over my shoulder, only just missing Cruz's face as he reaches around me and grips the handlebar.

We hit the main road and I can't help but laugh, only now just realizing that in all that, I never actually learned his mother's name. I'll have to ask later, because right now, Cruz is taking me for the ride of my life. I know it's fucking stupid and just asking for trouble, but I trust him blindly with my life. He won't let me fall. Besides, how could I possibly resist the joy that spreads across his face while having his two favorite things between his legs and the opportunity to forget the damaged world around us?

17

My bedroom door swings open, and I fly up out of bed only to find Ember standing in my doorway. "What the fuck happened yesterday?" she demands, walking straight in and dropping onto the edge of my bed. She crawls in beside me and lays her head down, only to cringe when the massive lump on the side of her head presses against the pillow.

She sucks in a sharp breath, her hand falling to the side of her head and gently feeling the evidence of yesterday's attack. She meets my stare, her eyes filled with panic. "Please tell me that's a zit the size of an egg on the side of my head and not a fucking lump from getting punched by a psychotic douchebag."

My face twists into a cringe and I take her hand, gently removing it from her head to examine her lump. "You're going to need to ice that," I tell her, taking in the deep purpling bruise that spreads right through the lump and around her eye, something that she wouldn't even come close to covering up with concealer. "How are you feeling? Do you have a headache? Do you need a painkiller or something like that? I'm pretty sure King put some on the bedside table in your room with a bottle of water."

Her eyes widen. "King was in my room while I slept?" she asks, not even swooning at the idea of being in his arms like the usual, chirpy version of Ember would have done. "Just tell me he wasn't being a creeper while he was in there."

"He carried you inside and put you into the bed so you weren't passed out by the pool and in the sun, but don't worry, he was extra careful with you. Very respectful for an asshole like King. We just didn't want you to wake up out there and be scared."

"So, you chose to put me in a room that I'd never been in before, in a house that I barely know that was just … I don't even know what happened. Burgled? Home invaded?"

I cringe. "Sorry," I say. "I guess I didn't really think that part through. I just wanted you to be comfortable, and I wasn't sure if you wanted me to call your parents or not, so I wanted to wait it out until you woke up, but then it was getting late and the exhaustion got me and I kinda crashed."

"It's fine," she grumbles, twisting her face in pain as she attempts to adjust herself on the pillow. "It's probably best that you didn't call them. They would have just worried and then you would have had them on your doorstep with an ambulance and the cops demanding a statement. They would have found a way to put the blame on you even though you literally couldn't help it, and they would have said that I can't hang out here … you know."

I press my lips into a tight line. Maybe her parents would be right to distance her from me. I'm bad news and she deserves better than that.

Her mouth drops open before quickly closing it again. "So, it's all true then? It's not just some crazy dream?"

"Unfortunately," I mutter, hating the images that replay in my mind on repeat.

Ember sighs and carefully relaxes into the pillow at a new angle. "I feel like I've been run over by a truck."

My heart breaks for her. I hate that she's been dragged into this bullshit, and because of me, ended up getting hurt. "Here," I say, pulling myself out of bed and trying to keep my voice quiet, knowing her head would be throbbing and aching in the worst kind of way. "Let me check my bathroom. I might have some painkillers in there."

I skip into the bathroom, trying to keep it quick as I'm more than aware that I've skipped over the explanation far too many times, but her health is far more important right now. As soon as she's comfortable and not hurting, I owe her the truth, or at least, the parts of the story which I can tell without exposing Dynasty.

I hurry through to the bathroom and scrounge around through the cabinets before finding what I need and grabbing a glass of water.

I help to get her comfortable and go as far as holding the glass while she swallows the small pills.

The second the glass hits the bedside table beside her, she shoots a heavy glare my way. "No more excuses," she tells me. "Sit down and tell me what the fuck happened before I go insane."

I give her a tight smile and make my way around to my vacated side. I scoot back in under the blankets, trying not to jostle the bed too much. I turn to face her and try to be strong. Telling Cruz's mom yesterday was easy, but breaking the news to Ember is like walking across hot coals. "From what we can gather," I start, "it was a home invasion. The guy scaled the gate while we were outside and tripped the silent alarm, which we would have known if we were inside and I had my phone on me. Grayson watched the security footage last night and told me that he'd tried to get into the house from the front, but the door has an automatic lock so that's when he came around back."

Ember groans, her eyes widening as she remembers exactly what I'm talking about. "Skip this part," she begs. "I know what happens here."

I press my lips into a tight line and nod, feeling a heavy guilt sink into my stomach at how I have to twist the truth. "Okay, well after you went down, he raced after me. I don't know if he was trying to get me to unlock the house or if he wanted something else, but he chased after me and I wasn't fast enough."

She sucks in a gasp and grabs my hands. "Please don't tell me that he …"

My eyes widen, realizing where her train of thought has taken her.

"Oh, no," I quickly rush out. "He didn't do that, but he threw me into the pool and tried to hold me down, but the boys made it just in time and dealt with him."

Ember's eyes narrow. "How do you mean 'dealt' with him?"

My jaw clenches as I try to figure out what the hell to say before I let out a soft sigh, regret sitting against my chest. "They beat the shit out of him and then dumped him behind some shitty bar to let someone else deal with him. But we're safe now. You don't need to worry about him, he's never going to hurt you again."

Tears well in her eyes. "I just … I was so scared."

"I know," I murmur, reaching across and pulling her into my arms. "So was I, but it's over and now all we have to do is focus on getting you better. Your head is probably going to hurt for a few days. Did you want me to take you down to the ER to get checked before I have to go to school or are you alright? You're bound to have a nasty concussion."

She gently shakes her head. "I think I'm all good. I mean, no offense or anything, but I just kinda wanna go home and spend the day sleeping in my own bed."

"Yeah, of course," I say. "Let me call the boys. Carver can drive you home and I'll get one of the others to follow with your car."

Any other day, Ember would have fought me on the decision to have someone else drive her car, but the fact she just nodded and let it go is a testament to how out of it she really is.

Wanting to get her home to her comfort place, I call Carver, and within the space of ten minutes, I have her at the front door with Grayson helping to get her down to the Escalade. I climb in the car beside her and go along for the drive. The trip to her place and back, plus the time it takes to get ready for school, will have us all late for homeroom, but what does it really matter?

We get Ember home just in time to find her parents trying to slip out of the house to get to work. Her mom instantly gasps and helps King and me usher her up into her bedroom. The other three boys stay downstairs with her father, charming him out of his pants and letting him know what happened—at least the Dynasty free version.

An hour later, I walk out of homeroom with a pretty pink detention slip for being tardy to class, and as I walk deeper into the hallway, I glance up to find the guys hovering around Carver's locker. I walk straight up to them, slipping right between Carver and Grayson.

I hold up my pink detention slip with a scowl. "Did you assholes get one of these as well or is today just my lucky day?"

King's lips pull up into an amused smirk. "I've never received one of them. The teachers here are too fucking pussy to even try."

I gape at him before glancing at the others, who all nod, but I have no idea if it's because they're confirming King's story or if they're trying to tell me that the same goes for them. I groan and reach forward to slip the little square piece of paper into the front pocket of Cruz's pants. "Screw it," I say. "If you guys don't have to suffer through detention, even though I'm sure you've done worse things than showing up late for homeroom, then I don't have to either. Mr. Bennett can go and suck a fat one."

King smirks and just as I'm about to ask them what's so important that they need to be huddled in front of Carver's locker, Sara Benson steps into Carver's side, and by 'steps,' what I really mean is that she tumbles into him and puts on a show of what a clumsy idiot she is.

Her hand falls to his chest as he catches her arm to balance her. My eyes instantly zone in on their touch, and an intense fire burns through me like an inferno threatening to destroy everything in its path, but why? Carver isn't mine and I sure as hell have no claim over him. He can be with whoever the fuck he wants to be with. I have no right to get jealous.

I stare, my top lip rising in a brazen growl as I watch her pathetically flirt with Carver, but even more so, I watch the way he eats it up as though she's feeding him his first meal in months.

"Woah, kitty," Cruz chuckles, keeping his voice low. "Retract the claws."

I shoot a lethal glare at Cruz as Grayson and King laugh at my unintentional performance. "Call me kitty one more time and I can personally guarantee that you'll never get a taste of this kitty ever again."

King sucks in a breath as though my threat is worse than me telling him his dick is about to be chopped off and skinned only so I can then stretch it over my head and wear it as a hat.

Carver shamelessly flirts back, giving Sara all the sexy winks and grins that would have me melting into a puddle of goo, but when he quickly glances up to see where my attention is, it suddenly all makes sense. It's a fucking show, purely for my benefit, and I got played like a fucking fool.

He doesn't want her, he just wants to make me sweat, and fuck it, it worked like a goddamn charm.

Sara flicks her hair over her shoulder, and it whips me right in the face, but unfortunately for her, my reflexes are on point and my hand snaps up, gripping the fake blonde strands securely in my palm.

Fuck it. She's pissed me off and I don't feel like holding back today; call me a petty bitch, but I don't fucking care.

I pull hard on her hair and her head tilts straight back, a loud, ear-shattering cry tearing out of her as I go. "Watch yourself," I warn. "You're in my way, and I think it's about time that you start backing up before I make you. Don't think I've forgotten what you did to me."

Her jaw clenches as she manages to twist her head to catch my eyes. "Let go of me, whore," she demands, the students around us stopping to stare. "You don't even belong here. Tell her Carver. She's hurting me."

Carver just laughs, watching the two of us.

Sara groans, reaching for her hair and pulling at my hand. "You're such a fucking bitch."

"Yeah, that may be true, but this bitch has had a really fucked up weekend, so I suggest you get lost before I start taking it out on you. What's it going to be? Have you seen Knox lately? I wonder how his face healed?"

Sara huffs and looks at Carver for help again. "Seriously? You're not going to do something about this?"

"I'm not her keeper," he tells her. "It's up to you how and when she releases you, but don't say that she didn't warn you. She really did have a fucked up weekend."

Sara lets out a deep sigh before twisting back to me. "Fine, I'll go, just let go of my hair, you crazy bitch."

In an instant, my hand comes loose, and her hair falls down her back like a golden mane. "Ahh, see? There are those magic words," I tell her as she spins around to shoot a nasty glare at me. "That wasn't so hard now, was it?"

She huffs and puffs, and after throwing one more glance at Carver, she disappears into the thinning students making their way to their first class of the day.

I instantly zone in on Carver, stepping closer to close the circle around us. "What the hell was that?"

He laughs as the others listen a little too closely. "Nothing," he says with a shrug, playing it off as though he didn't just hijack my emotions and shit all over them. "She was just asking to hook up tonight. What's it to you? You're not jealous, are you?"

"That's not what I'm talking about," I demand, more than fucking jealous, despite not having the right to feel that way, especially when Carver is the one who watches me fawn all over his friends day-in and day-out. "Why did you so easily send her away? It's obvious that you were just keeping her around to get under my skin. So why bother? Why go to all that fucking effort if you were just going to let her walk away?"

Carver clenches his jaw, hating being called out on his bullshit as a heavy breath comes sailing out of him. He quickly glances around us, making sure the lingering students aren't close enough to hear. "If you really must know," he starts, "I need to talk to you—all of you—and to do that, I needed her gone."

King's brows furrow as Grayson raises his chin, always ready for whatever bullshit fuckery is going to go down. Cruz on the other hand, leans in, wanting to hear every last word with eager ears.

Carver's gaze comes back to mine with a strange darkness filtering through his stormy depths. "Sam's back in the country. I just got his call during homeroom."

My brows instantly shoot up. I know Carver told him that he had two days to come back and deal with whatever bullshit lie Carver had fed him, but a part of me hadn't expected it. Sam is a self-righteous, self-important bastard, and he doesn't work on someone else's schedule. The fact that he stopped what he was doing and got straight back on a plane for Carver speaks volumes.

Grayson discreetly steps closer into my side so that my arm presses up against his stomach and chest and I find myself leaning into his touch. "So, what now?"

"You tell me," Carver says as I feel King and Cruz's heavy stare boring into my face. "I told you to have a plan ready, so what's it going to be?"

Panic soars through me. "I …" I shake my head. "I don't know. My weekend was a little … busy, so forgive me, but I haven't exactly had a minute to come up with some groundbreaking plan to take out a whole sex trafficking organization."

"Well, if you didn't spend all of your time focusing on getting dick, maybe you would have found a minute to think it through."

"Woah," Cruz says, holding up a hand. "Back off her. You know how easily she'll fire back, and we need her in the right mindset if we're going to do this."

"Going to do this?" I ask. "Why does it already sound like the groundbreaking plan has been talked through and agreed on?"

"Because it has," Grayson says, his hand discreetly finding my lower back and making me wonder if he even realizes that he's doing it. Though, this is Grayson Beckett, nothing ever gets by him. "I don't mean to offend you or anything like that, but we figured that you didn't have any … uhh … experience in the area and we went ahead and figured out how we're going to play this."

"And?" I ask, searching each of the guys for any kind of information. "What's the plan?"

"The plan," Carver says, "is that we hide you with Cruz's mom while we go and deal with it. You're not ready."

"Bullshit I'm not ready," I seethe, spitting the words through my teeth and trying to keep my voice down as the anger rolls through me. "You don't get to tell me what I'm ready for. I'm coming. After the weekend I just had, I deserve to make some heads roll. Besides, I was the fucking victim in all of this. Sam kept me in a cell, dressed me up as one of his sex slaves, and sold me. I'm coming, and there's not a damn thing you can say about it, so tell me the goddamn plan so I can make the fucker pay."

The guys quickly glance at one another, secret messages passing between them all, but when Carver's stare comes back to me, I see his decision before he's even said a word. "You better be fucking ready because if we're doing this, then we've got to go now."

I nod. "I'm ready."

"Okay then," he says. "Here's what you need to know."

18

Leaning through to the front of the Escalade, I meet Carver's focused stare. "I thought you told Sam you were meeting at the auction house?" I question, quickly glancing at the property Carver had pointed out as Sam's private home not two seconds ago.

"I did," he grunts as I notice all four of the guys' attention focused heavily on the house. Their eyes scan over every inch of the property, counting the security guards who case the joint, watching the way the cameras swivel and check to see if they leave any blind spots. They even watch the dogs that Sam has trained to walk circles around the border of his property.

"What's going on?"

Grayson raises his chin and leans to the side, getting a better view of the side entrance of the property. "Sam would have sent the majority of his security team to the auction house in preparation for a meeting tonight. They would have gotten there early to set up security in case Carver was planning a raid. That way, they would have time to catch it and bail before Sam was caught. That's how he runs his ship, but in doing that, he's left his home vulnerable," he explains. "We're going to hit him here where it hurts and take the whole thing down with it."

Fuck me. Grayson's so damn hot when he talks like that.

My brows shoot up as excitement pulses through me. "You guys really have thought this through."

"Mmhmm," King rumbles. "We value our lives. We don't go into reckless, unpredictable situations without a fucking plan. Our names aren't Winter."

"Hey," I snap. "Low fucking blow."

King just shrugs. "Try and change my mind," he says. "It's true and you damn well know it."

Well, shit. He has a point. I live for reckless and unpredictable situations. That's exactly where the adrenaline comes from and makes me feel alive, but now I have the boys giving me a whole new type of adrenaline rush. Maybe it's time for me to be a little smarter about my little outings to the back alleyways behind clubs and seedy bars.

"So, what's the plan? What do I need to do?"

Carver spins around to face me, his eyes boring into mine like a heavy weight. "All you need to do is stick to Grayson like fucking glue, you got it? If you can't manage that, then tell me now, and you'll stay in the fucking car."

I clench my jaw, wanting nothing more than to fuck up his pretty little face, but I hold my tongue. It'll have to wait until after. I have a feeling that I'm going to need my energy. "What's the plan?" I repeat, my tone a little more forceful.

Carver sighs and looks back at me again. "Cruz is going to eliminate as many guards as possible and search out receipts or a ledger of his transactions. Hopefully that will help us find the girls he's sold. You and Grayson are going in search of the chick Sam intended to replace you with. King has his own agenda," he adds, making my gaze momentarily sweep across to King, but Carver's next words steal my attention right back. "And me … I'm going after Sam."

I shake my head. "No. Get fucked. I want Sam."

"Tough shit. Stick to the plan."

"But—

Cruz cuts mc off. "No," he says. "We've already been over every variation of the plan and this is what's best. You need to do what Carver says."

"I—"

"What do you think this girl is going to think if one of us comes at her, huh?" Cruz questions. "She's probably already fucking terrified as it is, and we're just going to make her think the worst. We need you to do this."

I clench my jaw and finally nod, completely understanding. When I was in Sam's cell and those two men came in, I thought I was done for. This girl is probably scared as shit and already would have gone through so much more. I don't want her to have to suffer like I did. "Okay," I murmur. "I'll go with Grayson."

"Good," Carver grunts, pleased that I'm not putting up more of a fight despite how desperately I want to be the one to go after Sam. I want him to see my face and know that he lost. I want to be there the moment he realizes just how badly he fucked up by having his men sneak into my room and screw me over. "We meet back here at the end. Don't fuck it up."

I narrow my eyes on him, knowing that last comment was aimed solely at me. "If anyone was to fuck something up, it'd be you," I point out, making a heavy scowl stretch across his face. "What are we waiting for? Let's get this over and done with."

"You need this," Grayson says, leaning forward in the front passenger seat and pulling out a gun. He presses it right into my hands and my eyes bug out of my head before I shove it right back at him.

"Oh, hell no," I say, a slight panic creeping into my tone as Grayson tries to hand it back. I shake my head violently. "No, I … I don't know how. I've never even seen a real gun before. I can't … I'll hurt somebody."

King reaches across and takes the gun out of Grayson's hand before holding it up for me to see. "It's easy," he explains, taking my hands and curling them around the gun. "Hold it like this and keep your finger away from the trigger until you need to shoot. When you're moving, keep it down. You'll be right behind Grayson for most of this, and trust me when I tell you, a fucking accidental bullet to his back is going to piss the fucker off. Believe me, he has the scar to prove it."

I nod, taking in every word with wide eyes as I feel the guys watching me intently. "What else?"

"There's not much else to it. It's already loaded, and Grayson has backup magazines if you run out of bullets. If you can, hold out on shooting, the longer it takes for them to realize what the fuck is going on, the better. Remember, see an enemy, raise the gun, aim, finger on trigger, squeeze. Simple."

"Simple," I repeat.

Grayson grunts. "Just don't fucking miss. These assholes will have guns of their own, and if you miss, I can guarantee a bullet will be coming straight back at you."

"I … I think I'll be more comfortable with a knife."

"No," Carver says, meeting my stare through the rearview mirror. "Sam has some of the best trained guards in the country. Disgraced ex-military, hitmen, bullshit like that. I don't want you getting close enough to need a knife."

"Okay, I get it," I say, feeling the intense adrenaline building inside me. "But I still want a fucking knife."

Grayson just sighs and reaches forward before opening the glove compartment and pulling out a beautiful silver dagger. "Be careful with this," he tells me. "This is one of my father's most prized possessions."

I scoff as I take it from him, examining the designs on the hilt. "You mean the guy who's going to screw me over after everyone else already has?" I ask, slipping the blade down between my tits and letting the underwire of my bra hold it firmly in place. I doubt letting it jiggle around in my pocket is a great idea. "Yeah, I'll be sure to be very careful with it."

Grayson rolls his eyes, but the second he reaches for his door handle and pulls the lever, seriousness washes over me. "Are you ready?" Cruz demands, meeting my eyes. "Now's your last chance to back out. No one is going to judge you if you're not ready. You know we've got this with or without you."

"I'm ready."

"Good. Then let's go."

The five of us bail out of the Escalade and we race toward the property. Grayson grabs my hand and pulls me behind him, while King and Carver take off to the left, sticking to the shadows and keeping out of sight. Cruz darts to the right and I have a feeling that's the last I'm going to see of them until this is over.

Grayson tugs me hard, forcing my strides to keep up with his. He watches the security cameras and brings me to an immediate stop, his arm slamming across my chest to keep me from taking another step. "Wait," he orders.

The camera swivels, and the second it passes, he yanks hard on my hand and we bolt for the front gate. There is a tall concrete pillar and we aim straight for it. "We have less than ten seconds to get over that thing," he yells back at me. "I'm going to throw you up there, but the second your feet touch it, you need to fly right off the fucker. Got it?"

"Yep."

Fuck. Is now the right time to tell him that heights scare the shit out of me? Nah, I'll let it slide and see how it goes.

We reach the pillar and I hardly have a chance to step up in front of it before Grayson's hands are interlocking and bracing under my foot. I jump at the same time he launches me up and I catch the top of the pillar. "Holy fuck," I mutter under my breath, pulling myself right up. My ass hits it and I look down, my heart racing.

"Get the fuck down," Grayson tells me, already pulling himself up behind me. I close my eyes and jump. My ass comes down in the grass as my back slams against the concrete pillar, but I don't have a chance to check just how bad it is as a loud ferocious growl hits my ears.

My eyes bug out of my head, seeing the feral dog racing at me. My hands instantly fly up to protect my face just as Grayson lands on the ground in front of me. His hand shoots out and I hear a strange noise before the dog falls to the ground.

Grayson whips around to find me, offering me his hand and instantly yanking me to my feet. "You good?"

I nod, glancing down at the dog. "Did you kill it?"

"No, just tasered it. It'll only be out for a minute, so we need to go."

He pulls me along and I can't help but glance back at the still dog. He's out like a light. Maybe I need to get one of these tasers and practice on Carver.

Sam's yard isn't nearly as big as mine or the boys' so getting to the side entrance of the house is a lot quicker than I'd expected, but as we get there, we find the door locked with a retinal scanner staring back at us. Grayson curses before pulling me toward a window. "Guess we're doing this the old-fashioned way."

He walks right up to the window and feels the glass, checking just how thick it is before a smug grin stretches across his face. "The dickhead gets the best security system money can buy but goes stingy on the glass. Dumb fuck."

And just like that, Grayson's elbow goes straight through the glass. A cut slices along his skin and he sucks in a sharp breath, but it's not enough to stop him from what he's doing. He steps back and pushes out the rest of the glass with his hands before reaching for me.

He grabs my waist and hoists me up through the window and my feet silently come down in the empty dining room.

Just like the pillar at the front gate, he pulls himself up and drops in beside me as I scan the room to find something to stop the bleeding. "Here," I murmur as I approach the table, tearing the runner off and hurrying back to Grayson's side to wrap his elbow. "It's not pretty, but it'll do," I tell him.

Grayson nods, and just like that, takes my hand and creeps toward the door. He peers outside of the room and confirming that the coast is clear, he steps out into the hallway and drags me along. "We need to find where he's keeping this girl," he murmurs, his voice so low that it's nearly impossible to hear. "Try to find an entrance into a basement or a hidden room. I don't know, he could have stashed her anywhere."

I nod, keeping the gun held tightly in my hand as I scan the walls and doors for any clues or signs, though honestly, I have no idea what fucking signs to look for.

We hear voices around the corner and Grayson instantly throws us into a small room, our bodies so close that he'd be able to feel the rapid beat of my heart through his own chest. His eyes remain glued on mine. "Shhhhhh," he whispers.

My hands shake as I hear the voice, and as if being thrown straight back into the past, I know that one of these guys is the one responsible for stripping me bare in Sam's cell and dressing me up in that filthy lace lingerie. My jaw sets into a hard line and as if reading my mind, Grayson nods.

The voices come closer and we wait a beat, listening as their footsteps round the corner and head straight toward the cupboard we're hiding in.

The men approach our hiding spot, and like lightning, Grayson flies out of the cupboard, the door smacking straight into the guy on the left, busting his lip as Grayson dives for the other. He grabs his head and gives a violent twist before the first guy even has a chance to yell.

Grayson is on him in mere seconds, and before I can step out of the cupboard, both the men are dead, lying on the floor, never knowing what hit them. I gape at Grayson. "What the fuck was that?" I ask. "Do you all know how to do this shit?"

He just nods and pulls me out of the way before shoving the bodies in the cupboard.

"Fuck me," I breathe. "And all this time I've been trying to beat up Carver when he could have killed me with the flick of his fingers. A little warning would have been nice."

"On day one we fucking warned you," he grunts, shuffling the bodies around. "You just chose not to listen. Now, come on. We have a job to do and not a lot of time to do it."

I shut up and let him pull me along, and it's not long before we realize the whole house is covered with secret rooms, false walls, and creepy bullshit that no person in their right mind should have in their home.

We find King silently making his way through the house and Grayson stops. "Find anything?"

"Not yet," he says, his eyes scanning up and down my body, checking that I'm still in one piece, and honestly, after being resuscitated just yesterday, I could really use a sit down and maybe a glass of water, but it's going to have to wait. "Sam's personal study is just down the hall from here. I went through it but couldn't find anything. Cruz is better at paperwork though. He might be able to see something that I didn't."

Grayson nods. "Have you done what you needed to do?"

"Almost."

"Good."

And just like that, we part ways and King continues down the hall, his gun securely in his hand.

We keep moving, but when we pass Sam's personal study, I find myself reaching for his door. "No," Grayson says. "King has already checked it. Leave the rest for Cruz. We're not wasting time."

I shake my head. "I just … no. I just have a feeling about something."

Grayson sighs and looks back down the hallway before stepping into the study with me. "Make it quick."

I nod and hurry around the room, scanning over everything as I go before coming to a stop at Sam's desk. It's huge and spans the length of the room with about ten drawers on either side.

I place my gun down on the table, and not giving a shit about keeping it clean, I start yanking out the drawers and tipping them on to the desk. The pens and stationery clatter out and I quickly dig through it before dumping the drawer and going for the next. "Could you be any fucking louder?" Grayson seethes.

I snap my glare up at him. "You told me to be quick," I remind him. "Shut the fucking door if you're too scared."

I laugh at the ridiculousness of my comment. A guy like Grayson isn't scared of anything, but just the fact that I insinuated it drives him fucking mad. He doesn't say anything though, he's got far too much control for that, but knowing is enough for me.

The fifth drawer is heavier, and as I yank it out, I find nothing but a few papers, papers that definitely shouldn't be this heavy. I look over the drawer, rattling it to hear noise coming from inside. Grayson steps closer looking over it with me. "There," he says, pointing to a small opening. "It's got a false bottom."

I shove the drawer down on the desk, smirking to myself as it scratches the shit out of the expensive wood. I carefully pull the knife from between my tits and use it to pry open the false bottom, and just like that, I find Sam's sick little collection of mementos that he's collected from the stolen girls over the years. There are rings, necklaces, bangles, and right on fucking top are my brass knuckles.

A grin stretches across my face as I pick them out of the drawer and slide them straight back on my fingers. It's like coming home after a long, shitty trip away, and for the first time in weeks, I finally feel like myself again.

I glance up to meet Grayson's eyes, seeing an understanding within his grey depths. "I don't care what you say," I tell him. "We're taking this drawer and reuniting as many of these things with their owners as possible."

Grayson just nods, and as I go to lift up the drawer, the study door flies open, and my head snaps up to find Knox welcoming himself into the room.

Well, well, this is a nice little surprise.

Knox comes to an immediate stop, his head flying up as he meets my wide stare. His mouth drops and it takes me a second to realize that he hasn't been in school after the guys had gotten to him, and as far as he was aware, his uncle stole me right out of my bedroom and sold me to a wealthy businessman.

"What's the matter?" I ask, a grin kicking up the corner of my mouth. "You look like you're seeing a ghost."

His gaze flicks between me and Grayson, and I curl my fingers into a fist, feeling the sweet familiarity of the brass knuckles tightening over my fingers. It's like getting rain in the driest desert.

I step around the desk and Knox instantly backs up, sure as hell remembering how I'd fucked him up all those weeks ago. "You … you can't be here," he tells me. "You were—"

"Sold? Yeah, thanks for that," I say, inching in closer. "I don't think I ever got the chance to truly thank you for the hell you put me through."

"What? I—"

My fist slams out and I hear the sweet, sweet sound of his nose shattering under my brass knuckles. He falls straight to the ground, clutching his broken nose as a rare laugh tears through Grayson. I look back at him to find a proud grin stretched wide across his face. "There she is."

I grin back, the happiness and adrenaline pulsing through my veins like a rocket. "I lost her for a second," I tell him, laughing as I inspect my fist, checking that I didn't break anything, but damn it, it would be so worth it if I did. I forgot how fucking good that kind of power felt.

Knox groans on the ground, and just as I go to slam my boot into his ribs, a loud BANG echoes through the house and my wide stare whips back around to Grayson's.

"Playtime is over," he says, a seriousness over his face as he scoops up Sam's sick box of mementos before grabbing my discarded gun and knife. "They know we're here. It's time to find this girl and get the fuck out."

19

Gunshots sound throughout the house as Grayson dumps the drawer into my hands. He bends down and grabs Knox, the panic in his eyes enough to send fear rattling deep inside me. He hoists Knox up, bringing his face to hover right in front of him. "Where the fuck is the girl?" he roars, his voice rebounding off each of the four walls of the private study and making me suck in a breath, only just realizing how scary Grayson can be.

"Fuck off," Knox grunts, trying to pull free and earning himself a devastating uppercut to the stomach. "Sam's going to fucking kill you, and he'll sell your bitch all over again."

Grayson grabs him again, blood streaming from his nose as three more shots sound throughout the house. "Last fucking chance," Grayson growls, the warning thick in his tone. "The way you answer this question will determine if you live or die."

Knox grunts and as Grayson flinches to finish him off, he holds up his hands. "Kill me then," he spits. "Sam is just going to kill me if he finds out that I gave the girls up."

"Girls?" I question, flying forward and grabbing a handful of Knox's hair, tearing it back to force his face to mine. "How many?"

When Knox doesn't respond, Grayson slams him against the wall, his head bouncing off it with a solid thud. "How. Fucking. Many?"

Knox shakes his head, staring at Grayson with wide eyes, finally believing that this guy he grew up with has exactly what it takes to end his life. "I don't know, maybe four or five."

"Fuck." He slams him against the wall again and Knox groans low. "Where are they?"

His gaze snaps to me before flying back to Grayson in defeat. "Third bedroom on the left. There's a false wall that leads down to the underground cells."

Fuck. Underground cells. What the hell is wrong with this guy?

Grayson punches him again, this time knocking him right the fuck out. He releases his hold on Knox and his body crumbles to the ground, his head lolling at an unnatural angle.

Grayson looks back at me. "Ditch the fucking drawer, we'll come back for it. We have to get these girls out."

My heart breaks as I drop the drawer against a shelf and Grayson forces my gun back into my hand. "Shoot first, ask questions later.

Got it? They're going to be distracted by the shooting upstairs, but someone is bound to come down here to check."

I swallow over the lump in my throat and nod.

"Follow me. Stay right on my fucking ass."

I don't hesitate and follow him straight out the door. He keeps his gun held expertly in his hand, and I stand behind him, my heart racing as fear pulses through me. I'm the kinda girl that beats up dirty perverts; I never signed up for shootouts.

Grayson doesn't bother being quiet anymore; he just barrels down the hallway until we finally reach the third bedroom. He kicks in the door, tearing it right off the hinges and keeps his gun raised, assuming the room will be guarded, but when we find it empty, we storm straight in.

My gaze sweeps over the room, trying to figure out where the false wall is. Grayson walks around, skimming his fingertips over the ugly cream paint, feeling for any abnormalities while I scan the paintings on each side of the room. Three of them are modern and bright while the painting on the wall directly across from the bed is old and worn.

"There," I tell him, pointing out the painting of the woman standing in an overgrown garden wearing nothing but a sheet and struggling to hold it up as her left tit hangs free. "There's something off about that painting."

Grayson walks straight to it and roams his fingers over the frame, his brows furrowing as the seconds tick by. He shakes his head, not figuring out how it's supposed to open a false wall when he gets frustrated and tears the painting off the wall and throws it carelessly against the back of the room.

Grayson scoffs seeing the small button on the wall right where the painting used to be and without hesitation, he presses it and takes a step back. The false wall peels back and I stare in astonishment. I've seen a few secret doors like this since I came here and it's something that I'll never tire of.

The secret door opens to a dark room and Grayson instantly looks back at me with a strange cautiousness in his eyes. "Are you sure you're ready to see what's down here? It's not going to be pretty."

I give him a hard, determined stare. "I can handle it."

Grayson watches me a second longer, but it's precious seconds wasted that we could be using to save these girls. I push forward, shouldering past him into the dark room, only the floor drops away and I begin to tumble.

Grayson's hand shoots out like lightning and catches me by the waistband of my ripped jeans. "Careful," he says, almost like a curse, pulling out his phone and turning on his flashlight app. Light filters through the secret room and I realize that I was only moments from falling down a steep set of metal stairs.

I let out a breath and try not to focus on the smell. It's just as bad as the cells that Sam kept me in. There's not going to be anything good down here.

We reach the bottom of the stairs and Grayson slides in front of me, not knowing what we might find. He raises his flashlight into the small room and we find four cramped cells, each with girls laying naked on the floor with not even enough room to sit up properly.

I suck in a gasp.

These girls are in dog cages.

"Oh, no, no, no, no."

I race to the first cage and instantly drop to my knees, the desperation sitting heavily on my chest. "We're going to get you out of here," I call, pulling on the metal bars and frantically searching around as the girls squint against the light.

Grayson manically searches the room, tearing at fixtures and scanning every little crevice trying to find the keys. "I can't fucking find them," he roars, the frustration sinking through him as we listen to the gunshots above, and while he wants nothing more than to free these girls, he also wants to be upstairs, having his boys' backs.

The girl in the cage behind me raises her arm and points across the room. "There," she murmurs, her voice a breathy, exhausted whisper.

Grayson's flashlight whips around to the section of wall that she's pointing to and we find four small keys attached to a single nail in the wall.

Grayson races for it.

He throws two keys at me before dropping down in front of the other two girls and quickly trying to figure out which key belongs to each cage. We get two of the cages open before he takes the keys from my hand and points back at the open cages. "Here, you start getting them out," he says while darting across to the other cages.

I don't hesitate and reach into the first one. The girl is young, maybe only fifteen. She holds up her hand and desperately latches onto my wrist. "Please," she whispers. "Get us out of here."

"We're working on it," I promise her. "You're going home."

I awkwardly get her out as she cries in pain, her body cramping and malnourished after being down here for so long. Her legs are wobbly, and she has no choice but to crawl across the floor as I start on the next girl.

It takes us far too long to free each of the girls, and after ten minutes, Grayson has carried each of them up the stairs.

They sit on the bed with a broken demeanor, but we're not out of trouble just yet. Realizing that getting each of them out of here is going to be harder than we originally thought, Grayson presses a few buttons on his phone and holds it up to his ear as he stands in the open doorway, peering down the hall. "What's going on?" he snaps into the phone.

There's a slight pause before he looks back at me. "Alright. We need help down here, and another fucking car." His gaze sweeps over the naked, shivering girls. "Make it quick."

He shoves his phone into the pocket of his jeans as he watches me. "Cruz has what he needs. He's coming to help." I nod and watch as Grayson peers back out the door. "You good here? I'm going to grab that box of jewelry and meet you back here. We'll go out the fucking window if we have to."

I nod again, my heart kicking up a notch as he slips out of the door, leaving me alone to protect the girls, but he'll only be gone a few seconds. Wanting to give them even a fraction of privacy, I start digging through the old-fashioned dresser and pulling out random clothes. None of it looks even a little bit good but it'll help cover them up. "Here," I say, dropping the clothes in front of them. "It's nothing great, but it'll do until we can get you out of here."

The girls don't say a word, but the way they dive for the clothes tells me just how grateful they are.

Hearing a noise down the hallway, my hand tightens on the gun as my body shakes with adrenaline. This is too much.

I put myself between the door and the girls and hold up the gun, my finger hovering over the trigger.

The noise gets louder.

Footstep after footstep.

Thump. Thump. Thump.

"Fuck, fuck, fuck, fuck, fuck," I murmur to myself like a chant on constant replay.

A shadow crosses in front of the open door, and within the blink of an eye, a large, bald man covered in tattoos fills the door frame, his wide eyes focused right on me. "Not today, princess," he spits as the girls shrink and panic with fear.

He barrels into the room, and just as my finger goes to squeeze the trigger, a loud *BANG* comes from down the hallway. The man crumples to the ground as a bullet pierces through the side of his head, splattering blood all over the wall.

The girls scream in horror, and fuck, I'm right there with them.

"Ugh," Grayson says, appearing out of nowhere and pushing his body aside in disgust. "Come on," he says, looking at me and the four clothed girls behind me as he walks into the room and shoves the drawer of jewelry into my hands. "We have to go."

The girls wobble on their feet and Grayson slips his arms around two of them while I try to help the other two as best I can. Cruz comes careening down the hallway and his eyes go wide, only just realizing what the hell we needed help with. "Fuck," he grunts, instantly picking up the girl on my right and lightening my load as I take note of his bloodied knuckles, scrapes, and cuts over his face.

"Where are King and Carver?" Grayson demands, looking back at Cruz.

"King's out front stealing a car and Carver's still searching out Sam. The little bitch went into hiding at the first sight of trouble. The rest of the guards are down, but someone would have called in backup by now."

Grayson nods, barreling through to the front foyer of the house. "I still want these girls out of this fucking house as soon as possible."

"I'm fucking with you."

After what feels like forever, we get the girls out into the fresh air just as King brings a blacked-out SUV to a screeching stop before us. The driver's door flies open, and King races around, peeling open every door he passes and helping to get them all loaded in.

I stand with King and Cruz as Grayson runs down the drive to get the Escalade. My hands ball into fists, keeping my eyes on the front door. "Where is he?" I demand, refusing to move.

"He'll come," King promises.

A minute passes and then two and when Grayson pulls the Escalade to a stop right behind the blacked-out SUV for a quick getaway, my patience reaches its limits.

I bolt back toward the door. "Fuck, Winter," Cruz yells racing after me. "You're not going back in there."

He grabs hold of my arm, pulling me to a stop on the top step of Sam's home and I instantly whip back to see his furious stare. "I swear to God, Cruz. Let go of me before I pull your fucking balls out through your throat. I'm not leaving Carver in there. Who the fuck knows what's taking him so long. What if he's hurt?"

"He's not."

"You don't know that."

"Carver's the best we've got. He can handle himself. He'll get the job done and meet us out here, just like we planned. Trust him."

I let out a regretful sigh and pull my arm free. "I'm going in there whether you like it or not, so you can either get your ass back down the stairs or come with me. What's it going to be?"

Cruz glances back down the stairs at the guys standing protectively by the doors of the SUV, keeping the girls safe. Knowing that they have everything under control, he curses. "Fine," he snaps. "Make it fast."

Cruz pushes himself in front of me and we start racing back through the house. He leads me right up the stairs, kicking down doors as we go. I stare with wide eyes, seeing men lying across the floor with gunshot wounds all over their bodies.

"You did this?" I ask.

Cruz's stare hardens and all he gives me is a sharp nod before turning back to the mess before him. We get right through the upstairs level of the home before hurrying back down. "Where the fuck is he?"

Cruz murmurs to himself.

We cut through the kitchen and I come to an immediate stop, hearing voices on the other side of the wall. Only the other side of this room is the main living area that we just raced through that was completely empty.

"Wait," I tell Cruz, slowly scanning the kitchen. "They're here somewhere. I can hear Carver's voice."

Cruz steps in beside me, straining to hear what I hear, and when Carver's deep, haunting tone vibrates through the kitchen, Cruz instantly starts scanning the cabinetry.

He steps into it, pulling open the cupboards until he gets to the floor to ceiling pantry only to find another door inside. "Here," he tells me, indicating with a nod of his head to follow him into the pantry.

I don't hesitate, gripping my gun tightly. I follow Cruz through the tunnel-like room, realizing that this is some kind of escape tunnel. Carver would never let Sam get away so easily.

We walk for less than thirty seconds through the dark tunnel before it opens into a small bunker and we find Carver standing over Sam with a gun pointed right at his temple. Sam looks shit scared, and the sight has all sorts of joy spreading through my chest, though it instantly fades away as I see Carver's furious glare aimed right at me.

Sam quickly glances at us and he immediately recognizes me, though why wouldn't he? My kidnapping earned him a hefty five million dollars. "You," he spits, only now realizing that Carver wasn't an authentic purchaser and I'm not as dead as he may have let on.

Carver brings his hand back and hits Sam across the face, instantly splitting his cheek wide-open. "You don't speak to her," he spits, adjusting the gun to sit right between Sam's eyes. "Any last words?"

"Go to hell."

A grin cuts across Carver's face. "I'll see you there."

I see the exact moment that Carver goes to pull the trigger and I fly forward. "NO," I yell, pushing Carver's hand before he gets a chance to shoot the prick between the eyes.

"What the fuck is wrong with you?" Carver demands, grabbing my arm and throwing me back into Cruz's chest. "I could have shot you."

"You were going to kill him," I yell, throwing my heated stare back at Sam who looks as though he's about to collapse.

"Yeah," Carver scoffs. "That's the whole fucking point. I thought that's what you wanted. That's why we're here."

I shake my head, the anger burning up within me and making it hard to control myself. "No, it's too easy. He kidnapped me. He threw me in a fucking dark, cold cell with no food or water for three days. He had me stripped and dressed up as a cheap whore and paraded around in front of a room full of men. I was sold, Carver. Fucking sold," I remind him, just in case he's forgotten exactly what happened to me there. "You saw the cell. You saw the cheap lingerie, the humiliation, the fucking nightmares you held me through, and you think one clean bullet between the eyes is enough? You think that's going to make up for everything he's done? What about the four malnourished girls we just pulled out of the dog cages? What about the girls who've already been sold and are getting raped every fucking day? No, Sam needs to pay for what he's done. He needs to be punished."

Carver meets my stare, his eyes boring into mine, and without looking away or even a second of warning, his gun sounds with a loud, haunting *BANG*.

Sam crumbles to the ground and my heart shatters for the revenge that I will never get. How could he do that? How could he take that away from me?

Tears well in my eyes. Those four girls deserved so much more. I deserved more.

My hands ball into fists at my side, and the devastation quickly morphs into a cold-blooded fury. My brass knuckles tighten around my fingers, and as I imagine the feel of Carver's face under my punch, a pained groan tears through the small bunker.

My head whips around to find Sam laying in a pool of his own blood, his hands clutching his knee in agony. I suck in a breath. Carver didn't fucking kill him, just put a bullet through his knee.

I still have my chance at revenge. I can still make him pay for all the lives that he's ruined, stolen, and lost. It'll never make up for all the pain and anguish those girls and their families face every single day, but it will certainly make them feel better knowing that he will never be able to hurt another woman again. After all, once I've thoroughly made him beg for death, I'm going to finally end his life, and I'm going to do it with pleasure.

Relief powers through me, and I flick my gaze back to Carver's to find him watching me closely, watching every little emotion that filters through my eyes, but before I can utter a single word, Carver tears his stormy gaze away and glances at Cruz. "Help me get him out of here. She's fucking right. This bastard is going to regret the day he ever decided to lay a hand on our girl."

Our girl?

Fuck me. This is too many things to unload in one go. I'll have to store that one away and come back to it once we get home. For now, we have a job to do.

Cruz instantly sweeps in and together they drag Sam out of the house, kicking and screaming while leaving a thick trail of blood behind. The guys haul him down the stairs and I get a small satisfaction out of the way his body drops down each one. That's gotta hurt, and Sam's grunts of pain only make it so much sweeter.

Grayson and King don't say a damn word, just go with the flow, and by the time Carver and Cruz get Sam around the back of the Escalade, Grayson is already there, spreading a protective black plastic across the back. The boys tie his wrists and ankles with rope, and just for good measure, stick duct tape over his mouth and eyes.

They throw Sam into the back of the Escalade with a heavy thud and I quickly make my way over to the blacked-out SUV and climb in. King sits in the driver's seat and the four girls are cramped in the back. Sam's backup security will be here soon and we're not about to be caught in the crossfire when it happens.

King peels out of the driveway and the gate automatically opens for the car, saving us one more hurdle to jump through.

The Escalade pulls out behind us and just as we take off down the road, King smirks and glances up in the rearview mirror. "Watch this."

My gaze snaps up just in time to see him pull a phone out of his pocket. He presses a few buttons, and not a second later, an explosion rocks right through the street, Sam's home blowing into a million pieces before flames completely take over.

The force of the explosion rocks right through the car and has me and the girls flinching while King drives as though today is any other day. A wide smile tears across my face as I sink down into my seat and enjoy the ride home, knowing that nothing could ever get better than that.

20

My ass hits the chair as my elbows come down on the table between Grayson and King. "Where's Lord of the Douches?" I ask, glancing across at Cruz who's busily flicking through a black leather-bound book.

"Carver has some … built up frustrations that he's currently working out," Grayson tells me, a deadly sparkle hitting his eyes. He digs into his dinner and acts as though our morning didn't just consist of rescuing four girls, killing a bunch of shitty guys, getting our hands on Sam, and 'accidentally' blowing up his house of horrors.

"So, by that, I'm assuming that you mean he's using Sam as a punching bag?"

King meets my stare and winks. "You got it, babe."

A sick, twisted enjoyment shoots through me as I relax into my seat. "Have you heard anything about the girls?" I ask, speaking to all three of them and hoping that at least one has an update for me.

Cruz keeps his stare down at the book resting on the table as he responds. "One of the girls was only taken last night and her parents have already been notified and are with her in the hospital now. The blonde was from out of state and her mother is flying in tonight, but the other two are struggling a bit. Apparently one of them hasn't spoken a single word while the other is too emotional and refusing to see the doctors. They have suspicions that one of them matches the identity of a missing foster child, but they haven't been able to confirm that yet."

I let out a defeated sigh, hating just how broken they must be. I only suffered for three days, but those girls look as though they could have been there for months. "I wonder if they might talk to me," I murmur. "I mean, I'm no expert or have any fancy degrees, but there's already a relationship there. They might feel safer talking to someone they know they can trust."

"It's not a bad idea," King says.

Cruz nods, still looking over the pages of the book. "Okay, sure," he grumbles. "The doctor said that he'd give me another call in a few hours with an update. I'll let him know that you're down to help, but hopefully when he calls, he's got good news."

I nod, never agreeing more. "What are you looking at?" I ask, needing the distraction. "Did you take that from Sam's place?"

"Sure did," he says, raising his head and sliding the book across the table. "It's his ledger. It has the information of every single sale he's ever made. There are pages of names, girls and boys. Some of them as young as five years old."

My eyes bug out of my head as I spin the book around to see what's written. Both King and Grayson lean in to glance over my shoulders, each of them making a disgusted grunt. Just as Cruz said, there are names and ages along with details of where they were taken, who they were sold to, and for how much. "Holy shit," I whisper, scanning over the countless names and flipping through the pages. "He must have been doing this for years."

"Yeah," Cruz says, reaching for his fork and playing with his dinner, his appetite completely gone. "You don't even want to know what kind of shit I had to do to get that book."

I glance up, meeting his eyes. "I can only imagine," I murmur, my heart heavy and broken. "This book could put him away for the rest of his miserable life."

Grayson shakes his head. "That's not what that book is about," he explains. "Sam is going to be long gone before the law gets around to putting him on trial. They've been trying to nail him down for years and he kept slipping through their fingers. So, if we wait for a trial, we'll be waiting ages because they'll want to cross their t's and dot their i's, but like I said, Sam won't be getting a chance for a trial. Whether it's you who finishes him, Carver, or one of us, he won't be leaving this house alive. The ledger is here to help us locate the children who were taken and fuck over the bastards who purchased them."

Everything inside of my chest warms, but I find myself staring at Grayson, my eyes narrowing. "I thought Dynasty doesn't get involved in this kind of stuff?"

"They don't," he says. "Dynasty would have our fucking balls if they were to find out what we did today, but you were right. If we had sat back and done nothing when we had the ability to make a difference, then that makes us just as bad as he is."

I reach across the table and place my hand on top of his, watching as his whole body freezes. "You guys could never be as bad as he is. You're all the best guys I've ever met, even Carver."

A rare emotion flickers in Grayson's eyes and I wish that I knew him just a little bit better to be able to read what it means. "You give us way too much credit," he tells me, letting his hand fall away. "But this whole thing with Sam has got me thinking."

"Oh, yeah?"

He nods, his eyes narrowed as Cruz and King watch on in curiosity. "I've been watching you pretty fucking closely over the past few weeks, and I think I've got you worked out—at least your intentions that is."

My brows shoot straight up. "My intentions?"

"Mmhmm," he murmurs, leaning back in his chair. "I think since your birthday, and officially claiming the leadership, you've been rallying to destroy Dynasty. I think you've seen just how corrupt it is, and you've been trying to work out how to take it down, but I also think that things changed after King's father showed you just what kind of power we have. I see it in you, Elodie. It's the reason your grandfather founded Dynasty in the first place. You want to be the difference in this world. You want to recreate Dynasty as something great, just like it used to be, but you don't know how to get there."

"I—"

He shakes his head. "Don't try to deny it. *I see you, Elodie.* I get you, and I think you need to know that if that is your plan, if you want to overrun the remaining seven heads standing in your way, then I'm on your side."

My eyes widen as I sense King and Cruz sitting straight in their seats, watching Grayson closely. "Are you serious? You'll make a stand against your parents?"

Grayson nods. "If it means turning Dynasty from a power-hungry, corrupt organization to something that actively does shit like we did today, then abso-fucking-lutely. I'll follow you to the ends of the fucking earth."

My heart races as he holds my stare, his words sitting heavy in the air between us as I find it impossible to look away.

Cruz clears his throat and stretches across the table for Sam's ledger. "I, uhh … I'm going to go and study up on this, see what else I can find in here."

"Yeah," King says, also standing and making it awkward as Grayson's intense stare remains locked and loaded on mine. "I, umm … yeah. Bye."

Fuckers.

The boys fly out of the room, leaving just me and Grayson in a heated stare. I glance away, not being able to handle his intensity. I feel as though so much has already happened between us, when in reality, it's been absolutely nothing. All I know is that after we spoke in the kitchen during the disastrous BDSM eighteenth the boys threw for me, things have been different. He's somehow become my biggest protector, and the more he throws his life in front of danger for me, the more this burning need grows within me.

I bite down on my lip, not sure what the hell to say to him. He's just like Carver, so hot and cold all the time.

"Stop," he tells me.

My brows raise. "Excuse me?"

"You're overthinking this."

I can't stop the scoff that comes tearing up my throat. "How can I possibly overthink this when I don't even know what this is?"

Grayson just continues to stare, leaning back in his chair and watching me as though I'm filled with secrets that he's desperately trying to work out. When he doesn't respond, I let out a heavy sigh, more than ready to get up and walk away. I'm not here to play games. These guys already have me so worked up and in a constant state of confusion. I don't need to make it worse. "You confuse me," I tell him.

"It's simple," he says, standing and stepping into me. He leans over the table, one hand on either side of me as I stare straight ahead, his face just by my ear. "I like you, and I know that you can see that. I've liked you since the day I first saw you two years ago, way before the guys even knew where to find you."

"You've been watching me for two years?"

"Mmhmm. I was there the first time you visited the back end of a shady club and discovered that adrenaline rush of beating the shit out of someone. You were out of control and you nearly broke your hand," he says, his fingers brushing over the brass knuckles that sit over my fingers. "Where do you think this came from?"

My head snaps around and I meet his stare. "This was from you?" I ask, remembering the day that I'd 'found' them. They were shoved into my locker at my new school and I figured the previous student left them, which meant that I had every right to take them.

Grayson just nods and continues. "I've watched you so closely, that for a while, I thought I knew you better than you knew yourself, but then you came bulldozing your way in here, and you're surprising the fucking shit out of me. I don't know you at all, Elodie, but a part of me wants to, while the other … that part is still waiting for this all to blow up in our faces."

"That's why you're keeping an arm's distance from me?"

"See," he says, a cocky tone in his deep voice, "you're getting it already."

I turn in my seat and he instantly pulls back from me, so I stand and step into him, making it impossible for him to avoid me. "Don't do that," I tell him. "Stop masking your emotions with your cocky, bullshit attitude."

His eyes harden but I don't let him get away with it. "You're not scared of it blowing up in your face, you're scared of falling for me," I challenge. "You're not the only one who's watching, Grayson. I see you too. I see the way you're always the first to throw yourself in front of me, always the first to stand in front of Carver when he gets in one of his bullshit moods. You always have an excuse, but *I see you.* You want me, but you're too shit scared to grab what you want and take it even when it's standing right in front of you."

He shakes his head. "You don't know what you're talking about."

I roll my eyes. "Here we go with the excuses again. What's it going to be this time? You're only protecting me because it's the right thing to do for Dynasty? Is it the best thing for your friends who are already emotionally involved? Are you protecting me from Carver, who'll never forgive himself if he were to actually hurt me? Be fucking real with me."

"I CAN'T TAKE WHAT I FUCKING WANT," he roars, grabbing me and spinning us around until I'm backed up against the wall. "Don't you see? You're already falling for Carver and you don't even like him. You have King and Cruz hanging off a string and pining for you, so am I just supposed to be the fourth dickhead who waits in line for his turn? Fuck off, babe. This sharing thing is all fun and games for now, but you're already messing with Carver's head, and you see how fucked up he is over you. He treats you like shit because he can't work out if he fucking loves you or hates you, and you, you fucking let him do it."

I stare up at him with fury burning beneath the surface, and that same urge to hit something is building rapidly. "You know what? I fucking love it when Carver throws me up against a wall and yells at me. Sure, he's toxic as fuck, but at least I get some emotions out of him, *something real.* I read him best when he's in my face and losing control. But you, you just treat me like shit because you're pissed at yourself for not having the balls to make a fucking move."

"It's not like that."

I shove my hands into his chest and push him back. "It's exactly like that," I tell him, pushing off the wall and stepping around him, the wild flurry of emotions brimming at the surface, so close that I could break.

Why does it have to be so hard with both Grayson and Carver? They're so fucking stubborn that it drives me insane.

I walk away with my hands pulsing at my side, terrified of looking back and seeing the raw emotions in his eyes. I feel the heat of his stare on me, and I don't doubt that if I turned around right now, I would run at him with my arms wide-open and throw myself at him. But because he's a stubborn asshole just like the rest of his friends, he would push me away, no matter how much he has to hurt himself to do it.

I take a deep, calming breath and walk straight out of the room, needing to stop the second I round the corner to take a moment to figure out what the fuck just happened. I press myself up against the wall and stare at the blank one in front of me.

That fucking asshole. Who does he think he is coming at me with all that 'I got you those brass knuckles and I know you better than you know yourself' bullshit? Does he actually think I'm being a misleading whore who's going to destroy all his friends?

Screw him. King and Cruz know exactly what's going down between us and not only do they agree with it, they fucking love it just as much as I do. What is with the guys here being too fucking stubborn to just take what they want? Why do they need to make this so complicated?

The fury burns brighter, and the more I stand here, confused and torn over Grayson, the more that itch builds within me. I have to hit something. I have to work it out of my system.

I push off the wall and clench my jaw as I start storming toward the other end of the house. I don't venture down here often, but there's one room that I've been dying to get into since the second we got home.

I shove my shoulder into the door and twist the handle so violently that it opens with a bang and rebounds off the adjoining wall.

I stride through the darkened home office and grab hold of the sliding bookshelf. Pushing it out of the way, I instantly hear the sound of fists pummeling against flesh.

The sound is like a beacon drawing me in.

My shoes hit the top step, and as they do, the pummeling fists stop. Dread sinks heavily into my stomach. I know exactly what I'm going to find down here, but for some reason, I don't feel ready.

I don't think I'll ever be ready.

I hit the bottom step to find Carver standing by a long workbench with an old rag in his hand, wiping off the blood that stains his warm skin. The room is dark with a single hanging light that gently rocks from side to side, right above Sam Delacourt.

His wrists are bound and hooked over a big meat hook with his body bruised and bloodied, his eyes frantically searching for an escape, not that I can really see his eyes through all the swelling.

It's fucking creepy down here, and judging by the drainage grate built into the ground, I'd dare say this room has been used a few times before.

I swallow over the lump in my throat and raise my gaze to meet Carver's. It's the first time I've been down here, and I don't miss the way he searches my eyes, waiting to see if I'm about to freak out. But that's not going to happen. All he'll see is the crazed desperation that Grayson caused.

Carver just watches me for a long moment before nodding and reaching back. His fingers curl around the top of a baseball bat, and in a brief magical moment, he steps into me and presses the baseball bat against my chest.

I take it eagerly, and as that familiar itch burns brightly within me, I turn my ferocious stare on Sam. I grip the bat at the top, and as I stalk toward Sam, I let the tip of the bat drag against the concrete floor. The metallic sound instantly grinds against my nerves, but I stick with it, knowing that it's so much worse for Sam.

As I step in front of him, a twisted grin stretches across my face. "Time's up, motherfucker." And just like that, I rear back and let the bat fly.

It smashes into his ribs over and over again, hitting the exact same spot. I let every bit of my anger out. The frustration toward Carver, the confusion from Grayson, the fear of the dark, the faceless monsters, and the hands touching my body.

I swing the bat with everything that I've got, hitting his arm, breaking his wrist, fracturing his shin.

I do it for the girls that he's hurt, the girls that cry for their mothers every single night, the families that think their sweet little babies are gone.

My breath comes in sharp, ragged gasps, panting for oxygen, but I keep pushing myself, hitting harder and harder and not relenting, not daring to give up because every one of those names in that ledger deserves this.

Sam cries out in agony with every hit of the bat, and every time he does, I push myself harder. I hit harder. I pick up my pace. I give it my all knowing that I'll never get this chance again. Once he's gone, I'll have to live with what I've done, and if I don't make him suffer and beg for death, then I'll regret it for the rest of my life.

Minutes pass when exhaustion creeps up on me and my hands fall to my knees as the metal bat clatters to the ground. I physically can't keep going, and as I take a moment to evaluate the mess of a man that hangs before me, I know that I gave it my all.

Carver steps in behind me and I feel his body pressing against mine. I straighten myself up, sticking my back right against his solid chest. Without saying a word, his hand curls around mine, and before I know it, a gun rests comfortably between my fingers.

He raises my hand until the gun is pointed directly at Sam and only then does he allow his own hand to fall away, letting me take Sam's final punishment into my own control.

I let out a shaky breath. After everything we went through today, I still didn't get a chance to shoot a gun, so this is it. I keep one thing in my head, the one warning the boys had given me—don't fucking miss.

Keeping a strong arm, my hips squared, and my chin raised with confidence and pride, I squeeze the trigger and let the bullet fly.

21

The bullet launches straight through Sam's skull, and I watch as his body goes limp, sending him straight to hell. The only sound I hear is the sound of my pulse thumping rapidly in my ear.

My heart races but as my arm lowers and the back wall of the small concrete room is splattered with blood, I feel completely elated. Every single one of my demons are released, every monster gone, every ache and pain that resides within vanishes into thin air, and while I'll always be haunted by the life that I've lived, I'll never be scared of what can't hurt me again. Never fear the dark, shadowed corners, never need to long for Carver's arms to keep the monsters at bay, never need to fear the faceless men.

I'm finally free.

Carver steps in behind me and just as silently as he had given me the gun, he takes it away, and as he walks back to the long workbench that holds his many tools, I find myself watching him, needing my gaze to be anywhere but on Sam's dead body.

Carver takes a black rag and wipes down the gun, removing my fingerprints even though nobody will ever find this secret room down here. He places it in a drawer before turning around and meeting my stare.

He watches me for a moment, and I wonder what the hell he's seeing. Do I seem haunted? Terrified? Or can he see how my soul is finally coming back to me and that I feel like a brand-new person ready to take on the world? Ready to take on Dynasty?

I struggle to catch my breath but with his eyes on mine, I feel as though I could run a marathon. He doesn't take his stare off me, and as the seconds tick by, the tension in the dark room grows. Need shines in his eyes, filled with desire, and wonder. He doesn't judge me for what he just witnessed, doesn't frown upon me or think that I'm less of a woman. He doesn't push me away with horror. Instead, he watches me as though I'm the strongest woman he's ever met; the bravest, fiercest, most aggressively perfect woman, and it scares the shit out of me.

His chest rises and falls with quick rapid movements and the longer I stand here, not saying a word, with his dark, stormy eyes boring into mine, the more intense it becomes.

I have to have him.

Why the fuck are we fighting this attraction? I have to feel his skin on mine, feel his lips roaming over my body as his fingertips knot into my hair. I want his sweet words whispered into my hair as his tight grip curls around my waist. I need to feel his thick, veiny cock slamming up into me and taking it all away.

I need him to make me forget everything.

I have to have everything that he is, and I have to have it now.

Fuck it. I don't even care if he pushes me away.

I storm toward him, instantly throwing my hand around his neck and jumping up into his open arms. My lips crash down on his as my legs wrap around his waist. It's free falling from the highest peak and not knowing what's waiting below, but the journey down is the most exhilarating ride I'll ever take.

Carver's lips tangle with mine as we fight for dominance, just as we always do. His kisses are bruising but I welcome it, needing it harder, needing so much more.

He spins me around until my ass is dropping down onto the workbench, and the idea of knives, guns, ropes, and weapons just sitting right beside me only seems to get me hotter.

Grabbing his shirt, I tear it over his head and instantly wrap my arms back around him. My hands roam over the tight muscles of his back, exploring every inch of it as my legs tighten around his waist and draw him in until his hard cock is pressed right up against my pussy.

It screams for him as wetness floods me. There are too many

clothes between us and not enough time. I need to feel him inside of me. I need to crush this ache that I've felt for him since the second I met him.

Dante. Fucking. Carver.

Take the goddamn wheel.

I give up control and let him take whatever the fuck he needs.

Who gives a shit about the sound of blood dripping down the drain? Who cares that a dead body hangs just beside us, still with a gentle sway? Who cares that my body aches from beating the living shit out of him with a baseball bat?

All that matters is his lips on mine and his hands roaming over my body.

Carver reaches around me and grips the material of my cropped tank before peeling it over my head. It's instantly thrown away, and as one hand comes down on my bare skin, the other unhooks my bra with a simple flick of his wrist.

My bra falls between us and he pushes in even closer, needing the feel of my skin right up against his, just as desperately as I need it. "Fuck, Carver," I groan, panting heavily. "Touch me."

He complies all too easily, and within seconds, his hand is at my waist, slipping inside my jeans. He finds my center and with a quick, hard thrust, pushes two thick fingers straight inside my dripping core.

I groan deep, his lips falling to the sensitive skin of my neck as his fingers work my pussy like magic. He winds me up so easily and it's as if he knows my body better than I do. "Winter," he breathes my name so softly, his breath skimming across my ear and making everything inside of me clench.

His fingers slide in and out of me, curling at just the right spot as my pussy drenches his hand with my excitement. I grind against him, needing more, but if I push it too hard, I'll be coming within seconds.

Carver works my body as though he was fucking made for it. His fingers pinch my pebbled nipples while his tongue roams over the soft, sensitive skin below my ear, answering every silent prayer I send his way.

There's no other way to put it. It's simple. Dante Carver is a fucking god and I'm the luckiest girl who ever lived.

A soft moan slips from between my lips, and as if calling for him, as if he can't possibly get enough, his lips come right back to mine.

My body burns, my release building higher and higher. "Come on, Winter," he urges me in a deep, guttural groan, his voice speaking to the darkest places within me and filled with a demanding authority. "I want your tight little pussy to come on my fingers. Give me what I need."

His thumb flicks over my clit and sends an electric shock shooting right through me as he pinches my nipples. A loud gasp pulls from deep within me, and as he slams his fingers back inside and massages my walls, my body falls apart beneath him.

My orgasm tears through me, so much wilder, hotter, and louder than the explosion at Sam's house. "FUCK, CARVER," I cry, the desperation coming through loud and clear in my voice.

Carver doesn't let up, he keeps moving his fingers, keeps flicking my clit, and massaging my walls as my pussy clenches around his thick fingers, convulsing with wild, erratic movements.

When I finally come down from my high, Carver's fingers slip out of me and I instantly miss his touch. His head tilts forward, his forehead leaning against mine for just a moment. Satisfaction pulses through me but I get the exact same vibe from him, and if I didn't know any better, I'd wonder if he was the one who just came within an inch of his life.

I reach for him, curling my legs around his waist and drawing him back into me, so ready for what else he has in store, but he pulls back. His gaze sweeps away and in an instant he pulls his shirt back over his head and shoves my bra and tank into my hand. "Go," he tells me.

I just stare, the confusion pulsing through me. "What do you mean?" I question, unable to take my eyes off him as he distracts himself with the shit on the table. "We were doing something here. I wasn't nearly done."

"Yeah, you were," he tells me. "You asked me to touch you. I did, and now we're done."

I just stare a little longer, watching as he takes a blade and walks across to Sam's hanging body. The blade slices through the binds with ease and Sam drops to the ground with a heavy thud, the blood beneath him splattering across the room.

How could he be so dismissive?

'You asked me to touch you. I did, and now we're done.'

He said it as though I held the same gun that I'd just killed Sam with up against his head. He acted as though it didn't mean a thing, that he was just crossing off another thing on his 'to do' list.

Screw him. That meant something. It was raw and filled with passion and desire. That wasn't just some random finger-fucking to pass the goddamn time. It was a huge fucking step that I thought we were taking in the right direction. I thought maybe we'd finally jumped over a hurdle and came down the other side.

Apparently, I read the situation wrong. Again.

I jump off the table and my hand instantly curls into a fist, my brass knuckles tightening on my fingers. If I wasn't so exhausted after beating the shit out of Sam, I'd force Carver up against a wall and refuse to leave until I had every little answer I needed. But instead, I just stare.

"What are you still doing here?" he asks, looking back at me. "Would you prefer to stay and deal with this mess?"

A breathy scoff comes flying from between my lips as I just watch him, unable to believe what the hell is happening. He turns his back and focuses his attention on the body, but I'm not quite done with him.

I walk right up behind him and grab his wrist so fast, tugging it hard and leaving him absolutely no choice but to spin around or risk dislocating his shoulder. I narrow my gaze on his and raise my chin, wanting to hate him so badly. "The second that bullet went through his skull, I felt fucking free. My monsters were gone, and

I knew that I could finally put it behind me. He was never going to hurt me again, never going to haunt my dreams, and I had no reason to fear him anymore. But you … fuck, Carver. You are the one that I should be watching my back around. I gave you a fucking shot and then you dismiss me as though it meant nothing. You are the one I should be terrified of. You are the one who's going to destroy me, and from now on," I step right into him, holding his dark, stormy gaze hostage, "I'm done playing your game."

Without a backward glance, I turn and walk out of the shitty little torture chamber, leaving my feelings for Carver behind and hoping that they die right along with Sam.

22

My fist raps against the door as I nervously glare across at Ember beside me. "Do you have any idea how badly this is going to do down?"

She shakes her head. "I don't care. You're eighteen. You don't need their permission to do anything," she tells me, her lips pulling up in distaste. "Besides, what's it matter to them what you do? They're not your brothers, and as far as I'm aware, you're not dating any of them, so they don't have the right to say shit. They should consider themselves lucky that you're even standing here and letting them know what you're doing. If it were me, I'd already be at the freaking party with six shots of tequila making their way through my system and about ready to start making some fucked up decisions."

"Dude," I laugh. "Are you even allowed to drink? Didn't you only just get over your concussion?"

"Dude," she mimics, making the word seem so much less cool than what I thought it sounded. "The doctor didn't technically tell me that I couldn't drink, so—"

The door opens, cutting her off as Cruz stands before us, his brows furrowed in confusion. "Why are you knocking?" he questions, quickly glancing at Ember before trailing his eyes down our bodies and shaking his head. "No. No fucking way. You're not going out."

Ember scoffs but I jump in before she says something that's only going to make it worse. "For the record, I want it known that I came here to politely let you know what's going down tonight. I'm not here asking permission. I'm doing you assholes a kindness and telling you that Ember and I are going out tonight so that when you inevitably make yourselves welcome into my home and find me gone, you don't go all caveman on me."

Cruz just laughs before his face goes deadly serious. "No."

I turn on my heel, hooking my arm through Ember's. "Well, it was nice seeing you. I'll catch you in the morning."

We start making our way down the stairs and Cruz quickly races out after us. "No. Fuck. Winter, stop moving that fine as fuck ass down the goddamn stairs and get back here. You can't go out or have you forgotten that—"

He cuts himself off, almost slipping up in front of Ember about the fact that I have a whole bunch of crazy old men waiting to watch my head roll.

Ember pauses on the step and turns to glare at Cruz. "And why the hell not?" she questions, crossing her arms over her chest. "She's eighteen years old, and so far, I haven't heard any good excuses as to why you think you have the right to tell her what she can and cannot do."

Cruz just stares at her, not appreciating her bullshit just as much as she disapproves of his, then without taking his gaze off her, he leans back in toward the door and calls out. "GUYS, WINTER THINKS SHE'S ABOUT TO GO OUT TO A FUCKING PARTY."

"Get fucked," I murmur under my breath before turning to Ember and grabbing her hand. "Quick, we have to go."

We start making our way down the stairs, going much slower than I'd hoped with Ember in heels. I need to teach this bitch how to run in these things. But within the space of two seconds, Grayson and King are standing in the doorway with the ever-so-pissed-off-and-broody asshat coming in behind them.

"Don't even fucking think about it," King says. "If you want to party so bad, you two can drink Carver's whole liquor cabinet dry here. Get fucking wasted, party and have a fucking fuck-fest on the couch if you want to, but you're not going out."

My jaw clenches. I knew coming and telling them the plan was a bad idea, but had they walked into my place to find me gone, they would have raised hell trying to find me. That's an outcome nobody wants.

I spin around and glare up at the guys who all have eyes on me, the same message hidden within each of their dark stares. "Like I said to Cruz, I'm not here asking permission, and I'm not about to sit back and accept your cavemen bullshit. I just wanted to let you know where I'd be in case of an emergency. So, have a good night, except for you Carver," I say with a sickly-sweet smile that makes his eyes narrow further. "I hope you accidentally trip and fall on a whole new personality, but if you don't, I have a glow-in-the-dark dildo in my bedside drawer that's bound to put a smile on anyone's face. Highly recommended. Ten out of ten."

I turn and start walking again and as though not one of them can hear a word I'm saying, both Grayson and King are down the stairs and carrying my ass back up. "Are you insane?" King murmurs in my ear, keeping his voice low. "You've been attacked twice already. You're not even close to being in the clear. Like hell we're going to risk you going out to some shady club. You'll either end up dead, or worse, trying to fight twelve guys at once. At some point, you're going to have to let that chip on your shoulder go and remember that you're not a fucking superhero, you're human, and humans bleed."

I pull myself out of their arms and glare heavily at King. "If I want to be a fucking superhero, then I'll be a fucking superhero, and for the record, I know I fucking bleed. Carver made sure to remind me of that, and I damn well know that I'm only human, which is why I want to go out in the first place. If I have people after me and there's a risk that my life is going to be cut short, then I want to be able to say that I enjoyed it."

"Babe," Cruz says with a regretful sigh. "I know you want to go out, and I'd do just about anything to make sure that you could, but it's too dangerous. Don't you remember just how easily that bastard got to you last weekend?"

"Do you honestly think that I could forget that? Or have you forgotten that I was the one being held under the water?" I question. "Here's the thing. I'm going out tonight whether you guys like it or not. I've had a beyond fucked up week, and I need to forget that the real world exists for just one night. I'm going to go and have fun, I'm going to drink and maybe get a little fucked up, but what I'm not going to do is spend another night pissed off or planning how I'm going to kill someone. So please, if you really have such a big issue with it, then come. We're not going to a seedy club, it's a house party ten minutes from here. I'm safe."

Carver just scoffs, his stare hitting mine like an electric shock. "If she wants to go, then let her go. She's a big girl, I'm sure she's got it all under control."

Asshole.

The guys gape at him as though they can't believe what the hell just came out of his mouth, and if I didn't realize that he was just being a dick, I probably would have been surprised too. Nonetheless, I give the guys a sweet smile and turn on my heel, meeting Ember halfway down the steps just seconds before I hear Carver's familiar grunt as a fist slams into his gut.

Within the space of fifteen minutes, Ember and I go from walking down the stairs to dancing on a makeshift dance floor. I'm honestly not surprised to find four stares piercing into me from all over the room.

I knew they'd come. They can't possibly resist a chance to play the role of overprotective alpha assholes, though secretly—and I'd never admit this to them—I kinda like it. It gets me hot watching the way they like to dominate me—at least they try. They very rarely succeed, and when they do, it's not done without a fight.

I try to ignore them but it's a lot easier said than done. Everywhere I turn, everywhere I look, they're always there, so instead of getting frustrated and annoyed, I play the game.

We're surrounded by people from school and I'm more than aware that the four boys of Dynasty are not the only ones looking my way, but they're sure as hell the only ones I'm interested in playing with.

I take hold of Ember and turn so my back is pinned right up against her chest, and just as I knew she would, her arm curls around my waist and our bodies move together. I find King straight ahead, his eyes heated and filled with desire. It's been a few days since he's fucked me until I screamed. I wonder if he and Cruz will be down to play tonight?

I quickly scan the room and just like that, I find Cruz, his stare on my body, watching the way it moves against Ember's as we both bring out our inner vixen and put on a show of a lifetime. I mean, if they're going to drool like this, then they might as well start throwing some dollar bills our way, let us know just how badly they appreciate us.

I spin in Ember's arms and find Grayson across the room, standing by the bar with a scowl torn across his face, but what's new? As I meet his heavy stare, a smirk kicks up the side of my lips and I tease and taunt him, knowing just how badly he wants me. The ball is in his court now, and after what happened earlier in the week, he's really going to have to step up his game.

Only one asshat left.

My gaze snaps across the room to find Carver standing in a darkened corner, and while dark corners would usually send shivers shooting down my spine, that irrational fear is now gone. Carver watches me just like the other guys do, but while hunger pulses in their eyes, there's nothing but heated anger bubbling beneath the surface.

As my eyes meet his, I'm instantly thrown back into that small concrete holding room with his fingers deep inside my pussy and his lips pressing against mine. It was explosive, exhilarating. How could he just deny that? How can he say that there isn't something between us? He's fooling himself.

I know how he feels. He wants me, maybe even more than the others combined, but after pushing me away so many times, I won't be stupid enough to put myself out there for him again.

Carver hurt me and hurt doesn't go unpunished.

I keep my body moving, tilting my head back and showing off the long column of my neck, both King and Carver's weakness, and while the stares from the other corners of the room fill with even more desire, Carver's just gets harder.

I roll my tongue over my lips to keep the smile from cracking across my face. If I were to break, the moment would dissolve between us all. That might make me a tease or a whore, but I fucking love their attention on me. Nothing gets me hotter.

I keep my stare on Carver's, my gaze heating more by the second and everything deep inside of me clenches, desperately needing him to finish what he started in that bloodied little room. Don't get me wrong, King and Cruz both helped ease the growing ache that's starved me all week, but it won't be the same, not unless it's Carver's body I'm feeling against mine.

A bottle blonde cuts in front of Carver and my jaw clenches, watching as his hand snakes out and takes her waist.

Fucking Sara Benson. It's like no matter what I do, she's always there, lurking in the background. Seeing that she has just a fraction of Carver's attention, she eats it up, and puts on the world's biggest show.

His hand curls further around her waist, and suddenly, this game isn't so fun anymore.

Carver pulls her in tight and her body presses against his, right where I desperately wish mine could be. His eyes don't leave mine and I know it's just a game to him. I was playing him, and now he's throwing it right back in my face, but he should know me better than that. I don't concede that easily.

If it's a war of messy emotions that he wants, then I'm all in, and damn it, I'm going to push until I have sweet, sweet victory.

I feel the other guys' hard stares narrowing, knowing this could get messy, but not one of them makes a move, letting it play out exactly how Carver intends. There's only so many times Carver will allow the boys to stand in his way, and I have a feeling that quota has already been filled a million times over.

Sara raises her chin to Carver, silently asking him to kiss her, and as he drops his head, something dies inside of me, but he bypasses her lips and drops straight to the curve of her neck. Her head instantly tilts the opposite way, opening up for more.

Even from across the room I can see the pleasure pulsing through her. She thinks he's taking her home tonight, and right now, I don't know how far he's going to take it.

His eyes are like deep, dark vortexes drawing me in, but I hold my ground. Dante Carver will not be getting the best of me tonight.

As if sensing the hurt pulsing through my chest, a cocky as fuck grin pulls up the corners of his lips, and just to add insult to injury, his hand falls to her thigh and slowly trails across her skin.

Nope. Fuck that.

If Carver wants this to get messy, then that's exactly what's going to happen.

I keep my eyes glued to his, watching as his lips move against her neck and she moans his name.

His eyes harden as he watches me approach, but he doesn't relent, doesn't pull away even to tell me to fuck off.

I step in right behind Sara, and as my tits press up against her back, her head turns and she narrows her eyes at me. "Fuck off, bitch. He doesn't want you."

I roll my tongue over my lips and watch as her gaze drops. I bring my hand up and gently brush my fingertips down her makeup filled cheek. "Maybe I want you," I murmur, watching her eyes widen in confusion.

I slip my other hand around her bare waist, feeling as she sucks in a breath, her skin on one side and Carver's solid abs on the other. Carver raises his head, watching me closely and keeping my eyes on him, I play him at his own game and drop my lips to the sensitive curve of her neck.

A breathy groan slips from between her lips and the way her back straightens for just the slightest moment tells me that she's surprised she likes my touch, but when she relaxes into it, I keep going, feeling Carver's stare harden while the guys behind me watch with an intense interest. I can almost hear the thoughts shooting through Cruz and King's minds, planning exactly what's on the agenda for tonight.

Sara's hand slips up the front of Carver's shirt, desperately trying to pull his attention away from me, but she has no chance in hell. She's just a pawn in a much bigger game, one she doesn't even know she's playing.

My hand curls around the front of Sara's neck and I gently squeeze, watching the way she reacts to my touch and I have to admit, I'm a little surprised how much she likes it. My lips keep working her neck and I slowly draw my hand higher until my fingers are curled around her chin.

I force her face to mine and with Carver's eyes on me, and the stares of the whole school, I drop my lips to hers.

Sara kisses me back and a strange awkwardness pulses through me. I'm not going to pretend she's not hot, but I seriously have absolutely no desire to kiss her. She's a good kisser though, so I guess that's a bonus.

My hand falls over Carver's hand on her thigh and my fingers instantly slip between his. Go hard or go home, right?

I slowly draw our hands up her thigh, sliding them under her short skirt and across the front of her leg, getting higher and higher with each passing second. She moans into my mouth and I take a silent moment to thank whoever lives above that she's been sipping on strawberry cruisers all night.

My eyes flash to Carver's, and fuck me, I've never seen them so dark. Even if this wasn't a game and the only way I could truly have Carver is to have Sara too, I'd fucking take it, and I think he sees that determination pulsing in my eyes.

Our hands continue to move, inch by inch toward her pussy, the challenge sitting heavily between us. He can obviously see that I'm willing to go as far as it takes, but will he? Does he have what it takes to truly touch another girl or is he going to concede and admit that this was all a ploy to get under my skin?

He knows I'm trying to call his bluff, but fuck it, he's just as stubborn as I am, if not more. Sara might just get fucked tonight if neither of us is willing to back down, but her neediness tells me that's exactly what she's hoping for, even if she does hate me.

I'm not going to lie; the whole thing is hot and makes me yearn for a threesome with Carver. I can only imagine how good it'd be with him taking control and not being a little bitch-ass pussy. He would dominate me, and it'd be the hottest thing I've ever experienced.

God, all four of the guys with just me. Now that's a dream come true.

Can I handle it though? I don't know, but I'm willing to give it a try.

Carver sees the hunger in my eyes, and I see the moment he realizes that I'll take this all the way. Just as our hands reach her pussy, I squeeze down, cupping it tightly. Sara grinds down against Carver's hand with a needy groan, and even with his hand between us, I can feel the heat coming off her pussy.

Regret flashes in his eyes.

Checkmate, motherfucker.

He tears his hand away, his eyes filled with anger as he's the first to break and back down, not having what it takes to go through with it. Sara pulls her lips away from mine, her gaze snapping back to Carver in confusion as he pushes us both back a step.

With his little game over, I tear myself away from Sara, leaving her high and dry and more confused than ever before with my plum lipstick smeared across her lips. Meeting Carver's stare over Sara's shoulder, I make a show of wiping my lips as a smug grin tears across my face. Without a word, I turn and walk away, silently reminding him that when he plays with fire, he's going to get burned, but when he plays with me, I'll get even.

As for the hurt that still sits heavily in my chest, pulsing with determination and threatening to take over my night, I can deal with that later. Because right now, I have a scratch that needs to be more than itched.

I walk back to the dance floor and I find King and Cruz, their eyes blazing with a fiery need from their positions against the wall. My body is on edge and desperate to be touched, and as if reading my mind, they both weave their way through the crowded bodies and head for the back door, more than ready to give me exactly what I need.

23

Cruz's hand slips around mine the second we step into the shadows behind the property. King steps in behind me as the desperation from calling Carver's bluff tears through my body. I don't know how it happened but I'm so fucking hot. I need to be touched, need to be fucked hard and I don't care who sees it.

Maybe I'm bisexual because *damn.* I was not expecting my body to be so worked up, but I would have taken that all the way had he not backed down and shown his cards. Hmm, I wonder how the guys would feel if I was to introduce another girl to the mix?

But who? I bet Ember would be down, but the thought of getting naked with her just seems weird. She's like a sister to me and I couldn't possibly cross that line with her. Though, adding another girl to the mix would mean having to share the guys with her, and honestly, call me a selfish bitch, but I'm not down to share them like that. The second they touch her, all I'll be able to see is red.

The boys and I made a deal when we first got together. We'd be exclusive to each other and they promised not to be with other girls, but then, how is that fair? I kissed another girl right in front of their eyes and put on a fucking show. I paraded it in front of the people at the party all to get at Carver.

My eyes bug out of my head just as King's hands slip around my waist and start pulling at my clothes. "I kissed Sara," I gasp, looking up at Cruz with wide, horrified eyes.

Cruz grins back at me. "You sure fucking did, babe."

I shake my head, the panic sitting heavily on my chest. "No. I told you guys that you couldn't be with other girls and there I was, about ready to finger fuck her just to piss off Carver. I'm horrible. I didn't even stop to think."

"Stop thinking now then," King tells me, his lips dropping to my neck and making my body come alive all over again. "I'm not going to lie, it was a fucking surprise to see you kissing her, and I can't speak for Cruz, but it was the hottest thing I've ever seen. Fuck, babe. If you want to go back there and fuck her, just say the word and I'll happily sit in the corner and watch."

I turn to face him, forcing his lips up off my neck as he meets my stare. "You're not mad?"

"Not even in the slightest," he tells me. "But if it was some random dude and your intentions were solely to get at me, then yeah, I'd have a fucking problem with it. What can I say? I've gotten used to this open relationship bullshit and seeing you come alive under someone else's touch is just as good as being the one who gets to do it."

I raise my brow and turn to meet Cruz's stare, knowing that he's the sensitive one out of the two of them. "And you?"

Cruz leans in and brushes his lips over mine. "All I ask is that if you feel like fucking another chick, that I get to fuck you straight after, so you know exactly what you were missing out on," he says, grinding his hard cock against me. "But don't act like after this, we're not going to talk about what the fuck is going on with you and Carver. Something happened and I want to know what."

A grin tears across my face as relief settles into me. I knew the Carver talk was bound to happen sooner or later, and I don't doubt that talk is going to extend to answering questions about me and Grayson too. "You're seriously both okay with it? It just kinda happened. I had no intention of kissing another girl tonight, but for the record, I don't have any desire to go and randomly fuck some chick. You guys keep me more than satisfied. I'd totally get it if you felt like you deserved one free night to do whatever you wanted—it would drive me in-fucking-sane, but I'd understand it."

King's hand curls around me, instantly sliding down my body and cupping my aching pussy. "We do keep you more than satisfied, and don't you forget it," he tells me. "But for what it's worth, your tight little pussy and sweet ass are the only things I want."

I grind down against him, my body burning with need. "Good,"

I groan.

Cruz steps in closer, his fingers roaming over my skin and making me burn with need. "If you're getting so fucking hot by touching Sara Benson, then that just tells me that we're not fucking you hard enough."

My brow raises. "I didn't think it was possible to fuck me any harder."

The guys meet each other's hungry stares above my head, and I watch the twisted grin stretching across Cruz's face. A far too cocky laugh bubbles out of him and the sound pulses right through me, making everything inside of me ache.

"Are you ready?" he demands, his eyes darkening as I see a whole new side of Cruz Danforth. He pushes me harder against King, and in response, King's hand curls around the base of my neck where I wear my thin black choker, just as I'd done to Sara not five minutes ago.

Desperation tears through me as I realize exactly what I'm getting myself into.

This is going to be hard, fast, and fucking wild.

I can't wait.

Cruz grips my waist, his fingers digging into my skin, and I know without a doubt I'll be left with bruises, but I'm so here for it.

My chest rises and falls with rapid, intense movements, but when the sound of a branch breaking in the bushes around us tears through the silence, King's hand moves up to cover my mouth, knowing damn well that a deep, needy groan is only moments from slipping out.

Cruz's eyes sparkle, the idea of getting caught so damn thrilling, but neither of them stop and it kills me to not moan their names.

King's lips move against my neck as his hand slips into the front of my pants, making my eyes roll, and when King moves his hand from my mouth, it's instantly replaced by Cruz's lips.

"She's here," the person in the bushes says, making my back straighten.

King's hands stop working my pussy as Cruz pulls back and meets King's stare over my head, something dark flashing in their eyes.

There's something familiar about that voice. But what? Why do I know it?

No response comes and I realize the guy must be on the phone.

"They're here with her, so you need to make it good, and fast. Get her alone and fucking take her out."

I suck in a gasp and King's hand instantly comes back to my mouth.

Jacob Scardoni.

Fuck.

Meeting Cruz's stare in front of me, I realize that they're more than aware of what I've just figured out, and fuck me, they're pissed.

A silent conversation passes between them, and with a sharp nod from Cruz, the two of them take off like lightning.

I race after them, struggling to keep up with their long strides, but refusing to be left in the bushes alone, especially after that shady conversation we overheard. I'm not about to suffer through another attack, but at least now we know who the fuck was behind the first ambush in the woods.

Fucking Jacob Scardoni.

It was always him. I fucking knew it. He's been using Ember to get close to me, and I have no doubt it's his bastard father he's making arrangements with.

They're both going down.

Fury rages through me as my feet pound against the earth. I move faster than I've ever moved, ducking and weaving past branches and desperately trying to keep up with King and Cruz.

I hear a panicked "fuck," rumbling through the trees as I see King and Cruz's backs flashing through my sight, but like lightning, they're gone in mere moments.

I feel like I'm running blind, not knowing what sounds I'm following. I'm an idiot for thinking I'd be able to keep up with them. I come to an abrupt stop, looking all around for a sign of the boys, but nothing. I don't know where they fucking went and I'm lost as shit in these bushes.

Jacob trained right alongside the boys. He can do everything they can, and in these bushes, alone, now that his cards are laid out for the world to see, I don't doubt that he's going to try and kill me.

Unease filters through me as I search the shadows, fearing who could be watching me. As soon as the thought crosses my mind, my body is shoved hard and I go sprawling to the ground.

I whip myself over and instantly scramble away as I find Jacob hovering over me, slowly stalking toward me with his intentions as clear as day. "They're going to kill you," I state, trying to keep the fear out of my tone but failing. If they trained together, then Jacob has the ability to kill me with his bare hands and he won't hesitate, not now.

"Oh, I know," he tells me. "I won't walk out of here tonight, but as long as I'm a dead man, I might as well make it worth my while. There's nothing stopping me now from taking matters into my own hands."

Fuck.

My heels dig into the soil, pushing me back, but not fast enough.

I'd give anything to get to my feet. At least I'd have a small fighting chance, but like this, I'm as good as dead.

"You're a piece of shit," I growl, pushing myself further and further away until my back is pressed up against a tree. "Ember fucking trusted you."

He continues stalking me and my heart races. Where the fuck are the boys? I've always said that I don't need them coming to my rescue—but fuck that. I need them now more than ever.

"Ember was a means to an end, and an annoying one at that," he spits. "She's been a fucking leech for the past two years, hanging off me and reeking of desperation. I'll be glad to get rid of her. That bitch won't stop talking. The only good thing is that she's down to fuck and practically obsessed with you. She's the reason I always know where you're going to be."

"She deserved so much better than that," I growl, hating how heartbroken she's going to be when she learns what a low-life piece of shit he is. After finishing me off, he'll vanish from her life and leave her devastated, but even more, she'll be confused as fuck wondering what the hell she did wrong.

I fucking hate him. I knew he was a bad apple the second I saw him in the council chambers, standing way too proudly behind his despicable father. I'm just glad that once this is over, the boys won't let him get away with it. They'll end him, and when they do, they'll make it unforgettable.

Jacob steps right up in front of me and bends down to grip my arms. I'm yanked up off the dirty ground, and just as his fingers tighten on my arms and his nails dig into my skin, a hard body comes flying through the bushes and crashes into him with a devastating blow.

Their bodies collide so fast that it's not until they've come to a complete stop that I recognize Carver's large body crushing Jacob's into the ground. A pained groan tears from deep within Jacob, and within seconds, Grayson appears at my right and moves in close while Cruz and King come from the left.

"What the fuck is going on here?" Grayson demands, making me realize that when Carver took down Jacob, it was done purely because he was standing way too close to me.

King's sharp glare cuts toward Jacob as Carver gets off him, pulling the asshole up with him. "We just overheard the dickhead putting a hit on Winter," he spits. "The fucker is responsible for the attack in the woods."

Carver's hold on Jacob tightens, and with one quick flick of his wrist, he pushes Jacob forward and sends him falling to his knees as the guys and I form a circle around him, keeping him trapped with no way out.

I step in closer, putting myself right in front of him as Carver grips his chin and forces his deadly stare up to mine. Not one of the guys move, allowing me to take control of how this is going to go down. "Nowhere to run," I taunt, loving how the tables have turned.

"Fuck you," he spits, knowing damn well that he's not going to make it out of this alive. "Kill me."

"Careful what you wish for," Carver grunts, pulling uncomfortably harder on his chin and forcing him to try and pull free.

Jacob's hard glare comes shooting back to mine. "You're fucked, Elodie. Whether it was me who killed you tonight, or someone else tomorrow, your clock is ticking. It's only a matter of time before these assholes turn their back and you get a bullet right through your pretty little head."

Cruz scoffs, clearly not on board with the idea of them ever turning their backs, but Jacob uses it to try and get in my head. "How long do you think these dickheads are going to have your back? Soon enough, saving your ass is going to get old, and where will you be when that happens? Better yet, how many times are you going to put their lives at risk just to save your own? You're a selfish bitch if you ask me. You'd have to have a magical fucking pussy to get me to throw myself in front of a bullet for you."

His words dig deep, but I don't let it show. I know it's all talk. He's trying to get in my head and it's fucking working, but it's a whole lot of bullshit that I'm going to have to unload later. It does nothing to save his life. He'll still be dying tonight, and I'll still be walking away with one less threat against me.

We could stand here all night and interrogate him. There are so many unanswered questions. Who's he working with? Who was on the other end of that call? Who was the female standing outside Carver's house setting up the last hit on me? There are all these questions that we've been desperately trying to work out, and I bet between the guys, they have all sorts of tricks for extracting information. But then, Jacob has probably been trained to sit back and take it. We'd just be wasting our time.

These questions aren't getting answered tonight, and even with Jacob out of the picture, I'm just as fucked as I was before.

Wanting to get this over and done with, I raise my blank stare up to meet Carver's, and as his eyes come to mine, all the bullshit between us falls away for a moment. "Do it," I tell him.

And just like that, Carver nods and adjusts his grip on Jacob's head before violently twisting and snapping his neck.

His lifeless body crumbles to the ground, and not wanting to hang around for some bullshit shallow grave burial, I turn and walk back toward the party.

24

I slam the shot glass down and it clatters against the bar as I look up at the guy standing behind it and demand a refill.

Tonight fucking sucks. It was supposed to be a night where I got to dance with Ember and forget the shitty world around me. I was having fun playing with the guys and even after screwing with Carver's head, I didn't think it could get any better. I'm just glad that we caught Jacob before the night could have taken a turn for the worst.

My shot glass is filled and before the guy can even pull his hand away, my fingers are curling around the cool glass and raising it to my mouth. I throw it back and revel in the burn that flows down my throat. "Woah," a familiar voice says, stepping in beside me. "Why didn't you come get me? If I knew we were doing shots, I would have come to play, but now I have to play catch-up instead."

I can't help but smile at Ember. I can always trust her to be down with whatever fucked up situation I throw her way. "Don't even think about it," I tell her. "After what you've already drunk, if you started playing catch-up, you're going to end up spending the night in the hospital getting your stomach pumped."

Ember laughs, grabbing my used shot glass and pushing it toward the bartender. "Hit me," she says to the guy before looking back at me. "Girl, you have to give me more credit. If anyone around here can handle their liquor, it's me."

"Okay," I tell her as a cocky grin stretches across my face. "But I think I'm up to my fifth or sixth shot."

Her eyes bug out of her head. "Six? Fuck. Umm … okay," she says as a nervous confidence settles over her. "I've got this. It's just a temporary setback. Six. Cool, okay. Let's go, just promise you'll hold my hair back later because I'll be pissed if you let me get chunks all through it. Do you have any idea what it just cost me to get it colored?"

I laugh and watch as she takes her shot, knowing exactly how much she paid to have her hair done and still reeling from it. I don't understand how it could possibly cost so much, though don't get me wrong, it looks incredible and has a liveliness to it that I could never even dream about recreating for my own. I'd love to experience the whole fancy salon thing just once, but for me, it's been cheap box dye from the store since I was fourteen and decided that darker was better. I was a golden blonde before that, and I've never looked back.

Once the shot glass hits the bar and she slides it back toward the guy, I quickly reach out and grab it. "I'm just screwing with you," I tell her. "I only had two."

Ember's eyes narrow in suspicion and it's clear as day that she doesn't believe me. "You're lying."

I shrug my shoulder. "Maybe," I grin. "But let's not pretend that you haven't been drinking since the second I went outside."

Ember laughs to herself, knowing damn well that I'm right. "Speaking of what you've been up to tonight," she starts, making my heart kick into gear. "What the fuck was going down with you, Sara, and Carver?"

My eyes bug out of my head. "You saw that?"

"The whole fucking room saw it. I'm not going to lie, I'm kinda jealous. It was hot as fuck. I'd be the filling in that sandwich any day, but whatever is going on between you and Carver, you've got issues."

"Tell me about it," I grumble under my breath.

Ember scans the room, knowing all too well that while my response was filled with hidden meanings and untold stories, that there's no point in asking. "Did you happen to see Jacob on your travels?" she asks, making my brow arch as nerves pulse through my veins. "I just texted him like twenty minutes ago and he said that he was just pulling up."

"I, umm …" I shrug my shoulder feeling like the world's worst friend as I spy King across the room and realize that he was the one sent to watch over me. I should tell her the truth and spare her as much heartache as possible, but how am I supposed to admit that the guys and I caught her boyfriend out in the bushes organizing a hit on me? Am I supposed to just come out and tell her we snapped his neck and buried him in a shallow grave? Well, partially buried him at least, I'm not sure how fast the guys work. "I haven't. Maybe he found some friends and just got caught up."

She nods, her gaze sweeping across the room once again and catching the way King watches us. "I'm going to go and check out back. I'd ask you to come but King looks like he's about ready to tear you a new asshole."

I scoff. "Unfortunately, that's just his face."

Ember laughs and gives me a stupid grin before falling away into the crowded bodies and leaving me standing behind, completely riddled with guilt. We killed her boyfriend. He was a complete asshole, but to her, he was everything. She's never going to forgive me, but then, she's never going to find out. She'll just be left wondering why she wasn't enough for him to stick around and that's on me.

Fuck. I'm such an awful friend.

Something in King's expression softens and he pushes off the wall and makes his way toward me, but I discreetly shake my head, wanting to suffer alone. He instantly stops and gently nods his head, but the deepness in his eyes tells me that he's ready to throw his arms around me and hold me for as long as I need.

Not being able to handle it, I push away from the bar and make my way through the party, and before I know it, I find myself at the front door, walking straight out of it. I mindlessly walk down the center of the quiet road, the night wrapping around me as the subtle glow from the street lamps light my way.

I don't stop until I come to a familiar pier, a place that has somehow become so much more than just somewhere I once partied. I walk down, right to the sand below and drop my ass into it as I watch the calm waves crash on the shore.

I hear people down the beach partying by a bonfire while I'm pretty sure a couple to my right are getting more than just a little freaky, and judging by the sound of it, it might just be an exorcism.

I hear someone coming in behind me and I don't even bother looking back. "How'd you know where to find me?"

King laughs as he drops down beside me, putting his arm around my shoulders and pulling me into his side. "Do you want the stalker answer or the I'm a fucking impressive boyfriend kind of answer?"

"Hit me with both," I tell him, keeping my eyes on the crashing water in front as I sink deeper into his hold, needing his touch so much more than I realized.

"Well, apart from the fact I followed you from the party, this is the place where you go when you feel lost and when your world is about to explode around you."

Warmth swirls through my chest. "I didn't realize you were paying such close attention," I tell him, raising my chin and gently brushing a kiss over his jaw. "But I should have known you'd follow me. Your stalking knows no bounds."

King scoffs. "Of course I followed you. Jacob just put a hit out on you, and even though he's gone now, no one else knows that. There's still some dickhead on his way to that party, ready to put a bullet between your eyes, so I wasn't exactly going to stop you from leaving. Though, I'm pissed you thought it was a good idea just to walk out on your own."

My eyes widen. "I … I didn't even consider that. I just wanted out of there. Ember … she was asking me if I'd seen Jacob and I just … I crumbled. I didn't know how to respond. She left to go find him, but she's not going to, and I hate that I lied to her, even if it's for her own good. She thought she was crazy in love with him and now she's going to be left wondering what she did wrong to make him leave. I'm an awful person, King. How could someone do that to a friend?"

"You're not awful, Winter. You're a survivor in a fucked up world and you've been facing the impossible every single day. No one blames you, and Ember is sure as fuck not going to hate you. You did the right thing."

"But—"

"No. What would have happened if she had overheard him making that hit? Or what would have happened a few months down the track if she accidentally found out something she shouldn't have? He would have killed her without a second thought. You made the right call, and even if you hadn't, Carver still would have snapped his neck."

I let out a sigh, knowing he's right. He wasn't good for her and it would have ended in tragedy.

I try to hold onto that tiny snippet of closure and let out a deep sigh. "You know," I say, adjusting myself to better look up into his eyes. "Even though I have you four guys and Ember, I don't think I've ever been so lonely."

He nods, understanding me completely, where someone else who wasn't so confident in himself would have been easily offended. "I get it," he tells me. "You have all these new people around you, most of them knowing you better than you might even know yourself, but not one of them is in your position. We've all had eighteen fucking years to adjust to this fucked up lifestyle, but you've been thrown straight into the deep end and told to survive while you're having shots taken at your head. None of us can even pretend to know how that feels."

"You know, I've been through eighteen foster homes, at least thirty different schools, and a million fake friends, and not one person has ever understood me until I met you four assholes, and even with the chips on Grayson and Carver's shoulders, I still prefer their company to anyone else I've ever met."

"Well," he laughs, a cocky as fuck grin ripping across his face. "What can I say? We're pretty fucking awesome."

"Yeah, and not cocky at all."

King winks and slips his hand into mine, lacing our fingers. "Are you intent on sitting here all night watching the waves do exactly the same thing over and over again, or do you want to do something with me?" he asks, a wicked sparkle hitting his eyes. "I've got an idea."

Do I sit on the beach and sulk all night or let this deviously delicious man take me on an adventure? Choices, choices. I grin back at him, the excitement bubbling deep inside my chest. "Well, fuck me," I laugh, letting him pull me up. "How am I supposed to say no to that?"

"You can't," he tells me, dragging me along through the sand, back toward the road. "I'm just that fucking irresistible. No wonder your bitch-ass is always throwing yourself at me."

"Look who's talking," I grumble. "Do I need to remind you that you were the fucking weirdo stalker who snuck through my bedroom window in the hopes of getting your dick wet? Actually, I think there's a special, fucked up place in hell for guys like that."

"Don't even start with me," he says. "Getting my dick wet that night was just an added bonus. I couldn't help it that you were just that desperate for me."

"Yeah," I laugh, grinning up at him, absolutely loving the chance to tease him. "I was so desperate for you that I decided to fuck Cruz instead. You must have really rocked my world."

He looks my way, his eyes narrowing. "Dick."

"Don't you forget it."

We reach the main road and King comes to a stop, glancing up and down the street. "Well," he says. "We have two choices. We can either walk twenty minutes back to the party and steal Carver's Escalade, but also risk running into whatever backup Jacob called, or …" he adds, a devilish smirk kicking up the side of his mouth as his eyes sparkle with the best kind of mischief, "we can hotwire one of these bad boys and take it for a spin."

My gaze shifts toward the cars lining the streets, and fuck it, I like the way the man thinks.

Not bothering to wait for me to agree, King grabs my hand and pulls me toward a black Mustang parked a little down the road, and the closer we get to it, the wider his grin becomes. "Do I even want to know how you learned to do this?"

He looks back at me, his eyes sparkling with a devilish laughter. "Probably not."

I roll my eyes and watch as he steps up to the side of the Mustang only to shake his head at the idiocy of the owner who left the driver's side window open just enough for King to slip his fingers in and shimmy the window down. "Fucking idiot," he mutters to himself. "He should have at least made it a challenge."

King's hand dives inside the Mustang and unlocks the door before pulling it wide and dropping down beneath the steering wheel. I watch in amazement as he fiddles around, and not a moment later, he grins up at me as the engine roars to life.

I can't help but laugh, he looks like a fourteen-year-old boy who just had the hot babysitter offer to suck his dick. "Well?" he asks, getting up and waving his hand toward the driver's seat. "Are you driving?"

My eyes bug out of my head and I instantly retreat, shaking my head as the dread sinks heavily into my gut. "No. No, no, no, no. You don't want me to drive."

His brows furrow as he watches me with a strange curiosity. "Why the hell not?"

"Because you guys have been going to the ends of the earth to keep me alive and I wouldn't want to put all your hard work to waste by throwing myself behind the wheel of a car."

King just stares a moment longer, a grin slowly stretching across his face. "You can't drive."

I shake my head. "Nope, and I'll deny it if you were to tell anybody, but the whole driving a car thing kinda scares the crap out of me."

"But …" he trails off, unable to comprehend a word I'm saying. "How is that possible? You drive that Ducati as though you need it to breathe. How could you not know how to drive a car?"

I give him a tight smile, watching him over the top of the Mustang as I walk around to the passenger's side. "I had to force myself to learn how to drive that Ducati, and it was shit scary, but a car … when would I have ever had a chance to learn that? I don't have a driver's license and I've been in shitty foster homes since, well … forever. None of them gave a shit about teaching me, and it's not like I have a car to learn in."

"Holy shit," he breathes in astonishment, dropping into the driver's seat and pulling the door closed behind him. "I've got to tell the boys."

"No," I rush out. "You can't tell them that."

He hits the gas and we take off down the road as he looks across at me. "Dare I ask why not?"

I glance out the window, not wanting him to see the embarrassment written across my face. "Because everyone my age knows how to drive. I'm probably the only chick around here who's never even sat in the driver's seat, but I'm too fucking scared to even try. The whole thing … I don't know, it's daunting. I don't want to drive."

"No, that's not happening," he says. "You're honestly the toughest chick I've ever met, and tough chicks need badass cars. Do you like this one? We could take it home. It'll take Cruz less than twenty minutes to get everything changed into your name."

My jaw drops as I stare at him. "We're not stealing this car … I mean, for good. After this, we need to ditch it somewhere the owner can find it, but it doesn't matter anyway. I don't need a car, there's a whole garage of my father's cars at home."

"Those cars aren't you," he tells me. "You need something that screams 'get out of my fucking way.' Besides, those cars are fucking expensive. You need to learn in something cheap that you can fuck with."

I shake my head. "I'm not learning."

King scoffs. "Just wait until Grayson hears that your ass can't drive. He'll have you speeding down highways and drifting around corners in no time."

I groan, watching as he expertly shifts through the gears and unintentionally turns me the fuck on. "You're really going to tell them, aren't you?"

He laughs and the sound grates on my nerves. "Just try and stop me, babe."

A heavy sigh pulls from between my lips as I relax back into the car and scan my gaze over the impressive dashboard. Maybe he has a point about keeping this car. I'm not going to lie, it's nice. Very nice. "Fine," I grumble. "But do me a favor and leave out the whole 'scared' thing. I don't care if Grayson and Carver hear that, but Cruz … he thinks the sun shines out of my ass. I kinda like how he thinks that I'm some kind of superhero who can do anything she puts her mind to."

His eyes soften and it somehow eases the pain that lives within my chest, helping me to forget just how shitty my night has been. He doesn't say another word, just drives through the silent streets with my eyes glued to his body. What is it about a guy who can drive a stick shift? Fuck me, it's the hottest thing I've ever seen, but just when I think it couldn't get any better, his hand finds mine and he uses his knee to steer the wheel.

Dead. I'm fucking dead.

Ten minutes pass before King pulls up at a familiar old house and my heart instantly races, and not in the good way. I glance across at him, confusion quickly taking over. What does he think he's doing bringing me here? "What are we doing?" I ask him, my tone sharp as I wonder if I was right for putting my trust in him. "Why'd you bring me here?"

A smirk kicks up the corner of his mouth. "You said you were lonely, and now we're going to fix that."

My eyes bug out of my head and I gape at him. "By hanging out with Irene?" I ask, swinging my gaze back toward the shitty foster home that I'd stayed in when I first came here. "Are you insane? I couldn't think of anything worse. What the hell are we going to talk about? The brutally messy way I slit her deadbeat husband's throat?"

King just sighs, and as he does, the sound of Irene's yappy dog fills the silence.

I watch him as it finally clicks. "We're not here to talk to Irene, are we?"

He shakes his head. "Irene's been gone for nearly two weeks and that dog has been left here to starve. It hasn't been washed, fed, walked, nothing. And from where I'm standing, it looks like that dog needs a friend, maybe just as badly as you do."

I look back at the house. "You want to steal Irene's dog?"

King doesn't respond, but I don't need him to. I already know exactly what he's going to say.

My gaze shifts back to King's just as a wide smile stretches over my face. "Let's do this," I tell him, and not a second later, we bail out of the Mustang doors and race toward the yard, putting 'operation save the yappy little dog' into place.

25

"What's its name?" Grayson grunts, leaning against the brick wall of the house as he stands between Cruz and Carver, all three of them only now just realizing what the hell King and I had gotten upto last night.

"I … uhh," I cut myself off, glancing at King across the yard as he fills up a water bowl for the dog. "I actually have no idea. Irene and Kurt never spoke about the dog and I wasn't going out of my way to talk to them about it, so I guess from now on it doesn't have a name, unless one of you wants to track Irene down to find out?"

Cruz shakes his head, looking horrified by the idea of having to actively search that woman out. "A new name it is," he announces, walking forward and looking over the dog who plays at my feet, begging to be scratched. "What is it?"

I shrug my shoulders. "How the hell am I supposed to know? A Pomeranian maybe?"

"It's a Yorkshire Terrier," Carver says in a brazen, dismissive tone, forcing my stare to his. I'm thrown back to the party where his eyes stared into mine as our hands slowly sailed up Sara's skirt, though that only reminds me of why I was so pissed and ready to play with him in the first place. I really don't need another day where all I can do is think about just how alive Carver can make me feel. "And that's not what Cruz meant. He was asking if it's a boy or a girl."

"Oh, umm …" the dog takes off, sprinting around the backyard and I've honestly never seen it so happy. It has food, water, a clean yard to play and run, even a pool to sprint laps around. "I actually have no idea. I always assumed it was a girl, but I can't say that I've ever tackled it to the ground, flipped it over, and checked to see what bits and pieces it has."

Carver rolls his eyes, less than impressed with my comments as Cruz comes to stand by my side, watching the dog as it races around the yard. "It looks like a girl to me."

"How does a dog either look like a girl or a boy?" King mutters. "It's not like it has a pink bow in its hair or comes fully equipped with a spiked collar."

"Then be my guest," Cruz tells him. "You're more than welcome to get on your hands and knees to find out."

"You know what?" King says, a cocky grin stretching over his face and he meets my stare. "I think you're right. She's definitely a girl."

I can't help but laugh as both Carver and Grayson scoff, letting King know exactly what they think of his desire to not go digging between the dog's legs in search of a set of hairy balls. Personally, I think both Grayson and Carver would revel in a job like that. They're always searching to see who has the biggest set of balls. Spoiler alert, it's me. Always me.

"So, what's it going to be?" Grayson asks from his perch against the side of the house. "What's the dog's name?"

I scrunch my face, my lips twisting in thought as I watch the dog run up and down the length of the property. This is too much pressure. What if I give her a shitty name? What if she doesn't like it or doesn't respond to it?

Fuck. Is this what new parents go through naming their babies? I want something strong, but I also want it to suit her personality.

I'm just about to start throwing out ideas when she stops running and catches sight of her own damn tail. She instantly starts barking at it, threatening to tear it right off the back of her ass as she chases it, darting around in circles and making herself dizzy.

A grin tears across my face as I look back at the boys. "I've got the perfect name," I announce proudly. "She's feisty, irritating, clearly very stupid, and I have a feeling that her bark is a lot worse than her bite, which could only mean that she's a super bitch. Probably hormonal too. So from this day forward, I declare my new pupper to be named Lady Dante, Queen of the Bitches."

King, Cruz, and Grayson smirk and discreetly smother their laughs as Carver just stares. "You're fucking kidding, right? You can't call her that."

"And why the hell not? It suits her perfectly, and it's not like you're using the name. The only time I've ever heard it being used is when it comes out of my mouth because you've managed to piss me off again."

Carver just glares while Cruz howls with laughter. "I think the name is perfect," he says, dropping to his knees in the grass and patting his thighs. "Come here Lady Dante. Come here."

The dog instantly bolts toward him and jumps into Cruz's arms, her excitement enough to have her falling all over herself. She jumps up frantically, licking Cruz's face and letting him know just how much she appreciates his attention. I bet she never got anything like this while living in Kurt and Irene's small, dirty yard.

"That's right, Dante. Kiss me. You fucking love it, don't you, my little dirty bitch?" Cruz coos, his eyes sparkling with laughter as he plays with the dog and Carver's nerves at the same time. Lady Dante rolls around in front of Cruz, exposing herself and proving once and for all that she is in fact a girl. "Do you want a scratch, Dante?" Cruz continues, giving the dog exactly what she wants. "Yeah, I knew you'd like it rough."

I drop down into the grass beside Cruz and the dog instantly jumps up and shoves her head right between my legs, giving my lady bits a good sniff in that irritating way that dogs always seem to do. I grab her head and push her back. "Dante, where are your manners?" I demand, pretending to reprimand her. "You need to ask a girl to dinner before you help yourself to dessert."

"Oh, really?" Carver scoffs. "Because that's the level of respect you held for yourself when King and Cruz wanted a taste of that sweet pussy."

King sucks in a sharp breath and looks between me and Carver. "Ahh, fuck. Shots fired."

I just laugh, getting up off the ground and walking back toward Carver. I step around him, loving how his eyes never leave mine. He doesn't move, not even a flinch or a slight blink as I walk right around him, but damn, Cruz, Grayson, and King are watching our showdown.

My finger trails over Carver's large shoulder until I do a full circle and step in right beside him. "Sounds like someone is a little jealous," I whisper, knowing that he can hear me loud and clear. "What's the matter, Dante? Does it kill you to know how easy it would be to throw me down and strip me bare? Just imagine how loud I'd scream your name as your tongue worked my clit. My taste on your lips and my fingers in your hair. You and me, it'd be like fireworks. But you're never going to get it, never going to taste me as I come, never going to feel my legs squeeze around your head, begging for more." A breathy scoff pulls from deep within as I watch his jaw clench and his stare harden. "And to think just how easily it all could have been yours."

Carver doesn't respond, just stares and I watch as he desperately fights for control. A smug grin stretches across my face. I thought he learned what happened when he tried to play with me last night, but I wasn't going to say no to a refresher course.

With nothing left to say between us, I turn and walk back toward the house, listening to Cruz's subtle laugh behind me. I can't help but look back at Grayson, and as I catch his eye, a million messages pass between us. His stare hardens just like Carver's had, and I know he understands perfectly clear that every last word I just whispered to his friend was meant for his ears too.

As I take myself back inside, I wonder just how many times I can push Carver before he breaks. Surely his patience is wearing thin. He used to fight back. He used to put me right in my place and I'd walk away feeling like a complete fool, but things have changed. Maybe he doesn't want to fight for it anymore, or maybe he's just completely given up. Who knows? Maybe he just doesn't trust himself around me anymore. He gave in to me in that little death dungeon below his house, but emotions were riding high, and now that he's had his fix, he might just be done.

I let out a sigh and get halfway back to the kitchen when I hear my phone rumbling against the marble countertop. I hurry after it. Only a few people have my number, and those that do know to text. I hate answering calls, but the fact that it's ringing tells me that it's got to be important.

I scoop the phone off the counter and glance down at Ember's name before hitting accept and bringing it to my ear. "Hey, what's up?" I ask, shoving the phone between my shoulder and ear as I search through the fridge for something to drink.

"Sara's on the warpath," she rushes out as I grab the bottle of OJ and step back from the fridge, letting out a sigh. "Apparently, she's pissed you kissed her last night, and now everyone's talking about it because it was fucking hot and she's all scared that people are going to think she's a les or something like that, which like … who even cares, right? We all know she's not anyway. That girl would sell her soul to the devil just to have Carver slap her in the face with his dick. But like, that's beside the point—"

"So, what actually is the point?" I ask, cutting off her rambling.

"Oh, umm … so apparently she just told Taliah Williams that she's going to go and find you and make you pay for it. Then Taliah told Haylee Martinez, who just got off the phone with me. So, if that's all true, then she's probably on her way to your place now, and I assume that means a bitch slap and some high-pitched ranting."

A loud groan bubbles up my throat. "Are you serious?"

"Unfortunately," she laughs. "But if you ask me, she's just pissed that she enjoyed it and now the whole school knows that she's down for a little girl on girl action."

"It's not like she was shoving Carver away and begging me to fuck her," I laugh. "It was just a kiss and a little touching. It really doesn't need to be made into something bigger than what it was. Besides, what's the big deal anyway? Most girls have hooked up with another girl at some point. It's like a rite of passage."

"Right," she says with a scoff. "Besides, I distinctly remember school camp two years ago. After we'd all been sent to bed, there was a party where she got wasted and let some girl finger fuck her for everyone to see. She didn't care about it then, so I don't understand why she'd care about this now."

I shrug my shoulders even though she can't see me. "Who knows?" I sigh, grabbing a glass and placing it down on the counter. I instantly fill it, adding just a bit more knowing Cruz will steal it and help himself, even if he isn't thirsty.

"Beats me," she grumbles.

"What are you doing?" I ask, just as the four guys come striding through the back door and I watch as Cruz instantly goes for my glass of OJ. "King and I sorta stole a dog last night, and now I have to spend the afternoon working out which room is going to be hers and find all the best food for her."

"Um … what?" she laughs. "There's so much to unpack there. First off … you stole a dog? Why the hell am I not surprised? And secondly, did you just say she'll be getting a whole room to herself?"

"Why not?" I laugh. "I couldn't fill all these bedrooms in a million years, so why not dedicate one just to Lady Dante? I might see if I can convince the guys to build a little doggy door so she can get in and out whenever she needs."

"Lady Dante?" she scoffs just seconds before a howling laugh bubbles out of her. I can't help but glance up at Carver and the way he glares back at me, suggests that he can hear exactly what's being said through the phone. "I bet Carver had something to say about that."

A grin tears across my face as I keep my stare on Carver. "Look, put it this way," I tell her as King steps in behind me and curls his arms around my waist. "He wasn't thrilled, but I think the name suits her perfectly."

Ember laughs but it quickly fades away. "I can't wait to see how you do being a doggy mommy. It'll be interesting."

"Then come over. You can help me adapt to this new crazy lifestyle."

"Nah," she grumbles, a hint of sadness in her tone. "I think I'm just going to chill out at home. I'm not really feeling up to it."

"What do you mean? What's going on?"

Ember lets out a sigh. "I still haven't heard from Jacob. He never showed up at the party last night even though he said he was just pulling up, so I don't know. That's not like him. Maybe I did something wrong and this is just his way of taking space. But I swear, I've done everything right. Maybe something else is going on, or he's just bored of me."

Fuck.

"No," I tell her, leaning heavily against King and letting him hold me up. "I'm sure it's not that. You're the best girlfriend any guy could want. If he's being a dick and not talking to you, that's on him. Don't let it get you down."

"Yeah, I know," she sighs. "I'm trying not to think about it too much. He'll call when he's ready, but in the meantime, I think I just want to sulk about it for a while. I'll be fine tomorrow."

"Are you sure?"

"Yeah, I'm just going to binge Netflix and stuff my face with popcorn, ice-cream, and chocolate."

"Damn, that sounds so good."

"It really is," she tells me as a loud knock sounds at the front door.

All four of the guys freeze, their backs straightening as they glance around at one another. "How is there someone at the door?" I ask, looking straight at Grayson, knowing that when it comes to the security systems, he's the best one to ask.

He shakes his head. "It's not possible," he says, looking across at

Carver who discreetly reaches around to his back and pulls a gun from the waistband of his jeans, making my brows arch in surprise. "No one should have been able to get through either of the gates without us knowing. They've been tampered with. Someone's been fucking with your security system, and I don't like it."

My eyes go wide, glancing around at the boys as my heart begins to race. "Hey, Ember, I have to go," I murmur, hoping that this is all some misunderstanding and I'm not about to endure another attempt on my life. "I'll call you back later."

"Okay, but it's probably just Sara at the door," she says. "So, make sure you record it because she's bound to say something stupid and I really don't want to miss out on it."

A forced laugh pulls from deep within me as I hope to everything above that's holy that Ember is right. "Yeah, okay. Bye," I say, ending the call and slipping the phone straight into my pocket.

The knock sounds again, and the boys silently work out a plan between themselves. As they creep toward the door, I fall in behind King, hating the way he pushes me right behind him so that I can't see a damn thing that's going down.

When we reach the massive front door, I hear a loud familiar groan from the opposite side just as the impatient knocking sounds again. I let out a relieved sigh, my eyes briefly closing. "Thank fuck. It's just Sara."

"Sara?" Cruz questions. "What the fuck is she doing here?"

"More like how the fuck did she get through both the fucking gates without a code and manage to put herself on Winter's doorstep without the alarms going off?" Grayson mutters.

"I can hear you in there," Sara calls through the door. "Open the fucking door so I can beat Winter's stupid ass."

"Well, shit. This just got a little more exciting," Cruz says, his eyes sparkling with delight at the thought of witnessing a girl fight. He steps right into the door and instantly swings it wide, only just giving me a slight second to step out from behind King.

"YOU," Sara roars, laying her eyes on me and glaring furiously. She welcomes herself right into my home and for a brief second, I'm wondering how the hell she knows where I live. She storms right up to me, shoving her fingers right into my chest and poking my left tit until it hurts. "Because of you, the whole fucking school thinks I have a hard-on for you."

I laugh, shoving her hand away and rubbing my sore tit as Cruz smirks. "Is that such a bad thing?" he asks. "She's fucking hot, just look at her. Fuck, I've got a hard-on for her right now," he adds, making a show of adjusting his dick inside his pants.

Sara glares at him. "Of course it's a fucking bad thing. She's a whore. Don't act like everyone hasn't seen the way she throws herself around all of you guys. I bet she's been sucking all your dicks. I cannot have my name connected with that. She's pathetic. Just a broken little foster girl who nobody wanted."

I step right into her. "Really?" I ask, my voice murmured and filled with a deathly challenge. I bring my hand up and run my knuckles across her collar bone, smirking as she sucks in a breath. "Because you sure as fuck loved it when my hands were on your body last night. You didn't think so lowly of me then. Don't you remember the way your tongue glided past mine, the way you moaned, begging for more? I fucking remember it perfectly, so don't come in here trying to tell me that you didn't want it just because you woke up this morning and decided that you wanted to be embarrassed about it."

Carver moves forward, his eyes boring into Sara's and making her catch her breath. "She's fucking right and you know it. You're just as much to blame as she is. Winter gave you the chance to pull away, but you let her kiss you and you picked up exactly what she was putting down. If you didn't want everyone thinking you had a hard-on for her, then you could have pushed her away. You could have made a scene, fuck knows you're good at that."

"But you didn't want to," King continues, stepping into my back and curling his arms around my waist again. "You liked it, didn't you? You fucking loved her hands on your body. That's why you're here now. Maybe you've forgotten that we've known you since we were kids, and you sure as fuck don't care what people think about you, especially when it comes to this. You hook up with your girlfriends at every fucking party trying to get Carver's attention, and last night was no different. Only he was more interested in Winter than you. You're pissed, but you're also intrigued," he says, slowly drawing his fingers up my waist and catching every bit of her attention. "You're not here to berate her for touching you, you're here to see if you can finish what she started."

Her eyes briefly flick back to mine and I see the hunger pulsing beneath the surface, but in an instant, it's gone, replaced by her usual hard exterior. "You're fucking kidding yourself, right?" Sara scoffs. "Look at her and then look at me. Why would I want that? She's a slut."

I step forward, my brow arching. There's a lot of things I can handle but being called a slut is not one of them. I don't like it. There are only a few people who can get away with calling me that, and they're in this room right now. But the difference is, if they were to call me a slut, they better be prepared to fucking treat me like one until I'm screaming their names.

"You heard me," Sara spits. "You're a slut. A dirty fucking whore. I wouldn't be surprised if you were prostituting yourself for these guys. I mean, how else would you have been able to get a place like this?"

Without even thinking, my fist rears back and slams hard against Sara's face, my brass knuckles instantly leaving the perfect imprint across the side of her jaw.

She goes down like a sack of shit, her head rebounding against the marble tiles, and for a moment, all anyone can do is stare.

Silence follows and my eyes bug out of my head.

Well, shit.

"Someone tell me I didn't kill her."

26

Ahh, fuck, fuck, fuck, fuck.

I stare down at the message of the two eggplant emojis and a donut that I just sent through to King and Cruz and the nerves instantly pulse through my body.

It's been a long shitty day, and after confirming that Sara was in fact still alive and breathing, she was carted away in the back of an ambulance with a nasty concussion. I haven't heard the last of that though. She's bound to have a few things to say about me spontaneously knocking her out. Though if you asked me, I'd say she deserved it.

Who makes the effort to come all the way out to someone's home, only to stand in their doorway and pick a fight? King was right. Sara is confused about what she wants and that pisses her off. She wanted a taste, just like Grayson and Carver do, but unlike them, the feeling isn't mutual.

I watch the message, and the second it comes up saying that King has read it, the nerves instantly get worse. I don't know why I'm being such a bitch about this. I've been with them both at the same time plenty of times, but I've never actually gone out of my way to ask for it. The opportunity has always just presented itself.

Yet here I am, sitting on my bed, all alone in this big house after a shitty few weeks, asking two of the best guys I know to come and rail me until I scream.

What girl wouldn't want that? Besides, after the hell I've been through, I could use a night to forget about everything and just feel good.

The three little dots appear at the bottom of the screen, telling me that King is in the middle of responding, and as I watch them, the phone shows that Cruz has now seen the message too. "Fuck me," I breathe before launching my phone right across the room.

I fly to my feet and instantly grab the plate on my bedside table. I move it across the room before scooping up a lone sock and throwing it toward my private bathroom.

What is it about sending a risqué text that makes people want to start doing chores?

After straightening the pillows on my bed, I scoop up last night's pajamas and attempt to fold them. Giving up, I straighten the TV remote on my bedside table instead.

Ding.

Ding.

Ding.

Ding.

My head whips toward the phone that now resides in the corner of my room, and I freeze, not wanting to open it, but then if I don't, how will I know if they're coming?

Shit. I hate this, but at the same time, it's the most thrilling thing I've ever experienced.

Ding.

Ding.

Fuck it.

I dive across the room and scoop my phone up, not bothering to race back to my bed before unlocking the screen and opening the message chain. A smile instantly tears across my face.

King - Fuck. Give me ten and I'll be there.

Cruz - HELL YEAH!!!!!! I'm on my way.

King - Get fucked, bro. Don't start without me.

Cruz - Snooze, you lose, dickhead.

Cruz - By the time your dumbass gets there, we'll already be done.

Just as I'm reading through their texts, I hear the familiar rumble of Cruz's Harley Davidson down the street and I laugh to myself, knowing it'll only be a minute before the show is on the road.

I keep reading.

King - Fuck off. You'll only have her warmed up. Winter

needs a fucking man for this job, not your little pindick, but thanks for getting her primed and ready for me.

Cruz - Careful, bro. I might accidentally slip this little pindick into the wrong hole while you're fucking our girl. Then you'll see just how big this pindick really is.

King - Dude … no.

Cruz - I bet you'll fucking love it too.

I get up from the bed and instantly pull off my clothes. If they'll be here soon, then I want to make it worth their while.

I dart across to my closet and step inside, dumping my clothes on the floor and digging into my drawers. Over the past few weeks since finding out I'm not actually a broke-as-fuck foster kid, Tobias helped me gain access to my parents' bank accounts. I've been busily filling every online cart I can possibly fill and having deliveries dropped at my front gate.

I'm not going to lie, I'm a little obsessed with finding new things online, but apart from clothes, I haven't really been spending anything. I already have everything I need.

Having these guys constantly in my bed has encouraged me to buy all sorts of sexy lingerie that I know they'll appreciate. I haven't had a chance to really try any of it on, but there's always a first.

I pick out a red lace bra and slide the matching thong up my legs, instantly falling in love with what I see in the mirror. The bra pushes my tits up, making them look even fuller and mouth-watering, while somehow managing to make my hips look like every man's wet dream.

I tie my hair up into a messy bun, knowing it's only going to get in the way before finding a pair of black fuck-me heels to add to my look. I scan my gaze over my body through the full-length mirror in my closet and instantly wish that Carver and Grayson were down for this too.

Finishing off my outfit, I take the black silk robe from its hanger and slide it over my body, pulling it closed and knotting it at my waist. I let the robe fall off my shoulder, and just like that, I feel like the sexiest woman who ever lived.

It's incredible what just a few pieces of skimpy clothing can do for a woman's confidence. Add the soft moonlight streaming in through my bedroom window and I feel absolutely perfect.

I walk back out through my room and grab my phone off my bed before bringing up the camera and quickly taking a picture, making sure that all my best bits are on display.

I grin to myself as I turn my phone around to look at the picture, finding Cruz standing in the open doorway with a hungry expression on his face. "Fucking hell," he mutters, welcoming himself into my room as I attach the picture to the message chain.

Cruz's hands fall to my body as his lips instantly drop to my neck. I groan, leaning into him and desperately needing his touch, but first, I need to play with King and let him know exactly what he's late for.

Winter - Don't be too long. I have a feeling Cruz isn't going to wait.

King - HOLY FUCK! Those tits.

King - Damn it.

King - Fuck. Cruz, don't fucking touch her until I get there.

I raise my phone and take another shot, this time getting Cruz's hands all over my body as his lips press deliciously against my neck. I hit send.

King - Fucking cocksucker.

King - Screw it, I'm coming now.

A wide grin stretches across my face as I throw my phone back onto my bed and slowly turn in Cruz's arms, loving how his fingertips glide across the soft silk of my robe. "He's on his way," I tell Cruz, really not wanting to start without him, but if Cruz pushes me, my control will break, and I won't be responsible for what happens next.

"I bet he is," Cruz grumbles, dropping his hands from me and taking a step back so he can really appreciate the view. "Tell me that you're not going to make me wait."

I step back into him and raise my chin before brushing my lips over his. "I sure am," I tell him just as he captures my lips and deepens our kiss. His arms come back around me, and I silently beg for him to roam his hands over my body.

I need his touch. I ache for him. My whole body burns for more, needing his hands on my ass, his tight grip on my waist, his tongue against my clit, and his cock in my mouth. I have to wait; I need to find control.

Stepping back out of his arms, I walk over to my bed, and while keeping my heels on, I crawl across the bed until I'm right in the middle. I sit on my knees and keep my eyes locked on Cruz's, loving the raw need that pulses through his gaze.

I slowly spread my knees, giving him just a glimpse of what's hidden beneath my black robe. He groans and the sound rumbles through him, speaking right to the vixen who lives inside me. "Fuck, babe. I'll give him thirty seconds, and if he's still not here, then fuck him. I have to have you."

My eyes become hooded and I watch as he peels off his shirt, slowly drawing it over his head to reveal his perfect body beneath. I must have seen him like this a million times by now, but it'll never get old.

My control is just about to break when I hear King at the front door, throwing himself through it and letting it slam shut behind him. An excited grin tears across my face, listening as he takes the stairs two at a time, and before I know it, he's falling through my bedroom door and coming to an immediate stop beside Cruz, his eyes focused heavily on my body as I sit on the bed, knees wide.

Keeping my heated gaze on them both, I slowly allow the soft black silk to slide down my body.

"Jesus Fucking Christ," King says, his eyes hungry as his gaze travels over my tits, taking in my curves and watching the way the black silk slowly falls to my waist and shows off what's hidden beneath. He adjusts his cock in his jeans and I don't doubt that it's pressing uncomfortably against the fly. "From now on, when we fuck, this is all you'll wear."

His voice is low and dangerous, and it makes something inside of me scream for more. I absolutely love when the guys are demanding and forceful. They're such alphas that it's a miracle they can even play nicely together and not get pissed about sharing their toys.

Wanting to put on a show, I bring my hand up and slowly trail my fingertips across my collar bone, watching as both of the guys follow the movement, their eyes becoming hooded and desperate with need.

I love how they respond to me, always needy, always wanting more, and never failing to worship my body just how I need it.

The desire pulses through me, but I don't want to rush. We have all night and I want to take my time.

My fingertips trail down the center of my body, skimming between my breasts and trailing over my waist as my other hand slowly moves toward my breast. I grab it gently and squeeze as my head tilts back, a shallow breath slipping from between my lips.

Cruz edges toward me but I catch his eyes and shake my head. "Watch," I demand, my tone filled with authority. He comes to a stop, his brow instantly arching as he watches me with excitement.

His tongue rolls over his bottom lip, and fuck it, I want to bite it so bad. "You wanna put on a show, baby?"

My gaze flicks to King's who silently watches, his lips slowly pulling into a devilish grin. "Only if I can trust you two to behave."

A low groan tears from deep within King's chest and I silently wish for this part of it to be over so they can bend me over and fuck me until I scream, but that would be such a shame. Something tells me that teasing and enticing them is going to be the best part of the night.

King shakes his head. "I'll make no promises," he grumbles, flicking his gaze to Cruz and meeting his eyes, only for the two of them to give each other ridiculously cheesy, boyish grins filled with excitement. They might as well cross the room and give each other a high five.

Their wicked stares come back to me, and as heat floods between my legs, I keep my hands moving, ready to give the best performance of my life.

My hand skims over my hip and I suck in a breath, gasping with the touch, still squeezing my breast as my other hand travels down. I cup my pussy and can already feel my wetness seeping through the red thong.

I rub and grind against my hand, watching intently as the guys struggle to keep themselves still. King works his belt buckle, refusing to take his eyes off my body as Cruz dips his hand into the front of his grey sweatpants.

I watch the outline of his hand curling around his thick cock, and seeing what caught my attention, he pushes his sweatpants down over his hips, showing me exactly what he's working with. But I guess now the tables have turned. It's not just me putting on a show anymore. The boys are more than ready to step up and tease me just as I've been doing to them.

King's jeans fall to the ground and his veiny cock springs free as he tears his shirt over his head, showing off his perfectly sun-kissed abs. His fist curls around his cock and he slowly works it up and down as I grind against my hand, desperately needing one of those thick cocks inside my mouth while the other slams deep inside my aching pussy.

My fingers dig into the cup of my bra and pull it down, freeing my breast. Cruz moans, licking his lips as my fingers roll over my pebbled nipple. "Do you want me?" I ask him, keeping my voice low in a seductive whisper.

"Fuck, Winter. I want to take you until you can't fucking walk," he growls, the desire pulsing in his eyes, almost too much for me to handle.

I push my thong aside and suck in a breath as my fingers graze across my clit. I'm soaking wet and desperate, and I can't resist sliding two fingers deep inside. I curl them around and a sharp gasp tears out of me as my fingers press against my walls.

I slowly draw them out and they glisten in the moonlight as I catch King's stare. "And you?" I ask, bringing my fingers to my mouth and gliding them across my bottom lip before slowly rolling my tongue over it and tasting myself.

His eyes darken. "Fucking hell," he mutters, the desperation of his tone hitting me right in the chest. "Ride those fingers, baby."

A devilish grin cuts across my face as I push my fingers back in and show him exactly what I do when I think about them both at night. My breath comes in needy moans as I watch them stroking their cocks faster, but it all becomes too much and my control falls, needing so much more.

"Fuck," I groan, my tone almost coming out as a desperate cry. "I can't. I need you to touch me."

They don't hesitate.

King steps right into the side of the bed and reaches forward, curling his arm around my waist and yanking me to the end of the bed but keeping me on my knees. I look up at him, and seeing the darkness swirling in his eye, I lean forward and take his heavy cock in my mouth.

His fingers curl in my hair as he groans my name, but when Cruz climbs onto the bed behind me, a whole new level of excitement pulses through me. His legs fall on either side of my knees, and in one smooth motion, my thong is torn from my body.

He lifts me up and my aching cunt instantly comes down around his throbbing cock, my knees pressing into the bed on the other side of his thighs, spreading my legs so much wider.

I balance above him, my eyes clenched as I adjust to his delicious, full intrusion.

"Oh, fuck," Cruz mutters, fucking up into me as he grips my hip with one hand while the other curls around my body and slips down between my legs, rubbing tight, desperate circles over my clit and instantly bringing my body to the edge.

I swirl my tongue over King's tip, adding both my hands, one of them gliding up and down with my movements and the other slipping beneath and cupping his balls, giving them a firm squeeze just how he likes it.

His hands tighten in my hair and I can't help but look up at him again, his eyes burning as he watches me fuck his cock with my mouth as his best friend slams deep inside my pussy.

If my mouth wasn't so full, I'd be screaming their names, instead, all I can do is groan, moan, and pant as I move on top of Cruz, slamming down over him and taking him so much deeper.

Cruz's fingers tighten on my hip as King lets out a deep guttural growl. They're both so close, we all are.

I need it harder.

Faster.

As if reading my body, the boys take control. King grips my chin and fucks my mouth until my eyes water, while Cruz holds me up above him and slams into me over and over again. With my hands free, I reach down between my legs and furiously work my clit as my other hand dives further to feel Cruz's cock moving in and out of me.

My orgasm explodes around me, completely overtaking my body and making me cry out. My pussy clenches around Cruz, and in an instant, he's coming with me, a deep roaring groan rumbling through his chest.

My pussy convulses, and before I've even come down from my high, King stills, and with a sharp "fuck," I taste his warm seed pouring down my throat.

He slowly pulls out of my mouth and I adjust myself on top of Cruz so that I lay across his wide chest. King falls to the bed beside us and instantly trails his fingers over my waist. "We need to get you some more of these lingerie sets," he mutters, brushing his fingers over the red lacy material.

I roll my tongue over my lips and crawl across the bed until I'm straddled over his waist, more than aware of Cruz dripping between my legs and mixing with my own excitement.

"You like it?" I ask, pulling him up until he's sitting.

King instantly reaches around me and unhooks my bra, letting it fall to the bed beside us. King dips his head and sucks my nipple into his mouth, making my head tip back in ecstasy. He doesn't bother answering my question, but he doesn't need to. His response is loud and clear, and damn it, I like what he's putting down.

A breathy moan slips from between my lips, his touch bringing my body alive once again. I feel Cruz's stare and glance at him to find his cock already hardening, and the deep hunger pulsing in his eyes tells me that he's ready for more.

I reach across and curl my fingers around his cock, working up and down as King hardens beneath me.

I adjust myself on top of him and he instantly slips inside before Cruz climbs off the bed and moves in behind me, tilting me forward, and preparing to rock my fucking world all over again.

27

"Where the hell is it?" I whine, my stomach growling as I clamber across the couch, throwing myself over Carver's lap and diving for Grayson's phone.

I quickly unlock it, using the code that's become all too famous around here—0225, my birthday. I lie half sprawled across Carver with my ass staring right up at his face, his hands up in the air as though he doesn't know what the hell to do with them now.

I can practically see his objections on the tip of his tongue, but I beat him to it as I focus on Grayson's phone. "It's just an ass, Carver. I know that you're a little gun-shy when it comes to women, and you clearly have no idea what you're doing, but chill the fuck out, it's not going to bite you." I hear King and Cruz smothering their laughs across the room, and I whip my head up, grinning right back at them as I wiggle my ass for good measure. "Go on," I challenge him. "I dare you to touch it."

Carver grunts, clearly not impressed, but if I'm being honest, I'd say Carver would know exactly what to do with an ass, maybe even better than King or Cruz. I flick through the pages of Grayson's apps, and before I even know what's happening, Carver's hands are ramming into my hips and I go flying off his lap.

My body topples to the ground as a loud squeal tears out of me. Grayson's phone flies under the coffee table as Carver's foot shoots out, breaking my fall so that I don't fuck my hip in the process. My chest hits the cold marble tiles and I gasp at the chill as Grayson snickers, desperately trying to mask his laugh, but failing miserably.

I roll onto my side and glare up at Carver, kicking my foot out only for him to catch it and throw it back at me, making me roll back against the coffee table. "What the hell?" I shriek, trying to get comfortable before sliding my hand under the table and feeling around for Grayson's phone.

Carver just laughs, more than pleased to have gotten the best of me. "Serves you right for shoving your ass in my face," he grumbles as my arm gets stuck under the coffee table. "Maybe next time you get up and walk around me like a normal human being."

"Maybe next time I might knee you in the balls," I mutter under my breath as I try to wriggle my arm free while Lady Dante decides it's a good idea to come and cover my face in slobbery doggy kisses.

Usually, I wouldn't mind too much, but she only just ate her dinner. Someone needs to remind this dog that she needs to take a mint before going in for the full tongue kisses.

Getting my arm free, I make myself comfortable on the ground, making a point of not moving off Carver's foot just to be a pain. I bring Grayson's phone up and go through the whole process of unlocking it and scanning through all his apps until I get to the final page. "Where did you order from?" I ask him, quickly glancing up and meeting his stare as my stomach grumbles again. "UberEats or Menulog?"

"Menulog."

I click into the app and look over our order, trying to figure out just how long until our dinner is supposed to arrive. We've been waiting for over an hour and my stomach can't possibly take it anymore.

My whole world crashes as I look up at Grayson with my bottom lip pouting out and the devastation washing right over me. "I don't know how you did it, but you've ordered our dinner from a store in Australia."

"What?" he grunts, reaching down and snatching the phone out of my hand. He quickly scans over the order and I watch as his face falls. "How the fuck did I do that?"

"Shit," Carver grumbles. "That's a long fucking wait for dinner."

"Pizza?" Cruz asks, pulling out his own phone as King laughs at the whole situation, somehow still concentrating solely on the TV screen as he plays some ridiculous game on the PlayStation.

Realizing that it's still going to be ages until I get to eat, I get up off the ground and cross to King. I duck under his arms and slide up onto his lap without interrupting his game, and only then when he thinks I'm here to cuddle, I tear the controller right out of his hands and take over, having absolutely no idea what the hell I'm doing.

"You're making me lose," King yells, reaching for the controller.

I dart out of his arms, more than fucking up his game. "You were going to lose anyway," I laugh.

I don't even get a step away from him before he catches me around my waist and instantly pulls me back to him, but I'm not giving up, not yet. I pull the controller in close, laughing as I attempt to sit on it, but King has other plans and just sits on me instead.

"No," I squeal. "Get your fat ass off me."

An alarm cuts through Carver's home and everybody freezes and whips their gazes around to Carver, the PlayStation completely forgotten. King instantly gets off me, pulling me to my feet and holding onto my wrist in a bruising grip, ready to haul me away if need be. "What alarm is that?" I ask, wide-eyed, looking around at the guys who are now on their feet with hard stares across their faces.

"It's the front gate," Carver says, pulling out his phone and bringing up the security footage. "Someone is trying to break onto the property."

"When will this fucking bullshit end?" Cruz curses under his breath, more than done with the random, fucked up attacks. He steps past me and grabs my elbow on the way, tugging me away from King and walking deeper into the living room, far away from the windows. He takes me to the massive fireplace. "Get in."

"What?" I grunt, pulling away from him, my brows pinched as

anger pulses through me. I get that he's protective and wants to hide me away, they all are, but that's never how I've done things, and I'm sure as hell not about to start now. "I'm not hiding out in a fucking fireplace while you guys are left to handle my shit. If someone is here to make a move against me, then I'm not going to hide away. I face my problems straight on and you fucking know that."

"Babe," he groans. "Please, I'm not about to fight you on this. Get in the fucking fireplace."

My jaw clenches as my hands ball into fists at my side. I've never felt the need to throat punch Cruz before. That's usually something I save for Carver and maybe sometimes Grayson, but right now, Cruz is moments from experiencing what it's like to be on the receiving end of my rage.

Carver's voice cuts through my fury and instantly has me turning back to meet his eye. "It's fine," he says. "It's just Preston Scardoni."

My eyes somehow go wider as the guys seem to relax. I walk over to Carver and peer down at his phone to see the security footage of Preston desperately trying to tear the front gates down with his bare hands.

Carver presses the volume button on the side of his phone, and not a second later, Preston's voice comes tearing through the room. "You have three fucking seconds to open this goddamn gate and tell me what the fuck you did with my son. I know something is going on."

"Fuck," I breathe, my eyes snapping back up to Carver's. "He knows."

He shakes his head. "He doesn't know."

"But—"

"No," Grayson says. "All he knows is that Jacob didn't come home last night and seeing as though you did, something must have fucked with their plans. He's thinking the worst, but he doesn't actually know. He's just assuming."

"But—"

"No," Carver cuts in. "There's no proof. For all he knows, Jacob wrote himself off last night and was too fucked up to get home. Preston is just taking a guess, but he's got nothing. For him to push this with the heads of Dynasty means he will have to explain why he's accusing us and come clean about their role in all this. They can't implicate us without implicating themselves."

My brows raise and I search his eyes, looking for some kind of hope. "Are you sure?"

King's hands fall to my waist as his chest presses into my back. "Positive," he murmurs, his lips right beside my ear before he drops a kiss to my shoulder. He raises his head and meets Carver's stare. "You might as well let him in. We're going to have to have a little chat with Preston."

"Agreed," Cruz says.

Just like that, Carver presses a button on his phone and the gate slowly peels open. Preston stands dumbfounded for a short moment before racing back to his car and screeching down the driveway.

"Are you ready for this?" Cruz asks. "Facing him after what we did is going to fuck with your mind, and your guilty conscience is going to come out to play, but you need to hold your ground. Don't let him see you break, and if in doubt, don't say anything at all. We'll handle it."

I nod, loving how he knows me well enough to know that I would have taken over the show and demanded Preston's attention, but for the first time, I don't think I know what the hell to say. I made the call to end his son's life last night, and despite knowing that Jacob was the one to put in the order for an attack last night and the one in the woods, I'm not sure that I'm strong enough to face his father.

Sitting around a massive table and telling Preston that he's an asshole is as simple as breathing, but facing him after taking his son away from him, that's an entirely different situation.

"So, what do we do?"

A grin cuts across Grayson's lips as he looks back at me. The devilish sparkle that hits his eye is enough to have something roaring alive inside me. I absolutely love when he looks at me like that; I'm a sucker for it. "Now, we let the bastard in and watch as he unknowingly admits to it all."

I laugh, rolling my eyes. "That's insane. A guy like Preston Scardoni isn't going to come in here and admit to everything that he's done. He's been playing this game for far too long. He's not stupid."

"You never know," King murmurs as both he and Cruz go and stand with Grayson and Carver. "Men who let their emotions control and rule over them have a way of fucking it all up."

I laugh to myself, eyeing Carver and Grayson and watching their stares harden when they figure out exactly what's going through my mind. "Yeah," I agree, a grin splitting across my face. "I have a little experience with that."

Grayson just rolls his eyes, almost as though he's completely over the little chat we had, while Carver looks even more pissed. I meet his stare, letting my smugness shine through. "Point proven," I tell him, before stepping right in between Grayson and Carver and turning to face the entrance of the big room.

The guys all turn with me, and in that one movement, we form an impenetrable line of intimidation. Like clockwork, the front door barges open and we listen as Preston storms through Carver's home as though he has every right to be here.

He reaches the living room in no time.

Preston comes to an immediate stop, his eyes slightly widening at the sight of us all waiting for him, but he quickly rights himself, acting as though the five of us watching him like a hawk who knows his darkest secret isn't scaring the shit out of him.

His eyes slice right to mine, his jaw clenching as the fury bubbles through him. "What did you do to my son?" he roars, racing toward me.

He gets just a step away when Carver's arm shoots up, slamming against his shoulder and jerking him to a violent stop, keeping me just out of reach. "Close enough," Carver rumbles, the deep tone of his voice sailing straight through me.

I hold Preston's stare. "The whereabouts of your son seems like a you problem. I'm not sure if you've noticed this or not, but your son is a dick. I don't exactly spend all my free time worrying about where he is at all hours of the day. So, thanks for this little visit, but perhaps you will have better luck checking in with the people who actually consider him a friend."

"Don't you speak of my son like that, you rotten girl," he spits, his eyes narrowing in anger. "Who do you think I am? You cannot fool me like that. I know you were at that party last night."

"What party?" I ask, slightly stepping closer to Preston and holding back a laugh as each of the guys flinch and somehow manage to find the self-control to not pull me back. "I was out with King last night getting a rescue dog."

As if realizing that I'm talking about her, Lady Dante barks from deep within the living room and the corner of my mouth kicks up into a smile. I'll have to get that doggy a treat; her timing is impeccable.

Doubt flickers through Preston's gaze, but it's gone in his next blink. "Who are you trying to play?" he demands, his gaze shifting up and down the line of men at my back. "I know you were at that party. Jacob called me and specifically said you were there."

"Checkmate, motherfucker," Grayson grunts, a soft laugh in his tone.

I glance back at him as a smile pulls at his lips. His eyes sparkle at the knowledge of being right, and I realize that this is exactly the moment he was talking about. Preston's emotions have gotten the best of him, and just like that, he's admitted to being the person on the other end of Jacob's call, a call that he stupidly assumed we knew nothing about.

"Excuse me?" Preston roars, his glare sinking into Grayson like volcanic lava hitting ice. "I am the head of the Scardoni family. You have absolutely no right to speak to me like that. What would your father say?"

Grayson just laughs. "My father won't say a goddamn thing when he realizes that you just implicated yourself as the person who's been orchestrating the attacks on our leader, the woman you vowed to follow."

Preston roars. "I did no such thing. Where the hell do you get off making such horrendous accusations?"

"You know what?" I say, stepping even closer, a grin pulling at my lips. "I think I remember that party now. It was crazy. I was fucking around with Carver, you know, getting under his skin and all, and then I was literally fucking around with King and Cruz out in the bushes behind the property. But the strangest thing happened."

I pause, watching as confusion and dread instantly take over his features.

"You know, I think I did see Jacob last night after all. I was trying to get my rocks off, but we were interrupted by someone. I was pissed because who doesn't want to be fucked by two dudes up against a tree in the bushes, you know what I mean? Though, something tells me you're not the kind of guy to have ever been so lucky, which honestly is a real shame."

"Get. On. With. It," he demands. "Where is my son?"

I suck in a breath between my teeth. "You know, that's just the thing. I really don't know. He could be to the left of the big tree that I wanted to fuck against, or maybe under some shrubby bushes."

"What the hell is that supposed to mean?" Preston roars, flinching toward me only to have King and Grayson fly out at him and push him back a few steps.

The boys move in closer to me, standing as one. "Take a guess who interrupted us in the bushes," I tell him, lowering my tone to let him know just how fucked he really is. "I wonder what phone call we overheard."

"I knew it. You fucking touched my son. Where is Jacob? What did you do?"

Carver scoffs, a soft, cynical laugh rumbling through his chest. "We did to your son what you had planned to do to Elodie. Call it self-defense."

Preston's face glows the brightest shade of red and he launches himself toward Carver, but King and Grayson catch him before he can even take a step. "WHAT DID YOU DO?"

Carver pushes past me, shoving right into Preston, and in an incredible show of strength, pushes him back five steps until he's slammed up against the wall of Carver's foyer. "Consider him lucky that all I did was snap his neck," Carver hisses, leaning into Preston and reminding me once again just how much he holds back with me. "Jacob deserved so much worse. I should have cut his tongue right out of his mouth for the calls he made against Winter."

"You won't get away with this," Preston snaps as I try not to remember the way Carver twisted his son's neck on my order. "I swear on my son's grave, I will make you pay."

"You see, that's just it, Preston," I say, stepping in beside Carver and watching as both of their eyes slice toward me, the guilt Cruz was talking about creeping up on me. "We've already gotten away with it.

How the hell do you intend on making us pay? Who are you going to tell? Who will you run to? *Dynasty? I'm their fucking leader.* How will you make us pay without telling them exactly what you and your son have done? No matter what you do from here on out—you're screwed."

Preston clenches his jaw, knowing damn well that I'm right. "You won't get away with this. I'll fucking end you myself if I have to."

Carver grabs him and slams his back against the wall, letting his head rebound until he's seeing stars. "Do you remember what I said that first time in the council chambers? I told every one of you old fuckers that I was going to find the people responsible for the attacks on me, I was going to find the man responsible for my parents' deaths, and I was going to make every single one of them regret it. You watched me come through on my promise to Royston Carver, and now your son. You're next, Preston, but it won't be so easy for you. There are still so many unanswered questions. Once I get exactly what I need, you'll finally be reunited with your son in hell. But not before you get what's coming to you."

And just like that, I nod at Carver and he instantly walks deeper into his home, dragging Preston Scardoni behind him.

The second they're out of sight, my knees go weak and I collapse to the ground. Cruz catches me just in time, proving once and for all, that while I put on a hard exterior, deep down inside, I'm just as broken and tormented as the rest of them.

28

"Alright, I'm out of here," Grayson says, looking back at me and Cruz as the soft, muffled sounds of King and Carver 'questioning' Preston in the hidden room beneath the study flow through the house, the same room where Sam Delacourt finally realized just how badly he'd fucked up by setting his sights on me.

I guess Preston is in the middle of learning the exact same lesson, and damn it, it's one hell of a good lesson to learn. The only difference between Sam and Preston is that we still need answers out of Preston, and so far, it's been two days and the bastard still hasn't broken.

It's been a constant flood of pained groans and curses. The guys have been taking turns, and I'm not going to lie, Carver and Grayson have been volunteering their time more often than not. Don't get me wrong, King doesn't mind beating the shit out of Preston, but he doesn't get off on it the way Grayson and Carver do. Cruz though, he always comes back from that little room looking like hell. He does what he has to do without complaint, but I can see how it bothers him.

The first night was the worst. Preston's screams were so loud that it sounded as though I was in the room with him. I had King take me home and stay with me there. I avoided coming over here for most of the day yesterday, but it made me feel weak, so I came back and have been sitting in this same spot ever since.

I've had each of the guys come and sit with me, even Carver, though not a word was said. We just sat in an awkward silence for over an hour until Cruz came and saved me from his silent torture.

Grayson collects his phone and a set of keys off the mantelpiece above the massive fireplace, and as he goes to walk out of the room, I find myself flying to my feet. "Where are you going?" I rush out, a slight desperation in my tone as another roar of pain comes sweeping through the house from the room of horrors below the study.

Grayson stops and glances back at me, his brows pinched as he scans his dark gaze over my face. "Why?"

I glance away, my eyes dropping to the expensive tiles. "I, uhh … I just, umm …"

Fuck. Why is it so hard to ask for help?

"You want to come," he states, not as a question but more as though he's reading my mind.

A grimace stretches across my face and I raise my eyes to meet his stare once again, hating how easily these guys can read me. Though it wasn't that long ago that Grayson declared that he knew me better than I knew myself. Maybe he was right. Maybe he really does.

"I mean … yeah. I'm not trying to get all up in your business or take over your afternoon. I just … need to get out of here for a bit."

Grayson raises his chin, his eyes narrowing as though he's trying to work out if this is even a good idea, though the way things have been going between us lately, it's probably the worst idea I've ever had, but the desperation keeps me from taking it back. "I'll be gone a while," he grumbles, his deep voice flowing through the room.

I don't miss the fact that he still hasn't told me where the hell he's going, but I don't think I actually care. Anywhere is better than here, and if I'm completely honest with myself, the thought of being alone with Grayson is pretty damn intriguing.

"That's fine."

He watches me for another long, drawn-out moment before finally giving me a sharp nod. He turns to walk out of the room. "Let's go," he throws over his shoulder, not giving me a chance to change or do my hair. I'm just lucky that I already have my shoes on.

I scoop my phone off the coffee table and scramble after him as I hear Cruz's soft chuckle behind me before a scoffed 'good luck' is grumbled under his breath.

I glance back over my shoulder and meet Cruz's eye as I hurry out of here. "Don't miss me while I'm gone."

Cruz rolls his eyes, softly shaking his head. "Just do me a favor and don't piss him off. He's an ass when things don't go his way, and I don't exactly want to deal with that when he gets back."

"Come and say that to my face, Cruz," Grayson calls from the foyer of Carver's home, only making Cruz's chuckles turn into a twisted kind of snicker.

Grayson flies out the door and I quickly race after him, knowing damn well that he'll happily leave without me. I hurry through the door and down the steps, getting there just in time to throw myself through the passenger side door of Grayson's black Dodge Challenger.

"What is it with you guys and black cars?" I ask, pulling the door closed and getting comfortable just as Grayson hits the gas and we go soaring down the long drive.

Grayson peers across at me, his eyes narrowed and filled with a suspicious curiosity. "You don't like my car?"

"That's not what I said."

"You didn't have to say it."

My brows furrow as I watch him drive through the streets. "What's that supposed to mean?"

"Most girls—"

"No. No, no, no, no," I say, cutting him off. "If you're about to compare me to those girls who throw themselves at you and all but beg to suck your dick just to be close to you for one night, then we're going to have a problem. I'm not them and just because I'm not drooling over how sleek and sexy your car is, doesn't automatically mean that I don't like your car. I like it just fine, I was just pointing out that everyone around here has black cars, even the Ducati is matte black.

Don't be such a boy."

A smirk pulls at his lips. "What's that supposed to mean?" he throws back at me, mimicking my tone.

I let out a frustrated sigh and meet his hard, but playful stare. "It means that a week ago, you told me that you knew me better than I knew myself, and right now, I'm wondering if you actually meant what you said or if you were just talking shit to prove some ridiculous point."

A soft, amused laugh pulls from Grayson as he concentrates on the road ahead of us. "I guess you'll have to figure that one out on your own."

I roll my eyes and drop back into my seat. "How is it that every single time I have even a small conversation with you, I end up confused as all hell?"

He grins and I don't miss the way his dreamy grey eyes light up like a New Year's Eve party. "Call it a gift."

Everything warms inside me, and as he drives, I find myself unable to look away. There's just something so intriguing about Grayson. There always has been since the second I met him. He's the dark, broody hero that's silently saved me from behind the scenes, always there, always protecting me, and never claiming the credit. "What are you looking at?" he grumbles, refusing to look back at me and making it clear that he knows I've been staring.

"You're not mad at me anymore."

"Mad?" he questions, his brows pinching as he pulls off the side of the road right outside an expensive-looking tattoo parlor. He puts the Challenger in park and turns to look at me. "Why the hell would I be mad at you?"

"Last week in the dining room," I start, "after we blew up Sam's house. We had that fight and I called you out on all your bullshit. I'm not about to claim that I know exactly what goes down in that fucked up mind of yours, but you looked pretty fucking mad."

A wicked grin cuts across his face and it sends a million different messages, all of which I can't even begin to figure out. "I wasn't fucking mad at you, babe. Well, for a hot fucking minute I was. There's just something about the way you manage to read me and use that shit against me. I'm not used to having chicks so easily call me on my shit, but mostly I was just pissed at myself because you were fucking right."

My brows instantly shoot up, recalling exactly what was said during our little discussion by the dining table, which somehow ended up with my back slammed against the wall in the most delicious way possible. He told me that he would stand behind me. He would betray his parents for me and follow me to the ends of the earth, but somehow it turned from discussing Dynasty politics into him being too fucking scared to make a move with me. The tension was heavy, hot, and desperate, so fucking desperate that I had to walk away and put a bullet between Sam's eyes, which only led to an entirely different situation all together.

"A lot of things got said during that conversation," I remind him. "What part was I right about exactly?"

His grin widens, and without another word, he pushes his door open and gets out before looking back at me with a cocky as fuck smirk stretching across his face. "Are you coming or what?"

Fucker.

I roll my eyes and push my door open with a loud groan, letting him know just how much I appreciate his casual avoidance of our conversation. I meet him on the sidewalk, and as he reaches for the door handle of the tattoo parlor and pushes it open, I meet his heavy stare. "You're getting another tattoo?"

He shakes his head. "Just adding more detail to the raven on my chest."

"Raven, huh?"

He looks away and pushes into the store with me following closely on his heels. Grayson is instantly greeted by a gorgeous pin-up looking girl with a red bandana tied around her dark curls. Her eyes go wide taking him in, and she looks like all her dreams just came true, that is until she sees me step in beside him. "Grayson," she beams, her eyes shining bright. "We haven't seen you in months. I'm so glad you found some time to come in."

"Yeah," he says, placing his hand over his shirt, right where his tattoo rests peacefully beneath. "I had to get this thing finished at some point."

"True that," she smiles, making me want to claw at her.

"Listen," Grayson says. "I know it's against your policies, but Winter's going to sit in with us."

"Oh, umm …" her eyes slice to mine and I see the exact second that she decides to put up a fight, so before she can say another word, I step closer to Grayson's side and curl my hand around his large bicep, clinging onto him as though my world can't possibly go on without him by my side, and making him look like a taken man. Her gaze slices back to Grayson's. "I guess I can make an exception, but she needs to sit still. I can't risk her running around my stall and bumping me."

My fingers dig into Grayson's arm as I give her a sickly-sweet smile, and not a second later, his hand comes down on mine, a silent warning for me to not race across the store and suffocate her with her own stupid bandana. "Let's get started then."

We walk deeper into the store and she leads Grayson into a private room. I follow behind them and drop down into the seat in the corner. "Alright, what are we working with?" she says, walking across the room and organizing her tools.

I watch her closely. I've never seen this before, and I can't say that I'm not intrigued, but the second Grayson peels his shirt over his head and his tattoo is on full display, my attention falls back to him. Or more, the black ink that covers his chest and shoulders.

It's fucking gorgeous. I thought that when I first saw it, and still now, but I can't help that gut feeling that tells me there is so much more to this tattoo. My eyes skim over the finer details of the impressive ink as Grayson reminds the artist about what he wants, but from the sound of it, they've already talked about it in great detail, and she's more than ready to get started.

She wastes no time, and within seconds, Grayson is laying back on the table with one arm propped behind his head, making his bicep bulge in all the best kinds of ways.

I watch her work, and despite the obvious lady boner she has for Grayson, she's pretty fucking great at what she does. I find myself creeping closer and closer, watching every last thing she does in awe while trying desperately to not get in the way. As much as I despise her warning out in the front of the store, the last thing I would want is for her to get bumped and fuck up this beautiful artwork.

She moves down around his ribs and a soft pained groan rumbles through the room. Without thinking, my hand shoots up and curls into his, our fingers lacing as I desperately wish that I could take his pain away. He meets my eyes and a connection burns between us, the tension building like nothing I've ever felt before.

My heart races, and for just a moment, I forget the girl and the tattoo, as all that exists is him. His thumb gently moves over the back of my hand, and just for a moment, I wish I could throw this girl out of here and then throw myself at him.

She moves just an inch, and as she does, even more of his tattoo is put on display. "Why a raven?" I ask, slowly roaming my eyes over his body as I raise them to meet his.

A seriousness pulses within his eyes as he silently watches me. "Why do you think?" he finally says in a deep, raspy tone, almost as though the answer should be obvious.

I shrug my shoulders. "Honestly, I've been thinking about this since I first saw it at the party in the cabin, and there are a few reasons why you could have chosen a raven."

"Well?" he pushes, his eyes never leaving mine.

I bite down on my lip, not sure I'm ready to know the answer to this. "Well, it could be the typical bird tattoo. You know, not being caged and flying free bullshit, but I don't think you're that cheesy."

He shakes his head. "I'm not," he says. "What else have you got?"

My gaze briefly flickers toward the tattoo artist before resting back on Grayson. "It could be a nod toward … you know, the family business. Andrew and Gerald Ravenwood. I don't know, maybe you're a little more into the whole thing than I realized."

He shakes his head, his eyes darkening by the second. "I'll give you one last guess."

I swallow over the lump in my throat, not once taking my eyes from him. "Me," I whisper before I can convince myself to back out of this conversation just like he had done in the car. "It's a raven to acknowledge me—Ravenwood."

Grayson doesn't say a word, but he doesn't need to. I can see the answer shining brightly in his stormy grey eyes. As he stares into mine, something stronger builds between us, something solid and unbreakable.

"I've been working on it for the past year," he tells me. "The boys thought I was fucking crazy, but I think they understand it now."

"But you didn't even know me a year ago, not really."

His eyes bore into mine, and without even realizing it, I move in closer. "Yeah, Winter. I did," he murmurs, his voice barely even a whisper as I become locked in a trance, unable to look away.

"Move," a voice cuts in, breaking our moment.

I suck in a breath and have to blink a few times to realize where the hell I am and that we're not alone. The artist steps right in front of me, getting nice and close to Grayson and forcing me to pull my hand free. She starts cleaning up the excess ink, and before I know it, he's standing in the corner of the room, looking over everything she's just done.

All she gets out of him is a firm nod, and just like that, she starts applying some sort of cream and then bandages him up.

After rattling off a list of care instructions, she walks out of the room, pulling the door closed behind her so she can get to her next appointment, leaving us alone with far too many unsaid truths and emotions dangling in the air between us.

Grayson grabs his shirt off the seat he'd thrown it on, but before he pulls it over his head, he stops and looks back at me, his eyes soft and full of resignation. "You were right," he tells me with a heavy sigh, leaning back against the table that he'd just spent the last two hours on. "Since the second you walked into our lives, I've been too fucking scared to make a move. You and me … I don't know. You're already with my friends. I don't want to be third in line, and I sure as hell don't want to take their girl. You're off limits to me, Winter, no matter how much I wish things were different."

I shake my head, slowly moving into him and sucking in a small gasp at the way his hand so effortlessly falls to my waist. "I don't want to be off limits to you, Grayson," I tell him. "I know you feel that there's something here, just like I do, which is why I've already spoken to Cruz and King. They know how I feel about both you and Carver and if something were to happen, they're down with that, but sharing isn't about who comes first and second in line—it's equal. I'm not going to lie, it's a learning curve, and as long as you're open to it, I don't see why we can't make it work, or at least give it a try."

Grayson pulls me in just a little bit more and I move into the space between his legs. "You've talked to King and Cruz?"

"Mmhmm," I nod, my tongue rolling over my lips. "Haven't you? You were down for a foursome two weeks ago."

"That was about sex, Winter," he tells me. "This is more than that. I want to be able to call you mine."

"That's not how it works," I murmur, knowing I should pull away, but the thought silently threatens to kill me. "I won't be yours, I'll be *all of yours.* You won't be able to hate on me when I slip into Cruz's bed instead of yours, and you can't get jealous if you walk in to find me fucking King, you can join, but you can't get jealous."

He shakes his head ever so slightly. "I don't know," he says. "I'm just like Carver. I don't like to share."

I press my hands against his thighs and push up onto my tippy-toes, putting my lips right in line with his. I lower my voice to a breathy whisper. "How will you ever know if you don't at least try?"

His hand at my waist slips around my back, pulling me even tighter against his body as my heart races with need. His eyes lock onto mine, so full of desire that if he doesn't kiss me right fucking now, I might just die.

"Please," I whisper so softly that I fear he might not hear me.

Something breaks in his resolve, and just like that, his lips finally come down on mine.

29

Grayson pulls me in hard, his soft lips moving against mine with a hungry desperation that feels so fucking right. It's like that final second before a firework explodes, right when you know that what comes next is going to be absolutely spectacular. It's as though my lips were made just for his, my body, my heart and soul.

My hands slide up his bare chest, being careful not to fuck with his tattoo. I loop them around his neck, and as I do, his hand slides under the fabric of my tank and I groan into him, loving the feel of his warm skin against mine. It's like fire meeting ice, both of us cancelling one another out until there's absolutely nothing left.

He moves back onto the table until he's sitting and instantly picks me up, the awkward angle just proof of his incredible strength. He pulls me right into him and doesn't put me down until I'm straddled over his lap, instantly feeling his hardening cock between my legs.

I grind down against him as our kisses grow faster, deeper, and even more desperate, and as they do, I know that I have to have him now. I can't possibly wait any longer. This has been too long coming and I can't wait a second more.

His lips drop to my neck and I moan into him, pressing my chest harder against his and aching for so much more—more that I'm not sure he's willing to give. At least, not yet, but Grayson Beckett has a way of surprising me. I think out of all four of the guys, Grayson has surprised me the most.

He's so strong and demanding, forceful and protective, yet at the same time, he's incredibly sweet, caring, and loyal. He's everything a girl could ever dream of. Not to mention, he's hot as fuck with a pair of grey stormy eyes that could leave a girl drowning.

A moan slips from between my lips as his dominant kisses work their way up to the sensitive spot beneath my ear. "Fuck, Grayson," I breathe as my nails dig into his warm skin.

My soft moan only spurs him on, and within seconds, he pulls my tank over my head and reaches for my bra. It falls between us and he quickly tosses it to the side. His gaze scans over me, getting hungrier by the second. "Fucking hell, Elodie. You're—"

My nails roam up into his hair as his eyes come back to mine. "Shut up and kiss me."

He doesn't disappoint.

Grayson's lips crush against mine, kissing me with a brand-new urgency. His hand travels down my body until it's firmly against my ass, squeezing tight and telling me exactly how this is going to go. He's going to be like King, hard and fast and filled with dominance. I'll be lucky if he hands over control and lets me take the reins, but I'm here for it. There's just something about Grayson that makes me trust him completely. If he wants control, then I'll fucking give it to him willingly.

We hear the soft thud of the store door opening and closing and Grayson reluctantly pulls back. "Shit, babe. We can't be doing this here."

"Don't you dare stop," I groan, pulling him back to me and roaming my lips over the sensitive skin of his neck. "We've been waiting too long for this. Who knows when you and I will ever be on the same page again. Lock the fucking door if you have to, but we're not leaving this room until I'm screaming your name. I want to feel you for days."

A grin pulls at the corner of his mouth as a deep growl rumbles through his chest. "Fuck it."

In one smooth motion, Grayson's arm curls around my waist and he flips us over until I'm laying back on the table. A soft needy gasp pulls from deep within me as I stare up at him with wide, excited eyes. What the hell is this? I don't even remember how we got here. One minute I was watching the tattoo artist work, and the next thing I know, Grayson is about to tear me to shreds in the best way possible. All I know is that I have to have him now, and if I don't, heads are going to roll.

Grayson stares down at me, and the hunger in his eyes is almost enough to have me coming on the spot, but I won't dare. I have a feeling that I'm in for a treat and I'll be damned if I fuck it up now.

The grin across his face is doing all sorts of things to my body, but it's his skin upon mine that really gets me. He's like fire, burning me up in all the best ways. I feel like I've been waiting a lifetime for this, but the look in his eyes tells me that he's been waiting a shitload longer.

Grayson pulls back, looking down at my body and scanning his heated, dark stare over my curves, my tits, hips and waist. He brushes his fingers over my skin and sends goosebumps soaring over me, making me squirm beneath his touch. A shiver trails down my spine and I can't help but clench my thighs as the need pulses through me.

Grayson doesn't miss a thing. His eyes burn and a cocky as fuck smirk twists over his delicious lips. "You're fucking hungry for it."

I laugh. There's no point in denying it. He can see it all over my face, all over the way my body responds to his touch. "Then hurry up and put me out of my misery," I tell him, my voice a soft purr filled with desire. Hell, I don't even care if it makes me look desperate. If it means that I get to have him, I'll fucking take it.

His fingers trail down my body, grabbing, touching, taking whatever the hell he needs until he comes to the waistband of my ripped jeans and ever so slowly, he drags the zipper down, teasing me with the promise of what's to come.

I bite down on my bottom lip, my chest rising and falling with sharp, needy pants, and then finally, he draws my jeans down my legs, taking my thong right along with it. His heated stare lingers on my body for a moment before he jumps down from the table and hooks his arms around my legs.

With one sharp tug, he pulls me down to the end of the table until my ass is hitting the very edge, and not a moment later, hooks my legs over his shoulders and leans into me. His hands twine up my body, teasing me with just how rough they can be while he turns his head and peppers soft, desperate kisses against my inner thighs, quickly working his way down to my pussy.

I flood with wetness, fearing my soul is about to leave my fucking body.

"Oh, fuck," I purr, my fingers combing into his hair and instantly curling into a fist, holding him there as his tongue finally hits my clit. My legs instantly clench around his head, the desire pulsing through me like never before.

I feel Grayson's cocky smile against my pussy, but he doesn't dare stop. Flicking, kissing, sucking, and teasing. He works my body until I'm groaning his name, his hands constantly roaming over my skin and showing me just how good it's going to get.

He brings a hand down between my legs and just when I think it couldn't get any better, he slides two thick fingers deep inside me and with that one perfect thrust, finds the spot that has my whole body shuddering beneath. "Shit. YES," I groan, the sound pulling from the deepest part of my chest.

A responding rumble tears out of Grayson and I tug harder on his hair, wanting so much more. His fingers glide out of me, massaging and moving on their way, only to be pushed back in, finding that spot all over again.

Holy mother of all things holy. If things continue like this, I think I might spontaneously combust into a ball of burning flames. Shit, maybe I already have. Hell, Grayson could do just about anything he wanted to me and I'd let him.

He keeps working my clit, sucking it just the way I like, and for a brief moment, I wonder if Cruz and King have been sharing all of our dirty little secrets because there's no way someone could so effortlessly know how to make a woman scream.

That familiar feeling begins to build deep inside me, tightening and pulsing with a desperate need for release. My fingers tighten in his hair, and at this point, anyone would wonder if he had any hair left. "Fuck, Grayson," I moan, my legs pulling tighter around him, squeezing as my body gets closer and closer to the edge.

His tongue flicks over my clit, applying pressure before he circles it, and just as he does, his thick fingers hit that spot that drives me wild and all hell breaks loose.

My orgasm explodes deep within me, completely taking over and sending me into a world of intense pleasure. My eyes clench as it rocks through me, and I have no choice but to throw my head back and arch off the table. My body spasms beneath his touch, but he doesn't dare let up, just keeps working me while my pussy convulses and my legs threaten to suffocate him.

My high continues to climb, so intense and forceful as I feel him lapping up my excitement, tasting everything I have on offer.

It's too much. *He's too much,* but at the same time, he's absolutely everything.

Shit, we haven't even gotten to the good stuff yet and he already has me falling to pieces beneath him.

My orgasm finally begins to ease, and just when my body starts to relax, Grayson pulls away from me, dropping a kiss to my inner thigh as he goes.

He stands at the end of the table, watching me as I desperately try to catch my breath, putting on a show of licking his lips, not wasting a single drop of me.

I groan, biting down on my lip as I watch him reach for the front of his pants. His body is absolute perfection, his tight, prominent muscles, his wide chest, and strong shoulders. He's a work of art, even without the tattoo, he's gorgeous.

How could one girl ever get so lucky?

Grayson pulls his fly down, and a second later his pants are gone, freeing an absolute monster. A fucking monster with a sexy as fuck frenum piercing that has my eyes bugging out of my head.

"Holy fuck."

A cocky smirk twists across his gorgeous face. "Something wrong?"

I shake my head, wondering just how that piercing would feel moving inside of me. "Something's right."

Grayson's hand curls around his thick cock and a twinge of nervousness pulses through me. Can I even handle a monster like that? I mean, I'm not going to say no to a challenge, but damn, that thing is going to bring a whole new meaning to the phrase 'filling me.' No wonder this tattoo artist is so interested in him. If she was the one to pierce his dick, then she knows exactly what he's working with.

Jesus. I thought King and Cruz were beasts. I didn't think it could get any bigger, but what can I say? Grayson has a way of surprising me. I've said it before, and something tells me that I'll say it a million times more.

He stalks back toward the table and I squirm under his stare, my pussy flooding with need all over again. My stare drops back to his piercing. Fuck, I can't wait to get that in my mouth.

All of the guys for that matter.

King, Cruz, and Grayson. The three of them together would be an absolute dream. So sensual, dominating, and full. There will never be anything better in this world than experiencing something like that. Now, I know I've been lucky so far when it comes to these guys, but surely a girl's luck is bound to run dry eventually.

I can handle my luck running dry, but another part of me running dry would be nothing short of a nightmare.

Grayson steps right up to the end of the table where my ass is barely hanging off the edge and he takes my knees, slowly drawing them open for him. They're hooked around his waist and he looks down at my aching, desperate pussy and trails his fingers through my wetness as his other hand clutches his impressive cock, slowly working up and down his long, thick shaft.

"Are you sure about this?" he rumbles, the sounds hitting my chest like a wrecking ball. "Once I touch you, Elodie, I'm not going to be able to go back to what we were."

"Fuck me, Grayson," I tell him. "Don't make me beg for it."

Just like that, he lines himself up with my pussy and pushes deep inside me. I suck in a breath, feeling him stretch my walls as the cool metal of his piercing drags up inside of me. "Oh, fuck."

"You good?" he questions, pausing once he's fully seated inside of me and giving me a moment to get used to the feel of him, as if having to pause and check is a regular occurrence for him.

"Remind me not to let you anywhere near my ass."

Grayson winks as he slowly draws back, making me groan with his movements. "Something tells me you can handle it."

Fuck me.

My body instantly craves more, and I tighten my legs around him, pushing him back inside me. Grayson reads me perfectly. He unhooks my legs from around his waist and pushes them back toward me, keeping them spread as far as they can go, and just like that, he gives it to me hard and fast, bending me like a pretzel while his heated, hungry stare remains locked on my pussy, watching the show like it's the best damn thing he's ever seen.

I watch his body roll and move with each thrust, and when his hand comes down and his fingers rub tight, fast circles over my clit, I feel like I've died and gone to whore-heaven. "Fuck, Ellie, you've got such a tight little cunt," he grumbles, the sound vibrating right through to my chest and making me feel like the most beautiful and desired woman on the planet.

He fucks me hard and I cry out his name over and over until someone starts knocking at the door.

"Hey, you can't be in there," a loud, demanding voice calls before it gets a little softer as though he's speaking to someone else. "Can you believe it? Some kids are fucking in there."

"Let them fuck," the other person replies. "I saw them when they came in. That shit would be fucking hot. All they need is a camera and they'll both be fucking stars overnight."

"Fuck," I laugh, looking up at the amusement on Grayson's face, feeling as though I'm seeing a whole new side of him, one I was certain didn't exist. I'm so used to his broody silence, but here he's lighter, playful, and goddamn, that smile. "You need to make this quick."

A heavy fist slams against the door and Grayson just winks. "Hold on, Ellie."

Grayson gives me all that he has, and I can't help screaming his name, desperately panting and trying to keep myself alive, as I'm damn sure that he's trying to fuck me into the deepest pits of hell.

Bang. Bang. Bang.

"THERE AIN'T NO FUCKING IN MY SHOP. GET OUT."

I laugh harder and have no choice but to grip onto the edges of the table to keep from falling off. "Shit, yes. Grayson, give it to me."

"Fucking hell, babe," he groans low, his tone enough to have my orgasm sneaking up on me and threatening to wipe me out of existence.

My pussy clenches down around him and instantly starts convulsing as my climax rocks through me, but he doesn't let up. Grayson hits me in that spot again and again as his fingers furiously rub tight little circles over my clit, making my eyes clench and my head tip back. My toes curl and I cry out his name, and just as I suck in a deep breath, Grayson tears out of me and comes hard with a loud, desperate groan, sending hot spurts of his seed shooting over my tits and making me feel like a fucking goddess.

Grayson grabs my hands and pulls me up so I'm sitting in front of him, and within seconds, his eyes are scanning over my body, looking at his handiwork with pride. He leans in and crushes his lips to mine. "You're so fucking perfect, Ellie. I could fuck you all day."

"Then take me home."

Bang. Bang. Bang.

"Two fucking seconds before I break this fucking door down and beat your asses. Out. Now."

"Fuck," Grayson laughs, pulling back and quickly looking around. He finds the disinfectant wipes the tattoo artist had used on him and grabs a few fresh ones before quickly throwing them at me. He grabs his clothes and hastily starts getting dressed as I wipe myself off and yank my tank back over my head, leaving the bra for the car ride home.

As I jump off the table and hastily pull my pants back up my legs, Grayson crosses the room to the big window that leads to the back alley behind the shop. "After you, my thoroughly fucked queen."

"Why, thank you," I laugh, grabbing my shoes and bra and hauling ass toward the window. Grayson takes my hand and helps me up onto the windowsill, and as I meet his eyes, I grin back at him. "Who would have known that someone who could fuck like that could also be such a gentleman."

"Trust me, I'm full of all kinds of secrets," he promises me, and not a second later, he pushes me out the window and I drop down into the alley.

Grayson comes flying out after me just as we hear the door breaking free. "Hey," the owner of the shop calls out.

Grayson's hand falls into mine, and not a second later, we go racing down the alleyway, both laughing like a couple of hyenas. "Come on," he roars.

I trip and fumble over my own feet, hardly able to contain myself as the laughter rips through me. We finally reach his Challenger and he all but throws me through the door as the owner comes storming out the front of his shop. "Get back here."

Grayson dives into the driver's seat, and before I even get a chance to catch my breath, he's tearing down the street and putting distance between us and the shop. Though, there isn't really a point in running. They know exactly who Grayson is and have all his contact information, but running is all part of the fun.

It takes us less than ten minutes to get back to our private road, and as Grayson drives past all the homes of our enemies, he looks across at me. "We have two choices," he says. "I can either take you back to Carver's place and share you with King and Cruz, or I can take you back to your place and have you all for myself."

A grin kicks up the corner of my mouth and I feel my eyes sparkling with excitement. "As much as the thought of having all three of you at once excites me, I've not nearly had enough of you yet. And besides, I kinda want to throw you around and ride you like a cowgirl."

His brow arches and a wicked smirk cuts across his face. "Just for the record," he tells me, "I don't give up control that easily. You're really going to have to work for that."

"Trust me," I laugh. "I'll have you begging for it in no time."

Grayson scoffs as he sails right on by Carver's gate and heads down the road toward mine. "So …" I continue. "Speaking of sharing, does this mean you're on board?"

His lips press into a thin line and he thinks it over for a short second before letting out a soft sigh. "Honestly, I think maybe, yeah, I am. After having you now, I get it. Your pussy is like fucking fire, and now I understand why the guys are so down with sharing, but just so you know, if I'd had you first, there's no way in hell I would have let you out of my sights for even a second to get close with one of the other guys. King is a fucking idiot for letting that happen."

"But is he?" I question. "Just you wait until the four of us are alone and you see just how fucking good sharing can be. Then you'll realize that with all this time wasted denying me, you were actually the biggest idiot of them all."

"Those are some big claims," he laughs, pulling up to my gate and leaning out to enter the code.

"Well, you've got some big competition."

The gate peels open, and as we drive on through, we find Ember's car waiting at the bottom of my step. "Fuck," Grayson groans. "It's not too late. We can turn around and go back to my place, though we risk my little brother walking in and asking to watch."

I laugh. "No way. I don't want to meet your brother for the first time with my ass up in the air. Besides, Ember would have heard the notification that someone was coming through the gate. We're fucked, but we can sneak off into the pool house."

"I can knock her out," he suggests. "I swear, she won't feel a thing and wake up thinking she just dozed off."

I roll my eyes. "You are not knocking out my best friend."

Grayson groans as though he's legitimately down about my refusal, but nonetheless, pulls up behind Ember's car and cuts the engine.

We climb the stairs together and I'm even surprised when he takes my hand and leads me toward my front door. He really can be a gentleman. I think I'm going to enjoy having three guys pining for my attention.

Grayson opens the door and ushers me in. "Ember?" I call, pausing as I listen out for her response.

"Upstairs," she says in a sharp, dismissive tone, the word coming out almost as a curse.

I glance back at Grayson with a cringe and he scoffs, taking my hand once again and leading me toward the stairs. "What did you do to piss her off?" he grumbles low.

I shrug my shoulders, thinking over everything that's gone down in the past few days, and apart from the whole murdering her boyfriend, I've got absolutely no idea. "I don't know but something tells me that we're about to find out."

We reach the top of the stairs and I scan the bedrooms, expecting to find her in my room, but when I don't, I turn around, my confusion instantly beginning to plague me. "Where the fuck is she?" Grayson grumbles as I look down the other end of the hallway and feel the dread sinking heavily into my stomach.

I pull on his arm and watch the color drain from his face as he realizes exactly what I have. “Fuck, no,” he curses under his breath, his hands pulsing into tight fists and probably wishing more now than ever that he could come through on his idea of knocking her out. Maybe then we could somehow convince her that this was all a weird dream.

I start moving, fearing the worst as I pass the staircase and move on past the master bedroom. I see the massive painting on the wall and hate that I know exactly what I’m going to find in the hidden room behind it.

The secret entrance is wide-open and as Grayson and I step into the doorway, we find Ember sitting in the armchair, staring right back at us with a thick, leather-bound book labelled ‘DYNASTY’ on her lap. “You’ve got a lot of explaining to do.”

Well, fuck.

Ember sits on my parents' good couch as I pace in front of her, trying to figure out how the hell I'm supposed to explain all of this. The big leather-bound book sits on the coffee table between us and all four of the boys stare at it, wondering how the hell I'm going to get myself out of this.

But the fact is, I can't.

Ember has heard whispers about Dynasty since she was a little girl. She's been dying to know the truth so badly that it's almost become an obsession of hers. Even before I had anything to do with Dynasty, before I'd even met the boys, she told me about the secrets she'd heard around Ravenwood Heights.

I'll never be able to lie my way out of this, the evidence is too strong, and besides, who knows how long she's been here snooping through my father's secret room. She probably knows more about the ins and outs of Dynasty than I do.

I let out a sigh and stop pacing, and as I do, my stare falls to Cruz who gives me a small nod, silently letting me know that whatever I choose to do, I'll have his support. Carver though, he looks like he's about ready to snap her neck just like he'd done to her bastard boyfriend. He never would though. Ember is important to me, and because of that, he'll protect her just as he protects me.

I meet Ember's pissed off stare and try to think of something smart to say, but all that comes out is a grunted, "ahh, fuck, Ember. Dynasty … it's all fucking true."

Carver groans and sits forward, dropping his head into his hands. "Fucking hell, Winter. Good job keeping the secret. You didn't even try to lie your way out of it."

Ember clenches her jaw, clearly not fond of Carver's easy attitude about me lying to her. "Are you fucking kidding me?" she demands, keeping her heavy, betrayed stare on me. "All this time you've known about Dynasty and you didn't say a goddamn word? Even when I brought it up, you just let me go on talking shit, wondering if I was going crazy."

I shake my head. "To be fair, I only found out a few weeks ago, but yeah, I guess I'm a shitty friend. It wasn't my secret to tell."

"Bullshit, Elodie Ravenwood," she scoffs, proving that she knows so much more than I had hoped. "I'm not stupid. I found the fucking birth certificates in that book. You lied to me. You told me the guys said this was your place and that you were the daughter of Andrew Ravenwood, but it was so much more than that, wasn't it? Andrew was the leader of Dynasty and now you are."

My lips press into a hard line and I look down at the book. "Just how much reading did you get through?"

"Seriously? You want to joke right now?" she scoffs. "I can't believe this. I thought we were friends."

"Look, I just ..." I let out a loud groan and drop onto the couch beside her. "I'm not lying. Dynasty isn't my secret to tell. It is so much bigger than me. There are seventeen families involved in this, I can't just go spilling my guts to whomever I want. It doesn't work like that. I mean, yes, I might be the leader of it, and yes, I'm still trying to figure out what that means, but it's also a dangerous world and I didn't want you pulled into it. If you only knew the amount of near misses I've had over the past few weeks ... fuck."

"Weeks?" King scoffs. "Try years."

Ember's brows furrow as she looks back at me. "What the hell is that supposed to mean? Has someone been trying to kill you?"

"Try many someones," I tell her, flopping back against the soft cushion of the couch.

Her eyes bug out of her head. "WHAT?"

My hands pulse with that familiar urge to hit something, as beating the living shit out of some scumbag loser sounds so much better than having to explain this all to my best friend. I turn to Carver with regret in my eyes. "I'm warning you now, twatmuffin,

I'm about to tell her everything so if you have a problem with it, you can fuck off. I'm not about to sit here and listen to your snide comments the whole way through."

Ember gapes at me, still seeing Carver and the boys as untouchable. She's shocked that I'd dare use a tone like that with them, especially Carver. He just groans and looks back at Grayson. "Why the fuck don't you have my back on this?" he questions, his eyes narrowing on his friend. When guilt flashes in Grayson's eyes, realization pulses through Carver's. "Fucking hell," he grunts. "You jumped ship."

King and Cruz both straighten, looking between me and Grayson for confirmation, and when I cringe, they both raise their brows, trying to figure out what this might mean for us, but now is not the place, and certainly not the time. I've already got one bomb to drop on Ember, I'm not about to drop another.

Ember waits impatiently, and as I bring my gaze back to hers, I let out a deep breath. "Okay, so you know the basics of Dynasty," I start. "It's a secret organization run by seventeen different families with the Ravenwood line being at the top, and seeing as though there is only one living Ravenwood left—"

"That makes you their leader," she finishes for me, eyeing the boys as though she's secretly impressed that I have something over them.

I nod and continue. "Yes, I'm their leader, but Dynasty has some pretty solid and fucked up traditions and values. The other sixteen families are evenly split. The way the guys described it to me is good versus bad with me being the voice of reason between the two sides."

Ember nods, her brows lowering further and further by the second, trying to follow along to every little piece of information.

"Anyway," I continue, "the tradition is that an heir should be male. So when I was born without a big swinging dick, all hell broke loose. The 'bad side' conspired against my parents. They couldn't handle the idea of a female taking over and becoming their leader, so Carver's father took it upon himself to murder my parents in their sleep and attempted to take my life along with it. Only he failed."

Ember sucks in a breath, her eyes wide as she swings her head toward Carver. "The fuck? Your father is a murderer?"

"Was," he grunts, clearly still a little dirty on the whole topic. "Winter here took revenge into her own hands."

Ember's head swings right back to mine, her mouth dropped wide and looking like one of those creepy clowns that swallows balls at a shitty carnival. "YOU KILLED SOMEONE?" she shrieks.

I shrug my shoulder. "What was I supposed to do? He stood over me and admitted it like he was discussing the weather. The knife was already in my hands. I can't help that my self-control needs a little work."

"A little work?" Carver scoffs.

"You're one to talk, asshole."

"Umm … no," Ember cuts in, stealing my attention right back. "You're not about to get lost in some bullshit argument with Carver. Get on with it. Explain."

"Wait. You're not freaked out that I killed his dad?"

"I mean, I'm definitely concerned, but not surprised. You kinda give off the 'don't fuck with me' vibe, and you know, there were all those accusations about you killing Kurt not that long ago, and then you just sort of got let off, which was definitely strange. It's kinda the reason I started snooping in the first place," she admits. "It was too easy. No one gets let off murder charges like that, so I kinda figured that Dynasty had something to do with it, but I was just guessing. Though, don't get me wrong, I definitely want to know what's up with that too."

I roll my eyes and let out another huff. "Alright," I tell her. "I'll explain all of that too."

"Dynasty first," she says. "What happened after you killed his dickhead father?"

"Hey," Carver cuts in.

We both ignore him and I continue my recap of my past few weeks. "So, I kinda killed the guy during my initiation ceremony and everyone saw. So, I was thrown into a cell for a few days, which were those few days that I kinda went missing and you'd asked me where I'd been."

"You gave me some bullshit excuse."

"Yeah, sorry about that. I didn't exactly know how to tell you that I'd just done time for killing some asshole."

"Okay, we'll come back to this, but what happened next?"

"Everything happened," I tell her. "I've had all the other people who supported Carver's dad trying to come after me. Like that attack by my pool the other week. That wasn't just a random break in like we'd told you. That was a planned attack, and what you didn't know was that after knocking you out, he drowned me in the pool. I was just lucky that Grayson knows a thing or two about resuscitation."

"Are you kidding me?" she gasps, wide-eyed. "I fucking knew it. Break-ins just don't happen like that. I knew there was more to the story. Holy fuck. So was that like some kind of assassin?"

"A hitman," King grumbles from across the room. "And you were fucking lucky. Had he hit you just a little bit harder, you would have been dead."

Ember just gapes. "That's … fuck. I have no words."

"That's a first," Grayson mutters, earning a hard stare from me, though as he stares back, I'm instantly reminded of the way he just fucked me on that table and my cheeks flush the brightest red, something that King and Cruz are all too familiar with. My thighs clench and just as I'd requested of Grayson, I can feel exactly where he'd been. Though judging by the heated look in his eyes, he knows exactly what I'm thinking.

I turn back to Ember, desperately needing to get back on track. "That's not the only attack we've had. Do you remember my stupid BDSM party the boys threw for me?"

"Holy fuck, how could a girl forget? That was the party of the year."

"For you maybe," I grumble. "For me, it ended with a shoot-out in the woods that we were lucky to escape."

"Fuck me in the ass sideways," Ember breathes. "Are you shitting me? This bullshit is like … a normal occurrence for you. These guys are seriously trying to kill you, but I just … I don't get it. You're awesome. They should be happy to have you as their leader, at least, I know I would be."

"Thanks," I tell her. "For the most part, they're happy to have me. I mean, most of them are assholes either way, but they've been welcoming. Like King and Cruz's fathers have been helping me adjust."

"What about Grayson's?" she asks, eyeing him warily.

"He's waiting for a good time to sneak up behind me and slit my throat, but he'll wait until everyone else has tried and failed first so he can look like a hero."

"Holy fuck," she says, sucking in a shocked breath.

"Yeah, we'll deal with him eventually, but we have bigger issues to handle first."

Her gaze scans around the room, meeting each of the guys' heavy stares before coming back to mine. "Like?" she questions, her eyes narrowing in curiosity.

I look back at Carver, still for some reason seeing him as the guy I go to for approval. His eyes drop, knowing exactly what's on my mind but leaving it completely up to me whether I let her in on the secret or not.

I let out a heavy breath and take her hand, giving it a tight squeeze. "There's something you need to know," I tell her, my heart instantly breaking with what I have to tell her. "Did you know that Jacob's father, Preston Scardoni is one of the eight families who stand against me?"

Her brows furrow as her back straightens. "Wh … what do you mean? No he's not," she insists, annoyed that I'm even suggesting it. "Jacob isn't a part of this."

"I'm sorry, Ember, but he most definitely is … at least, he was."

Her eyes go wild, flicking around the room at each of our stares as she throws herself to her feet. *"Was?* What the hell is that supposed to mean?" she panics, her voice hitching higher. "Jacob has nothing to do with Dynasty. He didn't even know what it was when I talked to him about it. You're lying. He's a good guy. He loves me. *He's a good guy."*

"Ember …" I let out a broken sigh, hating that I have to break her heart. I get up and walk across the room to her, taking her hand once again. "Jacob was his father's son. You can see their house from here, just like the rest of the Dynasty families. Together, they were planning to take me out. I don't know what their end game was, if it was to just get rid of me or to take over the leadership like Carver's father planned. Preston stood by Carver's father. They're not good people, Ember. All they care about is power, money, and leadership, and they'd do absolutely anything to get what they wanted, even using a teenage girl's best friend and playing with her heart. Jacob was the one who put the call into the hitmen the night of the BDSM party, and a few nights ago, we caught him red-handed putting in another call, all while you were inside that party searching for him, and because of that, we had no choice but to deal with him. It was either his life or mine. You have to understand that."

Tears brim in her eyes. "I asked you that night," she whispers. "I looked you in the eye and asked you if you'd seen him and you said no."

"I—"

"What did you do?" she questions, cutting me off, not wanting to hear my pathetic excuses. "What did you do to him?"

My gaze flickers to Carver, unease brimming in my chest.

Seeing my helplessness, he gets up and walks over to us, crowding Ember as he looks down at her hard, broken stare. "We did what we had to do to make sure that he'd never be able to hurt Winter … ever again."

Ember's mouth drops and she instantly starts backing away, looking at me in horror. "Y … you killed him," she breathes, tears springing from her eyes. "All this time I thought I'd done something wrong, but you killed him. You took him away from me. How could you do that to me? You're supposed to be my best friend, but it's all been one big lie."

I rush toward her, desperately needing her to stay and see things from my perspective. "Ember, I—"

"NO," she yells. "Stay away from me. You … you *murderer.* You're dead to me, Winter … or Elodie Ravenwood. I don't even know who the hell you are anymore. I probably never even knew you at all."

My heart shatters, and just like that, Ember runs out the door, letting it slam shut behind her.

I crumble to the ground and with Carver being the closest, he's the first to catch me. "Go," he roars toward King and Cruz. "Make sure she doesn't talk."

They nod and within seconds, they're out the door, rushing after her as Grayson looks on with a broken stare. Carver looks up at him as he scoops me off the ground and drops back to the couch with me in his lap. "Let me talk to her for a minute," he tells Grayson. "There's some things that need to be discussed."

Grayson looks back at me. "You good?" he asks, the need to stay right by my side flashing brightly in his eyes. I nod and he doesn't waste a single second backing out of the room. "I'll come back later on," he tells me. "We probably have a few things that need to be discussed too."

Grayson leaves me sitting on Carver's lap and the second we're alone, a perfectly round tear falls from my eyes. "Don't cry," he tells me, wiping it away with a simple brush of his thumb. "She'll come around. She's just hurting. She thought she was in love with him, and learning that he was just using her … that would have sucked."

"I know," I whisper. "It's just … she's the only real friend I have here and because of Dynasty, I had to betray her trust. It's been weeks and I still haven't been able to tell her what happened with Sam in that cell, and sometimes, all a girl needs is to talk to a friend about all the bullshit going on in her life."

"I get it," he murmurs, tightening his arms around my waist and holding me so close that I can feel his chest rumbling with the vibrations of his words. "Sometimes all I need is to see my little fucking sisters running around and annoying the shit out of me, but life happens."

I let out a sigh and raise my head, meeting his dark eyes. "I'd give anything to be able to change that for you. If I knew you were risking losing your family, *your sisters* … I never would have pushed you to vote for my freedom. I—"

"Don't," he whispers, brushing my hair back off my face and showing that rare softness that speaks right to my heart. "I knew the risks of giving you your freedom and I took it anyway. My father went against my mother's wishes three times over the past twenty years, and each time she came back to him. So don't you worry about me," he tells me. "I might never have a good relationship with my mother, but they'll be back. It might not be tomorrow or the next day, but they'll come back. I couldn't bear to see you locked up like that, though. If my father never did time for the crimes he committed against your family, then you shouldn't have to do time for the ones committed against mine."

I adjust myself on his lap, turning around until I'm straddled over him and meeting him eye to eye. "Are you sure?"

"I'm sure," he tells me, his hands falling to my waist, something I've been craving since being alone with him in the small dungeon below his father's study. "I know things have been fucked up between us … well, since the fucking beginning, and I hate that. That's never what I intended for our relationship, but you're so fucking headstrong. You fought me every step of the way and that's not something I'm used to. I like to be in control, and you … you fucking love to challenge that."

"No shit," I whisper, the words getting caught in my throat.

Carver just watches me as though he's deep in thought, and

without even thinking, I dip my head toward his and capture his lips in mine. I kiss him softly, barely brushing my lips across his, but when he kisses me back, it's like two worlds colliding.

Our lips move together like the sweetest dance, and when he reluctantly pulls away from me, a tiny piece of my heart breaks, knowing that it could be a lifetime before I get to experience it again.

I pull back and meet his stare, both our hearts sitting on our sleeves. "I don't like fighting with you, Carver."

A soft grin pulls at his lips as his eyes remain locked on mine, his emotions loud and clear for the world to see. "I know, but we're so fucking good at it."

A soft laugh bubbles up my throat. "If I'm completely honest with you, I think I pick fights with you because I like seeing you lose control. It's really the only time I get anything real out of you."

Carver grins back at me. "This isn't real?"

"You know what I mean."

His tongue rolls over his bottom lip as a seriousness pulses through his eyes, making my heart race with fear of what he might say. "I'm not going to share, Winter," he murmurs, pointing out the obvious elephant in the room—the fact that we both desperately want each other. "I don't know how you managed to get Grayson on board with this whole sharing bullshit, but it's not for me."

"I get it," I whisper. "If I had you, I wouldn't want to share you either, but just because we can't make something work between us, doesn't mean that there has to be hostility every time we walk into a room."

Carver nods. "I agree," he says, his hands still on my waist as his thumb moves back and forth over my skin, making me desperately wish that things could be different. "I know it's going to take a lot more for things to truly be okay between us, a lot of things were said, and I know I hurt you last week, but let me extend an olive branch."

My eyes narrow. "What exactly does a Carver version of an olive branch entail?" I ask, slightly nervous about his offering.

"Let me escort you to the annual Dynasty Ball next weekend. You don't have to be my date or anything, but let me pick you up and deliver you to the party where I'm sure you'll have three … *boyfriends* waiting for you."

I skim over his 'boyfriends' comment because labels don't sit well with me, and if I'm honest, I'm not even sure if that's what they are. "Ball?"

Carver nods. "Yep, the annual Dynasty Ball. It's to celebrate the anniversary of when Dynasty was founded all those years ago. I don't know, I think this is the seventieth year running. It's a traditional thing."

"And I've got to wear a dress?"

"Yep, you'll even have to do your hair too."

"Shit."

An amused smirk pulls at Carver's warm lips. "The guys didn't tell you about this? Cruz's mom has been organizing it for years. The whole party planning thing is her jam. She loves it."

"And you're sure I have to wear a dress?" Carver nods and I let out a loud, frustrated groan. "Fuck."

"This is only a recommendation, so don't feel like you have to take this to heart," he starts. "But I know how Dynasty is with making new traditions, though can I suggest that you don't kill anyone during this party? I mean, it kinda fucked with the whole vibe of the last one."

My mouth drops. "You are not seriously joking about that."

"So what if I am?" he smirks. "But I'm still waiting. What's it going to be? Are you going to let me escort you to the Ball or what?"

"I think the guys might have an issue with it."

"Fuck them. What's it going to be?"

I let out a teasing sigh and lean back into him, pressing my lips to his in a quick kiss. "I guess I can let you escort me, after all, you're practically desperate for it. It's the least I can do."

Carver pushes me off his lap, making me sprawl out across the couch. "Fuck, you're such an asshole," he laughs, getting up off the couch, shaking his head in amusement. "If you're one second late, I'll be leaving your stubborn ass behind and making you walk."

"Aye, aye, captain," I laugh, throwing myself off the couch and getting the slightest glimpse of Carver rolling his eyes with a wide smirk across his face as he disappears around the corner. I can't help the cheesy as fuck grin that stretches across my face as he slams the front door behind him.

31

My legs rest comfortably in Grayson's lap as his hands roam up and down, reminding me that today really did happen. "So, we're really doing this, huh?" I ask, meeting his lazy stare. "Are you sure you're okay with it? There's not going to be any issues?"

"I'm not going to lie, just like the guys, I'm sure it's going to be an adjustment, but I'll need to speak with them and make sure they're really cool with the idea of me … joining? I don't know. Is that even the right word for this shit?"

I laugh and shrug my shoulders. "I honestly have no fucking clue. We're just making it up as we go, but so far, it's working. It's been the best of both worlds. I get dicked whenever the fuck I want and don't have to worry about all the bullshit that comes along with having a boyfriend."

"So … no dates?" he questions. "No labels?"

I shake my head. "I'm not a labels kind of girl, and I mean, I'm not going to say no to a date if you want to take me on one, but what I meant by all the bullshit that comes along with it, is that I don't have to deal with jealous guys fighting over me because I'm both of theirs … and well, yours now too. There are no secrets. Everything is out in the open, and like I said to King and Cruz, it won't work if we're not honest with one another."

"I agree," he says. "I'm not really one of those guys who can handle a chick hanging off me all the time, not that you're one of those girls, but maybe sharing is exactly what I need."

"First off, I'm not one of those girls who can put up with a guy constantly nagging for *my* attention all the time, so let's just make sure you're not one of them," I tease. "And secondly, who the fuck wouldn't want me hanging off them all day long? I know I would."

"Fuck me," he grumbles under his breath. "Your arrogance knows no bounds. You're lucky you're so fucking hot, otherwise I might have left you at that tattoo parlor to face the firing squad."

"Bullshit, you would have been worried that I'd fuck them too and your alpha, overprotective bullshit would have come out to play."

Grayson narrows his eyes more than ready to throw down with me, but instead, he grabs me around the waist and hoists me up onto his lap. "Say it to my face, Ellie."

I grin and just as my lips crush down against his, the front door swings open and two broody assholes come storming right in as though they own the place. My head snaps up and I grin back at them as they come striding into my living room. "How was Ember?" I ask, my desperation to know that she doesn't hate me pulsing rapidly through my body.

"She's alright," Cruz says. "She went straight home. We watched her for a while, but I don't think she's going anywhere. At least, not tonight. She was fucking pissed with you. I wouldn't be surprised if she's the one who orders the next hit on your ass."

I groan, hating the thought. "She probably just needs some time," I tell them, hoping to god that she can see this from my point of view. "She'll come around. She's hurting."

King nods. "Probably. Where's Carver?" he asks as he eyes me straddled over Grayson's lap, my face dangerously close to his.

I scoff. "Probably licking his wounds and nursing his ego."

"Huh?" Cruz says, dropping down in the seat I was in only two seconds ago. He meets my stare with a narrowed, suspicious gaze. "What did you do to him this time?"

"What?" I gasp. "I'm offended. I'm nothing but an angel. I didn't do a thing."

Grayson laughs and rests his hands against my waist, curling one of them right around and holding me close. "The dickhead wanted to play nice and asked her if he could escort her to the Ball next weekend."

"Ahh, fuck," King laughs, flopping back into his seat with an amused smirk pulling at his lips. He looks at me, his eyes sparkling like the most beautiful set of diamonds. "Let me guess, you fucking played with him."

I give King the most innocent smile I can possibly come up with. "I mean, would I do that? I was a perfect lady."

"Yeah, you fucked with his head," Cruz laughs. "The poor bastard. How'd he take it?"

I bite down on my lip, more than ready to keep those details to myself, and instantly regret that I'd just finished telling Grayson all about it. "The fucker just walked out of here with his tail between his legs. She told him that she'd go with him, only because he seemed so desperate to take her."

Cruz and King double over in laughter which only makes Grayson do the same. Despite already having heard the story, nothing but guilt pours through me. These guys have been friends for years so I'm sure they've seen more than their fair share of teasing, but there's just something about Carver, and I hate the thought of others laughing at his expense. "To be fair," I tell them. "Grayson totally exaggerated that story."

"Either way," King says. "Nothing's better than having you put that bastard in his place, especially after the way he's treated you over the past two months. You deserved better."

"I don't know," I say, shrugging my shoulders. "I give it to him just as hard as he gives it to me."

"Speaking of giving it to you," Cruz says, eyeing Grayson's hands on my waist. "It seems like Carver isn't the only one who's been giving you something today. What's going on here? Did my competition just double?"

I look over at Cruz, my lips pulling into a guilty grin. "If you consider the size of the monster between his legs, I'd say it didn't just double, it tripled," I laugh before looking at him with seriousness. "But we talked about this, right? You're still cool with me being with Grayson, too? This doesn't complicate things?"

His gaze briefly flickers toward King's before settling back on mine, and as he looks between me and Grayson, he shakes his head. "I stand by what I said," he tells me. "I'm cool with sharing as long as you're not worn out by the time I get my hands on you."

I give him a stupid grin before looking the other way at King. "And your stubborn ass?"

"My stubborn ass is good as long as your stubborn ass is."

The boys both look at Grayson. "Are you good with this?" Cruz asks. "It's not the same as when you dated Kristy Wakehurst. You can't get all possessive when her eyes start to wander."

"Kristy Wakehurst was supposed to be an exclusive relationship," Grayson grumbles, reaching out and knocking Cruz on the shoulder for even bringing it up. "This is different. I get it. We share, but don't come crying to me when she decides that I get her off best."

"Bullshit," King says. "We all know that it's my dick she's dreaming about, isn't it, Winter? Don't be shy, you can tell them what's up."

I bite down on my bottom lip, my gaze flicking between each of the guys. "Do you really want to know what I've been dreaming about?"

Cruz grips my ankle and starts dragging me back across the couch until I'm flat on the cushion with my legs over his lap. "I think I know exactly what you've been dreaming about," he tells me, pushing my knees apart and crawling in between them until his lips are brushing over my inner thigh.

I laugh as his peppered kisses tickle my skin, but my laugh only prompts him to do it again. I squirm under his touch, but a second later, his kisses trail higher until his face is pressed right between my legs. A soft moan slips from between my lips and I arch up off the couch, tilting my head back as desire sweeps through me.

My legs instantly curl around Cruz's head, holding him there as he continues to tease me above my clothing, his hands trailing up my body and roaming over my tits.

I look up and find Grayson staring down at me, his eyes hooded and full of lust. "What are you waiting for?" I murmur. "Touch me."

The desire in his eyes turns into a flaming need, and within seconds, his hands are on my body as Cruz peels my jeans down my legs. King's deep rumble comes from across the room and I look his way to find his tongue rolling over his full lips.

Holy shit. Is this going to happen?

King pushes up off the couch just as Grayson adjusts himself to lean down and kiss me upside down—Spiderman style. Hands shove my tank over my head, and not a second later, I'm as naked as the day I was born in a room full of the most attractive men I've ever met. If someone had told me before coming to Ravenwood Heights that I'd be in this exact situation, I'd never believe it. The thought of having three men ogling my body at the same time would have daunted me, but I would have been wrong because the way they worship my body, the way they look at me with their adoring gazes is the best thing I've ever experienced.

King drops down to his knees beside the couch, reaching over his head with one hand and gripping his shirt from the back. He tugs it effortlessly over his head, putting that amazing body on display. My hand instantly reaches out and I graze my nails over the sharp ridges of his abs just as Cruz's lips finally come down on my clit.

I suck in a gasp, and feel Grayson's heated stare on my pussy, watching the way Cruz touches me and seeing just how much the whole sharing thing turns me on, and damn it, the approval in his eyes makes me the happiest girl who ever lived.

I look up and meet Grayson's stare just as King's fly comes down and his rock-hard cock springs free from his pants. "Yeah?" I ask Grayson, double checking that he's on board.

A grin pulls at his lips. "Fuck yeah."

The boys shuffle me around to make things a little easier, sitting me up on the couch with Cruz on his knees in front, his tongue still working my clit, flicking, and teasing, getting my body all kinds of worked up.

Grayson kneels at one side while King kneels on the other, both their dicks in their hands, watching Cruz work my body. Getting myself comfortable on the couch, I reach up and curl my hands around their cocks as Grayson leans in and rolls his tongue over my nipple before gently nipping at it and driving me wild.

A shot of electricity pulses through me, leading right down to my core, and as I tip my head back on the couch, King's lips come down on mine, swallowing my moans.

Six hands roam over my body, so delicious and sensual that after a while, I have no fucking idea whose hand belongs to whom. At least, I can pinpoint which hand is Cruz's when it disappears between my legs and two thick fingers thrust up into me, making me gasp into King's mouth.

"Holy shit, Cruz," I pant, feeling King's lips pull up into a wicked grin against mine.

"You fucking love your pussy getting eaten," King murmurs before glancing up and meeting Grayson's eyes. "Watch this."

King's hand comes up and he gently pinches my nipple before roaming his thumb over it and giving it a flick. "Oh, fuck," I groan, thrusting my chest up toward his hand again, desperately needing more.

Grayson's brow arches and a smirk pulls at his lips. "Fuck, yeah," he rumbles low, the sound vibrating right through his chest. He doesn't waste a second giving it a go himself and with King, they each do it again at the same time.

"Shit," I cry, bucking up against Cruz and making his hands come around me to hold me still.

"So fucking responsive," Grayson mutters, bringing his lips back to mine and kissing me deeply as my thumb roams over the tip of both of their cocks, making King shudder beneath my touch.

"Get on your knees," King tells me.

I pull back from Grayson and briefly look his way, but the hunger in his eyes has me moving faster than lightning. I get to my knees, and within seconds, Cruz is back working my clit and this position has his fingers pushing even deeper within me, but when King's hand slips down behind me, I'm seeing stars.

His finger mixes with my wetness before drawing back to my ass and teasing me there. He applies a little pressure, testing the waters and as I push back against him with an eager moan, he presses up, giving me exactly what my body is craving.

"Oh my, God," I groan as Grayson's lips move to my neck, right in the sensitive spot beneath my ear that drives me insane with need.

I ride both King and Cruz's fingers knowing that from this moment, it could only get better. My hands tighten around the guys' dicks, and for a slight beat, my heart aches for Cruz as I only have two hands, and from this position, I wouldn't be able to reach him anyway.

"Fuck, Ellie," Grayson grunts, his soft breath grazing over my skin and sending shivers right down my spine. "I've been dreaming about those soft hands working my cock for fucking years."

I pull back and meet his eyes, and as I do, my hands work faster, my thumb constantly rolling over that silver metal piercing at his tip. I watch as his gaze darkens. I feel my orgasm building deep within me and a breathy moan slips from between my lips. "I'm going to come," I warn them, knowing that this one is not only going to tear me to pieces but most likely bring the whole fucking house down around us.

My pants only spur Cruz on, hitting that spot over and over as his tongue glides up and over my clit, nipping, circling, and sucking as he goes. He's relentless, drawing my orgasm out of me, building me higher and higher, and pushing me closer to the edge just how I like it.

My groans get louder, my hands move faster, and their touch becomes so much sweeter. Hands roam, my tits ache, tongues sweep. It's like running through bushes and having every single leaf and branch brush over my skin, only those leaves are tongues and lips, and the branches are skilled fingers that know exactly where to touch me.

I could die right here and know that my life was as good as it was ever going to get. If only Carver …

Fuck it, I'm not going to let him ruin this for me.

King presses deeper just as Cruz's fingers find that magical spot, and without warning, my orgasm rips through me. "OH, FUCK," I cry with Grayson's lips on my neck, his fingers pinching my nipples as Cruz's tongue flicks against my clit.

"Fucking give it to him," Grayson mutters in my ear, sending shivers shooting across my skin. "Let him taste your sweet cum."

My high only grows, intensifying with each passing second as the guys refuse to stop. "Fuck, fuck, fuck." It becomes a desperate plea as my eyes clench and Grayson grabs my chin, forcing my mouth back to his as he kisses me violently, making me melt into him.

My climax finally eases and I desperately try to catch my breath as Cruz's all too handsome face appears from between my legs with a proud as fuck smirk stretching far across his face. "Well, well, aren't you just the fucking hero of the hour."

His eyes darken as he gets to his feet and makes a show of unbuckling his belt. "You can fucking count on it."

Within seconds, Cruz's pants are gone and his heavy cock rests in his hand as his other slips around my waist and he tears me away from the guys, leaving both their impressive cocks unattended and very unimpressed.

Cruz drops down onto the couch, laying back and in the same, swift motion, sits me down on top of him, filling me with his large, veiny cock. I groan out, having to catch myself against his wide, chiseled chest as I get used to his welcome intrusion, but only a second passes before I start rocking my hips, riding him just the way he likes.

Cruz licks his lips and brushes his knuckles over my pebbled nipples that are pink from King and Grayson's gentle pinches, but damn it, it was so fucking worth it. Cruz's hand cups the curve of my breast, almost as though it's fragile. "Your fucking body, babe …" he says, leaving the ending of his sentence dangling in the air, but I don't need it. I already know exactly what he thinks of my body.

The couch dips behind me and I look back to find Grayson leaning into me, his arm curling around my waist as I feel his piercing gently moving against my back. "Just how fucking serious were you about staying away from your ass?"

King laughs. "Trust me, she can handle it."

My eyes beam with excitement as I look back at King, wanting to hate on him for answering for me but also wanting to give him a proud as fuck high five for knowing my body so well.

King just winks while moving in closer, and everything clenches within me, making Cruz groan.

I look back over my shoulder feeling a slight nervousness travel through me, but King is right. I can handle it. I just need to relax. If I tense up, it'll never happen, but there's no reason why I can't enjoy this. My arm curls around the back of Grayson's head and I pull him in closer, brushing my lips over his. "Just take it easy with me," I whisper, silently begging him not to hurt me.

He nods, skimming his fingers over my ass and making me jump, once again clenching down on Cruz. "I'd never fucking hurt you, Ellie," Grayson promises with a soft, sweet murmur, his lips moving against mine. He gives me one more kiss before pulling back and just like that, I lower myself down onto Cruz's chest, bringing my lips to meet his just as King steps into my side.

My fingers curl around his thick cock as Grayson works my ass, mixing my wetness and getting me ready. The nerves still pulse deep within me, but I trust them all. They'll keep me safe.

I feel the cool metal of Grayson's piercing at my ass as I pause on top of Cruz, letting out a slow, deep breath. Grayson pushes into me, guiding his monster cock with one hand while clutching my hip with the other.

"Holy shit," I breathe against Cruz's cheek as his hand falls to my back, slowly rubbing up and down and silently letting me know that I was born for this.

"You good?" Grayson's deep, gruff voice sounds through the room as he pushes deeper, stretching me wider and making my eyes roll to the back of my head.

"Just give me a sec," I whisper before I slowly push back against him, adjusting my hips until it's just right. "Okay," I finally breathe. "Let's do this."

Cruz stays still and lets the movement come from Grayson as he slowly draws out of me, making me burn in all the right ways. He goes back in and my eyes instantly roll, but Cruz is there and slips his hand between my legs and gently circles my clit, somehow making everything alright. Once my body finally accepts this beautiful punishment, I turn my heated stare on King, loving the way his eyes travel over my body, his hand stroking his cock as he watches his friends fuck his girl.

I put my hand down beside Cruz's shoulder and push up just a little, and as King meets my stare, I roll my tongue over my lips, letting him know just how hungry I really am. I mean, we haven't come this far just to stop at two dicks. I might as well take them all. "Are you happy watching or are you going to come and put it in my mouth?"

His brow arches and he instantly steps closer, curling his hand around the back of my neck as I open wide for him. Needing to keep my balance, King guides his cock into my mouth, and I watch the satisfaction slice over his features as I close my lips around him and let my tongue explore.

I start moving up and down his thick cock, keeping with the slow, torturous pace that Grayson keeps in order to literally not tear me a new asshole. Cruz groans under me, getting an up-close view of me sucking King's dick as my eyes roll, feeling his fingers flicking over my clit.

Grayson's hands tighten on my waist as we all hear his low, guttural growl, knowing that he's experiencing something special back there. It's a fucking tight squeeze for me, especially with Cruz's big dick already deep inside of me, but does that make a difference for them? Can Cruz feel it as Grayson moves? I don't fucking know, but not wanting him to miss out, I rock my hips up and down, making both of them groan with satisfaction.

All three of them slowly move in and out of me, and for a moment, I feel like a wet-as-fuck, human pin cushion, but instead of pain, all I feel is the greatest pleasure. Though I'm not going to lie, I'm going to need an ice bath after this, but I'm kinda hoping that all three of them will come to bed with me and spend the night with their arms around me. Though, I know that's a long shot.

Grayson's fingers tighten as I feel Cruz suck in a breath. "Oh, fuck," he murmurs in my ear just as King bites down on his lip, all three of them on the edge and ready to blow.

I push back against Grayson, taking him deeper as I drop down hard against Cruz, taking him rough. His fingers press down harder against my clit, rubbing faster as all three of the boys start to pick up their pace. I groan against King's solid cock, desperately wishing I could cry for more, but they read me perfectly.

They all fuck me harder. Grayson leans back and hits me at a new angle while also giving Cruz the freedom to move a little more, and fuck up into me, thrusting harder and making my eyes water. King's hand curls into my hair, fisting around my ponytail and controlling exactly how fast and deep I take him.

All three of them give me exactly what I want, holding out despite how desperate they are to come, until finally, I come undone beneath them. My pussy clenches hard and begins to spasm, and fuck me, I know Grayson feels it too.

King comes hard, his warm seed shooting to the back of my

throat as Grayson pulls out and spurts his hot cum all over my back. Cruz though, he just lets me have it and shoots his load deep inside me just as he always does, and the second King slips out of my mouth, I collapse down onto Cruz's chest, my body completely and utterly spent.

"Holy fuck," Grayson mutters, the impressed and awed astonishment clear in his tone as he climbs off the couch and crosses the room to grab the box of tissues from the hallway table. "I think I finally get what you mean about sharing."

A grin splits across my face but I don't have the energy to even raise my head to tell him what a dork he is. Instead, I just lay on Cruz's chest listening to the boys' congratulatory laughs and high fives as Grayson wipes himself off my back, finishing with a perfectly delicious spank to my ass that has me grinning like a fool, and knowing damn well that later on tonight, we'll be doing that all over again.

32

I let out a deep breath as I stare up at the door before me. It's been four fucking days and she still hasn't spoken a word to me, not even at school. Ember just scowled and looked at me as though I was the worst person in the world, but I know she doesn't really think that. Not really. She needs me just as much as I need her, she's just angry that she had to find out like that.

We have to be okay. Apart from the boys, Ember is all I have in Ravenwood Heights, and when the boys are being their usual, alpha asshole selves, I need her the most.

My knuckles come down over the door and I take a small step back, feeling the dread washing through me. Ember can be just as stubborn as I am, and I have a feeling that this isn't going to go down well, but I have to try. I can't walk away from this without trying.

I take a shaky breath, impatiently waiting for the door to open, and after what feels like an agonizing lifetime, I hear someone grabbing the door handle from inside.

The massive wooden door pulls open just a fraction and I see Ember through the gap. Not a second later, a scowl stretches over her face and she instantly pushes the door closed again. "Nope. Not today, Satan."

Fuck, that stung.

I shove my foot in the door and push my hand against it, but with the size of this door, it's got quite a bit of weight behind it, a weight that my foot is so not pleased about, but I suck it up. I can handle a sore foot for a minute longer. "Come on," I groan, pushing the door just wide enough to squeeze through to Ember's foyer. "Just hear me out. I hate that you're not talking to me."

"Welcome to my world," she sneers, reaching for the door and opening it again, not so subtly suggesting that I get my ass out. "We've been friends for nearly three months and I feel like you haven't really talked to me at all. I don't even know if you're a coffee or tea girl."

I lean back against the door, letting it fall shut again as I give her a blank stare. "You know that's not true," I tell her. "You know all that shit about me. I've shared every part of my life that I've been allowed to share."

"Oh yeah?" she scoffs. "What about those eighteen years spent in foster care? You've never once told me about that shit."

I shrug my shoulders as a soft groan pulls from deep within me. "What do you want from me, Ember? Those eighteen years aren't exactly something I'm comfortable talking about. I purposefully go out of my way to not even think about it, let alone share it with someone who's going to force me to face it."

"I … I wouldn't do that," she argues. "I just want to know you. You're supposed to be my best friend."

"I know that, but can't you be happy knowing that I've shared the parts of myself that I actually like? I have way too many demons, ones that you couldn't even begin to understand, ones that would shock you."

"Yeah," she scoffs, the distaste in her tone coming through loud and clear. "Trust me, I know all about the bullshit you've been getting up to that would shock me. Tell me, Winter … *or Elodie,* whichever one you go by now, have you killed anyone else's boyfriends lately?"

My stare hardens. "Come on, that's not fair. We explained that. It's not my fault that Jacob was secretly plotting against me and using our friendship to do it."

"No," she says, softly shaking her head and letting me see the real Ember, the one who is riddled with pain and hurt from my betrayal. "But it's certainly your fault that you hid it from me. How long have you known that he was a part of Dynasty and that his father was bad news?"

I let out a broken sigh and meet her pained stare. "A few weeks," I admit in a quiet, timid voice.

"Exactly," she mutters. "You could have told me, you could have *trusted* me, and none of this would have happened. I would have broken up with him straight away, and I never would have told him every time you were coming to a party with me or when we were hanging out at your place alone. You would have been safe, and had those hitmen actually gotten through and hurt you, that would have partially been my fault. Don't you see that?"

I shake my head. "I don't," I tell her. "I see you as an innocent. You don't have to be involved in this mess, and I don't want that for you. This world … it's not nice. I wanted to protect you from it, but Jacob insisted on dragging you right into the middle of a shit fight."

"You *killed* him, Winter. You and the boys *killed a man. Killed my boyfriend."*

I nod. "Trust me, I'm more than aware of that. Every single day something happens where I'm reminded of the shitty things I've had to do in the name of Dynasty. I hate it."

Ember lets out a heavy sigh and backs up a few steps until her ankles are hitting the bottom step of her massive staircase. She sits down and leans on her elbows, keeping her stare on the expensive tiles at her feet. "I … I really don't know what to say to you."

"Yes, you do," I tell her, walking toward the stairs and dropping down beside her. "Not once since the day that I met you have you ever been lost for words. Just hit me with whatever you've been wondering about, because I know damn well that there's a whole list of things, but first, tell me that we're okay."

A small smile pulls at her lips before she flattens them into a tight line. "I'm not giving in that easy," she tells me, proving just how stubborn she really is. She raises her head and meets my stare, the curiosity in her eyes shining brightly. "What's the deal with Knox?" she asks. "One minute we're hanging out with him at a party and the next thing I know we're waking up here and you're telling me that his uncle was a sex trafficker, but then a few days later, he completely disappeared and no one has seen him since. Does he have something to do with Dynasty?"

I shake my head, letting out a heavy sigh. "Knox has nothing to do with Dynasty, but are you sure you really want to go there? What happened with Knox isn't exactly a happy story, and fuck, it's going to be hard to tell. Once I tell you and open you up to that, there's no going back. You're going to see me differently."

Her brows furrow as she watches me. "What's that supposed to mean?" she questions, her back straightening. "What happened to you? If he's got nothing to do with Dynasty, why haven't you told me? What did he do?"

"His uncle was a sex trafficker," I say, even though she already knows that. "That night when Knox took us to Sam's club, he was putting me on display, trying to sell me to make a commission."

"I know that," she cuts in, "but the boys got to you first and you beat the shit out of Knox. That was over."

I shake my head. "That was only the beginning," I tell her. "Do you remember the night of the pier party?"

She nods. "That was the night Jacob and I first got together. I felt like a bitch because I ditched you and you went home early."

"Yeah," I whisper, glancing away. "When I got back to Kurt and

Irene's place, two of Sam's men were waiting for me in my room." Ember sucks in a breath but I don't stop, knowing that if I did, I might not be able to continue. "I tried to fight them off. I screamed and a part of me hoped that maybe Kurt or Irene would come to save me, but they never showed. The men shoved a black bag over my head and I was knocked out. The next thing I knew, I was being pulled out of the back of a van."

Tears well in Ember's eyes as she reaches out and takes my hand. "No, please don't tell me Sam hurt you."

I shake my head, hating my own tears that threaten to spill down my face. "I was put in a cold cell for three nights and it was awful. It was wet and dark. I couldn't see a damn thing. All I could hear was the sounds of the girls in other cells screaming for help and cell doors banging. There was this constant dripping, which I know doesn't sound bad but on repeat like that, it's fucking horrible. After the third night, I'd basically given up. Nobody knew I was gone and even if they did, how were they going to find me?"

I let out a shaky breath and meet her eyes again. "That night, two men came into my cell and dressed me in black lingerie. They forced me into this big room filled with men. Hands were grabbing at me, touching me, and they spit comments about my body and what they were going to do to it. I was taken onto a stage with harsh lights on my face and I couldn't see anything beyond that, only hear as the auctioneer sold me for five million dollars."

"What?" she breathes, her eyes wide. "No, please tell me this is some kind of joke."

"I really wish I could," I tell her, the tears now staining my cheeks. "It turns out that Dynasty was responsible for that five million dollars. Carver and the boys used some fancy tech and beat the living shit out of Knox until they got some information out of him. They found me just in time, but because of that, the past few weeks have been hard. Like really fucking hard."

"What happened? I know that's not the end of the story. Those guys wouldn't just let it go like that."

"Dynasty isn't big on revenge plans. They wouldn't let us go after Sam because they don't involve themselves in crimes like this. To them, the matter had been resolved, but I couldn't let it go."

"What did you do?" she asks, wide-eyed, reaching up and wiping away my tears.

Another shaky breath comes tearing out of me. "Last week, Carver put in a call. Sam remembered him from 'purchasing' me and he said that he wanted a new girl. So Sam flew back into the state and we royally fucked him up," I explain. "Do you remember seeing the house explosion on the news the other day?"

Her brows furrow and she quickly nods her head. "That was you?"

"Uh-huh. Well, King, actually. Apparently, he knows a little something about explosives," I say, a wicked grin pulling at my lips. "We took Sam back to Carver's place and gave him what he deserved."

"Holy fuck, tell me that you beat his ass?"

A grin stretches across my face as I meet her eyes. "With a fucking baseball bat."

"HELL YEAH," she cheers, throwing her arms around me. "I'm

so sorry. The past few days, I've been sulking because you wouldn't let me in, but you were just trying to protect me from all of this."

"I really was," I whisper. "You don't know how much I wanted to tell you, to have someone to talk to about all of this shit, because fuck, Ember, this world is fucking twisted and I've hardly been able to wrap my head around it."

She nods and grips my hand before pulling me to my feet. Despite us already being alone in her house, she leads me right up to her bedroom and closes the door for privacy. "I just have one more question," she tells me. "Then I promise, I won't bug you for information unless you want to tell me."

My eyes narrow. "What is it?"

"What's the fucking deal with the guys? Are you sleeping with them or what?"

I bite down on my lip, desperately trying to squish the smile that tears across my face, but the truth is as clear as the sky is blue. "HOLY FUCK," she shrieks. "YOU'RE FUCKING THEM ALL."

"Fuck," I grunt under my breath, letting the smile fly free. "I'm not doing them all, just King, Cruz, and Grayson. Carver is a stubborn asshole who insists that he doesn't share."

She just stares at me, her mouth hanging open. "Holy shit, girl. You've really been holding out on me. Like … what the fuck?"

I laugh. "Well, to be fair, I only started screwing Grayson over the weekend, but King and Cruz, I've been screwing them since the very beginning."

"I … fuck," she breathes, backing up to her bed. "I need to sit down."

I watch Ember for a second longer as she wraps her head around it and when she raises her gaze to meet mine, I can't help but laugh.

"So … how? Do you just fuck them all behind one another's back or do they know?"

"Babe," I grin, "they don't only know about each other, they join in."

A weird squeaky, grumbled sound comes tearing out of her and she grabs her pillow, hugging it to her chest as she stares blankly at the wall ahead. "You just … fuck them all at the same time?"

"I mean, wouldn't you if you were in my position?"

"I just … I just need a minute."

I nod, completely understanding and let her continue to stare at the wall as I cross her room and drop down onto her couch. I put my feet up and start scrolling through social media. It's not until five minutes later that she finally has the ability to string together a proper sentence. "You've had it rough over the past eighteen years in the foster system, and the bullshit with people trying to kill you, plus being kidnapped from your room the same night that I was supposed to be staying with you. Like, you've had some serious bad luck, but fuck, this more than makes up for it."

"Tell me about it," I grumble as a smirk cuts across my face.

"No, no. You tell me about it. All fucking about it."

I laugh and I can't help but bound back to her bed. I throw myself down next to her and finally let out all the steamy details that I've been dying to share with her. I'm not usually one for spilling secrets, but sometimes just having a girlfriend to talk to is better than any kind of therapy.

I tell her as much as I can while also protecting the guys' privacy, and after an hour, she's still gaping at me, absolutely speechless.

Once I've shared all the hot and heavy details, my lips press into a tight line as I contemplate asking her this next question. "Look," I tell her. "I might seriously be crossing a line here, but you're my best friend and I want you involved in my life, and if I'm completely honest, I doubt that I'm even allowed to ask you this, but …"

"But?" she prompts.

"There's kind of this big fancy annual Dynasty Ball over the weekend and I was hoping that maybe you might dress up in a ridiculous gown and come with me? Call it my big apology gesture."

Her mouth drops open. "A ball? Like an actual ball? Like Cinderella kind of bullshit?"

"Apparently," I say, shrugging my shoulders. "I didn't really ask too many details, but that's my take on it."

"HOLY SHIT, YES," she shrieks, her eyes going wide and glistening with excitement. "Count me in."

"Are you serious?"

Ember grabs her phone and instantly brings up her Pinterest app and starts creating a new board. "Fuck yeah. I am all over this."

"Good, because I'm going to need as much help as I can possibly get."

33

My Fadel Jaber black tulle halter gown sits across my body perfectly. Two thick tulle columns fall from around my neck and are pulled tight over my tits, meeting at my cinched waist and leaving my cleavage fully on display as my back is left completely bare.

The tulle poofs out at my waist and drops down to the ground with a small train behind. It's absolutely beautiful, so much more than I thought it was going to be. It hugs my body just right and makes me feel as though maybe I might just belong in this world after all.

I'm not the kind of girl who gets off on having fancy dresses, and I sure as hell have never dreamed about going to balls and grand parties, but this is my life now, and I think getting on board won't be such a horrible task. This ball gown though, it's fit for a gothic barbie. The tulle even comes right up and winds around my neck like one of my many chokers. It's as though it was designed just for me.

I slip my heels on and take one final look at myself in the mirror. My hair is pulled up into a bun with soft strands flowing freely around my face. I was all about keeping my hair down tonight, but the back of this gown, or lack thereof, deserves to be shown off.

I lean into the mirror and paint on one final coat of my favorite deep plum lipstick while glancing over my makeup. Ember convinced me to try fake eyelashes, and damn, I'm all about the fake eyelash life now. I wonder how I'd look with extensions.

"What did I tell you about being even one second late?" Carver's deep baritone voice comes shooting up the stairs from the open space of the foyer.

I roll my eyes and light up the screen of my phone. 7:58 p.m. "I'm not late," I yell back at him, "but keep yelling bullshit like that and I'll make sure that I am. You know, I'm not really feeling this dress. I think I need a whole outfit change, hair, and makeup as well."

I grin to myself as I hear his muttered grumbling from downstairs. "Either get your ass down here, or I'm coming up to get you."

"Ooooooh," I tease. "Should I be scared? Are you going to tie me up, throw me over your shoulder, and spank my ass?"

"You're an asshole, Elodie Ravenwood."

"Come up here and tell me that, Dante Carver."

Not a second later, I hear the sound of Carver on the stairs, taking them two at a time.

My stomach drops.

Oh, fuck.

I run to the door grabbing hold of it and slamming it shut, only I'm not fast enough as Carver reaches the other side and pushes against me. "No, no, no," I squeal, nearly tripping over my dress. "Get your douchey ass out of here."

"Why don't you get your douchey ass out here?"

My strength is absolutely no match to his and he quickly overpowers me, pushing the door wider with ease. I groan and grunt, trying my hardest, but I have absolutely no chance of winning this. Sometimes it's just best to know your limits and work out a way around them.

Being far too stubborn to give up without a fight, I dart out of the way, letting the door fly open under his pressure and watch with a wicked smirk as he comes tumbling into my room, only just catching himself before he trips and smacks his head against the frame of my dresser.

"Have a nice trip?" I laugh, watching as he straightens out only to be struck by how fucking amazing he looks in his black suit. His messy hair looks as though it's actually had some attention put into it, while that light smattering of stubble across his jaw makes me weak. He's like a dark knight, but not the kind who's there to save the princess at the end of the day. He's the one who the princess is going to think about while she's screwing her Prince Charming.

Dante Carver is fucking everything.

His suit shirt is black and he's ditched the whole tie thing, leaving the top two buttons undone and making everything ache within me. "Holy shit," I breathe, taking him in from head to toe only to notice the way his dark eyes scan over my body in awe. "I didn't think it was possible, but you actually look a little alright."

Carver scoffs, having to clear his throat before quickly glancing away as though the rest of my room suddenly just became extremely exciting. "Right back at ya, babe."

"Smooth," I laugh, grabbing my phone and shoving it deep into the hidden pocket of my incredible dress. While that was the worst kind of compliment a girl could receive, from Carver, it means the fucking world. "Are you this awkward with all your dates? Maybe you need to spend some more time with Cruz. I'm sure he could teach you a thing or two about talking to a girl."

Carver laughs. "Cruz doesn't know shit about talking to a girl, all he has to do is flash a fucking smile and chicks go stupid," he says, giving me a pointed stare. "Case in point."

I roll my eyes as I walk right into him, tilting my head as his hand falls to my waist, his fingers gently digging in. "I think you're underestimating Cruz," I tell him. "The things he's murmured in my ear that have gotten me on my knees would make even you blush."

Carver's stare hardens, and for just a second, his rigid exterior fades away and his emotions come screaming out, hitting me right in the chest. "What's the matter, Carver? You look jealous."

"So what if I am?" he questions, his voice deep and gruff, filled with everything he refuses to say out loud.

I push up, hovering my lips right in front of his. "It doesn't have to be that way," I remind him. "You're the one putting limitations on us. All you'd have to do is open yourself up and you'll see just how good it is."

"Is that the bullshit line you used on Gray?"

A smile pulls at my lips and the way he watches nearly has me melting into a ball at his feet, making me wonder for the millionth time how he managed to have such a hold over me. Who would have ever known that I'd have such a weakness for asshole guys with alpha complexes? "Trust me, you're not ready for the lines I've used on him."

"No, Winter," he says, his voice filled with authority as his fingers pinch at my waist. "You're not ready. Now let's go. I have a ball to escort you to."

Without another word, Carver's hands fall from my waist and he steps around me, disappearing straight through the door. My heart races and I brush my hands down my dress, giving myself a moment to collect my thoughts.

I step back in front of the mirror and quickly scan my gaze over my beautiful dress. This right here is as good as it's ever going to get.

"Are you coming or what?" Carver calls.

I groan and follow him out the door. "I should have known letting you escort me wasn't going to be anywhere near as good as it sounded."

"Bullshit," he fires back from the top of the stairs. "You're having the time of your fucking life."

I roll my eyes as I step into his side and he instantly takes my hand to help me down the stairs. He's right, I am having the time of my life, but I'm not about to go admitting that to him. There's just something about this playful, teasing version of Carver that makes me feel as though there might just be a future between us. It gives me hope, and damn it, I know all too well that hope can be a dangerous thing.

Don't get me wrong, I also love that moody version of him. When he throws me up against the wall and loses control, he oozes sex appeal, and if I wasn't pretending to hate him so much, I would have let him have his wicked way with me ages ago. Sex with Carver when he's in a mood like that … shit. Now that would be the definition of explosive.

We reach the bottom of the stairs and I don't miss the way that he doesn't release my hand as we walk to the front door and then down to his Escalade that waits patiently for us. "King called," he murmurs as we hit the final step. "Ember arrived about ten minutes ago. They're keeping an eye on her for you."

A beaming smile lights up my face and I turn to meet his stare. "Oh, good," I breathe, feeling the excitement drumming inside me. "She's going to have a great time. This is the kind of shit she lives for."

"Most chicks do."

I shake my head. "Most, but not me."

"You're not excited?"

"Not in the least. The last big Dynasty party ended up with me in a cell. Not to mention that Tobias said I had to give some ridiculous speech and that's really not my thing." A devilish grin stretches over my lips as we reach Carver's Escalade, and he reaches out to open the door for me. "I'm more excited about what happens after."

"I don't want to know," he mutters under his breath, helping me up into the car and going above and beyond to shove all the tulle in after me so it doesn't get stuck in the door.

"Maybe you should."

Carver meets my stare and watches me for a minute, his emotions screaming loudly in his eyes. Without another word, he steps back and closes the door between us. As he walks around to the driver's side, I take a breath, knowing the second he opens his door and climbs in, this car is going to fill with an unbreakable tension.

It takes less than three seconds for the tension to hit me, and as he gets in and closes his door, my heart begins to race. Carver quickly glances my way as he starts the engine, and not a second later, we're sailing down my long driveway.

We hit the road in no time, but when Carver pulls right up to the main gate of the communal private road, I look his way. "Is this not happening here?" I ask, recalling the massive party room we'd been in during my initiation ceremony.

He shakes his head. "No, the venue here is too small."

My eyes bug out of my head. "Too small?"

"Mmhmm, this is going to be every member who's ever walked through Dynasty and their extended families, starting right from those original families who helped found Dynasty. Their children grew up, married, and had children of their own, and in most families, this goes back three, some four generations. There's going to be at least two thousand people there tonight."

I just blink. "I never thought about it like that, which I guess is kinda stupid, but it makes sense. I don't know, I guess I never gave a second thought to just how big this really is," I tell him before my eyes go wide and my head whips around to meet his stare. My voice kicks up a notch. "I have to give a speech in front of that many people?"

Carver just grins as the main gate slides open. "Sucks to be you."

Fucker.

We drive through the streets for ten minutes, neither of us really knowing how to have a casual conversation with one another. Not even the soft music from the radio fills the silence between us.

Carver brings the Escalade to a stop after exactly eleven minutes of driving, and just like with the underground city beneath our homes, he pulls into a parking garage that takes us deep underground. "Dynasty really is built right under Ravenwood Heights."

"You haven't even seen the half of it," he tells me. "Just wait 'til you see the size of this ballroom. It'll blow you the fuck away."

"And here I was thinking that nothing could blow better than me."

Carver just scoffs and brings his car to a stop right in the very front space that's reserved with a sign 'RAVENWOOD.'

"Ahh, it finally makes sense," I tease as Carver pushes his door wide, stopping to look back at me through narrowed eyes, knowing me all too well that whatever comment comes out of my mouth is going to be as stupid as they come. "You escorted me just so you could get the best parking space."

He rolls his eyes and gets out of his car as the words "fucking hell," are muttered so lowly under his breath that I'm left wondering if I even heard them at all.

I start helping myself out, but Carver rushes around and takes my hand, not wanting me to fall in this big dress. His hand is firm on mine, his thumb gently brushing over my knuckles. He meets my eyes, but not a word is muttered as he leads me through the parking garage and toward a door.

We walk through and it's like walking through to the lobby of a grand, five-star hotel. There are waiters rushing around the brightly lit room, people are checking their jackets, and hostesses are handing off glasses of champagne to guests in the most stunning ball gowns. For just a brief moment, I feel severely underdressed.

At the end of the room, there's a set of massive double doors, and I have a sneaking suspicion that's the main entrance of the grand ballroom. We're offered a glass of champagne and I take it gratefully before Carver leads me toward the main entrance. He offers me his elbow and I instantly raise a brow, looking at him in shock. "Don't start acting like a gentleman on my account."

He scoffs, still holding out his elbow until I reluctantly take it. "It's tradition. A lady must be escorted properly into the Ball. Cruz did the same for Ember, though the term 'lady' is being used lightly when it comes to you."

I ignore Carver's last comment with a roll of my eyes as my heart flutters thinking about how damn sweet Cruz is. He is honestly the most kind-hearted person I've ever met. The fact that he's also a badass, alpha, overprotective killer with a devilish smile is just the cherry on top.

We reach the doors and Carver pauses for just a second. "Are you ready for this?" he asks. "Everyone's going to be looking at you, and they're going to expect you to be as graceful as a fucking swan."

"Well I hope they don't disappoint easily because I'm about as graceful as a ham sandwich."

Carver rolls his eyes and brings me to a stop in front of the massive doors. I hear the music pulsing from behind them and I swallow back the fear that threatens to rise in my throat. This is going to be great. The guys are all going to be there, looking all sorts of delicious, while Ember will be keeping me sane. I can do this. The attention will only be on me for a minute, and once all the bitchy ladies judge my dress, they'll forget about me and get back to the party.

There's no need to kill anyone's father tonight.

Carver nods toward the two men in tuxedos waiting by the door, and for a brief second, I'm left wondering who these guys are and what their relationship to Dynasty is. If they were part of the organization, they'd be on the other side of the door enjoying the party, but they're working and are clearly privy to the fact that we have an underground world. So who the hell are they? I thought Dynasty was supposed to be some big secret, but there are outsiders working the party. That doesn't make sense.

Before I have a chance to question Carver about it, the two men step toward the handles and begin opening the massive doors.

We're instantly flooded with loud music and conversation, and as the doors completely open, I suck in a breath as I find myself standing at the very top of a grand staircase, staring down into a sea of beauty.

The room is massive, so much bigger than the one beneath our homes. It's been completely decorated with white drapes hanging from the high ceilings with fairy lights and designer bouquets. Everything leads back toward the massive chandelier that hangs in the very center of the room, directly above the dance floor.

Everything is laced with a soft gold trim, making the room look like it was plucked straight out of a fairytale. Tables are scattered around the left-hand side of the room, each of them perfectly set with marvelous centrepieces. The right-hand side is lined with tables of food, enough to feed the whole freaking country, but it's the people who stand at the bottom of the stairs who really have my attention.

There must be at least two thousand people in this room, each of them dressed amazingly. The men look drool-worthy in their expensive suits with their Rolexes and sharp jawlines, while the women—holy shit. The women look as though they just stepped off a runway. The gowns that flood this room are incredible. There are big ball gowns of every color, and sexy mermaid style dresses that show off perfect figures. It's almost like a competition between the women of who can come with the most extravagant gown.

Not a hair is out of place and every single female lip in the room is painted perfectly with a color that compliments her gown. It's a sight I've never seen before, something I never thought I'd ever be lucky enough to be a part of. Hell, I didn't even think my senior prom was going to be in my cards, but this out does any function Ravenwood Heights Academy would be able to put on a million times over.

Carver leads me toward the first step, and as he does, I grip his hand tighter, terrified that I'll fall. He shoots his devastatingly handsome smirk my way, silently reminding me that I've got this, and everything settles inside me. Why am I being such a bitch about this?

I'm Elodie Ravenwood. This is what I was born to do.

I hold my head a little higher and as my heel hits the very top step leading down into the grand party below, every eye turns my way.

It's like being a princess for a moment. You're the center of attention and you know that nothing could ever beat this. Awed gasps and whispered encouragements filter through the room as the younger kids blatantly stare with slack jaws.

A soft blush creeps into my cheeks, and as we hit the second step, I finally find them—King, Cruz, and Grayson.

They stand beside Ember who looks flawless in a deep red, satin gown that sits just off her shoulders with a short train that would have her non-stop gushing. I hope the guys told her how beautiful she looks tonight because I've never seen her look so amazing.

She looks up at me with a proud smile on her lips and her eyes shimmering with unshed tears. "You look beautiful," she mouths, making a big, cheesy smile stretch across my face.

But the guys.

My mouth instantly waters and I suck in a breath. They look like the best kind of nightmare.

My gaze travels over King first, scanning over his sharp jaw and dark messy hair, that for once isn't hanging forward into his ocean blue eyes. He wears a four-piece grey suit that fits his strong body perfectly, and I know that when I get to the bottom of the stairs, I'll probably find each of them in designer suits that I won't be able to pronounce.

Seeing that I have his attention, King smirks, and I have no choice but to shift my gaze toward Cruz before I become a fumbling mess for the whole organization to see, but I'm lost for words. Cruz looks like my next meal. His suit is a softer shade of grey than King's but looks just as good. He went without the vest, leaving the top button of his white dress shirt open and hinting at the deliciousness hidden below.

He licks his lips and I just about die.

These boys better be meeting me in my room after the party, still wearing these suits. I think I just got a whole new fantasy that's going to get played out before the night is over.

A small smile pulls at my lips, and as I turn to Grayson, I find his stormy eyes already on mine. They seem to smile up at me despite the hard set of his strong jaw, trying to appear as though he isn't having the time of his life.

His suit is as black as night, just like Carver's, and he somehow looks like the sharpest one in the room. It matches his personality perfectly, and I find myself desperate to tear it off him. He's dressed a lot simpler than Cruz and King, yet it makes him seem so much more unapproachable, but now I know better.

Carver and I get just over halfway when King's head whips up and I look back at him, watching as he scans the upper mezzanine level of the ballroom with his brows furrowed. "What's going on?" I murmur as Carver clutches my hand tighter.

He shakes his head ever so slightly. "I don't—"

King's loud, booming tone tears through the ballroom as his panicked gaze cuts back to me. "GET DOWN," he roars just as he reaches for Ember and throws her to the ground.

Carver launches himself at me. His body crashes against mine and as we fall down the stairs with the eyes of the whole organization on us, a deafening, burning explosion tears through the ballroom, throwing Carver and I clear across the room.

BOOM!

34

Screams tear through the ballroom and my head spins as I fade in and out of consciousness, but as the seconds tick by, the screams only get louder.

My brows furrow as I try to push myself up and have to blink a few times to really see anything that's going on around me. As I put weight down on my arm a sharp sting cuts through me. I suck in a pained gasp, falling to my other side and glancing down at my arm to find a deep cut just above my elbow.

"Fuck," I grunt, sucking in a breath through my teeth and rolling over debris until I'm on my back. I push up on my good hand and finally get a look around me.

People are running around as the stairs that I was just standing on with Carver are completely destroyed. The room spins and I blink a few more times, pressing my hand to my head and trying to will the dizziness away.

I look through the screaming people, ignoring the smoke and flames that tear through the room, licking up the walls and catching onto the white decorative drapes hanging from the roof.

I have to find the boys and Ember. Where the hell are they?

"WINTER?"

I hear my name and desperately try to search around but can't find any of them. My head spins so much that I can't even work out who's calling my name.

"WINTER? WHERE THE FUCK ARE YOU?"

I shakily get to my feet and wobble on my heels, more clearly able to see the horrifying destruction around me. People lay injured on the ground, screaming in agony while parents run around, yelling their children's names and fearing the worst.

The flames grow quicker, licking up the side of the building as the smoke gets caught in my throat. We have to get out of here before it's too late, but the stairs are gone, completely torn to pieces. We're in an underground ballroom. There's no emergency exit in a room like this. We're fucking trapped in here.

What the hell am I going to do?

This had to be another attack. Someone let off that explosion, someone in this room who knew exactly where I was on the steps, but Carver … oh, fuck. Carver. He was standing right beside me, in the middle of trying to protect me with his life. If he's hurt …

My breath comes in short, sharp gasps. I have to help, but I don't know how. Children are bleeding on the ground while others are caught under big chunks of concrete.

Blood pours from the cut on my elbow and my head continues to spin. I won't be helping anyone if I pass out from blood loss. I bend down to grip the bottom of my skirt, wiping the tears and dirt off my face. I tear a long, thick piece of tulle from the bottom of my gown and start wrapping it tightly around the cut on my elbow, doing my best to bandage it up. It's a shitty job, but for now, it'll have to do.

I start aimlessly moving through the room, having absolutely no idea how to help, but knowing I have to do something. People are dying, children are lost, and a shitload of people are far too close to suffering the effects of smoke inhalation.

"WINTER?"

It sounds like Cruz but my head is too foggy, and the smoke is getting thicker.

As I scan the room, I find a little girl sprawled in the middle of the dance floor. She screams in agony, her leg at a distorted angle as adults race past her, crushing her fingers beneath their shoes and knocking into her, not even noticing her there.

I race toward her, my heart breaking for this sweet, sweet little girl.

A loud crack echoes through the room and everyone seems to stop and look around, trying to figure out where the sound is coming from but when nothing happens, the chaos continues. I shove people out of the way. "MOVE," I roar, pushing them hard, not giving a shit as they tumble to the ground. All that matters is that little girl.

"WINTER."

King, maybe. I don't know. It's too loud in here.

The cracking sound continues, and having absolutely no idea what it is, I just keep running until I'm crashing down beside the little girl. She looks up at me with wide eyes, eyes that look so damn familiar, so blue and beautiful that in an instant, I know this has to be King's baby sister, Caitlin.

"I'm going to get you out of here," I promise her, desperately looking around and knowing that's going to be a shitload harder than it sounds. There are no stairs out, no lift or escalator. We're just left here in a fiery pit to perish.

I reach down and grab her, seeing that her hand is crushed and her leg more than just broken. She must be in agony. The sharp squeal that tears through her as I grip her arm and desperately pull her up is proof of that. "I know it hurts," I cry for her, "but I have to move you. I have to get you out."

Tears stream down her face as she nods, showing me just how strong and brave she is, just like her big brother.

As I get her standing on one foot, someone bumps into us, sending her sprawling back down to the ground. "FUCK," I yell, desperately grabbing at Caitlin and pulling her into my arms. I lift her and get her to wrap her arms around my neck then call over the deafening noise for her to hold on as best as she can while the cut on my arm screams in protest. Her legs get tangled in the tulle of my dress, but I don't stop to fix it. I have to get her out of here now.

Where the fuck is King? "If you see your brother, tell me," I call right into her ear, making her nod as I feel her tears dripping off her chin and landing on my shoulder.

The loud crack sounds through the room again, this time coming with the sound of live electricity. The lights in the room flicker, and with the fires taking over the roof, it sends long, creepy shadows soaring across the ballroom.

"WINTER. FUCK."

I stop. "CRUZ?" I yell, desperately searching around, the panic rising high in my chest. I don't want to die here today. I can't. "WHERE ARE YOU?"

The crack continues, getting louder and pounding against my aching head.

"FUCK, WINTER. MOVE."

Two strong arms collide around me and throw me and Caitlin across the dance floor. She screams in my ear as we crash to the ground. The arms wrap around us, protecting Caitlin's head as we hit the dance floor hard.

"KEEP YOUR HEAD DOWN," Cruz yells in my ear just as the massive chandelier above the dance floor breaks free from its hinges and crashes to the ground, sending sharp glass shards flying through the room like a wave of destruction.

People scream as I feel the exposed skin of my back being blasted with glass, but for the most part, Cruz covers me, doing his best to protect us both as our weight pressing down on Caitlin only makes her scream louder.

Cruz quickly gets off us, his eyes scanning over me with a deep relief, but he doesn't waste a single second and looks down at Caitlin, the recognition instantly flashing in his eyes.

Without hesitation, he takes Caitlin from me, scooping her off the ground and holding her with ease. "Fuck, her leg's broken," he curses as I get up beside him.

"I know," I say, scanning my gaze over her beautiful little face and meeting her eyes that are so much like her brother's. "Be careful. I think her hand is crushed too."

"Fuck."

Cruz instantly pulls me along, gripping me tightly and moving fast as we race through the bodies. "Where's Ember?" I call as I notice more people laying on the ground, covered in blood, some of them not moving at all. I look back at Cruz and instantly get an elbow to the side of my face. "Are the guys okay? Fuck, Cruz, tell me they're okay. Carver … he was right beside me. I haven't seen him."

"Fine. Ember's fucking terrified, but she's helping someone. She isn't cut out for this though. The smoke is getting to her."

Dread sinks heavily into my gut, but I can't get caught on little details. I need the whole picture. "The guys?" I ask as I notice people trying to scale the walls to get up to the mezzanine level that leads to the only exit, only half of them drop and crash to the ground with a sickening thud.

"Grayson is hurt, but he's been through worse," he tells me, instantly making my chest ache. "They're all helping to put the fires out, but if we don't get them out soon, there are going to be more dead than survivors in here. There are too many people, all fucking terrified. My little fucking brothers are in here somewhere."

"Shit. Okay, just tell me what to do and I'll do it."

Cruz just nods as he brings me to a stop near a table that has a whole bunch of injured children crowded around it. "Stay with them," he yells back at me, already a few feet away.

I nod, watching him go and anxiously looking around at the destruction as Caitlin grips onto my hand so tight that it hurts. I watch Cruz go and as he runs to help, I finally catch sight of the boys.

Carver stands dangerously close to the flames as they wrap around the white and gold trimmed drapes. He pulls on them, bringing them closer and putting himself in more danger as he tries to contain the fire and minimize its spread.

Grayson stands just by him with a pained expression on his face and a bad limp. He holds a fire extinguisher up to the flames, and while it's helping over here, the flames are spreading throughout the whole room. But at least the injured people who occupy this corner of the room are just that bit safer.

King though, he stands with Cruz, both of them looking back at the little girl who grips my hand. Cruz says something, and within a heartbeat, King is racing back toward us.

He drops to his knees in front of his little sister, his eyes scanning over her in a panic. "Fuck, Caitie," he says with a raw emotion hitting his voice as he takes in just how bad her injuries are. He leans forward and presses a lingering kiss to her forehead, the pain in his eyes shining so brightly that I wish I could do anything to take it away. "You're going to be okay, I swear. Just stay with Winter and we'll find a way to get us out of here. I promise. Have I ever broken a promise?"

She shakes her head, her tears only running faster.

"Exactly," King says, straightening and taking my hand. He gives it a tight squeeze before looking back at me and letting me see the true pain in his eyes, a pain that nearly cripples me. He looks over me. "Are you alright?"

All I can do is nod.

"Good," he murmurs, looking back to his little sister. "I have to go and help. Winter is going to stay right here with you. You're safe with her. I promise, Caitie. We'll find Mom and Dad soon, and the pain will go away."

Without waiting for her answer, King rushes back to the guys, and as I glance up, I see Cruz stepping in beside Carver to help. "Did you find Winter?" Carver roars over the sound of the flames.

"She's good," Cruz yells back. "A little banged up, but fine. She's just over there."

As if on cue, both Grayson and Carver look back toward the table, and I meet their panicked stares, watching as the burning relief pulses through them like a wave. Carver nods as Grayson's stormy gaze sails over my body, and just like that, their stares fall away and they get back to saving all of our lives, along with the other courageous men and women in the room.

Not wanting to do nothing, I turn toward the injured children and instantly start tearing more long strips off my dress and grab bleeding arms and legs, wrapping them up as best as I can as each of them cry for their parents.

"Elodie," a high-pitched wailing tone cuts through as a hand pulls at my arm. I spin around to find Cruz's mom looking at me in desperation. "My son," she begs with dirt and grime smudged across her pretty face. "Please, tell me you've seen him."

"Cruz?" I ask, knowing that she has three sons. I point around her, showing her exactly where he is. "He's fine. He's a hero, but I need help. These kids are all hurt."

She lets out a shaky breath and now knowing that her son is safe, she nods. "Okay," she says, swallowing back the same fear that's been threatening to overtake me since the second the explosion went off. "How can I help?"

We get into it, mending up the children as best we can while the fire still flourishes around us. I start to sweat, the heat beginning to burn my skin as the people in the corners of the room are forced to start moving in.

Burned pieces of wood are falling, but I try to hold it together, knowing we don't have much time.

People are collapsing, the smoke becoming too much as others are having asthma attacks, finding it impossible to breathe. I hold my dress to my face, desperately trying to keep the smoke out of my lungs, but they're starting to ache.

More children get dumped at the table as the other adults work tirelessly to try and contain the fire. I see Tobias King cutting through the people, shoving desperately as he runs toward the edge of the room with a large piece of paper in his hands, papers that kind of look like blueprints.

He looks up at the wall, coughing from the smoke and then double checking the papers. "HERE," he yells to anyone who will listen. "THE OLD TUNNELS ARE HERE. HELP ME KNOCK THIS WALL OUT."

Grayson is the first to run with the other men hot on his heels. He uses the back of the fire extinguisher to break through the wall, but it's not fucking easy. These underground buildings were built to last.

I see Cruz's father, Matthew Montgomery, even Earnest Brooks in there, all of them getting in and doing their part to save their families and what's left of Dynasty. If we all perish here tonight, that will be the end of Dynasty, but right now I'm wondering if that's even such a bad thing.

Everybody grabs something and starts banging against the hard walls of the ballroom and as the first hole begins to appear, hope surges through everyone. The men work harder and faster, but they don't have much energy left and have to work as a team.

The hole gets bigger and as the fires continue raging around us, only getting bigger with the new oxygen breathing into the room, I realize that while Cruz told me that Ember was alright, I still haven't actually seen her.

I desperately look around, but the hole finally gets big enough and the crowd rushes toward it, anxious to get out.

"WOMEN AND CHILDREN," Tobias hollers through the chaos. "WOMEN AND CHILDREN FIRST."

They don't listen and rush toward the hole, squishing their way in and hurrying out into the long tunnel, not knowing what they're going to find on the other side, but anything is better than this.

I look down at Caitlin, knowing that rushing her into that mess of bodies isn't going to be good for her. We need to hang back a bit and take our time otherwise she could end up worse, but she looks as though she's about to pass out from both the pain and thick smoke.

With the majority of the partiers pushing toward the tunnel, it gives us a clear view of the remaining bodies left scattered over the ballroom. Many of them have passed out from the smoke, but there are three of them left crushed under a large piece of the stairs that had fallen. There's debris everywhere and the glass and crystal from the shattered chandelier sparkles across the whole room like a deadly, enticing weapon.

There are people left crying for help, and blood smeared all over the room, but not a damn thing I can do to help them right now. "We have to go," King demands, rushing into me with so much momentum that he crushes into me and throws me back a step. He scoops up Caitlin as Cruz, Grayson, and Carver come back to help the other stranded children.

They all start leaving, taking as many kids as they can possibly handle, leaving the rest for the other men to help, but I hesitate, looking back at the people on the ground and scanning once again for Ember. "Now, Winter. We have to go," King insists.

"But all these people. They're going to die in here."

"We need to get these kids out of here," he tells me. "I know you understand that. Once they're safe, we'll come back for the others, but we have to go NOW. The smoke is too much for them."

A tear sits in the corner of my eye as I reluctantly nod and let King pull me away. We get to the tunnel and I look back, being one of the very last people to leave the burning ballroom with guilt resting heavily in my chest.

King tugs on my hand one more time and I tumble after him, having to skip a step to keep up with his fast pace. Carver looks back over his shoulder, holding two kids, one on either side as blood seeps through his clothes. "Keep up," he grunts at me, his jaw clenched as his muscles strain and bulge.

We quickly catch up to the rest of the crowd desperately trying to escape as the smoke follows us down the tunnel. We walk for another five minutes when we finally break out into a usually quiet street, only we find it swarming with people.

There are ambulances all around. The fire department is shoving their way past us as women in stained ball gowns cry on the floor. Others search the arms of the boys, desperately seeking out their lost children, while people lay on the ground, the smoke too much for their lungs to handle.

Tobias meets us just as we step out onto the road. Relief cuts across his face seeing both his son and daughter alive, but when he sees the state she's in, he runs with King to the back of the ambulance and instantly gets in with her. King doubles back with the rest of the guys, anxious to get back in there and save as many people as possible.

I rip off my heels and turn back with them, starting to race back into the tunnel when Grayson shoves a hard hand against my chest.

"No," he growls, the authority loud and clear in his tone. "Get back there and address your people. Let us do this. You're not going back in there."

"But—"

"NO," he roars. "GET THE FUCK OUT OF HERE."

I pull back, never having seen him so angry with me, but he's right. There are two thousand people out here, all scared, all confused, lost, and grieving. *They're my responsibility. They're mine to deal with.*

I swallow hard and nod, and without missing a beat, Grayson turns back around and shoots down the tunnel with the rest of the fire department.

I look back at the chaos on the road, and just as I go to find the heads of Dynasty to put together a plan, Ember comes crashing into me, her face burying into the curve of my neck as she lets out a breath of relief. "Holy shit, Winter. I thought you were dead."

35

"What the fuck was that?" I roar through my living room as fifteen heads of Dynasty, Cruz, King, and Grayson stare back at me. They all look exhausted. We only just got back from the night from hell ten minutes ago, and within seconds, the heads of Dynasty were barging down my door, ready to get to the bottom of it.

One of these men is guilty, and I want to know who. I *need* to know.

Any normal group would have waited until morning. Everyone would have gone home with their families, showered, and thought on their night, but not Dynasty. These fuckers are all about the here and now, and for once, I actually agree with them.

The guys look like shit. Carver's suit is practically non-existent. His jacket was burned to a crisp and his shirt ended up in pieces, yet for some stupid reason, he still wears it. His pants somehow survived though.

Grayson came out the best. Though, he might just look the best because his suit was black, whereas Cruz and King's grey suits look like an absolute mess. There's no salvaging that shit. Cruz is missing his jacket, only two buttons remain on his dress shirt, giving me a good peek at the masterpiece beneath, and his hair is as unruly as can be.

King on the other hand just looks like shit. His pants are torn, there's black smudges of ash and soot all over his face, half of his dress shirt is gone, and his jacket lays on the floor at my feet after being hung over my shoulders for a good portion of the night.

The majority of the men in this room look just as bad, except for the few who got their priorities wrong. Though maybe that was a blessing because now I know to watch them even closer than before.

It's well past two in the morning and my beautiful dress is now barely holding on. What was once full and dazzling is now torn to shreds and burned, just like what remains of Dynasty.

A wave of violent anger burns through me and I pace frantically, teetering on the edge of losing control. If Cruz weren't here keeping me grounded, I'd be off the fucking rails by now. "I know one of you motherfuckers has something to do with this, and I swear to God you'll pay. It's one thing going after me, but there were children in there. *Children.* Caitlin King just spent three hours in surgery. Both her leg and hand are being held together by pins."

"How dare you assume we had something to do with this," Michael Harding demands, shooting to his feet and spilling his bourbon all over my parents' expensive tiles, but what else should I have expected for a shallow asshole like him? He was basically Royston Carver's best friend. I wouldn't be surprised if he used to wipe Roy's ass for him too. "Where's Scardoni? He's been gone for days. If anyone did this, it was that shady bastard."

"Oh, is that how things are going to go now?" Grayson's father demands, slamming his empty glass down on the coffee table and leaning forward to refill it. "We're just shooting blame at one another without any rhyme or reason? If that's the case, I think you did it. You've been gunning to get rid of the Ravenwood line for years."

Earnest Brooks stands. "Let's keep this civil," he demands. "We should be discussing how we're going to rebuild, how we're going to earn back the trust of our people. They're scared. Over thirty of our own died tonight. Let's talk about that instead of putting the blame on one another."

Michael Harding ignores Earnest and storms toward Harlen Beckett, who gets to his feet just in time to block a punch from Michael. "You fucking bastard. I could kill you for this. I had nothing to do with it. My brother is lying in the fucking morgue as we speak."

Harlen clenches his jaw, his hands balling into fists, and for an old guy, I don't doubt that he could throw down just as well as his son, but Grayson steps in before I get the chance to find out. He shoves his hands against each of their chests, giving a violent push, sending his father sprawling back into the couch and proving that he's had way too much to drink, all of them have, but maybe that's a good thing. Their tongues are getting a little loose.

Michael shakes it off and walks around the back of the couch, glaring back at Grayson and his father while trying to calm himself. "I stand by what I said. Scardoni is all over this. The bastard has been a no-show for a fucking week. His son too. They've been planning this and now they're running scared. You know they planned that fucking shooting on the King property."

My brow raises as the room falls silent. "You knew about that and didn't come forward?" I question, stepping toward him and letting him see just how dangerous I can be, especially now that I'm fucking pissed. "You know there's a special place in hell for people like you? How do I know that you weren't working with them?"

Harding's jaw clenches, clearly seeing just how badly he fucked up and knowing all too well that he just put himself at the top of my suspect list. After all, Preston and Jacob weren't working alone. There's still a woman involved and who knows how many others.

"I had nothing to do with it," he spits, his eyes narrowing on me until Tobias King pushes him back a step and silently pulls him back in line, remembering who the fuck he's speaking to right now.

"Preston had nothing to do with it," Carver says from the other side of the room, his voice low and deadly, daring Harding to come at him as he gets the conversation back on track.

Matthew Montgomery scoffs, drinking his rum right from my father's expensive bottle. "How the hell do you know? You're just a kid. Fuck off out of here and let the real adults discuss this."

The corner of Carver's mouth twitches and Matthew flinches, slinking back into the couch and taking another swig of rum. "You want to know how I know Preston had nothing to do with it?" he asks, both King and Grayson smirking with the knowledge. "That fucker got caught. His son slipped up and got caught red-handed putting a hit on Elodie, so after I snapped Jacob's neck, I took Preston and put him in my fucking cellar last week. I'm surprised you fuckers haven't heard his screams. It's been quite soothing."

Mr. Danforth turns to Cruz. "Is that true?" he demands, ballsy enough to question Carver's statement in front of him.

Cruz nods. "Yes. Like Harding said, they were behind the attack in the woods, and Preston admitted to having part in another attempt on Elodie's life. Though, that being said, we know there's still someone else involved, perhaps a few someone's."

"How do you know that?" his father prompts.

Cruz just shakes his head and makes a show of stepping in beside me, away from his father, which at any other time would seem insignificant, but during a meeting like this, despite how informal it is, it speaks volumes. "If you want those details, you can arrange to meet with Elodie in private. We don't trust half the men in this room."

Mr. Danforth narrows his eyes at his son, his jaw clenched and the anger radiating off him. "You better know what the fuck you're doing, son," he says, though while his words might be harmless, the venom in his eyes says something entirely different.

Cruz steps forward, putting himself slightly in front of me but not blocking me, acting as a protector. "I stand with Elodie," he announces, not afraid of his father in the least.

Tobias stands, holding up his hands to diffuse the situation before it becomes something more. After all, there are much more important things to discuss other than Cruz's affection for me. "Either way," he says, looking at Carver, "you should have brought your accusations against Preston to the table. If you suspected him of harm against our leader, then we should have had a proper trial. You of all people should know that, after what happened with your father last month. You're to release him immediately, and as a group, we will decide his fate."

"No can do," Carver says, standing and stepping up in front of Tobias, making King twitchy. "This isn't a trial. Preston has admitted his guilt and he will be staying right where he is until I decide that I'm done with him. I have Elodie's approval."

All eyes fall to me and I nod. "Preston will remain in Dante's cellar until we get the information we need out of him. He will not be released a minute sooner, and depending on what information is retrieved, Dante has my full approval to deal with him the way he sees fit."

"That's not how we do things," Earnest spits.

"You know what?" I throw back at Earnest. "I'm hearing a lot of 'that's not how we do things' lately, but screw it and screw you … all of you. You're not the one who's dodging bullets every fucking day. You're not the one who's getting drowned in her own fucking pool, and you're sure as hell not the one who was nearly blown up on a fucking grand staircase tonight."

I throw back a shot of vodka and go for another, but being on a roll, I keep the words flowing free, letting them have a piece of my mind. "I'm done playing by the rules of corrupt men who don't give a shit about the value of life. King's little sister was nearly trampled tonight. Harding's fucking brother is dead along with thirty other people, and thousands of lives were put at risk. So fuck you, and fuck all the goddamn rules. We're playing by mine now, and shit is about to change around here. If you don't like it, there's the fucking door," I tell the room, throwing my hand out toward the entrance.

"Elodie," Tobias warns.

"No." I throw my hand up, cutting him off as another shot of vodka goes down. "Once things have settled down and the people responsible for this shit have been dealt with, then we can all sit down and discuss this, but not a second before. I want to be proud of Dynasty. This is all I have left of my family, and right now, it's nothing but a pile of steaming horse shit thanks to all of you morons. You killed what was once something great, and I'm tired of standing up and being the face of a corrupt organization that its own people fear. How the hell are we supposed to ever put on another function without your wives and children being terrified of being blown up? I mean, fuck. This is ridiculous."

"You have no right," Dion Luca argues. "You're just a kid. You don't understand our traditions. You're not about to come in here and shit all over what we've built."

"YOU HAVEN'T BUILT SHIT," I yell back at him. "You've

destroyed it. What would my grandfather say if he was looking in on this now? I'm sure he didn't intend for the seventeen families of Dynasty to constantly be at war. He wanted unity, because with unity comes strength."

"She's right," Tobias says. "Gerald founded Dynasty to be a revolution. We were going to be powerful, but we've become petty. Brothers at war. We should be standing together like our fathers before us. We were once great."

Matthew Montgomery scoffs. "That'll never happen. It's too far gone. I'd rather give my life than concede to this child."

"Then get the fuck out," I tell him. "I'm sure there are millions of families out there who would happily take your place and stand as proud and powerful members of Dynasty. So get on board, or you can go and hang out with Scardoni in the fucking cellar. I won't stop until I can stand in front of the seventeen families of Dynasty and tell them that we are united as the great Gerald Ravenwood fully intended."

"You can't do that."

I step up to him, raising my chin and narrowing my eyes. "Then challenge me," I dare him, listening to the gasps of the men around me. "Take the leadership from me. Put it to vote." Montgomery raises his brow and glances around the room, knowing damn well that the men around him aren't going to vote him in, but he can't resist trying. "In fact, I put it to everyone here, raise your hand if you would like leadership."

One by one, every fucking hand in the room raises and I look around at the fifteen remaining heads of Dynasty. "Then let's vote.

Majority rules."

"Are you sure you want to do this?" Cruz murmurs beside me.

I shrug my shoulders and swallow another shot of vodka. "What have I got to lose?"

"Everything," he grunts.

I just smirk, way too confident.

Carver stands and looks directly to his right. "All in favor of appointing Earnest Brooks into leadership."

Earnest raises his hand, and we wait a second until we confirm that no one else will vote for him.

Carver nods and moves around the circle, the tension building in the room like never before. "All in favor of appointing Michael Harding."

Michael raises his hand and none other.

It goes on and on, every single individual voting for himself until it gets to the last three—me, Carver and Tobias King. Carver continues. "All in favor of appointing Tobias King."

All eyes fall to Tobias and I watch as his gaze subtly flicks between me and Carver. A beat passes and then another when Tobias nods at Carver. "Continue."

My brow raises and I watch him a second longer. He didn't vote for himself which could only mean one of two things. In the next thirty seconds, either I will walk out of this as the leader of Dynasty, or Carver will.

I swallow over the lump in my throat as Carver continues. "All in favor of appointing myself, Dante Carver."

Not a single hand moves, not even his own and I suck in a breath, realizing that not only does he have to vote for me, but when he does, he's publicly declaring in front of the other heads of Dynasty that he will support me.

"Right," Carver continues, studiously ignoring the stares and murmurs of the men around him. "All in favor of appointing our current leader, Elodie Ravenwood to continue in her role as leader of Dynasty, raise your hands."

Just like that, Carver, Tobias, and I raise our hands, proving once and for all that this is where I need to be. Though I have to be honest, I'm surprised that Tobias didn't vote for himself just as everyone else had. I silently nod and he gives me a tight smile in return.

Not able to meet Carver's heavy stare, I raise my chin and get back to business as usual. "Then it's settled," I say, desperately trying to hide the odd mix of nerves and pride welling within me. "We will rebuild Dynasty in the true vision of Gerald Ravenwood, and we will flourish, but not before I make the fuckers who have done me wrong bleed."

I instantly refill my glass and as it's the time for making declarations, King comes and stands behind me with Grayson stepping in on Cruz's other side. The four of us make a stand with Carver's intentions known, and just like that, we change the game in one hell of a big way.

"What the hell is this?" Grayson's father demands, getting to his feet and glaring at his son as Tobias King just raises his chin, making it damn clear that he and his son will be having a private conversation, but not here, and certainly not for every head of Dynasty to witness. Grayson and his father don't have those same reservations though, especially with the way his father has been drinking tonight.

"My loyalties are to Elodie now," Grayson tells his father while also making it crystal clear to every other bastard in the room. "You've been sitting on the wrong side for far too fucking long, father. I will not be your legacy, not anymore."

"You are my heir," he roars. "I have raised you to stand in my place, now quit this foolishness. I will not allow you to throw away everything I've worked for on a piece of easy pussy."

Eyes widen all over the room and as Grayson's hands curl into fists, I press my hand to his chest, calming him down. "Allow me," I tell him, walking up to his father with a wicked smirk stretched wide across my face.

In one sharp snap, I curl my fingers into a tight fist, rejoicing in the way my brass knuckles tighten over my skin. I bring my fist back, and calling on every ounce of anger, hatred, and pain swarming deep inside me, I let my fist fly and smack him right in the fucking nose.

He roars, his arms flailing as he falls back, and I watch it happen, almost in slow motion. His ass crashes down into the couch and it rocks back, nearly threatening to tip right over as I turn and look back at Grayson, shaking out my hand. "How was that?"

"Fucking beautiful," he tells me.

"Alright," Sebastian Whitman groans and rests back in his chair, less than impressed with the halftime show. "Now that we've wasted half an hour learning absolutely nothing new, can we please get back to the topic at hand. There are thirty-four men, women, and children currently waiting to be buried, and I demand to know who is responsible."

"My thoughts exactly," I tell him. "And my gut tells me that one of the men in this room has a death sentence. I guess the fun will be figuring it out."

I look back at Carver, watching as he refills his drink and then refills Tobias' and shoves it down in front of him. The guys take their glasses and Tobias quickly throws his down his throat before going for another. Carver slowly leans back in his seat, resting his head on the couch, completely exhausted.

I wonder what my luck is like tonight. Maybe he'll let me sneak through his bedroom door for old times' sake and sleep with his arms curled around me. I hate that he's had such a shitty night, but then, we all have. Maybe King needs me more tonight. After trying to save as many lives as possible while waiting to hear about his sister, he could really use some comfort.

"Alright, so what's the plan?" Sebastian continues. "I have a few ideas, but—"

Carver launches out of his seat, crashing to the ground in front of Tobias. He throws his full glass clear across the room, letting it smash into the fireplace. Rum soaks the wall as his hand reaches for the glass moving towards Tobias' lips. "NOOOO," he roars, knocking it out of his hand just in time.

But it's already too late. That's Tobias' second glass.

Tobias grunts, his furious glare shooting toward Carver as rum soaks through his already destroyed clothes. Everyone watches on wide-eyed, not a damn person having a fucking clue what's going on.

"What the hell do you think you're doing?" Tobias demands, flying to his feet.

Carver stares up at him, genuine fear shining in his eyes. "Cyanide."

Panic sets in and my heart instantly races. I don't know much about cyanide, but I know that it can be deadly.

Tobias stills and looks down at Carver on his knees before him, his eyes wide and the terror clear on his face. He falls to his knees, his hands coming to his throat, almost as though he's choking. Carver holds onto him, desperately searching his face. "SOMEONE CALL A FUCKING AMBULANCE."

"No, no, no," I begin to chant, my hand gripping Cruz's beside me as silence falls through the room.

Tobias looks at his son as Michael Harding whips out his phone, urgently dialing 911. "Hunter," Tobias breathes as King watches on in horror, not able to believe what's happening right before his eyes.

His father begins to fall, and Carver gently lowers him down, but the second his head hits the expensive tiles, he begins frothing at the mouth as a violent seizure rocks through him.

"DAD," King cries, rushing forward, knocking past me and shoving Carver back until he's sprawled out behind him. King slides in, cradling his father's head with hot tears stinging his eyes, killing me as I see such a strong man break. "No, Dad. Don't you fucking go. We're not finished yet. DAD." King shakes him in desperation. "Open your fucking eyes. You're going to be alright. The ambulance is on its way. Just hold on a little while longer."

King holds his father as we all watch on in fear, my heart shattering in my chest as my body trembles under Cruz's desperate hold. I want to run to King, I want to hold him and tell him that it's going to be alright, but it won't. There's no escaping this.

Tobias King will die tonight.

"No, Dad. Please, no," King sobs, dropping his head down to his father's as his violent seizure eases and his body becomes limp in his son's arms. Tobias finally gives in, allowing the cyanide to shut down his organs, and I watch in heartbreak as this great man is brought to his knees and we lose another soldier to the war that's better known as Dynasty.

36

King's arm curls around my body, pulling me in tight against his chest as he lays awake, staring up at the dark ceiling. I finally got him into bed at five this morning, but we've both just laid here, neither of us saying a word as we soak in one another's comfort.

I've drifted in and out of sleep over the past few hours, but I don't think King has even closed his eyes to blink, he's just stared up at the ceiling with his hand propped behind his head.

"Are you alright?" I murmur into the quiet room, placing my hand on top of his and lacing our fingers, holding him as tight as I possibly can. I can't even begin to imagine what he must be feeling, watching his father fall like that … fuck, it broke him. I've never seen devastation like that before.

"No," he grumbles as a sliver of morning sunlight begins to shine through my bedroom window. "But that doesn't matter. I'll figure it out and learn how to cope, but my little brother and sister … I just … Mom's going to have to tell them this morning and I can't stop thinking about how this is going to destroy them. Dad always treated me as an heir. Our relationship was strained, but with the twins … they got to have the relationship that I always dreamed about. They were just his kids, not his protégé, and they fucking loved him. They're never going to be the same."

I roll over, curling into his side and raising my head to meet his broken stare. "I haven't met your little brother, but from what I saw of Caitlin last night, it's clear that she's strong just like you. She's a survivor. She's going to be alright because she has you watching out for her, and honestly, I couldn't think of anything better."

King's arms just tighten around me, holding me as though I'm his only lifeline. "I don't know about that," he whispers into the quiet room before dropping the softest kiss to my temple. "I couldn't think of anything worse for them."

"You're wrong," I murmur. "They're going to lean on you. They're going to need you more than ever before, and you're going to be everything they need. They know you're hurting because they feel it too. They don't need you to replace your father, all they need is for you to tell them that everything is going to be alright, wrap your arms around them, and tell them that you're never going to leave them."

"What if I let them down?"

I shake my head. "That's not possible."

King lets out a sigh and buries his face into my hair. He's so fucking broken that it kills me, and seeing him like that last night just proved to me that I'd do absolutely anything to make sure that he never has to feel like that again.

Taking his hand, I scoot to the edge of the bed and pull him up beside me. "Come on," I tell him, getting to my feet and turning around to look at him sitting on the edge of my bed, looking exhausted as shit, while also knowing that he'll refuse to sleep until he physically can't stay awake anymore. "Let's go."

"Where?"

"The hospital." His brows furrow as I cross my room and grab a pair of pants and a tank. I quickly pull them on before looking back at him and explaining myself. "You said that your mom is going to have to tell them this morning, so now is your last chance to see them before their worlds change for the worse. Put on a smile and go tell Caitlin how fucking strong she is and how proud you are of how she handled herself last night. Soak up her light and laugh with her because for a little while, you might not get a chance to hear it again."

King just nods and offers me his hand. I take it and give a light tug and he gets up beside me, dropping another kiss to my forehead. His hand falls away from mine as he crosses the room and grabs the sweatpants and shirt that he left here last week.

Within seconds, he's walking out the door and I follow him out, knowing that while we have every intention of going to the hospital to make his little sister laugh, it might just be one of the hardest things he'll ever have to do.

With his car still parked in his garage at home, King goes straight for my bike and hands me my helmet. I know better than to argue with him, so I pull it on and climb on behind him, curling my arms right around his waist.

We pull up at the hospital within the space of five minutes and make it up to her room before breakfast is even served. King stands outside her room, peering in while desperately trying to find the strength to give her what she needs.

He lets out a shaky breath and instantly takes my hands. "You can do this," I tell him. "I'll be right here waiting for you."

He shakes his head and pushes the door open, tugging me in right along with him. "Hey Caitie," King beams, slapping on a fake smile and striding deeper into the room, seeing that she's wide awake and looking up at the cartoons on the TV. "What's going on? Are these doctors treating you alright or do I need to kick their butts?"

Her leg is held together with pins while her hand is completely casted, and I'm sure also filled with little pins holding everything together. It kills me. No little girl should have to suffer through this. They should be out in their yards playing and having the time of their lives. She shouldn't have to look back on her childhood years and remember going through months of physiotherapy to retrain herself how to walk and run properly. She should get to remember the times her big brother threw her so high in the air that she accidentally threw up all over him.

She must be in so much pain, but hopefully there's enough meds pulsing through her little system that she can forget about being in the hospital.

"Move," Caitlin screeches when her big brother walks right in front of the TV, blocking her view. "I can't see my shows."

"I brought someone who wanted to meet you."

Caitlin's gaze snaps away from the TV and quickly scans over my face. Her little eyes widen and a bright smile stretches over her lips as I see the memories of last night flashing through her mind. "Don't be silly," she laughs, making King's eyes sparkle with raw happiness. "I already met her. She's the girl who saved me. Don't you remember? She picked me up off the floor when everybody else was squishing me."

"How could I forget?" he tells her.

"She needs to work on her muscles though," Caitlin grins, knowing exactly what she's doing, and I don't doubt that she learned it from her big brother. "She's not very strong. She couldn't pick me up very well, not like Cruz. Do you know he could pick me up with one hand?"

King just shakes his head, letting out a soft breath. "Please don't tell me that you have a crush on Cruz."

She just beams, but like … girl, same. Who could blame her? Cruz is fine.

"Crap," King mutters. "What happened to Carver? I thought you liked him last week."

"Yeah, but he's kinda scary. Cruz smiles a lot."

"Fuck me," King murmurs under his breath, tugging on my hand and pulling me right into his chest. "Where's Cody and Mom? Are they here yet?"

Caitlin shakes her head, a frown pulling at her face. "No, Mom gave me Dad's phone so she could call me, but she hasn't called me yet. I think she forgot about me."

"Trust me, kid," King tells her, moving around the side of her bed to sit in the chair and bringing me with him. "Mom hasn't forgotten about you. How could she? You're too special."

"I know," she laughs, her gaze shifting back up toward the TV. "I'm her favorite. She always tells me that you boys stink and have cooties, but I'm the best because I'm a princess."

King just nods, a heaviness coming over him. "You sure are, Caitie. Always."

Sensing the change in his tone, she whips her head back toward us and this time takes note of the way King pulls me into his lap with his hand securely wrapped around mine. She sucks in a sharp breath, her eyes bugging out as a wide smile stretches over her face. "YOU'RE IN LOVE WITH *THE* ELODIE RAVENWOOD."

Ahh, fuck.

I laugh and start shaking my head and King leans back in the chair. "So what if I am?" he asks her. "Who's going to believe you? She's the leader of Dynasty and I'm just your stupid big brother."

My mouth drops and I whip back around to King, my eyes wide as he refuses to look at me, clearly already dealing with far too many other things to face this bomb straight on.

Caitlin laughs from her space on her bed, furious about his comment while also clearly very happy for him. "You are stupid," she tells him. "But you're also an heir. You're practically royalty around here. Everyone is going to believe me."

A smile pulls at King's lips, and in a flash, his eyes come back to mine.

I see it all there, all of that raw emotion telling me that every word he just said is true. I want to talk about it, make him say it again, but I can't push him on this. Not today, and certainly not now. I would never forgive myself if I ruined this time with his sister. So instead, I simply lean in as my heart races with fear of what this could mean and gently press a soft, quick kiss to his lips.

"EWWWWWW," Caitlin groans before a high-pitched laughing squeal takes over her, making her sound as though she's somewhat possessed. "Yuck. That's gross. No kissing in my room."

"Careful," he laughs. "If you hate it so much, I might just let her do it again."

"Gross," she mutters to herself, dipping her head as her lips twist into a disgusted cringe.

"Hey," he says, forcing her attention back to him. "You never told me how you were feeling? Are you okay? Did you sleep well? What about your leg? Is it hurting? Do you want me to get the doctor?"

Caitlin rolls her eyes, and just as she goes to reprimand her big brother for asking a million questions, the door swings open and King's mom and little brother come striding into the room.

His mom looks like death warmed up, and I can't even begin to imagine what she's feeling after spending her night in the hospital by her daughter's bedside to then come home and get the news that her husband was murdered in front of her eldest son.

"Mom," King says, flying to his feet and taking my waist to balance me. He steps around me and instantly pulls his mom into his warm, welcoming arms. It's such a contrast to the version of the man I met after he snuck through my bedroom window back at Kurt and Irene's place.

King murmurs something in her ear and her face drops onto his shoulder for a long moment before she takes a deep breath and pulls back, nodding and giving what she thinks is an encouraging smile, but all I see is a broken woman who's doing everything she can to try and be strong for her kids.

Her gaze sweeps back to me and she gives me a polite smile before looking up at her son. "What are you doing here? Is everything alright?"

King nods. "Yeah, I just wanted to sit with Caitie for a while before … you know."

"Oh," she says, peering over his shoulder at the two kids squished on the bed who are glued to the TV. She gives his shoulder a tight squeeze. "Thank you. You didn't have to do that, but I appreciate it. She would have loved spending time with you and getting to meet Elodie Ravenwood properly."

"I hope so," he whispers, reaching back for my hand. "We'll go and give you some space to talk," he says, drawing me back toward the door before stopping and looking back at his mom. "Just call me if you need anything."

She gives him a tight smile, struggling to hold it together and walks to the door with us, taking the handle and gently closing it behind us as she gives herself and her babies some privacy to break their hearts.

A hollowness sits in my chest as King and I make our way back to my place, but being able to sit behind him on my bike and keep my arms wrapped around his waist goes a long way in easing that ache.

We just get into my drive when the skies open up around us and a storm tears through Ravenwood Heights. King hits the throttle, sending us soaring down the driveway, but what does it matter? We're already soaking wet.

As we walk through the door, I hear a murmured conversation coming from the kitchen and warmth instantly settles through my broken heart. I keep my hand tightly held in King's as we walk through my home to find Cruz, Carver, and Grayson hovering around my kitchen making breakfast.

The second they see us, the boys instantly stop what they're doing and make their way over to King. Cruz pulls him into his arms, not giving a shit that we're soaking wet, and pats him on the back, silently telling him that he's here for anything he needs. Carver simply reaches out and puts his hand on King's shoulder, giving it a tight squeeze, his silent messages always speaking much louder than his words.

As Cruz pulls back, Grayson steals his place, giving King exactly what he needs from his friends.

Cruz steps into me and drops his arm over my shoulder, pulling me into his side and quickly capturing my lips with his own. "Are you good?" he murmurs, knowing just how hard last night was for me.

I nod, feeling as though what I went through is nothing compared to the night King had, or any of them for that matter. "Fine," I tell him as Carver gets back to cooking while Grayson steps in closer to me, pulling my arm away and checking over the gash above my elbow with a scrunched-up face. If he doesn't like that, I should remember not to show him my back from the falling chandelier. "I just want to sleep for about a year, and after that, we need to figure out who the fuck put cyanide in Carver's bottle of rum and who thought it'd be a good fucking idea to blow up a room filled with innocent people."

"I'm going to fucking kill them," King declares, grabbing a chair from the dining table and yanking it back, only to drop down into it a second later. "One of them hurt my baby sister, and the other killed my father."

"The other?" I ask, pulling out of Cruz's arms and peeling off my wet tank, hating the feeling of being wet. I gather my hair into a bun. "You don't think they're the same person?"

He shakes his head, but it's Carver who responds. "No, the bomb was a direct attack on you that got out of hand. Whoever did it was trying to make a point by killing you in front of everyone, making you look weak and sending a message, but they fucked up. This was done by someone who doesn't have any kind of training, either someone young, or someone who wasn't raised around Dynasty. But the cyanide," he says, quickly flashing his gaze at King and hating to talk about it while it's still so fresh in his mind. "That was too coincidental and done by someone in that room. I'd been drinking from that bottle for over an hour before it was hit with cyanide, but for it to happen right after I pledged to support you … that's too fucking coincidental. Tobias though, I believe that was just an unfortunate incident. That cyanide was meant for me. His support for you has been clear from the start, but me, I jumped ship and that pissed someone off."

"So, what's the plan?" I ask.

Grayson just shakes his head as a rumbling of thunder shakes the foundations of my home and instantly sends the house into darkness. "Fuck," he grunts, walking over to the stove and cutting the gas, a firm believer in better safe than sorry.

I lean up against the counter, wanting to stay close to the guys as with the dark clouds outside, and the electricity out, there's not a lot of light shining through my home. I point toward the half-cooked breakfast. "Is that still good to e—"

A loud bang sounds through the house and the words fall from my mouth as my eyes widen in horror. That was more than just a crack of lightning.

There's someone in my house.

The boys come to the realization just as fast as I do and are gone within seconds, sprinting toward the stairs, intent on ending the dickhead who's been responsible for helping Preston and Jacob Scardoni—at least that's who I assume it is. "Fucking hide," Cruz yells back over his shoulder. "And don't come out until we come and get you."

I'm not fucking stupid. I've been through enough attacks to know to listen to them straight away.

I slip straight into the massive floor to ceiling walk-in pantry and close my eyes, desperately trying to calm my racing heart as I rely on my other senses. Besides, it's dark in here and trying to peer out of the gap in the pantry door is just going to end up freaking me out.

So, I wait … and wait.

I hear the guys upstairs, racing round and double checking every little space, but after ten minutes, I hear Cruz calling out from upstairs. "Babe, you can come out. There's no one up here," he tells me, making a heavy sigh of relief pour out of me, my knees instantly going weak. "Ember left her fucking bedroom window open again and the storm blew a frame off the wall."

I nod to myself, gripping the pantry shelf as I give myself a second to relax. Far too much has gone down over the past twenty-four hours; I'm so much jumpier than normal. Though, speaking of Ember, I should probably check in with her today. She was certainly rattled last night, and I need to make sure I haven't scared her away for good.

I push through the pantry door and step out into the kitchen, aiming straight for the two pancakes Carver managed to cook before the power went out, and as I reach for them, a soft laugh bounces through the room. "Don't fucking move," a familiar voice says just as a feminine body presses into my back and a sharp sting hits the base of my neck.

I suck in a gasp, my body freezing as my eyes snap up to the mirrored backsplash and find a familiar face staring back at me, *my face staring back at me.*

It's the woman who stood outside of Carver's home, the one who worked side-by-side with Preston Scardoni and planned for an innocent eighteen-year-old girl to be drowned in her family's pool.

She's a fucking monster.

My whole world stops as I stare back at the woman who stands beside my father in all the pictures, only now eighteen years older.

London Fucking Ravenwood.

My mother.

"No," I breathe, unable to believe what I'm seeing as I meet my mother's cold and calculating stare. "You're supposed to be dead."

A grin pulls up the corner of her mouth. "Surprise, daughter," she spits, pressing harder against the knife as a twisted, sick laughter sounds in her tone. "Now, move."

I swallow hard and the movement only makes me feel the sharp sting of the knife more. A trickle of blood seeps down my throat and she pushes me through the kitchen. I keep my feet moving, knowing better than to piss off the woman who's been trying to kill me for God knows how long.

We get through the foyer and she leads me toward the internal door of the garage. She silently opens it as my mind reels with questions, the main ones being how the fuck is she still alive and where the hell has she been hiding for all these years?

My mother pushes me down the steps leading into the garage, and I follow her lead as I'm pushed toward the side of the room. Keeping her knife on me, she leans across to the table and pulls out a secret drawer and my brows raise as I find every key for all of my father's cars lining this impressive garage. I didn't know they were there, but I guess it doesn't matter now because it looks like I won't be living long enough to drive any of them. Not that I ever had a chance to learn to drive anyway.

"Move," she orders, shoving me in the back.

I do as I'm told, silently wishing the boys would hurry the fuck up. I could speed up the process by calling out for them, but that's just asking for a slit throat.

"Why?" I ask as she presses a button on the key fob and the trunk of the car glides open.

London just laughs. "Why else?" she tells me, indicating for me to get in. "It's the same reason every other bastard in this godforsaken town wants you dead. Money, power, and Dynasty. They were all supposed to be mine until you came along and ruined it."

I let out a breath, filled with disbelief. How could she be so shallow? All this time I've been mourning and grieving for my mother who I never got a real chance to meet, and then this is what I get? Who the fuck did I piss off in the underworld?

Though, one question still bugs me—why the hell do I find her voice so familiar? There's no way I would remember it from being a newborn baby.

"Don't. Fucking. Move," Carver's smooth, deep tone echoes through the massive garage as I hear the soft movements of the guys stepping in around him.

My mother laughs, turning and bringing me with her to find all four of the guys standing in the garage, watching with wide eyes as they take in the knife at my throat, but not only that, realizing that the woman who was supposed to be dead eighteen years ago is standing before them, alive and well … though 'well' probably isn't the word I'd use for it. She's definitely sick in the head.

"Take one more step," London purrs. "And you'll never see your little pet again."

Carver calls her bluff, slowly pulling out a gun and holding it up, aimed straight between my eyes. "Drop your knife and I might just let you live."

London laughs. "Drop your gun, and I might not slit your girlfriend's throat."

Silence fills the garage and after a long, drawn-out minute, London starts to get nervous. "Put your gun down," she yells at him as the boys slowly begin to creep closer. My eyes flash around, meeting Cruz wide stare and then Kings. They both looking fucking sick, while Grayson just looks pissed.

Catching their movements, London starts pulling me toward the driver's door of the car and I close my eyes as she shuffles around, the knife pressing too hard against my throat and making me want to hurl.

She gets the door open, realizing just how far the boys will go to keep me alive, even if it means risking me in the process. She thought her plans were seamless. She thought they would just give up and let her drag me away with a knife at my throat.

Yeah fucking right.

She thought wrong.

"You have two fucking seconds," Carver tells her, his voice low and thick with a dark, menacing promise that on any other day would have a chill sweeping down my spine. "Let her go, or I will shoot."

"Back off," she yells, keeping her body hidden behind me.

"One," Carver says, his voice cutting through the garage like the deep rumbling thunder coming from outside.

"Two."

London pushes me hard, throwing me forward, directly in line with Carver just as he pulls his trigger, sending a bullet spiraling toward me. A loud scream pierces through the garage but the deafening *BANG* from his gun completely drowns it out.

The car door is slammed just as an agonizing burn shoots through my body, feeling like I've just been stabbed by a sharp branding iron.

I suck in a gasp, hearing three more shots ring out, but I fall to the ground, my eyes wide as I meet Carver's horrified stare.

Tires squeal on the polished concrete floor and the car behind me flies out through the closed garage door, tearing it right off its hinges and getting away as my hand falls to my stomach, instantly drenching in blood.

He shot me.

The blood pours out of me in waves and just as I look across at King, Cruz, and Grayson, and find them racing toward me, my head starts to spin and I fall to the ground, feeling the life quickly draining out of me.

Darkness swallows me and as I hear a loud, panicked "WINTER" tearing through my father's garage, my world fades to nothing.

Don't worry, Daddy. I'm finally coming home to you.

Boys of Winter Series Playlist

Blood // Water - Grandson
Evil - 8 Graves
11 Minutes - Yungblud Ft. Halsey & Travis Barker
Hate The Way - G-Eazy Feat Blackbear
Control - Halsey
Play With Fire - Sam Tinnesz
You Should See Me In A Crown - Billie Eilish
Everybody Wants To Rule The World - Lorde
Courage To Change - Sia
You Broke Me First - Tate McRae
Yellow Flicker Beat - Lorde
Sweet Dreams - Marilyn Manson
Wicked Game - Daisy Gray
Nobody's Home - Avril Lavigne
Stand By Me - Ki: Theory
Paparazzi - Kim Dracula
Bringing Me Down - Ki: Theory (feat. Ruelle)
Therefore I am - Billie Eilish
I see Red - Everybody Love An Outlaw
In The Air Tonight - Nonpoint
Tainted Love - Marilyn Manson
Saviour - Daisy Gray
I Put A Spell On You - Annie Lennox
Heaven Julia Michaels
Heart Attack - Demi Lovato
Dynasty - Mia
Weak - AJR
Redemption - Besomorph & Coopex & RIELL
Legends Never Die - League of Legends & Against the Current
Time - NF
Rumors - NEFFEX

Thanks for reading!

If you enjoyed reading this book as much as I enjoyed writing it, please leave an Amazon review to let me know.

https://www.amazon.com/gp/product/B08TKN387H

For more information on Boys of Winter, stalk me online –

Facebook Page - www.facebook.com/SheridanAnneAuthor

FacebookReaderGroup–www.facebook.com/SheridansBookishBabes

Instagram – www.instagram.com/Sheridan.Anne.Author

Other Series by Sheridan Anne

www.amazon.com/Sheridan-Anne/e/B079TLXN6K

YOUNG ADULT / NEW ADULT DARK ROMANCE

The Broken Hill High Series (5 Book Series + Novella)

Haven Falls (7 Book Series + Novella)

Broken Hill Boys (5 Book Novella Series)

Aston Creek High (4 Book Series)

Rejects Paradise (4 Book Series)

Black Widow (A Rejects Paradise Novella)

Boys of Winter (4 Book Series)

NEW ADULT SPORTS ROMANCE

Kings of Denver (4 Book Series)

Denver Royalty (3 Book Series)

Rebels Advocate (4 Book Series)

CONTEMPORARY ROMANCE

Men of Fire Rescue One (4 Book Series)

Until Autumn – Happily Eva Alpha World

URBAN FANTASY - PEN NAME: CASSIDY SUMMERS

Slayer Academy (3 Book Series)

Made in United States
Orlando, FL
16 April 2024